ROMANTIC TIMES RAVES ABOUT CONNIE MASON! WINNER OF THE *ROMANTIC TIMES* CAREER ACHIEVEMENT AWARD!

PIRATE

"Ms. Mason has written interesting characters into a twisting plot filled with humor and pathos. If you enjoy pirates and romance, you'll enjoy *Pirate*.

BEYOND THE HORIZON

"Connie Mason at her best! She draws readers into this fast-paced, tender and emotional historical romance that proves that love really does conquer all!"

BRAVE LAND, BRAVE LOVE

"*Brave Land, Brave Love* is an utter delight from first page to last—funny, tender, adventurous, and highly romantic!"

WILD LAND, WILD LOVE

"Connie Mason has done it again!"

BOLD LAND, BOLD LOVE

"A lovely romance and a fine historical!"

VIKING!

"This captive/captor romance proves a delicious read."

TEMPT THE DEVIL

"A grand and glorious adventure-romp! Ms. Mason tempts the readers with . . . thrilling action and sizzling sensuality!"

SHEIK

"Ms. Mason has written another winner. . . . This story that will certainly keep you warm on a cold winter's night."

HOT TIP

"What is the meaning of this, you big lummox?" Maggie sputtered angrily.

"Sorry, lady," Chase mumbled, "I need your help. Take off your blouse."

"What! Are you some kind of pervert?"

"Hurry, lady, I don't cotton to being hauled off to jail. Move your tail, take off your blouse and hop in the bunk before they start searchin' the rooms."

"I'll do no such thing!" Maggie returned huffily.

With grim determination, Chase drew his pistol. "Look, lady, you heard them call me a killer. You gonna make me prove it?"

Maggie eyed Chase's tall, imposing form narrowly. He was everything a gentleman was not. His language was crude and unfit for a lady's ears, his manners despicable. She looked at him again. This time through the eyes of an inquisitive reporter with the makings of a hot story within her grasp.

"I'll help you, Mr. McGarrett, on one condition," Maggie said brusquely. "Once the sheriff and his men leave, I want your story."

ICE &
Rapture

CONNIE MASON

LEISURE BOOKS NEW YORK CITY

A LEISURE BOOK®

August 1999

Published by

Dorchester Publishing Co., Inc.
276 Fifth Avenue
New York, NY 10001

ISBN 0-8439-4570-2

To my daughters Jeri and Michelle.
Though the mountain seems insurmountable,
we are never given more than we can handle.

ICE &
Rapture

Prologue

July 16, 1897, from Seattle Post-Intelligencer:

Gold! Gold! Gold! Gold! At three o'clock this
morning the steamer, *Portland*, from St.
Michael, Alaska, passed up the sound with
more than a ton of solid gold aboard. A tug
hired by reporters from the Seattle Post-Intelligencer steamed out to meet the Portland.

Later, when the ship docked and was greeted
by hails of "show us the gold," more than one
passenger held up a sack. More than a ton of
gold arrived on the ship (actually it was more
than two ton). Interviews with the prospectors
aboard reflected prosperity, optimism and a
determination to rejoin as quickly as possible
a partner who was left behind working their
claim.

* * *

11

News spread around the world by the next morning when the *Portland* approached the dock in Seattle, producing a stampede to the Yukon by Americans and Canadians alike.

Chapter One

Seattle—July 17, 1897

"Please, Mr. Grant, can't you forget I'm a woman this one time and treat me like one of the other reporters?" Maggie asked, swiping ineffectually at a stray lock of honey-blond hair dangling on her furrowed brow.

Maggie was angry, damn angry. Everyone knew she was the best reporter and photographer on the Seattle Post-Intelligencer, but being a woman prevented her from being assigned to the Yukon to report on the Klondike gold rush. It was nearly 1900, for heaven's sake, and Maggie Afton was a young woman poised on the threshhold of a bold new century where countless opportunities awaited her. If going to the Klondike would help other women break out of the mold in which men cast them, then go she would, with or without Mr. Grant's blessing.

"For the last time, Maggie, you don't belong in that frozen wasteland," Fred Grant, managing editor of the highly respected newspaper pronounced with firm conviction. "You're a damn good reporter, but there's a limit to what you can do. There are plenty of men here at the newspaper eager and willing to go. For God's sake, Maggie, you've seen some of the wretched souls coming down from the Klondike—hollow-eyed emaciated creatures dressed in rags with frozen hands and feet. You've interviewed them, heard the harrowing tales they told of hardship and deprivation. Not everyone comes back rich. I'm much too fond of you to allow something like that happen."

"Surely those were extreme cases, Mr. Grant," Maggie argued, growing desperate. She wanted to go to the Klondike—needed to go to prove to the world that she was as good as any man at her profession. "When the *Portland* steamed into Puget Sound yesterday, I fought to be one of the first reporters aboard. I saw the gold—tons of it—took pictures, listened to their stories. Of course it was difficult, but they survived and came home wealthy. If they did it, so can I. Only I won't be going to stake a claim on the Bonanza or Eldorado, but to send back stories and pictures for posterity."

Peering over the lenses of his thick glasses, Fred Grant glared at Maggie Afton. Tunneling stubby fingers though his sparse gray hair, he recalled vividly the day headstrong Maggie Afton had walked into his office seeking a job. Cool, tough, yet lovelier than a woman had a right to be, she had more experience than most men he hired. He soon learned that she was possessed of guts and determination to match. Furthermore, he could depend on Maggie Afton when all others failed him.

Fred Grant had offered Maggie a position on the paper, at first wasting her talents on society and women's affairs, until the day she scooped all her male counterparts with an exciting interview and pictures of a condemned murderer. Since that day Maggie had been given more responsible assignments that made use of her journalistic talents. But send her to the Klondike? Preposterous!

"It's out of the question, Maggie, I won't even consider it," Grant blustered.

"Then I'll go on my own," Maggie defied him stubbornly. "I'm not without resources. I've saved every cent of the money I got from the sale of Father's newspaper in California."

Her eyes, a warm amber gold, darkened with determination, a sign that Fred Grant grew to recognize as the beginning of a confrontation—which the lovely young woman usually won through sheer bullheadedness.

Maggie Afton was argumentative, tough, stubborn; she knew what she wanted and went after it with a single-mindedness unusual in the women Fred Grant knew. Wide amber eyes, a beguiling smile, honey-colored hair shimmering with golden highlights, and a slim but nicely curved body gave one the distinct impression of softness, but her looks were deceiving. Hidden beneath that lovely exterior lay a steely resolve and firmness of purpose seldom seen even in men. It was rumored that Maggie was engaged once, but what happened to her intended remained locked within Maggie's heart.

Literally raised in a newspaper office, Maggie was at home with the smell of printer's ink and the clatter of presses. Maggie's father had been a much respected owner of a small newspaper in Eureka, California, when he died suddenly of a heart attack. Maggie continued to operate the paper alone for a time, but later sold out and moved to Sacramento before finally settling in Seattle when opportunity beckoned her northward. She was lucky in finding

Grant, who immediately recognized her potential
and hired her. At the advanced age of twenty-five,
Maggie was considered a spinster by many, but she
appeared more amused than disturbed by the title.

"I'm a damn good reporter and you know it, Mr.
Grant!"

Grant rolled his eyes heavenward, calling on all
the patience God gave him. "No one is belittling
your work, Maggie, but I've grown too fond of you
to see harm come to you. Leave the Klondike with
its harsh climate and hardships to men equipped
to handle it. I'd be better served if you remained
in Seattle to cover the news while all those damn
fool men rush north in search of quick wealth."

"Don't patronize me, Mr. Grant," Maggie returned
testily. "You know I'll do a good job for you. I'd
prefer to travel as an employee of the Seattle Post-
Intelligencer but if not I'll do it as a free agent and
sell my articles and pictures to the highest bidder."

Fred Grant wagged his sparsely thatched head
slowly from side to side, recognizing defeat in Maggie's defiant glare. Obviously this determined young
woman couldn't be talked out of this crazy venture.
And if she was set on going to the Klondike then the
Post-Intelligencer might as well benefit.

"You realize, of course, that passage will be hard
to come by now that word is out of the gold strike.
You may have to accept passage on a garbage scow."

"I'll risk it," Maggie grinned, aware that she'd surmounted the first hurdle of her great adventure. Her
impish grin lent her the appearance of an adorable
pixie, belying her tough resolve and the impossible
goals she set for herself.

"I know I'll live to regret it," Fred Grant sighed
wearily, "but if you insist on going to the Klondike
you'll go as an employee of the Post-Intelligencer.
I'll arrange passage."

"I knew I could count on you, Mr. Grant," Maggie

said eagerly. "You won't regret it, either. I'll send you the best damn stories ever to come out of the Yukon."

August 10, 1897

"Take care of yourself, Maggie, and for God's sake don't let anything happen to you."

"Thanks, Mr. Grant, I'll start sending articles back as soon as I arrive in Skagway. There's probably lots of stories available right here aboard the *North Star*."

"I've done all I can to pave your way. I'm sorry accommodations are so lousy. The *North Star* is a mail packet, little better than a scow, but at least I've secured a cabin for you. Once you get to Skagway, you'll be on your own to find transportation over White Pass to the Klondike. It's not too late," he added hopefully, "to back out."

"I'm not a quitter," Maggie returned, her chin jutting out at a stubborn angle. "My father once told me that being a woman had nothing to do with the goals I set for myself. He taught me to be tough and self-reliant so I could get along in a man's world. Besides, this is something I need to prove to myself. I appreciate your concern, but my mind is made up."

Nodding grimly, Fred Grant watched Maggie's trim figure as she picked her way up the gangplank of the insignificant little barge and slowly wound her way through the throngs of men milling about on deck waiting for the last passengers to board. There hadn't been time to purchase the entire eleven hundred and fifty pounds of food the Canadian government insisted upon before allowing stampeders to cross into the Yukon, but Grant assumed the rest could be purchased in Skagway, Alaska. It worried him that Maggie would be on her own in Skagway. If reports could be believed, Skagway was a lawless town teeming with swindlers and criminals of every nature.

Actually, Fred Grant hoped Maggie failed to find someone willing to take her over White Pass to Bennet Lake and downriver to Dawson City in the Klondike. He knew of few women willing or able to endure the hardships, harsh elements, and deplorable conditions at the gold fields. But then, Maggie Afton was like no other woman he'd ever known.

Pausing at the door to her cabin, Maggie swung around to catch a last glimpse of Fred Grant's departing back. Her warm golden eyes darkened with satisfaction over how easily she had gotten her way. Of course she wasn't *in* the Klondike yet, but she was confident of her ability to find suitable escort across that desolate wasteland.

Born twenty-five years ago on Christmas day, she was named Margaret Ann after her grandmother, and promptly called Maggie. Maggie's parents had moved to California from Illinois, where her father had owned and operated a newspaper in Springfield. Lured by adventure, Walt Afton pulled up stakes and took his small family west. He settled in Eureka, where he promptly began publishing a weekly newspaper. Pleased with the town and their reception, the family had remained.

Walt had been the driving force in his daughter's life, raising his only child to be independent, self-reliant, and as tough as her feminine nature would allow. Maggie's mother, Sarah, died in childbirth when Maggie was ten, and Walt chose not to remarry. Instead he devoted his life to reporting the truth and teaching his daughter everything he knew about publishing a newspaper, which was considerable. After Walt's death three years ago, Maggie had floundered for a few months, trying to decide what to do with her life.

Enter Matt Creed, a handsome rogue who nearly succeeded in talking Maggie out of her inheritance as well as her virginity. Vulnerable and at loose ends, Maggie nearly forgot all her father's teachings, allowing the soft, feminine side of her to obscure all but the way Matt's kisses made her feel and the need to be loved and protected.

Maggie rudely came to her senses when she found Matt Creed with another woman and overheard him telling her he'd soon have enough money to set her up in a place of her own. It was the last time Maggie ever let a man's smooth words and false promises lead her astray.

She promptly sold her father's business and moved to Sacramento, where she found a place with a local newspaper. Two years later she felt herself stifling with the assignments allowed her and moved to Seattle, hoping for that one big break to make a name for herself. Through fortitude and perseverance, that day was now at hand. Soon, she vowed, her name would be recognized the world over for her work in the Yukon. But the biggest thrill of all would come with being the first woman to brave adversity and the elements to send back reports of life in the Klondike.

Suddenly a commotion along the dock diverted Maggie's attention, and she turned to watch a herd of noisy, complaining cattle being driven down the pier and into the belly of the barge. It wasn't a large herd, but a strange sight indeed when most ships of every description were used to carry hordes of men to Alaska.

Fascinated, Maggie saw the captain leave the bridge and call down to the dock to the tall cowboy who appeared to be in charge. "Get a move on, Chase, we're behind schedule. Almost left without you."

"Had a mite of trouble on the trail, Cap'n Bates," the man hollered back. He lifted his face, pushing the wide-brimmed hat to the back of his head, and Maggie was treated to the electrifying sight of startling blue eyes in an interesting face bronzed by exposure to the sun. She couldn't help but admire the way his six foot plus frame sat in the saddle with an air or undisputed authority and the wiry strength of his magnificently honed body.

A thin cotton shirt hugged his lean torso and was tucked into the waist of tan cord pants that fit much more snugly than Maggie thought decent. A leather holster hung from his slim hips, cradling a lethal-looking pistol that he wore with such an air of casual menace it was frightening. His body was as hard as steel, and the elements had tanned his skin to a deep bronze, with tiny white lines radiating from the corners of those fascinating blue eyes. His lips were full and sensuous, his hair a burnished copper. The hard planes of his face indicated he was a man who showed scant mercy to his enemies— and asked for none. A tiny shudder traveled the length of Maggie's slender body as their eyes met across the expanse of deck and water.

Abruptly he smiled, a crooked grin displaying a wide expanse of strong white teeth. The effect was devastating, to say the least. When he tipped his hat and winked, Maggie flushed, embarrassed that the bold cowboy had caught her staring at him. She whirled, fully intending to enter the cabin assigned her, when suddenly a harsh cry froze her to the spot. Her reporter instincts and natural curiosity would not allow her to ignore the strong possibility of a story.

"That's him, Sheriff! Arrest the killer. He murdered my buddy in cold blood."

The man pointed a grubby finger directly at the blue-eyed cowboy, who was now trudging up the gangplank with his saddlebag slung over one shoulder. Hearing the cry, the cowboy turned, surprise and disgust wrinkling his wide brow. At least half a dozen men wearing badges sprinted from the crowded dock to give chase.

Still hanging over the rail, the captain shouted, "Chase, hop aboard, quick!"

Leaping the last few feet, Chase landed on deck with a thud, aware that the law was hard on his heels. "Damn!" he cursed beneath his breath. It wasn't in his best interests to be detained now, not when he'd fought weeks of choking trail dust to bring his herd this far. Not when everything he owned was tied up in those one hundred and twenty head of cattle. Not when Rusty was waiting for him in Skagway. He'd worked too dadburned hard to end up in jail for killing a skunk who tried to steal his grubstake to the gold fields. The thieving bastard got no more than he deserved.

But what could he do with the sheriff and his deputies hot on his tail? Chase wondered frantically. Careening around trunks and supplies stacked on the deck, Chase paid little heed to the sheriff's warning to stop, scaling the ladder to the deck above, where the few passenger cabins were located. Skidding to an abrupt halt, he came face to face with Maggie, who had ducked into the doorway of her cabin when she saw the wild-eyed cowboy leaping up the ladder in her direction.

Glancing behind him, Chase saw that his pursuers had yet to reach the top deck, and his natural instinct for survival brought him to a hasty decision. Grasping Maggie around the waist with one hand and the doorknob with the other, Chase opened the door and thrust her inside, following close behind.

"Why—why—what is the meaning of this, you— you big lummox?" Maggie sputtered angrily.

"Sorry, lady," Chase mumbled, slinging his saddlebag beneath the bunk out of sight, "I need your help. Take off your blouse."

"What! Are you some kind of pervert?"

"Listen, lady, I don't aim to hurt you, not if you cooperate."

The sound of raised voices and racing steps brought a tenseness to Chase's large frame and an icy hardness to his blue eyes. "Hurry, lady, I don't cotton to being hauled off to jail. Move your tail, take off your blouse and hop in the bunk before they start searchin' the rooms."

"I'll do no such thing!" Maggie returned huffily.

With grim determination, Chase drew his pistol. "Look, lady, you heard them call me a killer. You gonna make me prove it?"

Maggie eyed Chase's tall, imposing form narrowly. He was everything a well-bred gentleman was not—a barbarian, totally uncivilized, offensive and rude. His language was crude and unfit for a lady's ears, his manners despicable. He wasn't worth a second glance. She looked at him again. This time through the eyes of an inquisitive reporter with the makings of a hot story within her grasp. Besides, he didn't look like a killer to her, and she'd seen enough of them to know.

"All right, Mr.—Mr.—"

"Chase. Chase McGarrett."

"I'll help you, Mr. McGarrett, on one condition," Maggie said brusquely. She was all business now, and Chase decided the lady was one cold fish despite her soft beauty.

" 'Pears to me you got no choice, lady." His bluff didn't fool Maggie.

"I doubt you'll kill me, Mr. McGarrett," she said with more conviction than she felt.

"Name your condition," Chase growled. God preserve him from bossy women.

"Once the sheriff and his men leave, I want your story."

"Story? What in hell are you talkin' about?"

"I'm a reporter with the Seattle Post-Intelligencer. I'm on my way to the Klondike to report on the Bonanza gold strike." She eyed him speculatively. "There's bound to be a story somewhere in this."

"You're a woman!" Chase exploded, astounded by the notion that a female would attempt such a daring feat.

"Obviously you're not blind," Maggie replied coolly. She found little humor in his disparaging tone of voice.

"What I mean, lady," Chase explained with exaggerated patience, "is that the Klondike is no place for a woman."

"We'll argue that point later. What's your answer? The sheriff will be here any second."

"Hell's bells, lady, if you can find a story in my life, you're welcome to it. Turn around."

"What!"

"I'll unbutton your blouse. As soon as you get it off hop in the bunk." Flipping her around, he had the buttons undone before Maggie could voice a protest. "By the way, what's your name?"

"Maggie Afton, but—"

That's as far as Maggie got as Chase dived into the bunk, spurs and all, burrowing into the far corner against the wall. As slim as he was, the bulge he made beneath the covers was slight. Comprehension finally dawned as Maggie realized what he intended. A loud racket at the door set her feet into motion.

"Damn," she muttered sourly, flinging off her blouse, "it never ceases to amaze me what I'm willing to do for a good story."

"Open up in the name of the law!"

Lunging for the bunk, Maggie slid beneath the blanket, draping herself in such a way that her reclining form all but hid Chase, who huddled between her and the wall.

The knocking grew more insistent. "Open up or we'll break the door down!"

"Say somethin'," Chase hissed.

"I—I'm resting in bed," Maggie called out. "What do you want?"

"There's a criminal loose on board, ma'am. We need to search the cabin."

"Surely you don't think . . ." She let her words trail off as if the thought shocked her.

"He has to be somewhere. I'm Sheriff Loomis, ma'am. No harm will come to you. Just open the door so me and my men can get on with our job."

"I have to let them in," Maggie whispered to Chase.

"No funny business," Chase warned. His ominous words were followed by the unmistakable feel of cold steel prodding her ribs.

"The door is unlocked," Maggie called in a voice loud enough to be heard by the lawmen standing outside the door.

Immediately the door burst open and three men stumbled inside. Striking a seductive pose deliberately meant to beguile, Maggie held the sheet to her scantily clad breasts in such a way as to titillate the bemused men's senses.

"I—I'm sorry to bother you, ma'am, but there's a killer on the loose," Sheriff Loomis stuttered, mesmerized by the beautiful woman displayed in charming dishabille.

"As you can see, Sheriff, there's no one here but me," Maggie said prettily, despising the deception she was forced to employ. She considered using feminine wiles a form of dishonesty and almost never resorted to such demeaning tactics.

The sheriff made a cursory inspection of the small cabin, his eyes skipping over the mounds of luggage, consisting mostly of cameras and photographic equipment, littering the floor. Suddenly his gaze

swept back to the cameras, then settled again on
Maggie.

"Why I know you! You're Maggie Afton, from the
Post-Intelligencer. We met when you were covering
a murder trail a few weeks ago, remember?"

"Of course I remember, Sheriff," Maggie smiled.
"How could—oh—" Her sentence ended in a harsh
gasp she attempted to smother with a cough.

That despicable cur hiding behind her skirts had
insinuated one huge hand beneath her petticoat and
slowly slid it up the long slim length of her leg,
over the enticing hill of a curved hip to rest boldly
on her silk-covered buttocks. The sheriff attributed Maggie's sudden intake of breath to the fact
that her privacy had been rudely invaded by three
strange men.

"Sorry, Miss Afton, but were obliged to search all
the cabins," the sheriff apologized sheepishly.

"I un—understand," Maggie said in a strangled
voice. The heat of Chase's hand was like a burning
brand on her flesh, a moist, scalding sensation she
felt in the most private part of her being.

"Looks like all is in order here, so I'll leave you
to your rest. Sorry to interrupt your nap." Sheriff
Loomis backed out of the room followed by his
deputies, who continued to stare gape-mouthed at
the small amount of exposed flesh displayed above
the sheet Maggie held tightly in her slim fingers.

"Are you satisfied, Sheriff? Unless you want to
go to Alaska, I suggest you debark immediately."
Captain Bates glanced into the cabin, then, seeing
Maggie's partially clad form reclining on the bunk,
hastily drew back. "Sorry, Miss Afton."

"We haven't found McGarrett yet," the sheriff complained testily.

"If you haven't found him by now, he's not here,"
Bates argued. "We sail in three minutes, Sheriff." He
waited politely for the three men to stomp off before

reaching behind him to close the door to Maggie's cabin.

Maggie collapsed in relief, until the warm hand caressing her bottom reminded her of a danger of a different sort.

"Don't know when I've felt anythin' so damn soft," Chase murmured, his hand becoming bolder as it slid across the slight indent of Maggie's stomach, inching downward. "I'm no authority, but I'd venture to say your underwear is a mite scandalous."

"Take your filthy hands off me!" Maggie spat, leaping from the bunk. In her haste to escape the cowboy's crude fumblings she had forgotten that her breasts nearly spilled over her corset.

Chase's amused gaze worked its way leisurely across those enticing mounds. He made no pretense of giving her the once-over. She could have slapped his face for thinking what she thought he was thinking. Snatching her blouse from where she had dropped it earlier, she held it before her like a shield.

"Anyone who wears underwear like that can't be as hard-assed as you'd like everyone to believe." Unwinding his long length from the bed, Chase bent Maggie an assessing look.

An angry flush crept up Maggie's neck. How dare that vulgar cowboy talk to her like a common— streetwalker! What business was it of his what kind of underwear she wore? The brief silk pantalettes imported from France were her one concession to feminine extravagance, one she felt safe in indulging, for no one would ever see them but the laundress. Now this obnoxious cowboy had discovered something so intimate about her it brought a blush to her cheeks. And along with it a rush of incredible rage.

Then logic took over and Maggie the newspaper reporter emerged. Years of experience had taught her to disregard her own feelings if they interfered with a story. With great effort, she swallowed her peppery retort, turned her back, and calmly slipped on her blouse. When she swung around to face Chase, she was as composed and business-like as one would expect of a top-notch reporter from the Seattle Post-Intelligencer.

"Now, then, Mr. McGarrett, about that story."

"Hell's bells, Maggie, you're a cool one. What do you have for blood, ice water?"

"I'd prefer you call me Miss Afton. If you'd—"

Her next words were lost to the blast of the steam whistle and the churn of engines. Two more blasts came in quick succession, followed by a wild cheer from the men crowding the decks, and Maggie felt a lurch beneath her feet. With firm purpose, she picked up a leather case lying on a table nearby, then rummaged around until she found a pencil and paper. "About that story, Mr. McGarrett," she repeated crisply, "where would you like to begin?"

Chapter Two

Chase couldn't believe his ears. Despite her beautiful face and curvacious body, Maggie Afton wasn't a woman like any woman he'd known before. She was tough, damn tough, yet he'd bet his favorite Stetson there was a softness beneath that hard-bitten exterior just waiting for someone to discover, a vulnerability she tried desperately to conceal. Too bad, Chase silently lamented, that he had no time to explore all the fascinating facets of Miss Maggie Afton, spinster and career woman.

Curiously, he wondered what made a beautiful, sensuous woman choose a career over a husband and family. At least Maggie would be sensuous if she allowed her softer side to emerge. Nor would it hurt if she smiled more and released her hair from the prim honey-blond bun she wore at the back of her neck. In all fairness, Chase had to admit the severe style detracted little from her vivid beauty. No matter what Maggie did to herself, she couldn't disguise her angel face or full, woman's body. Hot damn, he'd like to be the one to thaw the ice in her veins, Chase thought wistfully. In fact . . .

Maggie realized Chase's intentions too late to utter a protest or react. Suddenly, she found herself in his arms, molded against his long, lean length, her head bent against the crook of his elbow. His lips swooped down to capture hers, driving the breath from her lungs. His kiss was not the kiss of a gentleman, but a bold, insolent assault on her senses that both intrigued and angered her.

Suddenly Maggie felt trapped in unfamiliar feelings. She wanted to run from Chase, from the closeness of his body, and from the strange lethargy creeping through her limbs. No one had the right to make her feel like this, she thought resentfully. Then all coherent thought fled as his kiss deepened, and he slid his tongue along the joining of her lips, then plunged inside when she gasped in shocked indignation. Ruthlessly he plundered her sweetness, seeking, forcing a response she sought to withhold.

But the final indignity came when Maggie felt his big hands slide down her ribs to cup her buttocks, bringing her hard against the unrelenting contours of his swelling loins. To Maggie's absolute horror, the sensitive nipples of her breasts reacted to the unfamiliar caress down below by growing pebble-hard and surging against the thin material of her blouse. A deep chuckle rumbled through Chase's massive chest. The sound brought Maggie abruptly to her senses, and she struggled to free herself from Chase's crude embrace. Reluctantly he released her and she staggered backwards, tripping over her luggage. She would have fallen if Chase hadn't reached out to steady her.

"Don't touch me!" Maggie hissed, shrugging away from his restraining grip.

"Sorry, Maggie." Chase grinned cheekily. "I just couldn't resist." His obnoxious leer told Maggie he wasn't at all sorry for manhandling her. "I had to see for myself if a real woman existed beneath that tough hide. And I'm happy to say I found nothin' lackin', Maggie Afton." His blue eyes sparkled with rare amusement and something else Maggie had difficulty interpreting.

But to her credit, Maggie kept her composure, summoning all her reserves to resist the impossible rogue's rugged appeal. "If you're finished with your games, Mr. McGarrett, may we begin the interview? You might start by telling me why you're being accused of murder."

Though still slightly breathless, Maggie managed to keep her voice crisp and impersonal. She was a professional, one of the few women accorded that position, and she sought to maintain the dignity her work demanded despite her racing heart and the heat generated by the crude cowboy's mysterious appeal. Later, after she obtained all the information necessary for her story, she'd find a way to put Mr. Chase McGarrett in his place and leave him there.

Admiration shone in Chase's eyes as he selected a spot on the bunk to settle his lanky frame. He reckoned it best he didn't show himself on deck for a while anyway, so he might as well sit back for a spell and give this determined lady the story he'd promised her.

"The man I killed tried to steal my cows. They represent all I own in the world and my grubstake to the Klondike goldfields. I intend to sell them in Skagway. My partner told me beef is so scarce I can name my own price once I get them there."

Maggie wrote furiously. "Where are you from, Mr. McGarrett?"

"My name is Chase. Mr. McGarrett makes me feel like I'm pushin' sixty when I'm only twenty-eight. I come from Montana, the most beautiful place in the world," he added wistfully. "Got me a small spread, not much, but it will be a big ranch some day, when I strike it rich in the Klondike. Aim to buy up more land and raise blooded horses, some cattle, and a passel of kids, once I find the right woman."

Maggie studiously ignored this last remark. "You mentioned something about a partner."

"Yep, Rusty Reed, an old army buddy. He's up in Skagway waitin' on me. When he got to the Klondike, he learned all the claims were taken, but fortunately he found a disgruntled prospector willin' to sell out. He says Eleven Above on Gold Bottom, a pup of the Bonanza, is a damn good site and I hope he's right."

"A pup?" Maggie's pencil slid to a halt.

"A little tributary creeklet, or a tributary of a tributary. They usually trickle in from the side of Bonanza Creek. Rusty filed the claim in both our names but lacked the money to buy the ton of food and supplies the Canadian government demands each person purchase before startin' out for the Yukon. That's where me and the cattle come in. They're our grubstake. So you can see why I couldn't let them arrest me for protectin' my property. Rusty is dependin' on me."

"Tell me, Mr. Mc—"

"Chase."

"Tell me, Chase," Maggie conceded, "do you truly expect to strike it rich?"

"Damn tootin', I do."

Maggie winced. Though accustomed to the rough language of her colleagues, Chase's crude words set her teeth on edge. She decided she had about all she could take from this uncouth cowboy. "I think that's all for now, Mr.—Chase. If I have any further questions I'll find you. This floating scow isn't all that big."

"You've got that right, Maggie girl," Chase guffawed. "Cap'n Bates is a friend of mine. An enterprisin' fellow, to say the least. In normal times fares up the Inside Passage are $150. News of the gold strike brought it up to $1500 overnight. A considerable sum for a converted mail barge. He's agreed to transport my cows for a five percent interest in Eleven Above."

Maggie girl! Chase's familiarity brought a scowl to her face. The big lummox, she thought, exasperated. Just because he kissed her didn't give him the right to treat her in so cavalier a manner.

"Thank you, Chase," she said, her jaw clenched tightly. "We've both kept our bargain, now we're quits."

"Quits?" Chase repeated, flashing a wicked grin. "Not on your life, Miss Maggie Afton. You're a fascinatin' woman, spinster or no, and I aim to find out what makes you so damn different from other ladies of my acquaintance."

"In four days we'll be in Skagway, hardly enough time, especially since I won't be seeing you again." Deliberately she held the door open.

"Don't be too sure, Maggie girl. We'll meet again," Chase promised, retrieving his saddlebag and tipping his hat at a rakish angle as he ambled out the door.

Enthralled by the maddening swivel of his lean hips and taut buttocks, Maggie's golden gaze followed his slow progress along the deck. When he reached the ladder leading to the lower deck, he turned, a crooked grin splitting his features, and winked with slow exaggeration. Somehow he knew Maggie would still be poised in the doorway, watching as he sauntered away.

"Oh!" Maggie muttered, disgusted with herself for being caught staring. It was the second time the big cowboy had caught her ogling him. It wasn't as if she were attracted to him. Heaven forbid! No, Maggie told herself firmly, it was just natural curiosity. Rarely, if ever, did she come in contact with men like Chase McGarrett, whose rough country appeal could make a lady forget her own name.

Carefully picking her way around the baggage and supplies littering the deck, Maggie aimed her camera at a youth lounging against a barrel. Decked out in brand-new miner's clothes, he looked barely old enough to shave, and Maggie wondered what he'd look like six months from now after spending a winter in the Yukon. He mugged outrageously for her camera and blinked after the resulting flash. Afterwards Maggie paused to jot down his name and address and a few sentences describing his circumstances.

She moved on to a nearly toothless, grizzled prospector, sporting a flowing gray beard but little hair on his head. His clothing was well-worn, and a wad of chewing tobacco filled his right cheek. When Maggie moved into place before him, he let loose a brown stream that just missed her swaying skirts. She slammed in a fresh plate, took his picture, name, and story and quickly moved on, stopping before a lanky man reclining against a piece of equipment, his wide-brimmed hat pulled down over his face.

"Do you mind if I take your picture, mister?" Maggie asked, focusing the bulky camera and shoving a new plate in the slot.

"Happy to oblige, Maggie girl." Pushing his hat to the back of his head, Chase grinned owlishly at the lovely photographer standing over him. "Shoot away."

Damn, Maggie thought, exasperated. She had hoped she wouldn't encounter Chase McGarrett again. He disturbed her in ways she had never thought possible. Deciding to humor the cocky cowboy, Maggie set her camera, stepped back, and snapped. She wanted his picture anyway to send in with her first story. It was an article on what drove man to desert home and family, facing hardships and possible death, for the elusive glitter of gold. But the real test of her talent would come not with writing the articles, but in finding a way to the Klondike. Surely someone would be willing to take her, Maggie reasoned, for the right price.

Everyone had a price, even the lanky cowboy who took indecent liberties with her body. Suddenly Maggie's thoughts slid to halt as the beginnings of an idea took root in her brain. Why not ask Chase McGarrett to take her to the Klondike? Obviously he wasn't rich, and she was prepared to pay well for his escort. At least she knew his story and what to expect from him. He might be crude, uneducated, and without manners, but Maggie thought him basically honest. The longer she considered the possibility, the more eager she became to present her proposition to him.

"Mister—er, Chase, do you have a minute? I'd like to speak with you—privately."

Chase's eyebrows shot upwards. "Sure thing, Maggie girl, got all the minutes you want," he replied agreeably, unwinding his long length until he towered above her. Despite her own willowy height, Chase stood a good eight inches above her.

Frowning in annoyance, Maggie noted that there wasn't a place on the entire ship, with the exception of her own tiny cabin, where she and Chase might converse in private. As much as she hated the idea of being alone with him, there seemed to be no alternative. Abruptly she whirled, motioning for Chase to follow. His blue eyes crinkling with wry amusement, Chase needed no further urging as he fell into step behind her. A few suggestive remarks followed their progress, which Maggie pretended not to hear, swishing past with the dignity of a queen.

Ascending the ladder to the cabin deck, Maggie had no idea that Chase was admiring her trim ankles, exposed with each upward step. He sighed regretfully when she reached the top and led the way into her cabin. Though Maggie had straightened up somewhat, her bulky equipment still dominated the small cabin. She turned to face Chase, staring up at him through a thick fringe of dark lashes. Chase thought it disconcerting as well as highly arousing. Obviously the lady had powers she wasn't even aware of. What did she want? he wondered, his eyes narrowing suspiciously.

"I'd like to hear more about your plans and how soon you intend to leave for the Klondike," Maggie asked with deceptive innocence.

"Why the sudden interest in my plans?"

"Just answer my question, Chase. Please," she added in a placating tone.

"Sure. Just can't see how my plans would interest you. Or is this some scheme to entice me into your bed? If it is, you sure as hell don't have to go to all this trouble. A simple request will do."

"Why, you conceited oaf! Enticing men to my bed is hardly my calling. What do you think I am?"

"A mite long in the tooth, Maggie girl," Chase goaded, deliberately raking her trim figure with suggestive boldness. "But I don't mind. Never did fancy those sweet young things, all innocence and battin' eyelashes. Give me a real woman who knows what she wants any day."

Stunned, Maggie's mouth flopped open. Never had she encountered such a rude, despicable creature. She had always considered herself an enlightened woman, but Chase's crude teasing rendered her speechless. She had never before felt the need to apologize about her age and marital status, but never before had it been thrown up to her in such a callous manner. She never made excuses to anyone for choosing a career over a husband and family and wasn't about to do so now. She was on the verge of spitting out a scathing retort when she decided that the best way to handle this offensive cowboy was to ignore his outrageous remarks. Besides, she wanted something from him and it wouldn't do to anger or insult him at this point.

"Can't you be serious for once, Chase?" Maggie chided, her amber eyes dark with suppressed rage.

"Believe me, Maggie girl, I am serious," Chase returned, his voice slow and lazy, with overtones Maggie chose to ignore. "What's so all-fired important that you'd invite me to your room?"

"Tell me about your plans once you reach Skagway." She perched gingerly on the edge of the bunk, ready to flee if Chase made an indecent move or suggestion.

"Same as every man aboard the *North Star*. Get to the goldfields as quickly as possible."

"Which route will you take?"

"The easiest and most logical, accordin' to Rusty, is White Pass and raft upriver from Bennet Lake to Dawson. Some still take Chilcoot Pass, pullin' their gear by dogsled, but that route has been all but abandoned by now 'cause it's more difficult. What's this all about?"

"I want you to take me with you. I'll pay whatever you ask."

"Anythin'?" Chase echoed, treating Maggie to an outrageous leer.

"Within reason," Maggie clarified, flushing. She wanted to smack his face but forcibly restrained herself.

Sighing regretfully, Chase shook his head. "Sorry, Maggie girl, the Klondike is no place for a woman. I'd be a liar if I said I wasn't tempted, and not because of the money," he added, twinkling. "But only a damn fool would attempt anythin' so foolish. If you want my opinion, you'll stay board the *North Star* and return to Seattle instead of debarkin' at Skagway. I hear the town is lawless and so corrupt murders occur nearly every hour of every day."

"I didn't ask for advice, only your help in reaching the Klondike. But if you insist on being stubborn, I'll find someone else to take me. If not, I'm prepared to go it alone."

She'd do it, too, Chase concluded, admiring Maggie's grit and determination but despairing of her reckless nature. He didn't much cotton to women with driving ambition who thought themselves better than men, but something about this feisty lady made him want to cheer her on. But not at his expense. He didn't want the responsibility of taking a woman where she didn't belong. Besides, Chase could well imagine Old Rusty's reaction to dragging a woman along with them to the Klondike.

"I doubt you'll find anyone willin' to take you, Maggie, but for what it's worth, I wish you luck. Who knows, you're so blamed determined you might just succeed."

"I *will* succeed, Chase McGarrett," Maggie promised softly, disappointed but not discouraged by Chase's refusal. She stood, waiting for him to leave. But Chase chose to linger, studying Maggie through eyes as vivid blue as the sea.

"You're some woman, Maggie girl."

Then he reached for her, dragging her into his arms as his mouth slashed over hers. Hot, eager, demanding, his tongue-tip prying them apart, her mouth yielding, he kissed her in a way that made her bones melt.

Chase groaned. What was there about this woman that made him want her so? His desire for Maggie was undeniable, the swollen ridge of his manhood a fiery brand through her clothing, its warmth sending heat through her loins. His musky fragrance warped her senses as she clung to him, drowning in sensations foreign to her.

His hand claimed her breast and Maggie shuddered. She knew this couldn't go on or she'd find herself surrendering all to him. Desperately, she threw herself away from his potent embrace, needing to put a safe distance between herself and this powerful mass of brawn and muscle who was turning her inside out, exposing emotions she usually kept under tight rein.

Chase's mouth slanted into a mocking grin. "Are you afraid of me, Maggie Afton? Are you frightened of how I make you feel?"

"I fear no man," Maggie denied vehemently.

Chase's eyes were so clear and sharp they pierced cleanly through her hard exterior, seeking the softness she tried desperately to conceal. "Then why won't you let me kiss you?"

Maggie asked herself the same question. Many men had kissed her, but Chase's kisses were an assault upon her senses. He was ruggedly handsome—impossibly, wonderfully masculine, broadchested and hard muscled—and he roused wicked, wanton instincts in her that she tried hard to stifle.

"Dammit, Chase, I don't have time for this." Irritation sparked her words. "I came to do a job and nothing or no one will interfere with the goals I set for myself. You're an adventurer, seeking wealth and collecting conquests along the way, and I'll not be added to your list. Now get out of here. If you change your mind about helping me, let me know."

A slow smile worked its way across Chase's rugged features. There was something intriguing about this golden-eyed witch with the face of an angel and the disposition of a tigress that made him want to make love to her one minute and wring her neck the next. She was infuriating, foul-tempered, and too damn independent to attract any man with marriage on his mind. No wonder she was still unmarried. But hot damn, spinster or no, Maggie Afton was one gorgeous hunk of woman, one he'd have a high old time taming. He'd bed her in a minute if she'd let him. Right now though it looked as if his chances of making love to her were virtually nil.

"I'll not change my mind, Maggie girl, but if you change yours I'll be around. If the sparks that fly between us are any indication, we'd be damn good in bed." Then he was gone.

"Ohhh," Maggie groaned, infuriated at Chase's audacity. That cowboy had more gall than any man she'd ever met. If one thing came from this adventure, it would be the certain knowledge never to tangle with cowboys from Montana.

Chapter Three

During the summer of 1897, boats of every size and description clogged Skagway Bay. More than two thousand horses and hundreds of dogs, goats, mules, and oxen were dumped overboard and forced to swim ashore in icy water. Freight bundles were dropped onto scows and rafts, with no concern for breakage or water damage, and moved from deep water across the shallow tidal mud flats, then tossed helter-skelter on the shore. The confusion and racket were unescapable day and night as men stumbled over trunks, boxes, food supplies, stoves, mining tools, and bales of hay in a frantic effort to locate their belongings and gather them into one place beyond the high-water line.

This was the bedlam Maggie found herself thrust into that August day in 1897 when the *North Star* steamed up the Inside Passage, down Lynne Canal, and into Skagway Bay. With hundreds of people pouring into town and hundreds more backtracking to carry their supplies over White Pass, sometimes making fifteen to twenty trips, the town took on the appearance of a grim carnival. Every known kind of criminal and crook flocked there. They swindled, stole, waylaid, drugged, attacked, and murdered men without restraint. Maggie was soon to learn that most were part of a complex outlaw group bossed by Jefferson R. "Soapy" Smith, an enterprising man who collected a fifty percent commission on various criminal ventures, promising protection when those who did the deed got in trouble.

The day the *North Star* hove to would live long in Maggie's memory. People had tried to warn her, but she had absolutely no idea things would be this bad. Undaunted, she stood on deck beside her fragile photographic equipment, ready to do battle with the first person who manhandled her valuable belongings. Like a knight of long ago, it was Chase who came to her rescue, lifting her things aboard the raft sent out to ferry them ashore. When she scrambled aboard the bobbing craft to accompany her equipment, she fully expected Chase to follow. Instead, he saluted jauntily and stood by as the raft pulled away.

Aren't you coming?" Maggie called out.

"Nope, got to get my cattle ashore. See ya 'round, Maggie girl."

What now? Maggie thought as she sat on one of her trunks dumped unceremoniously on the beach by the bargeman. As far as she could see, thousands of tents lined the beach up and down for many miles.

At least the scenery was spectacular, she reflected as she gazed in awe at the magnificent, snowcapped mountains hugging three sides of the narrow valley on which Skagway was built. The open side faced the Lynne Canal with its mud flats and shallow water.

"Need help, lady?"

Maggie heaved a sigh of relief. At least there was one gentleman in Skagway, she thought. But the man standing before her scarcely resembled any gentleman she'd ever seen. He wore an assortment of rags; his hair and scraggly beard were long and unkempt. His shoes were wrapped with rags to hold them together and most of his teeth were missing.

"Yes, thank you. I'd appreciate it if you'd carry my baggage to the nearest hotel."

A loud guffaw followed Maggie's words. "There ain't no hotel in Skagway fit fer a lady. But Mr. Smith will rent ya a place on the beach to pitch a tent. What in the hell is a lady like you doin' in Skagway anyways? Where's yer man?"

"That's none of your business. Just tell me where I can locate Mr. Smith and I'll find him while you move my belongings to high ground."

The man scratched his head in a most disconcerting manner. "You'll find Soapy at Soapy's Parlor, most likely. If he ain't there, try the Ice Palace."

"Soapy?"

"Folks 'round here call him Soapy. His real name is Jefferson Randolph Smith. He kinda runs things in Skagway."

"Thank you, Mr.—"

"Just call me Hank."

"Thank you, Hank." She turned to leave, lifting her skirts to keep them from dragging in the mud.

"Fifty dollars, lady."

"What!"

"It'll cost ya fifty dollars to move yer belongin's above high-water line."

"That's highway robbery!" Maggie blustered.

Hank shrugged. "Take it or leave it, makes me no nevermind."

Damn, Maggie cursed beneath her breath. She hoped she'd not be forced to linger in this hellhole long. Opening her bag, she produced half the required amount, placed it in the greedy man's grubby paw, and trudged off across the wet sand. "I expect you to guard my luggage well for that money," she threw over her shoulder. "When I return you'll receive the balance."

Unaccustomed to the sight of a well-dressed woman in this rough wilderness, dozens of pairs of admiring eyes and numerous covetous glances followed Maggie's progress—as did catcalls, hoots, and whistles, which Maggie did her best to ignore.

Maggie paused before the Ice Palace, debating whether to look for Soapy Smith inside or continue on to Soapy's Parlor. She'd never been inside a saloon before, and she looked around for someone to send inside with a message for the notorious Mr. Smith. Suddenly the thud of hooves and the sounds of complaining cattle brought people rushing from the saloon and buildings lining the single street, oddly named Broadway. Maggie turned her head just as Chase, assisted by an older man with a shock of graying red hair and a full beard, drove his cattle though the main thoroughfare.

As Chase passed by, two middle-aged women dressed in an odd assortment of men's clothing rushed up to intercept him. "Whose cows are those, mister?" one of the the women asked excitedly.

"Mine," Chase replied, tipping his hat politely. "Got a corral hereabouts where I can pen them for a spell?"

"There's a corral behind the Ice Palace you can use."

The feminine voice was soft, low, and provocative, and Chase reacted instinctively, craning his neck in the direction of the speaker. A flamboyantly garbed woman stepped boldly forward. "I'm Belle

Delarue, owner of the Ice Palace."

She was of medium height and voluptuous, with lustrous strands of thick, copper-colored hair piled atop her head in an elaborate style that framed her exotic features perfectly. Wide mouth, sloping eyes, and high defined cheekbones all added to her allure. Though her dress was bold and colorful, it wouldn't have been considered decent by most standards.

Chase's male instincts leaped out to devour the flaming beauty. He found no fault with her looks except perhaps for the hardness lingering around her green eyes and too-bright smile. A man could find a heap of comfort in those soft white arms, he thought idly. Then he turned his head slightly and met Maggie Afton's contemptuous glare. Her amber gaze slid over him with the knowledge that she knew exactly what he was thinking. And blast it all, she was right!

"Wait!" The woman who had first accosted Chase rudely shoved her way to his side, interrupting his silent observations. "Are them cows fer sale?"

"Yep. All hundred and twenty head."

"I'll give you five dollars a head. I'm Hannah Brown and this here is Kate Sites. We own the Hash House Restaurant. My customers are sick of bear meat and can't say as how I blame them. A beefsteak sure would taste good."

A crooked smile hung on the corner of Chase's lips. "Sorry, Hannah, you'll have to do better than that. I brought these cows clear up from Montana."

"Ten dollars," offered Hannah, growing desperate.

"I'll give you twenty." All eyes turned to Belle, who had just entered into the bidding, tossing a gloating look at Hannah and her partner.

"Thirty!" Hannah responded, prompted by Kate.

"One hundred dollars!" bid Belle, well aware that the two women couldn't afford to outbid her.

"We can't afford to go no higher and you know it!" Hannah retorted, her voice ripe with disgust. "Come on, Kate, we got supper to prepare. Bear stew tonight, men!" she called over her shoulder, drawing a groan from prospective customers.

When Belle loudly proclaimed, "Beefsteak at the Ice Palace tonight," it started a small stampede toward the saloon door.

Happy to see another woman in this godforsaken town, Maggie hurried after Hannah and Kate. She hoped they'd know of a place to stay other than a tent pitched on a beach crowded with men of all description.

"Excuse me," Maggie called out. "May I have a word with you?"

Both women turned in unison, their eyes widening at the sight of Maggie, impeccably dressed in the latest fashion. "Land sakes, child, where did you come from?"

"I'm Maggie Afton. I just arrived on the *North Star*."

"Pleased to meet ya, Maggie. I'm Hannah Brown and this here's Kate Sites. Where's yer man? Ain't safe in Skagway fer a woman alone, lessen they look like me and Kate." A loud guffaw followed her words.

Maggie couldn't help but smile at their friendly manner, or react in kind. "I'm alone and I'm sorry about the cows. Perhaps there'll be others come through."

Hannah shrugged philosophically. "Mebbe. What ya doin' by yerself in a place like Skagway?"

"I'm a newspaper reporter with the Seattle Post-Intelligencer," Maggie explained. "I'm on my way to the Klondike to cover the gold strike as soon as I find someone to take me."

"I'll be damned!" Kate exclaimed, bug-eyed. "A woman reporter. 'Bout time a woman got a decent job. I sure wish ya luck, honey, but don't expect miracles. Don't rightly know of any man willin' to take a woman to the Klondike. I'm sure a woman will get there one day, but most likely it will be a woman accompanying her man."

"Kate's right, Maggie," Hannah concurred. "And Skagway is no place fer a woman alone. Gettin' to the Klondike is no picnic. I respect yer gumption, but yer too young and purty to be on yer own in this part of the world. Gold fever makes men do crazy things."

"Thanks for the advice, ladies, but I'll find a way to the Klondike, just you wait and see."

A gap-toothed smile split Hannah's weathered face. "I believe ya will, honey. Meanwhile, ya gotta have a place to stay."

"Exactly," Maggie concurred. "Do either of you know someone willing to board me for a while? Or a good hotel in town?"

"Only women in town besides me and Kate are saloon girls and whores. Hotels here ain't fit fer a lady. The saloons sometimes rent rooms," Hannah advised, "but don't reckon you'd be interested in that."

"I could always pitch a tent on the beach," Maggie grimaced, suppressing a shudder. "It won't be for long. Only until I can hire someone to take me over White Pass to Yukon Territory."

Hannah and Kate exchanged worried glances over Maggie's head. "Tell ya what, honey," Kate suggested. "I can bunk in with Hannah fer a spell and you can use my room behind the Hash House. It ain't much, but it's clean and yer welcome to it."

"Oh, no, I couldn't take your room, Kate!" Maggie cried, touched by their generosity.

"Sure ya can. How's twenty dollars a week room and board sound?"

"Sounds wonderful, but . . ."

"No buts," Kate grinned, "it's all settled. Come along, ya can send fer yer things later."

Chase sat across from Belle Delarue in her cramped office behind the bar in the Ice Palace. "What's your name, Cowboy?" she asked archly. She made no bones about sizing up Chase's lanky frame and masculine attributes, evidently liking what she saw.

"McGarrett, ma'am, Chase McGarrett."

"Just plain Belle will do, Chase. Now what do I owe you for the cows?"

"One hundred and twenty head at one hundred dollars a head comes to twelve thousand dollars."

"I suppose you're planning on using it for a grub-stake to the Klondike," Belle said, moving to the safe and flipping the dial. "I'll have to pay you in nuggets and dust, that agreeable with you?"

Belle experienced the full radiance of Chase's crooked smile. "Gold is just fine, Belle. And to answer your question, I'll be leavin' for the Klondike soon as me and Rusty can buy the food and equipment we need."

"Rusty?"

"My partner, Rusty Reed. We bought a claim on Gold Bottom from a prospector who had his fill of the weather and hardships."

"Too bad," Belle said huskily. "I like you, Cowboy, like you a lot. I could use someone like you around the Ice Palace. The salary is excellent and a man like you should find the . . . fringe benefits to your liking." Her sultry tone and seductive green eyes promised lust and passion and more—much more. Though Chase exhibited normal male interest, he couldn't banish the picture of flashing amber eyes and warm golden tresses from his mind. It shocked him to think that an exasperating female like Mag-

gie Afton made every other woman pale in comparison. Even flamboyant Belle Delarue.

"Your offer is mighty temptin', Belle, but so is the
Klondike. 'Sides, can't let Rusty down, he's countin'
on me to help work the claim." He rose to leave,
tucking the two pouches of dust and nuggets in his
jacket pockets.

"If you change your mind, Chase, look me up.
In case you have trouble remembering me, here's
something to carry along with you to refresh your
memory."

Her hips swaying seductively, Belle sidled up
beside Chase until her breasts brushed the front
of his shirt, their hardened tips etching fire through
the material to his chest. Her soft white arms came
around his neck and her full red lips pressed against
his with bold insistence. With a will of their own,
Chase's arms came around Belle, pressing her softness into his own hardness. Her mouth opened,
inviting his tongue, and Chase obliged. Until his
good sense returned. His arms dropped and he
backed away, wondering what in the hell he was
doing here fooling around with Belle Delarue when
Rusty was waiting on him.

Chase had known many women like Belle before.
Plenty of them. They were users, seekers of pleasure
who grabbed you by the short hairs and kept you
dangling till someone better came along. They were
all right for a night's dalliance, but he tried to steer
clear of involvements with whores. And he certainly
recognized Belle for what she was—a discriminat-
ing whore who had found a gold mine in the Ice
Palace. She might not have to whore for a living
now, but the instincts were still there.

Yet Chase had to admit that bedding a beautiful
woman like Belle wouldn't be too difficult. In fact,
he'd probably enjoy it if—if what? If he didn't have

gold fever? Or if he hadn't met Miss Maggie High and Mighty Afton? Truth to tell, he'd rather bed Maggie than any woman he knew. Sighing wistfully at something that was as unlikely to happen as snow in hell, Chase moved toward the door.

Belle's question stopped him just short of the exit. "You need a room, Chase? The hotels are rat's nests. I got a spare room upstairs if you're interested."

"Much obliged, Belle, but Rusty pitched a tent down on the beach. We'll only be in Skagway a day or two anyway. Gotta get over the pass and to the Klondike before the river freezes over." He tipped his hat.

"So long, Chase. Stop in again if you come back through Skagway."

"So long, Belle. Enjoy the cows."

Suddenly the door opened before Chase touched the knob, admitting a tall, slim, bearded man with a long, narrow face and cold, almost colorless eyes. He stared at Chase narrowly before settling his probing gaze on Belle.

"Who's the cowboy, Belle?"

"Chase McGarrett," Belle said, licking her lips nervously. "I just bought his cows."

"Ah, the cattle in the pen out back. I'm Jefferson Randolph Smith. Folks call me Soapy." He extended his hand to Chase.

"Howdy," Chase greeted him, pumping Soapy's hand.

"Soapy is—an important man in town," Belle offered. "He owns Soapy's Parlor over on Holly Street."

Chase nodded, mumbled an appropiate reply, and made a hasty exit. Truth to tell, he didn't like Soapy's looks. A straight-forward man himself, Chase thought Soapy looked like a shifty, greedy character who'd stop at nothing to further his own interests. He wouldn't have been surprised to find

out later that Soapy had his hand in every crime
committed in Skagway.

Soapy watched Chase narrowly as the cowboy
ambled out. He hadn't seen anything quite like him
since he arrived in Skagway a few months earlier as
a soap salesman. When his sales lagged, he wrapped
fifty and one hundred dollar bills inside the wrap-
pers of selected bars of soap in order to spur sales.
Needless to say, sales soared. But Soapy made certain only his henchmen received soap with money.
From that day on he was known as "Soapy."

"How much did you pay the cowboy for his cows?"
Soapy asked Belle.

"Twelve thousand, and worth every cent. They'll
bring in lots of business. Don't know how long it's
been since the Ice Palace offered a good beefsteak."

"Does McGarrett have the money on him?"

Belle nodded, understanding Soapy perfectly.
"Him and his partner are going to use it to
grubstake them to the Klondike. They bought a
claim on Gold Bottom."

"Hmmm. Some pretty good samples coming down
from Gold Bottom. Thanks, Belle." He turned to
leave, then thought better of it. "You seemed mighty
taken with the cowboy."

Belle grinned. "Wouldn't mind having him stick
around a spell."

"Maybe I can arrange it," Soapy said, his colorless
eyes glinting deviously.

The grin remained on Belle's red lips long after
Soapy left.

"Hot damn, twelve thousand dollars!" Rusty
whooped as Chase poured the dust and nuggets
into the older man's hands. "That oughta tide us
over till we hit pay dirt."

Slender and wiry, Rusty carried his fifty years
well. Years of fighting Indians had taught him how

to survive through any adversity. He was a crusty sergeant when he met young Chase McGarrett, a fresh young private. He took the green rookie under his wing and taught Chase all about survival. Soon the two became fast, albeit unlikely, friends.

Since Chase was an orphan whose family had died of influenza, he adopted Rusty as a substitute father, and when Rusty mustered from the army, Chase tagged along. They pooled their savings and bought a spread in Montana, where they struggled along trying to hold together the ranch they both grew to love.

When first word of gold in the Yukon reached civilization, Rusty and Chase talked it over and decided it was worth the effort for one of them to go and look over the prospects. Rusty was elected and he left immediately, only to find no claims left to file. But luck was with him when he met a down-and-out prospector eager to unload his holdings. Chase mortgaged the ranch and sent Rusty money to purchase Eleven Above, but little was left for a grubstake or to work the claim.

Chase did manage, though, to scrape up enough money to buy a small herd of cattle with the intention of driving them to Skagway. According to Rusty, beef was so scarce men would pay "dang near anything" for a tasty steak. Pinning their future on the small herd of cattle might seem foolhardy, but it proved a good investment, one that had paid off handsomely. The one drawback was that if they failed to find gold, they stood to lose everything, including the ranch that they'd both struggled so hard for.

"When you drove them cows ashore I was never so glad to see anyone in my life," Rusty admitted. "Time's gettin' short. We gotta get over the pass before bad weather cuts off travel. I was right, wasn't I, son? Them cows was a dang good idea."

They sat in the small tent Rusty had set up on the beach and outfitted with two cots and a camp stove.

"The best," Chase agreed. "How soon can we leave?"

"In a couple of days, I reckon. We need to buy just about everythin'. The Canadian government demands that each man have eleven hundert fifty pounds of food and a ton of supplies in order to enter the Yukon. They got Mounties stationed at the foot of the pass to make certain everyone complies with the law and to collect customs."

"Customs?"

"Yep, twenty-five percent on American-made goods."

Chase chewed on that for awhile before asking, "Will the four pack horses I brought be enough to carry our supplies?"

"If they ain't, we'll buy sleds and dogs. We got enough money now to travel in style."

"Whatever you say, Rusty," Chase grinned, "you're the expert. Here," he said, shoving the sacks of gold at the older man. "You know what's needed, why don't you see to the supplies. I—there's some unfinished business I need to attend to."

Rusty scratched his head, ruffling his shock of gray-streaked red hair. "You just got in town, son. What kinda business could you have already?

Chase grinned foolishly. "It's personal."

Suddenly comprehension dawned. "Don't know how I could be so stupid. You go on, Chase, take care of your—business. You'll find the purtiest and cleanest girls at the Ice Palace. You got money? Whores don't come cheap up here."

A slow flush crept over Chase's face. "You got me wrong, Rusty. I'm gonna find a woman, but not a whore. This is a woman I met aboard the *North*

Star. A newspaper reporter who's lookin' for someone stupid enough to take her to the Klondike."

"A woman newspaper reporter?" Rusty repeated,
aghast. "Is the damn fool woman loco? This ain't no
place fer a lady."

"That's what I tried to tell her, but you don't know
the lady, Rusty. She's stubborn as a mule and twice
as feisty. She's obstinate, bullheaded, and as beautiful as an angel. I just want to make sure she's all
right before I leave Skagway."

A look of disbelief marched across Rusty's weathered features. Not once since Rusty had known him
had Chase voiced concern over a woman. He'd
almost given up on Chase finding a good woman
and settling down. Whenever he brought up the
subject Chase always said he hadn't met a woman
yet he'd want to spend the rest of his life with. What
kind of woman was this newspaper reporter who
had captured Chase's senses so thoroughly?

"You go ahead, son, I'll take care of things at this
end," he said, "but if you ask me, the lady sounds
like someone you hadn't oughta tangle with."

"I don't aim to tangle with Maggie, Rusty, I'm just
gonna make sure she's okay. I'll meet you over at the
outfittin' store in a couple of hours."

Leaving Rusty muttering to himself about career
women and what they can do to a man, Chase
left the tent, jammed his hat down on his head
and ambled off toward town. He had no idea he
was being followed until he was shoved into a
dark alley between two buildings. Automatically
he reached for his gun, but one of the two men
who accosted him clubbed him with the butt of
his pistol before his hand touched his holster. The
last thing he heard before he plunged into the bottomless pit of unconsciousness was a voice saying,
"Soapy says he's carryin' twelve thousand in dust
and nuggets."

"Soapy . . ." Chase repeated groggily. Then he knew no more.

"Dammit, Bandy, there's nothin' in his pockets but lint," one of the men complained.

"There's gotta be, Zeke, keep lookin'," Bandy replied, growling with impatience.

"Shit! The old coot must have the gold," Zeke swore after all Chase's pockets were turned inside out. "What'll we do now?"

"We find his partner," Bandy replied, rising and drawing his gun. "Soon as we finish here."

"We gonna kill him?"

"I gotta gut feelin' we oughta, but Soapy says to let him live. 'Pears like Belle's gotta hankerin' fer the cowboy. Come on, let's get outta here. He won't wake up fer a good long spell. Should give us plenty of time to find his partner and relieve him of his gold."

Rusty made one short stop before heading over to the outfitting store to purchase the ton of supplies required before entering the Yukon. Rusty Reed was a hard drinking man who liked his liquor, but he knew his limit. He rarely appeared inebriated and was wise enough to stop short of falling down drunk. With the comfortable weight of gold lining his pockets, he saw no reason why he shouldn't wet his whistle before beginning the tedious task of purchasing supplies. His mind made up, he wheeled into the Ice Palace, where he promptly treated his newfound friends to a round of drinks. He paid with a shiny gold nugget carefully weighed by the bartender. That's where Bandy and Zeke found him after leaving Chase unconscious in the alley.

"That's him," Bandy hissed, nudging Zeke in the ribs and nodding toward Rusty, who stood at the long curved bar amidst a crowd of men.

"Yeah, do we take him now?"

Bandy slanted Zeke an oblique look. "I swear you ain't got no more sense than a jackass. We wait till he leaves, then we follow. Don't let the old bastard outta yer sight."

Rusty allowed himself two drinks of poor whiskey. Nearly every saloon in Skagway sold whiskey adulterated with two-thirds water. When whiskey became scarce they sold "hootch" consisting of sourdough and brown sugar, flavored with blueberries or dried peaches. Home-brewed beer was also sold when supplies became short during the long winter. After bidding his cronies good-bye, Rusty sauntered out into the twilight. Halfway down the block he was shoved into a dark alley, the same one where Chase lay unconscious a few feet away.

"What the hell . . ." Rusty's eyes widened with shock when he whirled to face the two toughs closing in on him.

Rusty went for his gun, and met with the saw fate Chase had a short time earlier. The cruel blow to his head sent him to his knees, then he keeled over on his face. Both toughs were on him in an instant, tearing at his clothes to get at the gold. They found it with little trouble stuffed inside his jacket pockets.

"Hot damn, it's all here!" Zeke crowed as he hefted the two sacks in his hands.

"Don't get no ideas," Bandy warned, "all we get is our cut. The rest belongs to Soapy. Let's finish off the old buzzard so's we can get outta here." He drew his Colt Repeater.

Groggy and disoriented, Chase struggled out of his stupor, shook his head, and rose unsteadily to his knees. What in the hell happened? he wondered as his vision slowly began to clear. His head felt as if he'd been butting it into a brick wall. Suddenly the murmur of voices caught his attention and he froze, his hand slowly inching toward the gun still strapped snugly around his hips. In the murky

dimness of the alley Chase made out the figures of
two men bending over something or someone lying
at their feet. Another poor hapless bastard getting
his brains bashed in and robbed, Chase thought
disgustedly.

When he saw one of the men aiming his gun at
the helpless victim on the ground, Chase reacted
instinctively. Roaring with outrage, he whipped out
his weapon and fired. But his head injury made him
too dizzy to aim straight, and Chase's shot went
wild.

"Shit!" Bandy spat, ducking. Through the gloom
Chase came stalking toward them, looking tough
and mean despite his recent clubbing.

"Let's get the hell outta here, Bandy, we got what
we come for." Without waiting for a reply, Zeke
turned and hightailed it out of the alley.

Unwilling to remain and face an enraged Chase
unaided, Bandy followed close on Zeke's heels. But
before he left he aimed a vicious kick at Rusty's leg
with a cleated boot. The loud crack that followed
brought a moan from Rusty's lips and plunged
· him deeper into unconsciousness. By the time
Chase reached him, Bandy and Zeke were long
gone.

Dropping to his knees before the injured man,
Chase attempted to turn him over. A damp stickiness stained his hands and he cursed. "They did
a job on you, didn't they, fella? Let me turn you
over and see what you look like." Carefully he eased
the man on his back, swearing profusely when he
recognized his partner. "Hell's bells! Rusty!"

Suddenly the import of what finding Rusty here
like this meant hit Chase with the force of a sledge-
hammer. "Jesus! No!" His hands slid over Rusty's
body, discovering nothing but turned-out pockets
holding a few loose dollars and change. "It's gone!
Everythin' we fought and saved for is gone!"

Not one to openly display his feelings, Chase was as close to tears as he had ever been in his life. And he couldn't ever remember crying. His head bent, Chase spent a few painful seconds silently marshaling his ragged emotions.

"That you, Chase? What happened, son?"

"Dirty dealin's afoot, Rusty," Chase choked out. "I was dragged into the alley and clubbed by someone who knew I had just collected a fortune in gold. When they didn't find the gold on me, they naturally assumed you had it. Don't know what happened after they hit me or how you got here."

"It's my fault, Chase, all my fault," Rusty lamented. "I shoulda been more careful. Why in tarnation did I stop in at the Ice Palace to wet my whistle? But I swear, Chase, I only had two drinks of watered-down whiskey. Those two toughs musta followed me out."

"It's not that simple, Rusty. Somebody deliberately set us up, and I know who."

"You do? Then let's go get the bastard." He tried to rise, let out an agonized shriek, and fell back.

"What is it, Rusty?"

"My leg, Chase, I think it's broken."

A string of obscenities shot past Chase's lips as he probed gently, finding the break immediately, halfway between Rusty's ankle and knee. "Yep, it's broke, Rusty. Don't move. I'll get the doc and find someplace to move you. A tent's no place for a man with a broken leg." He staggered to his feet, still groggy from the blow to his head and not completely himself.

"Chase, wait, you started to tell me who clubbed us."

"You ever heard of Soapy Smith?"

"Damn right I have. Soapy Smith is bossman here-abouts. He controls everythin' in Skagway. You can bet your ass he didn't do it hisself, though. He hates violence. They say he's got two hundred men workin' fer him. Takes his cut in every crime committed in this hellhole. We might as well kiss our money good-bye, son."

"We'll talk about that later, Rusty," Chase said. "Will you be okay while I go get help?"

"Sure, son. I got my gun. The first man who steps inside the alley gets his head blowed off."

"Don't get trigger-happy, Rusty. I don't hanker to get blowed away by my partner."

Waving him on, Rusty watched as Chase left the alley, his face a grimace of pain. He didn't want to let on in front of Chase, but his leg hurt so damn bad it was all he could do to suppress the groan lurking at the back of his throat.

Chase emerged from the alley, grabbing the first person he saw on the street. "Where can I find a doctor? My partner's been hurt."

"You won't find no doctor in Skagway, mister. There's one in Juneau, though. Heard tell there's one in Dyea, too. Take your friend there."

"You don't understand. His leg is broken, and he can't be moved," Chase growled, growing impatient.

"Well, if that's all, Kate Sites is the closest thing to a doctor in town. She set more than one broken bone that I know of. You'll find her at the Hash House."

Chase groaned. Kate Sites. One of the women who wanted to buy his cattle. Why did it have to be her? She was probably still mad at him for selling his cows to Belle and raking in a hefty profit. Still, Rusty could be crippled for life if he didn't get help. Stiffening his shoulders, he raced off toward the Hash House.

It was the supper hour, and Chase found both women busy preparing and serving food to their hungry customers. Hannah saw Chase first and approached him, hands on ample hips. "What's the matter, Cowboy, don't you like beefsteak? Thought you'd be over at the Ice Palace enjoyin' yer profits. But if yer hankerin' fer bear stew, set yerself down."

"Sorry 'bout that, Hannah, but I needed the money. I also need help. My partner and me were attacked and robbed tonight. They stole our gold and broke Rusty's leg. I was told Kate knew some doctorin'."

"Oh, the poor man," Kate said, hurrying over when she heard Chase's plea.

"Sounds like Soapy Smith's doin's," Hannah grunted, not unduly surprised by Chase's disclosure. "Happens all the time. If he can't cheat a man outta his money, he'll steal it."

"Will you help me? I'm not even sure I can pay, but I can't let Rusty go unattended and end up a cripple for the rest of his life."

"Where is your friend?" Kate asked.

"I left him lyin' in the alley between the general store and the assayer's office. I was afraid to move him."

"I don't know. . . . Got customers here to think of, and it being supper time and all . . ." Though Hannah expressed reservations, Kate had already made up her mind.

"Chase, what are you doing here?" Chase whirled, surprised to find Maggie standing at his elbow.

"Maggie!" Despite his urgency, the sight of Maggie's beautiful face brought a sigh of profound relief to his lips. Once he found out what this town was like, he'd been damn worried about her. But apparently Maggie had escaped unscathed while he and Rusty had fallen victim to unscrupulous men before one day had elapsed. "I was worried about you."

"You know this man?" Hannah asked.

"Yes," Maggie freely admitted, "we met aboard ship. Mr. McGarrett was kind enough to help me with my baggage. He also provided me with a story for my very first article to leave Alaska."

"You're acquainted with these ladies?" Chase asked, surprised.

"We just met today, but Hannah and Kate kindly offered me a room until I find someone to take me to the Klondike. Are you here to sample their bear stew?"

"I wish it was nothin' more serious than an empty stomach that brought we here," Chase said, managing a shaky smile. "Me and Rusty were attacked and robbed tonight."

"Oh, no, your grubstake," Maggie groaned, expressing true sympathy for Chase's predicament. "Are you hurt?"

Gingerly he fingered the egg-sized lump on his head. "Nothin' serious. It's Rusty who's injured. I left him lyin' in the alley nursin' a broken leg."

"Have you summoned a doctor?"

"Doctor! Hrumph!" Kate said with a hint of disgust. "If one ever came to Skagway, he'd only stay long enough to buy supplies and join the stampeders to the Klondike."

"Oh, poor Rusty, what can we do?"

"Well," Hannah, the more outspoken of the two women, conceded grudgingly, "if you know this cowboy, I guess it's okay to help. I'll round up a couple of boys to carry Rusty back here so Kate can treat him. She's the best doctor hereabouts, even if I do say so myself."

"You'll have to splint the leg first, Chase, can you do it?" Kate asked anxiously.

"I don't know, but I sure as hell can try," Chase said, his mouth set in determined lines.

"Wait here, I'll be right back." She hustled off, leaving Chase and Maggie alone as Hannah turned back to her customers.

"I didn't know Kate was a doctor," Maggie mused.

"She isn't, but she's all I got right now."

"Chase, I—I'm sorry. About the money, I mean. And your partner. What are you going to do now?"

"Damned if I know," Chase admitted shakily. "We might be forced to sell our claim. Neither of us has more than a few dollars in our jeans, a tent, and some supplies."

The gleam in Maggie's eyes should have alerted Chase, but he was too worried about Rusty to notice. Then Kate returned with two burly men carrying a wide board, several short pieces of wood, and strips of cloth.

"I'll talk to you later, Maggie. 'Pears I'll be around longer than I expected." Motioning to the men, he hurried off.

"Chase, wait, I'm coming with you. Maybe I can help."

As it turned out, Maggie's help was greatly appreciated by Rusty, who by now was nearly senseless with pain. Maggie's steady hand was called upon to splint Rusty's leg when Chase's clumsy fumbling only added to his partner's torture.

Rusty passed out long before Kate snapped the bone into place with amazing skill. Afterwards they moved him to a small storeroom sparsely furnished with cot, table and lamp located behind the Hash House. Chase sprawled on the floor beside Rusty. When Maggie stopped by a short time later with a tray of food, both men were sound asleep.

Chapter Four

Maggie had a lot to think about after she returned to the crackerbox room Kate had been good enough to vacate for her. She felt real sympathy for Chase and the dilemma facing him, but she still couldn't help the jolt of elation his predicament brought. Wouldn't he be more amenable now to considering her offer of payment for taking her to the Klondike? She'd much rather go with someone she knew than trust a stranger who was likely to take advantage of her.

Chase McGarrett might be a crude, uneducated cowboy, but Maggie knew he'd do nothing to harm her. He was the kind who, once committed, would keep his word. The only problem was that he was too attractive, too well endowed with masculine virility for Maggie to be completely immune to his appeal. Close contact with Chase for weeks on end would be dangerous, in more ways than one, Maggie decided, but no more dangerous than trusting her life to strangers.

Why did she have to be so attracted to the big ox? Maggie asked herself as she undressed for bed. He was the complete opposite of the men she normally associated with. He thought nothing of kissing her and taking liberties where none were given whenever he pleased. She'd have to be on her guard at all times if she traveled with Chase, but Maggie considered herself a match for any man—especially one like Chase McGarrett, who constantly challenged her resolve.

Though Maggie arose early the next morning, she found she was the last one up. Hannah was already in the kitchen flipping flapjacks and Kate had just walked into the kitchen with an empty tray.

"Mornin', Maggie." Kate grinned, her brown eyes alive and friendly in a face showing more than her forty-odd years. "Did ya sleep well?"

"Very well, thank you," Maggie returned.

"Help yerself," Hannah invited as she sped by with a huge tray of flapjacks, which she placed on a long trestle table where several men were seated.

"How is the patient?" Maggie asked Kate as she fixed herself a plate of the tempting flapjacks. They smelled delicious.

"Fair to middlin'," Kate replied, smiling shyly. "He's a bit testy, due to pain, no doubt, but I gave him some laudanum last night, and Chase said Rusty slept for several hours. Poor man," Kate clucked sympathetically. "All that money and now they're broke."

"Do you know what their plans are?"

"Beats me. Chase and Rusty were discussin' it when I left a few minutes ago."

Unable to sleep because of the hard floor beneath him and Rusty's moaning, Chase had awakened early. He thought about looking for a cup of coffee in the kitchen when Rusty groaned and opened his eyes.

"How are you feelin', Rusty?" Chase asked solicitously.

"Ask me in a week," Rusty grumbled. He tried to shift his position and a jolt of pain shot through his leg. "What happened?"

"What do you remember?"

"Nothin' much after leavin' the Ice Palace and—and—oh shit, I was robbed! Did the bastards get everythin'?"

"All they left were the few dollars and change in our pants pockets. They were only interested in the gold."

"I'm sorry, Chase. I shoulda knowed better. I know what Skagway is like and ignored the danger. You can bet your ass Soapy Smith is behind this."

"I sure as hell aim to find out," Chase said grimly.

"What we gonna do now?"

Before Chase could answer Kate arrived with Rusty's breakfast. She fussed over him like a mother hen, plumping his pillow and washing his hands and face with a wet cloth she brought along with her until he began to sputter and protest that he didn't need no dang fool woman motherin' him.

"Come to the kitchen when yer ready fer yer breakfast, Chase," Kate called over her shoulder when she turned to leave. "In a few minutes the place will be full of hungry men." She flashed Rusty a shy smile, then hurried off.

"Looks like you made a conquest, Rusty," Chase remarked cheekily.

Rusty's face turn beet red beneath his beard. "Kate's a mighty fine-lookin' woman, but I ain't got time fer such nonsense. We're damn near penniless, son, we'll have to sell the claim and maybe lose the ranch."

"Not if I can help it," Chase said tightly.

"Don't do nothin' foolish, son. This is Soapy's town."

"I'll think of somethin'. Eat your breakfast, Rusty. I'll be back later."

When Chase entered the kitchen, Kate and Hannah were too busy to talk and Maggie had already eaten and left, so he helped himself to a plate of flapjacks and drank three cups of coffee. Afterwards he walked directly to the tent Rusty had erected on the beach, retrieved a clean set of clothes from his pack, and headed over to the bathhouse. He still had a few dollars in his jeans and intended to spend them on a shave, haircut, and bath.

Maggie rapped lightly on Rusty's door, not wanting to awaken him if he was napping.

"It ain't locked." Rusty's gravely voice still hinted of pain but sounded much stronger than the night before.

Maggie stepped into the room. "How are you feeling, Mr. Reed?"

"Like hell. Who are you?" Evidently he didn't remember her from the night before.

"Maggie Afton. I'm a friend of Chase's."

"Yer the damn fool newspaper reporter who's tryin' to get to the Klondike. Ain't ya got no sense, girl? You should be thinkin' 'bout a husband and younguns instead of traipsin' around the country lookin' fer trouble."

Maggie flushed. If Rusty weren't flat on his back and in considerable pain, she would have lambasted him thoroughly. "Thank you for the advice, Mr. Reed, but I'm old enough to make my own decisions. I came to see if you need anything, but if you prefer to be alone I'll understand." She turned to leave.

"Whoa, girl, I ain't chasin' ya off. Chase ain't back yet and I could use some company. Might take my mind off the pain. And I'd feel more comfortable if ya called me Rusty."

"Is it unbearable, Rusty?" Maggie asked, concern coloring her words. "Would you like me to ask Kate for some laudanum?"

"No, girl, not yet. I'll need a clear head when Chase returns. We got some important decisions to make."

Maggie nodded, well aware of the problems facing them. Looking around for something to sit on, she spied an empty crate and drew it close to the bed. She made appropiate smalltalk for several minutes before Rusty blurted out, "I can see why you got Chase all tied up in knots. Yer a beautiful woman, Maggie Afton."

"Why thank you, Rusty," Maggie replied, flustered. "But you're wrong about Chase. If he's tied in knots, it's not over me."

"Suit yerself, girl," Rusty said, a twinge of pain bringing a grimace to his face.

"Do you still plan on going to the Klondike?"

"Don't see how. I'll be laid up the rest of the summer, and then we'll have to hole up here for the winter. Chase can probably find work to pay for our keep, but it won't be enough fer a grubstake or to save the ranch."

Maggie cleared her throat. "Did Chase tell you I offered to grubstake him if he took me along to the Klondike?"

"Yeah, he mentioned it."

"The offer still stands. He and I can go, and I'll see that you're taken care of here. You can follow when you're fully recovered."

"If I know Chase, he ain't gonna agree to no such outlandish notion."

Maggie bristled indignantly. "My work might not

be important to you, Mr. Reed, but to me it's my life. I'm constantly being belittled and ridiculed by my male counterparts, and I worked hard to make a place for myself in a man's world. Because I'm a woman I'm forced to go a little bit farther, put out a little more effort to prove myself. Can you blame me for wanting to scoop everyone else with this story?

"I begged and pleaded to be allowed to come up here," Maggie continued relentlessly. "Mr. Grant, my editor, finally consented when he learned most of the male reporters were likely to abandon their assignments and join the stampede once they got to the Klondike."

Throughout Maggie's heated argument, Rusty suppressed the smile hovering at the corner of his lips. Maggie Afton was all Chase said she was and more, he thought, eyeing her with unconcealed admiration. She was a damn plucky female, too stubborn to listen to reason and determined enough to succeed. Suddenly it occurred to Rusty that Maggie was exactly the kind of woman Chase needed, someone who would never bore him but would keep him on his toes at all times. When those two came together—if they ever came together—it was likely to produce fireworks all the way to the Arctic Circle. He wondered if Chase and Maggie would ever discover they were perfect for one another without a certain amount of meddling from an old fool.

Though Rusty wholeheartedly endorsed Maggie's ideas, he still thought it too risky for a woman to travel to the Klondike. Also, driving ambition in a woman was something that would take some getting use to. He reckoned Chase felt the same way or he would have accepted Maggie's offer immediately.

"I can't speak for Chase, Maggie. If he wants to take you to the Klondike, he'll do it with or without my permission."

"He has to do something," Maggie argued logically. "You're both broke, you're injured, and you can lose your ranch if you don't make good in the Klondike."

A sadness crept over Rusty's weathered features when he thought of the ranch in Montana Chase loved so much. Seeing his expression, Maggie thought she had tired the injured man with her rather lengthy visit and made to leave. "I've overstayed my welcome," she said, offering a shy smile. "I'll come back again. If you need anything, please let me know."

"I appreciate your concern, Maggie. I reckon I am a mite bushed." His eyes closed and Maggie tiptoed from the room.

Chase felt like a new man after his bath, shave and haircut. His clean clothes resembled those he just taken off—cord jeans, cotton shirt, and denim jacket. His pockets might be empty, but he felt a whole lot better.

While he bathed he did a heap of thinking, coming to one conclusion. Since Rusty was unable to travel for a spell, Chase knew he would need some kind of work to support them through the summer and winter. He fully intended to stick around Skagway long enough to recover his twelve thousand dollars. Selling the claim was another option, though he fought it. If rumor could be believed, claims all up and down Gold Bottom were paying off handsomely. It stood to reason theirs would produce equally as well once they were able to work it. Damn, if only there was some way for him to get to the Klondike, someone willing to grubstake him and provide for Rusty in his absence.

Inexplicably he thought of Maggie and her offer to grubstake him if he took her along. He scolded himself soundly for even thinking of accepting, no matter how desperate he was. Besides, he'd never be able to keep his hands off the beautiful reporter during the time it took to reach the Klondike. Her voluptuous body and angel face would tempt a saint and Lord knew he was no saint. He'd end up in all kinds of trouble; he might even end up with a wife he wasn't ready for. That chilling notion abruptly jolted him to his senses, and he directed his thoughts elsewhere.

After Chase had made himself presentable, he made his way to the Ice Palace, his mouth set in determined lines. Just as he surmised, Belle Delarue was more than glad to see him.

"Come in, Chase, and close the door," Belle greeted him when Chase entered her small office behind the bar. "What brings you here this time of day? I thought by now you'd be joining the stampede to the Klondike."

A frown darkened Chase's brow. He'd met Soapy Smith in Belle's office yesterday. Could she have anything to do with the robbery? It was a thought, one that might bear pursuing. It seemed no one in this hellhole called Skagway was above suspicion. "Does that job offer still stand?" he asked.

"It sure does, Cowboy, but what made you change your mind? Can I hope it had something to do with those fringe benefits I mentioned?"

A wide grin slashed across Chase's face. "You sure don't beat around the bush, do you?"

"Why be coy? When I see something I like, I go after it. Stick with me and I'll make you richer than that claim of yours. The sky's the limit as long as we don't rile Soapy. By the way, what *did* make you change your mind?"

Chase knew he had to tread carefully so as not to let on that he suspected Soapy of robbing him of his money. "I lost my grubstake, Belle."

"Damnation! All twelve thousand? I thought you

were smarter than to gamble away your poke."

"Didn't gamble it away," Chase said sourly.

"Then how . . ."

"Some bastards clubbed me in an alley, and when they didn't find the gold on me, they went after my partner. Rusty suffered the same fate, only he didn't fare so well. They would have killed him if I hadn't come to and chased them off. Rusty got his leg broke and will likely be laid up the rest of the summer. Not only that, but it will take years to save enough to build our poke up again. I need to work to support us until Rusty is on his feet."

"You weren't hurt, were you?" Belle asked anxiously.

"Nope, and that's the funny part. Why didn't they kill me like they were gonna do Rusty? I was out long enough for them to do anythin' they wanted to me."

"This town is full of unscrupulous men," Belle contended. She had a good idea who was behind the robbery, but as long as Chase wasn't hurt she accepted it as the way of things in Skagway. Besides, it would keep Chase where she could work her wiles on him. She was long overdue for some excitement in her life, and Chase looked ready and able to provide all she required. "I should have warned you before you left here with so much money. Still, I'm not sorry it turned out like this. And I swear you won't be either." Belle's voice was low and sultry, her eyes filled with seductive possibilities.

"When do you want me to start?" Chase asked, returning Belle's bold scrutiny.

"Have you ever dealt blackjack?" Belle asked, suddenly all business.

"Nope, but I've played enough to know what to do."

"Can you start tonight?"

"Yep, reckon I can." He uncoiled his long length

from the chair he had sprawled into and prepared to leave.

"Wait. A room goes with the job—are you interested? You can't live in a tent on the beach in the winter."

Chase considered Belle's offer carefully. A room with a real bed was mighty tempting. And once Rusty could be moved, he'd bring him here from the little storeroom at the Hash House. Not that he didn't appreciate Kate and Hannah for caring for Rusty after he had refused to sell them his cows. "I'll take it if it doesn't mean too big a cut in pay," Chase replied.

"Two hundred dollars a week and room and board," Belle said, shocking him with her generous offer. Cowhands worked six months for the same money he'd make in a week.

"That's a heap of money, boss lady, are you sure I'll earn it?"

"You'll earn it," Belle purred, her voice a husky promise. "Now, about clothes—you can't dress like that. Do you own a suit?"

Chase laughed, an outrageous sound in the small room. "Never had no use for a suit."

"Well you do now." Belle reached in a drawer, fumbled around for some loose nuggets and handed Chase three choice specimens. "Consider this an advance on your salary. Get yourself something decent to wear and report back here at eight tonight. The first night or two you can watch and get acquainted."

"You gotta deal, boss lady." Chase saluted smartly, then stuck out his hand to seal the bargain.

Rising, Belle pointedly ignored his hand, slipped her arms around his neck, and brought their mouths together in a searing kiss. With the lusty exuberance of a virile twenty-eight-year-old male, Chase returned the kiss. When Belle grew giddy from lack of air, Chase released her abruptly, turned, and sauntered lazily from the room.

"My gawd!" Belle gasped, sucking her breath in noisily. Chase McGarrett was one helluva man. Mesmerized, she stared raptly at the sway of his lean hips and taut buttocks as he strode out the door.

Maggie spent the day putting the finishing touches on her article to send back with Captain Bates on the *North Star*, along with the exposed plates of the pictures she had taken. She hoped Mr. Grant would like what she'd done so far and intended to arrange with Captain Bates to regularly deliver her stories and pictures to the paper.

She'd seen nothing of Chase today and wondered what he was up to. She couldn't wait to see him and repeat her offer. She wanted to start her journey to the Klondike as soon as it could be arranged. Making a neat package of the plates and article to be sent back to Seattle, Maggie left her room at the Hash House, walking at a brisk pace toward the beach.

Maggie's sharp eyes missed nothing as she strode through town. A steady stream of pack horses were being led one after another toward White Pass. Men without animals carried their equipment on their backs, making many trips through the pass to carry it all across. Maggie wished she had brought her camera, but vowed to do so tomorrow, setting up the tripod at the foot of the pass.

In front of the outfitting store, supplies were being bought and inspected by men who knew exactly what was required by the Canadian government. Some kind of altercation was taking place in front of the store, and Maggie's nose for news demanded she investigate.

Two men stood before a huge pile of supplies. One read from a long list while the other glared at him belligerently. "Seems to be all here. Four hundred pounds of flour, two hundred of bacon, one hundred each of beans and sugar, twenty-five pounds butter, eight pounds baking powder, seventy-five pounds dried fruit, fifty each of onions, potatoes, oatmeal, rice, and cornmeal, twenty-five pounds coffee, three dozen yeast cakes, tea, matches, soap, spices, candles, and whiskey. Comes to exactly eleven hundred and fifty pounds. Now for your equipment," the inspector droned on. "Stove, buckets, cooking and mining implements, ax, saw, shovel, files, chisels, nails, rope, tent, sled, mosquito net, and clothes. You also have candy, cloth, and kerosene. Everything seems in order. Soapy Smith's cut is two hundred dollars."

"It ain't fair!" complained the prospector. "I sold everything I owned to get here. Why should I pay some unscrupulous citizen for the privilege of crossing White Pass? Once I get to the Yukon, the Mounties will collect twenty-five percent customs tax."

"You'll pay 'cause Soapy says so," the man snarled, pulling his coat back to reveal a pair of pistols strapped to his waist.

Maggie was stunned. Why did Soapy Smith's name strike fear in the hearts of men? Finally, she could stand it no longer. What was happening here was unlawful and needed to be exposed. Was there no one brave enough to defy Soapy Smith?

The prospector was still grumbling when he reached into his pocket, fully prepared to shell out the illegal tax. "Wait!" Maggie cried out, rushing forward. "You don't have to pay this—this crook. What he demands is illegal."

"Who in the hell are you?" This from Soapy's henchman.

"Maggie Afton, reporter with the Seattle Post-Intelligencer."

"A woman reporter," the man scoffed derisively.

"Why ain't you home where you belong, takin' care of yer man?"

Maggie flounced indignantly. "I'm exactly where I want to be, mister—mister—"

"Casey. Liam Casey."

"Where is the law in Skagway, Mr. Casey? How can people meekly give in to Soapy Smith's demands?" Maggie wanted to know.

"It's all right, miss," the prospector interjected, unwilling to draw the attractive young woman into his problems. "I'll pay just like everyone else. Soapy Smith *is* the law in Skagway. Ain't but one U.S. Marshal and one commissioner in the entire territory of Alaska—not like Canada with all the Royal Canadian Mounted Police to keep the law."

He reached in his pocket, counted out the required amount, and handed it to Liam Casey. Then he tipped his cap at Maggie and went on his way.

Maggie had never known such rage, and she whirled to face Liam Casey, her eyes spitting amber fire. "You tell Mr. Smith he won't get away with this—this miscarriage of justice. I'm going to devote my next article to his illegal dealings and send them to the Post-Intelligencer for publication. Once law-abiding citizens learn what's going on up here, there will be such an outcry that the law will be forced to put a stop to his practices. Good day, sir!"

Turning on her heel, Maggie marched away, her body taut, head held high. Behind her, Liam Casey slunk away, certain that Soapy would want to know about the nosy woman reporter snooping into his business.

Chapter Five

Maggie dispatched her packet to the *North Star*, which she learned was to depart the following day. That taken care of, she retrieved a notebook and pencil from her bag and began interviewing men lounging outside their tents. Unaccustomed to seeing a lady in Skagway, most cooperated out of sheer delight in talking with a refined female. Some remembered her from the *North Star*, and those that followed her progress with lust-filled eyes she steered clear of. Through these interviews, Maggie learned more of Soapy Smith, and the list of crimes attributed to him both angered and amazed her.

She learned from her carefully phrased questions that Soapy sent toughs to the Seattle docks for the purpose of luring men to Skagway, where he promptly fleeced them of their hard-earned money. In return for promised protection, the unsuspecting stampeders, as those men flocking to the Yukon were called, doled out large sums to Soapy's men.

Before Maggie started back to her room much later, she had compiled an entire dossier of atrocities committed by the notorious Soapy Smith and his gang of toughs.

Lost in contemplation of her next story, Maggie did not notice the two brawny men who sidled up beside her until both her arms were seized and she was hustled into an alley. If anyone noticed, they gave no alarm, going about their business as usual.

"What's the meaning of this?" Maggie demanded, a jolt of fear nearly paralyzing her. Things like this just didn't happen to her.

"Mr. Smith wants ta talk to ya."

"Well I don't want to talk to him. Take your filthy hands off me."

"Feisty little piece, ain't she, Bandy?" Zeke guffawed, beady eyes gleaming.

"Yeah, tough as nails," Bandy Johnson agreed. "I pity the man who mounts her, she'll cut him down ta size." They both laughed uproariously over Bandy's little pun.

They shoved her farther down the alley. "I'll scream," Maggie threatened.

"Go ahead," Bandy challenged. "You'll find no one cares enough ta interfere. Come along quiet-like and ya won't be hurt. Soapy just wants ta talk to ya nice and friendly-like."

Giving in to the inevitable, Maggie stumbled down the alley. At the other end, she was met by a tall, slim, sandy-haired man with the coldest eyes she'd ever seen. Intuitively she knew she was face-to-face with the notorious Soapy Smith.

"Much obliged, boys," Soapy smiled, grasping Maggie's arm. "I won't need you any longer."

His chilling smile turned Maggie's blood to ice water. "Take your hands off me!" she insisted. Obviously her false bravado gained her naught, for Soapy's hold only tightened.

"I just want to talk to you, Miss Afton," Soapy said smoothly. "Come along."

Digging in her heels, Maggie balked. "I'm not going anywhere with you, but go ahead and talk. I'm listening."

"Not here." He began dragging her toward a door at the rear of one of the buildings. It led directly to his small office behind Soapy's Parlor. Due to his superior strength, Maggie was forced to follow.

The room Soapy shoved her into was an office of sorts, with furnishings far superior to anything she'd seen thus far in Skagway. He locked the door behind him and pocketed the key while Maggie studied her surroundings with mild curiosity.

"Now then, Miss Afton, have a seat." His politeness did not fool Maggie for a minute.

Moving with exaggerated slowness, she selected a chair and seated herself with noteworthy aplomb, considering the circumstances.

"All right, Mr. Smith, what is it you want?"

Soapy regarded Maggie with considerable interest. Any other woman would be quaking in her boots, but not Miss Maggie Afton. She confronted him boldly, a challenge on her tongue, bristling with hostility and anger. He'd always pictured spinsters as thin, timid women wearing spectacles, hair pulled back into a severe bun and clothed in dark, baggy garments that concealed their sex. This fiery creature was definitely no retiring old maid. Nor did she frighten easily.

"I understand you've been asking questions about me, Miss Afton. This is a small town, and word travels fast. What possible interest could I be to you and your paper?" Maggie easily saw through his facade of mild-mannered businessman and community benefactor.

"I've been here just two days, Mr. Smith, but already I've gathered enough material to send you to prison if you were anywhere but in Alaska," she said, her voice dripping with contempt.

"Ah, but we *are* in Alaska," Soapy replied with deceptive charm. "Here we do things my way. I want you to stop interfering in my business."

"Business! Ha! It didn't take long to discover that you're involved in dirty business," Maggie shot back. "Every violent crime in this city can be laid directly on your doorstep."

"Did you also learn that I collected two thousand dollars for two widows, stopped an illegal lynching, and promoted business, labor, and the church? Because of me, the citizens of Skagway are protected against outlaws."

"I see," Maggie said, her voice honey-sweet yet ripe with mockery. "I had no idea you were such a paragon of virtue. What about all the man passing through Skagway who are robbed outright or cheated out of their money? I talked to numerous men who are stranded here because of one or another of your schemes. You've a whole gang of toughs ready to do your dirty work while you sit back and reap the rewards."

"You're a foolish woman, Miss Afton," Soapy said pointedly. "Foolish for coming to Skagway in the first place and foolish for snooping into things that don't concern you. I strongly urge you to return to Seattle at your earliest convenience."

Maggie bristled indignantly. "I'm sure your advice is well-meant, Mr. Smith, but I'm not leaving until I accomplish what I set out to do."

"And what is that, Miss Afton?"

"To go to the Klondike."

"It's not an easy trip for a woman."

"I'm aware of that. May I go now?"

"As soon as you hand over that notebook you've been scribbling in."

"Absolutely not!"

"I don't doubt your bravery, Miss Afton, but it will do you no good. Give it to me!"

"Do you think me stupid? I've a good memory. Much of what's in here can easily be duplicated."

"But you won't." His voice had a hard edge to it that warned of dire consequences should she disregard his advice.

"Are you threatening me?"

A tight-lipped smile split his sly features. "Let's just call it a friendly warning. I abhor violence. Must I search you for the notebook?" His look implied that he'd derive great pleasure from doing so. "I find you quite attractive, Miss Afton—Maggie. Perhaps we would find it mutually satisfying to form an alliance of sorts. If you must write about me, perhaps it could be about the beneficial aspects of my life, the good I do for Skagway. Perhaps history will remember kindly all the good works I performed for the community."

"I write the truth, Mr. Smith," Maggie sniffed disdainfully. "I'm sure you'll go down in history, but it certainly won't be for your good deeds. I must go. Hannah and Kate will be worried about me."

"As well they should. Strange things happen to people in Skagway," he said ominously.

Rising abruptly, Maggie moved toward the door, but found her way blocked by Soapy, holding up the key in one hand. "The notebook," he demanded with quiet menace.

Maggie's hand tightened on her bag. Soapy's keen eyes noted her reflexive action, and he grabbed her around the waist with one hand while snatching away her bag with the other. A struggle ensued, and eventually Soapy wrested the bag from her hands and shoved her hard while he removed the notebook and placed it in his jacket pocket. Losing her balance, Maggie screamed as she hit the floor, stunning her and knocking the breath from her lungs.

*   *   *

Glancing into the alley, Chase couldn't help but remember what had happened to him and Rusty in that same alley just two short days ago. It now became habit to glance warily into every dark nook and corner where outlaws might lurk so that he wouldn't be caught unawares again. Not that he had anything left to steal. What he saw caused the blood to curdle in his veins. Two men were hustling a struggling woman through the murky passage and out the other end. The woman appeared wildly reluctant, but what made Chase break out in a cold sweat was the fact that he could have sworn the woman was Maggie.

By the time Chase collected his senses and willed his feet into motion, the trio had already left the alley. Racing through the passage, Chase groaned in frustration when he found no sign of either the men or the woman. Obviously they had entered one of the rear doors leading into the buildings lining Holly Street.

Chase grew frantic. Was it Maggie he had seen or just one of the saloon girls with a customer? He couldn't take the chance. Maggie might think she could take care of herself, but she was an innocent among a pack of wolves. He had no idea why he cared so much, but in the short time he had known her, Maggie Afton had made a strong impact on his life.

Testing door after door, Chase worked his way down the line of buildings, encountering mostly empty storerooms. The next door he tried was locked, and he started to turn away. But the sound of voices coming from within changed his mind. A feminine scream released his frozen limbs, and without a thought for the consequences he hurled himself against the door, his broad shoulders breaking the flimsy lock with the first thrust. He hurtled into the room in time to see Maggie sprawled on the floor and Soapy Smith leaning over her. A roar of outrage left his lips.

"What have you done to her, you bastard?"

Startled by the unexpected intrusion, Soapy rose abruptly, cursing beneath his breath when he saw Chase bearing down on him with murder in his eyes. He was sorry now he didn't have the cowboy killed instead of saving him for Belle. "This doesn't concern you, McGarrett. I haven't harmed the lady."

"This sure as hell does concern me!" Chase gritted from between clenched teeth. "Get away from Maggie."

Soapy backed away, his right hand easing toward his pocket. "I wouldn't try it if I were you," Chase warned.

Just then Maggie's vision cleared and she groaned, momentarily diverting Chase's attention. Thinking to catch Chase unaware, Soapy dove for his concealed weapon. But Chase was not as inattentive as he appeared. His hand lashed out, his pistol appearing like magic, and he caught Soapy full in the face with the butt. Stunned, Soapy sprawled on the floor, watching groggily as Chase scooped Maggie up into his arms.

"I'd kill you, but first I'm gonna get back the money you stole from me," Chase growled, stepping through the ruined door. "I don't care how many men you've got workin' for you, me and Rusty slaved too hard and long for that money to let some two-bit outlaw rob us blind. If I don't get you, someone else surely will."

Cradling her tenderly in his arms, Chase carried Maggie all the way back through the alley to Holly Street. "You can put me down now, Chase, I'm all right."

Carefully Chase set Maggie on her feet. His arms

steadied her when she swayed, but after a few minutes she was ready to move under her own steam.

"What happened, Maggie girl?" Chased asked, concern etching his brow. "What were you doin' alone with a skunk like Smith? I warned you Skagway was no place for a lady."

They were beginning to draw unwanted attention from passersby, too much attention for Maggie's liking. "Come back to the Hash House with me and I'll explain everything," she suggested.

Nodding grimly, Chase took her arm and they proceeded down the street to the Hash House, now jammed with the usual supper crowd of hungry, clamoring men. Little heed was paid them as they slipped past the kitchen where both Hannah and Kate toiled furiously to provide palatable meals for their throng of customers.

"Where we goin'?" Chase asked.

"The only place where we might talk privately is my room. Of course I'll expect you to behave."

Chase's blue eyes gleamed wickedly. "I'll keep that in mind."

The moment they entered Maggie's small room, she released a tremulous sigh.

"Are you sure you're all right?" Chase asked anxiously.

"I'm fine, Chase, really," Maggie insisted. "That terrible man had the gall to threaten me."

"But why? Sit down, Maggie, darlin', and tell me everythin'."

Darling! He called her darling! A thrill of anticipation shot through her. Why should a tender word from a crude cowboy set her heart to thumping and her knees knocking? she wondered curiously.

Perching on the edge of the bed, Maggie took a deep breath and told Chase about being hustled from the street by two thugs and taken by Soapy Smith to his office. She related nearly word for word their entire conversation and how she had ended up on the floor.

"Are you convinced now that you should go back to Seattle?" Chase asked softly.

"Not at all," Maggie returned calmly. "I'll not let that unscrupulous character frighten me. He might have stolen my notebook, but most of the interviews are committed to memory. I'll have my story ready to send back on the next mail steamer."

"Listen, darlin', I know you're a brave girl, but what can you hope to accomplish against Smith and his network of spies and toughs?"

"I want the whole country to know what's going on up here. I intend to make Soapy Smith's name synonymous with crime and injustice. I want—"

"Whoa, Maggie girl, you're only one woman, and I'd sure as hell hate to see you hurt. Today was merely a taste of what Smith is capable of. Go home, Maggie. The longer you stay in Skagway, the more danger you face."

"I—I realize that, Chase. That's why I want to leave here," Maggie agreed, stunning Chase—until he heard her next words and realized she had learned nothing from her encounter with Smith. "Take me to the Klondike. We can leave as soon as you're outfitted. I'm sure Kate can be persuaded to look after Rusty until he's on his feet again. It's obvious she has a soft spot for him."

"Haven't you given up on that damn fool notion yet?" Chase said, exasperated.

"Did you expect me to?"

He studied her determined face through eyes as blue as a cloudless sky. "Nope, not really, but I hoped you gained somethin' from all this. I'm not gonna change my mind, Maggie."

"But you're broke," Maggie argued with relentless logic. "You have every reason to accept my offer. You get to your claim and I get to the Klondike."

"Dammit all, Maggie, I know I'm flat busted, but I got a job today. A damn good one."

"You got a job?"

"Yep, at the Ice Palace. Belle was quite generous."

"I'll bet," Maggie muttered dryly. "That still isn't getting you to your claim."

"It's a livin' 'til Rusty mends and we decide what to do. Do I detect a note of jealousy there?"

He moved closer, finding the shape of her full lips fascinating. When he dropped down on the bed beside her, Maggie's mouth suddenly went dry. He was so close she could smell the virile male scent of him, and the masculine aroma of sexual arousal sparked an answering response in her. Her heart did flipflops when he looked at her with eyes warm and compelling, and oh, so tender.

"I'm gonna kiss you, Maggie girl."

Maggie felt like a puppet on a string, answering the pull of Chase's magnetism as she lifted her face to accept his kiss. His lips were warm and moist, his tongue a hot brand as it outlined the shape of her mouth, then gently pushed between her lips. Her mouth opened beneath his, and his tongue slipped inside. Chase groaned, the taste and feel of her so wonderful he could have gone on kissing her forever.

"Sweet, so sweet," he whispered against her mouth. "I want you, Maggie girl. I want you so damn bad I could die of it."

He pressed her down into the surface of the bed, his body hard and demanding against her softness, one hand traveling upward with maddening slowness over a curving hip to cup the fullness of her breast. Maggie gasped, feeling her nipple pucker into painful erectness beneath the material of her blouse.

A jolt of longing turned Maggie's bones to rubber. No man had ever touched her so intimately or with such tenderness. Chase didn't seem to be at all intimidated, as most men were, by her unfeminine career or the tough veneer she had deliberately adopted to conceal her vulnerability to those who ridiculed her age and ambition. The crude cowboy had a way about him, Maggie thought, that suddenly made her virginity a burden. That thought made her stiffen beneath his gentle caresses.

Suddenly Chase's mouth and hands were everywhere at once. Feeling her resistance, he concentrated on stroking it away. A tiny moan bubbled in her throat as he unbuttoned her blouse and brushed it away from her shoulders, his kisses tracing a path across the tops of her breasts, leaving a trail of fire in the wake of his tantalizing explorations. Then he shoved aside her chemise, and she felt the moist warmth of his mouth claim the throbbing pink bud of her breast. First one, then the other, kissing, teasing, suckling like a starving babe. When he unfastened her skirt to push it down her thighs, Maggie deliberately stayed his hand.

"Chase, no, this is crazy. We don't really know each other. Once we leave here we'll never see each other again."

"You're probably right, darlin', this is crazy. I'm crazy—you drive me out of my mind. Let me love you. You won't be sorry. I'll make it so good for you you'll forget every lover you've ever had."

Other lovers? Of course, why wouldn't Chase think she had had lovers? She was twenty-five years old, independent, and unconcerned with propriety. She opened her mouth to set him straight and the wet blade of his tongue slipped inside, playing leisurely within, and Maggie's control fled like ashes before the wind.

Taking her silence for permission, Chase shrugged out of his jacket and shirt, the bronze expanse of his chest glowing like dull gold in the dimness of the room. Maggie thought the sight entrancing, the copper mat of curling hair too inviting to resist as her hands made bold contact with the naked wall of his chest. Her fingers tangled in the furred expanse before curiosity moved them downwards to trace the thin line disappearing into the top of his jeans. That simple act transformed him into a quivering mass of desire. A groan of sheer pleasure rattled in his throat, leaving him oblivious to all except this wild, breathless need for her that bordered on madness.

"Say somethin', darlin'," Chase said, sucking his breath in sharply as her fingers played mindlessly against his sensitive skin. "Tell me you want me as much as I want you."

Unable to lie effectively, Maggie answered truthfully. "I want you, Chase. God help me, but I want you."

If she never had anything more from this attractive cowboy, she'd have this moment to savor. Marriage had passed her by, but at least she would experience passion once in her life. Never before had Maggie desired a man enough to let him make a woman of her—until Chase came along with his crooked grin and teasing kisses.

That was all Chase needed to hear as he rose up on his knees and skimmed the skirt down Maggie's hips. Her petticoat followed, then the scanty French panties that had enthralled and shocked him the first time they met. Last to go were her stockings and shoes. Then she was nude, and curiously Maggie felt no embarrassment as Chase's hot gaze swept over her with obvious enjoyment.

"You're damn near perfect," he breathed, his voice tinged with awe. "But I reckon you've heard that before."

Almost reverently, Chase trailed his hands along the elegant length of her body, teasing her breasts, molding the twin mounds of her buttocks, massaging the thickly thatched mound at the joining of her legs. Maggie moaned, a foreign sound deep in her throat. She could feel her warm wet desire for him on the insides of her thighs when he began exploring that secret part of her no man had touched before. His fingers stroked her satiny fold and his thumb teased the tiny button he found there, sending her passion soaring past all limits of endurance. When his finger found the small hidden opening she jerked in response.

"You feel so tight, darlin', and so warm and wet. I'm crazy with wantin'."

Her breath came in short, harsh gasps, and her breasts arched upwards against his chest. Sensing her need, his lips found a taut nipple, drawing it deeply into his mouth. Below, his fingers continued to work their magic on her sensitive flesh, driving her further and further from reality, until shock waves of pleasure exploded through every fiber of her body.

While Maggie was lost in the throes of the first sexual response she had ever experienced, Chase quickly stripped off his pants. When she felt the full length of his magnificently aroused body pressing her down, a tiny thread of reality forced itself into her brain. She knew there was something she should tell Chase, but for the life of her she couldn't remember what it was. His relentless probing dulled her memory and stole her words. Then Chase was pushing inside her, stretching her, filling her with his incredible length. Maggie hadn't been prepared for the pain—the searing, brutal pain of penetration.

Tears sprang to her eyes. "Chase, stop! It hurts! I can't bear it."

Too far immersed in passion, Chase barely heard her plea until she cried out in agony, struggling beneath him. Then the head of his manhood met resistance and he understood. He went still, his blue eyes full of wonder. "Damnation, you're a virgin!"

"Th—that's what I wanted to tell you," Maggie hiccupped.

"I can't stop now, darlin', don't ask it of me." Desperation rode him as he flexed his hips and broke through the barrier, sheathing himself deeply—oh so deeply—into her hot tightness.

A strangled gasp left Maggie's throat, effectively stifled by Chase as his mouth swallowed her cries. Once he was past her maidenhead, he willed himself to remain still, allowing Maggie time to adjust to the feel and size of him.

"I'm sorry, Maggie girl, I didn't think—that is—" he gulped, searching for the right words. "I just didn't think someone your age and with your beauty could still be a virgin. But it had to happen some time. I'm glad it was me."

Once the initial pain was gone, Maggie began to relax, enjoying the feel of his hard-muscled chest against her breasts, savoring the way their bodies fit together, so snugly—so right. Yes, she admitted, she wanted this, wanted it from the moment she had laid eyes on the outrageous cowboy, and she wasn't going to deny herself the pleasure he offered.

"Tell me what to do," Maggie gasped. Her breath was soft and sweet against his neck.

"Oh, sweet darlin'." Her words sent his passion soaring, but he deliberately held himself back, not wanting to hurt her, waiting for her to tell him she was ready to proceed.

He moved his hips, not withdrawing completely but caressing her tenderly until he felt the gentle rocking response of her muscles around him. "Are you still hurtin'?" Chase asked.

"N—no," Maggie gasped, his subtle movements transporting her once again to the sensual, dreamy world of passion. "You seem so good at this, Chase."

Thrilled by her innocent words, Chase brought his mouth to her breast, spiraling light kisses on her tender flesh until he reached the hardened tip. His lips closed around it and his tongue caressed it, making it wet and eliciting a husky murmur from Maggie's lips.

"Lovin' you is easy," Chase responded, his warm breath whispering against her heated flesh. "Move your hips," he instructed, moving slowly to teach her the rhythm. Almost shyly she followed his direction. "That's it, darlin'. God, you're so responsive I want to explode."

Soon they were moving faster, Maggie's breath coming in short gasps, her mind cleared of everything but this powerful man straining above her, bringing her pleasure she never knew existed. The intimacy was unbearable, something she hadn't considered. He was a part of her. He lay atop her and inside her, his huge calloused hands guiding her bare buttocks to meet his strokes. All that she held private and vulnerable lay open and naked to him. Their breath mingled in shared passion and their heartbeats pounded in unison.

"Chase, I—something is happening!" Maggie cried out. "I feel—oh God—I *feel*!"

"I know, Maggie girl, I feel it, too. I'll try to wait for you. Hurry, sweet darlin', hurry."

Her breath was a hot brand searing her throat, her limbs weightless, the sensation that began where their bodies joined so intense it bordered on pain. Chase was equally carried away. Sweat dripped from his slick torso and his burnished head was thrown back, his teeth clenched from the effort it took to hold his passion under tight rein.

Suddenly Maggie found what she was striving for as tiny bursts of sensation exploded inside her body, and she cried out. Her response seemed to break something loose in Chase as he stiffened above her, then began to shudder with the force of his climax. Maggie could feel that part of his body buried deep within her quiver, then convulse, keeping her own sweet throbbing alive. It went on so long that Maggie felt certain she would die from the pleasure. She seriously doubted anyone could make love as well as Chase. When her breathing returned to normal, she told him so.

Despite his rapid breathing and pounding heart, Chase roared with laughter. "How would you know? I was the first." Though he didn't say so, her words gave him nearly as much pleasure as their loving.

"Women know these things," Maggie insisted.

"Well, I sure as hell didn't know you'd have so much passion in that slender body of yours. You were fantastic." Sighing regretfully, he eased himself to his side, wishing he could stay and make love to her all night long. "I don't know how you've managed to stay unwed all these years. What about the men in your life? Surely there were some."

Maggie's eyes dulled to tarnished gold as a flush rose up from her neck to claim her cheeks. "There were none that mattered."

Wisely Chase didn't pursue the subject, astute enough to realize Maggie didn't wish to discuss her personal life. "Maggie girl, you're an incredible woman. I've never met anyone like you. If I didn't have to leave, I'd like nothing better than to make love to you all night. But it's probably best I don't. You'd be too sore to get out of bed tomorrow."

He planted a playful kiss on her nose, swatted her luscious backside, and uncoiled his lean length from the narrow bed. As he pulled on his clothes, Maggie watched with unabashed admiration. She wasn't sorry she had given herself to Chase. He was a special man. Though she was unclear what exactly made him special, she just knew he was. Tall, lean, and strong, he was blessed with shining, burnished hair that curled endearingly against the back of his neck, brilliant blue eyes, roughly handsome features accented by a firm chin and a devastating smile. Maggie looked forward with relish to their journey to the Klondike. Though he'd said nothing more about it, Maggie assumed their lovemaking had changed Chase's mind about taking her to the goldfields.

Still thinking along those lines, Maggie asked, "How soon do you think you'll be ready to leave?"

"I'm ready now," Chase replied, mistaking her meaning. "I'm expected at the Ice Palace and don't want to be late for my first day on the job."

"You still intend working tonight?"

Chase smiled owlishly. "Darlin', makin' love, enjoyable as it is, won't feed me and Rusty. I need this job."

"But—but, I thought—"

"You thought what?" Chase asked sharply.

"That after our—after tonight you'd change your mind about taking me to the Klondike."

"What!" Chase exploded, his face a dark cloud. "You planned this—this seduction just so's I'd agree to take you to the Klondike, didn't you? No wonder you were so willin' to surrender your virginity. Was I just handy or would any man off the street have served as well?"

"Chase, no, it wasn't like that!"

"Wasn't it? No man likes to be used, Miss Afton, or manipulated. You're a cold-blooded bitch, and I'm a besotted fool. You were good, Maggie girl, but not that good. I reckon you'll have to lure some other poor sucker to your bed to get what you want. Better luck next time. Too bad I can't replace your maidenhead so you can use it again."

Whirling on his heel, he stomped from the room, leaving Maggie stunned as well as thoroughly shaken. How could that stubborn jackass think she had

enticed him to her bed with a purpose in mind?
What happened had been a spontaneous reaction,
one fueled by desire and passion. She could wring
Chase's neck. Didn't he know the difference between
real need and playacting?

The hell with Chase McGarrett, Maggie thought
crossly. No matter what he thought about her, her
plans hadn't changed. Somewhere in Skagway a
man or men existed whose price she could meet.
Somehow, some way, she'd get to the Klondike.

Chapter Six

Before leaving for the Ice Palace, Chase stopped in to see Rusty to tell him all—or nearly all—that had transpired that eventful day.

"Where in tarnation you been, son?" Rusty asked peevishly. "Been waitin' all day fer ya ta show up."

"Busy," Chase said curtly, still upset over the way Maggie tried to manipulate him—though in the end she had gained nothing and lost her virginity in the bargain. Chase had to admit he suffered a mite of guilt over that, but Maggie certainly had enjoyed it, probably as much as he had, if that were possible.

"Too busy fer an old friend and partner?" Rusty sounded bored, in pain, and very much put out for being neglected. "If it wasn't for Kate, I'd probably rot away in here. Tell me what you been up to, son."

"I got a job, Rusty, just till you're well enough for us to continue on to the claim."

"You know blamed well that ain't gonna be any time soon," Rusty complained. "What kinda job?"

"I'm workin' for Belle Delarue at the Ice Palace."

"What! You gonna be her fancy man?" Rusty sounded bitterly disappointed. "I can't believe it. I reckoned you had more pride than that."

"Damnation, Rusty, there you go, always jumpin' to conclusions. My duties will consist of dealin' blackjack, nothin' more."

"I heard Soapy Smith has his finger in the business."

"Don't rightly know, but I can keep an eye on the man and earn our keep at the same time. I aim to get our money back."

"Ain't likely," Rusty scoffed. "The man rules the town with an iron fist. There's some who thinks he's a saint. He's head of the welfare department that helps widows and children."

"He also hires thugs to steal and kill. One way or another, I'll get our money back. In the meantime, I'll be stayin' at the Ice Palace. A room goes with the job. As soon as you're up to it, I'll have you moved. Looks like we're gonna be holed up here for the winter, and I aim to make the most of it."

"I'm gettin' kinda used to this storeroom," Rusty claimed. "Besides, you can always take Maggie Afton up on her offer. From what I seen of her, she ain't no fragile flower, and if she's as anxious to get to the Klondike as she lets on, you and her oughta make a good team. Old Sam Cooper is probably gettin, a mite anxious wonderin' where we are. I told him we'd be up there by the first of August, and that day passed weeks ago."

Sam Cooper was an old prospector Rusty had hired to protect their claim in their absence for five percent of the profits. An abandoned claim was an open invitation to claim-jumpers and thieves.

Chase didn't want to be reminded of Maggie. The way she used him still rankled. Evidently she expected him to feel guilt over robbing her of her

virginity and offer to take her to Dawson as a means
of salving his conscience.

"It'll be a cold day in hell before I take Maggie to
the Klondike," Chase bit out angrily. "No woman is
gonna manipulate me."

Rusty looked thoughtful. "Did you and Maggie
have a fallin' out?"

"You might say that. I'd better get goin', Rusty, I'm
due at the Ice Palace. I'll come by tomorrow and ask
Kate how soon you can be moved."

"Don't reckon it'll be any time soon," Rusty grumbled, reluctant to leave Kate's care.

Chase hurried off, refusing to glance at Maggie's
closed door or think about what had passed between
them. The incredible satisfaction she had given him
and the unaccustomed feelings she had stirred in
him were far too confusing to delve deeply into
at this time. As far as Chase was concerned, Miss
Maggie Afton was a scheming bitch who used her
body to gain her own ends.

Yet why did his hands sweat and his body tremble when he thought about what Soapy could have
done to her if he hadn't shown up when he did?
Obviously Soapy wanted Maggie out of town, but
that contrary little vixen wouldn't listen to reason.
She deserved whatever she got, Chase thought, not
really believing it. Though he thought her a contrary
female who resorted to devious methods, he knew
he'd not hesitate to come to her aid as many times
as necessary.

Still stunned over the way Chase had left her the
night before, Maggie was up bright and early to take
pictures and conduct more interviews in order to
complete her article on Soapy Smith. She learned
that the next mail packet was due any day. She set
her tripod up on the beach but was dismayed to find
few people willing to talk, unlike the day before.

Only those on their way home, broke and disillusioned, could be persuaded to talk about Soapy. It
appeared that Soapy's toughs had circulated around
town issuing warnings to anyone who cooperated
with the lady reporter, unless they said only good
things about Soapy. It was difficult, but Maggie was
still able to gather sufficient information for her
purposes.

It was late afternoon when Maggie put her notebook away and began dismantling the bulky camera, eager to begin her article that would label
Soapy Smith a crook. She felt pleased with her
work, and a smile hovered at the corner of her
mouth. She still hadn't abandoned the notion of
going to the Klondike and had specifically made
mention of it to more than one stampeder during
her interviews, stating that she would pay well.
A few expressed interest, but as yet she was still
stranded in Skagway, and it was nearly the first
of September. Maggie understood that both White
Pass and Chilcoot Pass were all but impassable after
October.

"What in the hell are you doin' back here? Didn't
you learn your lesson yesterday?"

Maggie whirled, the smile on her lips turning sour
when she saw Chase glowering at her. "I've a job to
do," she said crisply. "What kind of reporter would
I be if I let men like Soapy Smith intimidate me?"

"One who valued her skin. Hell's bells, Maggie,
don't you know Soapy's toughs have been watchin'
you? Why are you dead set on provokin' that man?"

"I only write the truth," Maggie shrugged. "Can
I help it if the man is afraid the world will learn
what's going on up here? He may be a benefactor
to some, but I know what he's really like."

"So do I," Chase muttered beneath his breath.

"What are you doing down here?" Maggie asked,
trying to ignore the strange stirrings in the pit of her

stomach. Just looking at Chase made her tremble with weakness.

She saw Chase as he had been last night, his massive bronze chest bare, pressed against the softness of her breasts, his smooth loins tightly enmeshed with hers. His strength, his sexual prowess, and the expert way he drew a response from her quivering body combined to make her want him again—and again.

Chase's unprovoked verbal attack after they had made such incredible love had hurt Maggie deeply. She had felt so wonderful after their loving that she naturally assumed Chase would feel the same way and would want her with him on the trip to Dawson. She had no intention of using her feminine wiles as a means of persuasion. Their loving was nothing more complicated than the result of two healthy people of the opposite sex desiring each other. She couldn't help it if Chase McGarrett acted like a spoiled child.

"Belle said I could use the storeroom at the Ice Palace to store our tent and equipment," Chase explained. "I came down to the beach to gather our gear. I couldn't believe my eyes when I saw you back down here. I can't be around to protect you all the time."

Maggie bristled. "I didn't ask for your protection."

"You were damn glad to see me when I showed up yesterday," Chase argued. "Then you paid me back by seducin' me, hopin' to get me to agree to your plans. But it did you little good to give up your virginity. You should have saved it for someone who appreciates it."

"Oh-h-h!" Maggie said, stomping her foot. "You're an obnoxious man, Chase McGarrett, and certainly no gentleman. Go back to the Ice Palace and Miss Delarue. I certainly don't need you." Hefting the camera and tripod under her am, she stalked off.

Chase watched Maggie walk away, momentarily distracted by the seductive sway of her hips. Then he shook his head to clear it of the disturbing thought of Maggie sprawled beneath him, arching to meet his thrusts, eagerly following his instructions. But shaking his head did damn little to dispel the memory of Maggie's white body responding eagerly to the touch of his hands and lips. Though Chase's hands were occupied with packing his and Rusty's belongings, his mind relived each tiny detail of the too-short minutes spent with Maggie in her bed. The only thing that his wayward thoughts settled upon was the fact that he wanted her again—and again.

Maggie put the finishing touches on the first installment of her articles titled "Corruption in Skagway." She bundled the pages in a neat package along with the exposed plates to take to the post office later. She'd worked two days on it and was quite proud of her work. She hoped Mr. Grant would be equally proud. What she needed now, she decided, was fresh air and a walk. But first she stopped in to visit Rusty, who proved as cantankerous as ever. The only person who seemed able to handle him was Kate.

Maggie didn't stay long and soon wandered along Broadway, wondering how long she'd have to remain in this corrupt town. Abruptly her mind was jerked back to reality when she saw Chase strolling across the street with Belle Delarue clinging to his am. He was dressed like a fancy gambling main in suit, high collared white shirt, and string tie. Shiny new boots and leather holster clasped to his slim hips added the finishing touches to the outfit. Though Chase cut a grand figure, he looked oddly out of place and uncomfortable in the stylish clothes. But evidently Belle thought he looked marvelous, for her eyes roamed possessively over his virile physique as if she wanted him for dinner. No doubt she'd already had him, Maggie thought, disgruntled. Maggie frowned, wondering why the notion of Chase in Belle's bed should disturb her so greatly. Who cared what Chase McGarrett did? Or with whom?

Chase saw Maggie watching him from across the street but chose to ignore her, instead devoting his undivided attention to the petite woman clinging to his arm. He didn't entirely succeed, for his eyes strayed more often than he'd have liked to the vivacious newspaper reporter with more beauty than sense. Chase had heard from different sources that Maggie was making inquiries around town for someone to provide her escort to the Klondike for a fee. He hoped to God no one volunteered. Maybe she'd go home, then, where she belonged.

"Chase, you're not listening," Belle pouted.

"Sorry, Belle. What were you sayin'?"

"I asked if you knew that nosy newspaper woman who's going around town asking questions."

"Yeah, I know her."

"I thought so, since you seemed quite interested in her just now. Plain little thing, isn't she? Well past her prime."

Plain? Maggie plain? "I wouldn't call Maggie Afton plain, boss lady." Chase had no idea Belle had been watching him so closely. "She isn't exactly over the hill, either."

"Still, she's quite brazen to want to go to the Klondike alone. There aren't any women that I know of at Dawson City. I've been told there aren't even any whores or saloon girls up there yet."

Chase continued to watch Maggie, disappointed when she disappeared into a store. Despite what he'd told her earlier, he wanted to be able to protect her always. Damn, why did Maggie have to affect him in ways that left him confused and vulnerable?

"Chase what are you thinking, honey?"

"Huh?" Reluctantly Chase shifted his flagging attention back to Belle. "Just thinkin' that the town 'pears full of newcomers. I reckon they're just passin' through to the Klondike."

"Are you envious?"

"Damn right! If we hadn't been robbed, me and Rusty would already be there."

"If you're careful with your money, you could join the stampeders next spring. It's so late in the year now, you couldn't accomplish much by the time you got up there anyway. Another month or so and you'd have to close down the claim for the winter."

"I reckon you're right," Chase allowed grudgingly. He didn't say that spring of next year would be too late to save his ranch. He had expected to pay off the loan with some of the money from the cattle.

"I know what will make you feel better, Chase," Belle hinted coyly, hoping to coax Chase from his dark mood. "Let's go back to the Ice Palace. We've several hours yet to kill before the evening crowd arrives and I know a most delightful way to pass the time."

For the past few days, Belle had tried most unsuccessfully to invite herself into Chase's bed. But to her chagrin, Chase found one excuse after another to fend her off, which she viewed as unnatural. It seemed abnormal for a virile male like Chase to deny himself the pleasure she offered. Belle knew for a fact that Chase was bedding no other woman. He spent most of his spare time over at the Hash House catering to that injured partner of his. Suddenly warning lights went on in Belle's head. Didn't that spinster newspaper woman live at the Hash House? Of course, why hadn't she suspected it before? Chase was bedding that uppity bitch every time he went to see his partner!

"Sorry, Belle," Chase said, surprised at himself for turning down her suggestion. "I promised Rusty I'd spend the afternoon with him. He's bored as hell."

Belle fumed in impotent rage. Why did this incredible man thwart her best efforts to seduce him at every turn? "I thought you'd have your partner moved over to the Ice Palace by now. Or is he still too ill to be moved?"

"It's the dangedest thing," Chase mused thoughtfully, "but Rusty don't want to leave. He seems perfectly satisfied with that little storeroom behind the Hash House, though I 'spect Kate Sites has somethin' to do with his decision."

"Kate Sites? That dried-up old prune?"

Chase frowned, not at all pleased with Belle's description of the kind-hearted Kate. "Nevertheless, the two have a lot in common, and Rusty seems to dote on the woman. You go on back to the Ice Palace, boss lady. I'll see you later."

Ignoring Belle's sputtering protest, Chase shrugged free of her arm and sauntered off. Belle had never been so humiliated in her life. She simply had to speak to Soapy. Something would have to be done, and soon, about that newspaper snoop who pretended to be so virtuous and upright but spread her legs just like any other woman.

Maggie lingered in the store, in no particular hurry to leave. The day was too fine despite being spoiled by Chase and his whore. Encountering him on the street had nearly ruined her day. Since their passionate encounter a few days ago and Chase's subsequent anger, Maggie had avoided him, making certain she was either out or confined to her room when he came to call on Rusty. That was another thing that bothered Maggie. She expected to stay in Skagway no longer than a few days and already over two weeks had slipped by. She felt guilty depriving Kate of her room, although that good woman insisted she wasn't being put out.

When Maggie finally arrived back at the Hash House, she stopped off first at Rusty's room. She knew how partial he was to peppermint candy and had managed to buy a few sticks for an exorbitant price. She hoped the sweets would help ease Rusty's grumpy disposition. She hadn't counted on finding Chase with the older man, and she paused in the doorway, poised on the verge of flight.

"Well, are ya gonna stand there or do ya need a special invite?" Rusty growled when he saw Maggie standing uncertainly just inside his room.

Chase swiveled his head, drinking in the sight of Maggie's slim form, flushed face, and warm amber eyes registering confusion and a hint of some other vague emotion. "Yes, join us, Miss Afton. Have you found someone willing to take you to Dawson yet?"

The air between the two crackled with electricity, the tension mounting until Chase had to look away or go up in ash and smoke. One frosty glance from Maggie Afton did more to arouse him than all Belle Delarue's feminine wiles.

Maggie sizzled with indignation. If not for Rusty looking at them as if he'd just made a great discovery, she'd give Chase a piece of her mind. A very large piece. "I'm considering several offers," she lied. "I'll make up my mind in a day or two."

"Yeah," Chase replied skeptically, "and Soapy Smith offered to give back the money he stole from me and Rusty."

"Mr. Smith stole your money? That's another black mark against the scoundrel. I'm glad I didn't give up on exposing him. The first of my articles and pictures are ready to mail. Now if you excuse me, there are things I have to do."

She turned to leave, then changed her mind. "I almost forgot. I bought some peppermint candy for Rusty." She walked into the room, placing a small package in Rusty's eager hands.

"Bless your heart, girl," Rusty chuckled, licking his lips in anticipation. "Always did have a powerful cravin' fer peppermint candy." He popped one of the treats into his mouth and rolled his eyes. "Much obliged Maggie. You warm an old man's heart."

"Go on with you, Rusty," Maggie teased, "you're not old, just set in your ways."

Though Rusty was well into his fifties, his weathered features and grizzled appearance added years to his age.

Chase was amazed at the way Maggie had brought Rusty out of his doldrums with her meager offering. Why hadn't he thought of it? He owed Rusty more than he could ever repay, yet had never thought to bring him sweets—or anything else.

"Good-bye, Rusty, I'll see you later. Enjoy your visit with Chase. I'm sure he's given up a—er, pleasant afternoon to be with you." Then she was gone, her skirts swishing about her slender ankles as she disappeared around the corner.

"What in tarnation was that all about, son?" Rusty asked, eyes twinkling with wry amusement. It was the first sign of humor Chase had noted in his friend since he was robbed and injured.

"Maggie saw me with Belle this afternoon and she naturally assumed—" A scream brought Chase's words to an abrupt halt and he leaped to his feet. "What in the hell! That sounds like Maggie."

It took Chase sightly more than five seconds to reach Maggie's door, which was flung wide open. His heart leaped to his throat when he saw her lying on the floor. "Maggie! Maggie, darlin'! Oh, my God."

"I'm all right, Chase," Maggie gasped, rising unsteadily to a sitting position. Chase bent and helped her to her feet. Strangely reluctant to leave Chase's supporting arms, Maggie leaned gratefully into his embrace.

"What happened?"

"I'm not sure, exactly. I must have walked in on someone, for he rushed past me when I entered my room. I tried to stop him, but he shoved me aside when he tried to get out the door. I fell, and then I screamed, and—and that's when you came."

"What's goin' on here?" From the kitchen Hannah had heard Maggie scream and came running to her aid, brandishing an iron skillet.

"Someone was in Maggie's room," Chase explained tersely. "I was too late. He got clean away."

Maggie made a slow inspection of the room. It didn't take long to discover what the culprit was after. "Oh, no, look what he did to my plates!" Scattered over the room were the plates she had already exposed, as well as the remaining photographic plates she had brought with her from Seattle, each one broken or mutilated beyond repair. Her papers and notes lay amidst the wreckage, torn into tiny bits. The willful destruction lent mute testimony to Soapy Smith's power. It was also a sobering warning meant to frighten.

"Tarnation, will ya look at that!" Hannah said, stepping into the room. "Who'd do somethin' like that?"

"Soapy Smith," Chase muttered sourly. "He don't appreciate Maggie's determination to expose him."

"You been messin' with that man?" Hannah asked, awed by Maggie's daring. "Honey, you oughta know better than that. You'd be wise to leave Skagway."

"I intend to," Maggie replied tightly. "As soon as I find someone to take me to the Klondike. Now if you'll excuse me, I'll clean up this mess."

"Stop by and tell Rusty what happened, will you, Hannah?" Chase asked. "I'll stay and help Maggie."

"Sure thing." Hannah left and Chase deliberately closed the door behind her.

"I don't need your help, Mr. McGarrett."

"Maggie girl, this has gone far enough. What happened here is just a warnin'. Smith wants you gone. Don't you know your life is in danger?"

"Why should you care?" Maggie challenged.

"Damned if I know, but I do. What can I say to convince you to leave Skagway?"

"Take me to the Klondike," she argued, "where Soapy Smith can't touch me."

"Will you never give up?"

"Never!" Abruptly she turned and began tidying up the room.

Chase bent to help, muttering beneath his breath all the while. When finally a semblance of order was restored to the chaos Soapy's toughs had created, Chase tried one more time to reason with Maggie.

Grasping her by the shoulders, he said, "Regardless of the way you tried to use me, I don't want to see you hurt."

Maggie sighed, weary of his accusations. "Don't you recognize a true response when you see one? If you weren't so damn hotheaded, you'd realize that we made love because of the way I felt, not as a means of cajoling you into doing my bidding. I thought you felt something special between us, something that had nothing to do with taking me to the Yukon."

"I did feel something special, Maggie. That's why it hurt to think you'd use that feeling to persuade me into doing something I had no intention of doing. But perhaps I was too hasty to judge. I know how badly you want to go to the Klondike."

"Don't you understand, Chase? I can't give up now. My pride won't allow it. I've begged and cajoled for this assignment, and to return now would mean I'd be back to covering society pages and book reviews. Every man working for the Post-Intelligencer expects me to fail. Oh forget it," she said dejectedly, "you're a man yourself, so how can I expect you to understand?"

Strangely, Chase understood exactly how Maggie felt. He even had an inkling of what drove her. But it didn't change his mind. What it did was make him want her, make him yearn to experience her love once more. He vividly recalled how she had given unstintingly of herself, deriving as much pleasure as he had from their union. Afterwards there had been no recriminations or tears despite his angry accusations and cruel words. Maggie Afton was a courageous young woman rushing headlong into a bold new century and bravely embracing every challenge along the way. Chase couldn't help but admire her and what she was trying to accomplish, not just for herself but for the benefit of all womankind.

"I understand how you feel, Maggie, but I can't help you. I don't think you realize how long the six-hundred-mile trip will take or what would likely happen when we're alone for so long a time. I can't keep my hands off you now—think how it would be if we were together day after day." His blue eyes turned smoky with desire and his voice grew oddly hoarse.

Maggie worried her bottom lip thoughtfully with her perfect white teeth. "I've considered that, Chase," she admitted slowly. "It will test our willpower, but I'm willing to take the chance if you are."

"Dammit, Maggie, don't you know I've got no willpower where you're concerned? I hate the way you used me, but I can't forget the softness of your skin or the way your body responds to my touch. I want . . ."

"Just what is it you want from me, Chase?"

"I thought I made it clear—I want you, any way I can get you."

Maggie glared at him with scornful mockery. "Evidently you don't want me badly enough to take me to Dawson."

Chase gleefully rose to the challenge. "Maybe not," he admitted, a lazy smile dangling on the corner of his mouth, "but I want you badly enough to take you here and now."

Maggie held her breath as his burnished head descended toward hers and his mouth took hers hostage, snatching her breath away, then offering it back.

"Do you remember what it felt like when I was deep inside you, darlin'?" he asked, his voice slurred with desire. "When I think of you tightened around me, I can hardly breathe I want you so badly."

Maggie's golden eyes grew wide with alarm, fighting her own demons as her treacherous body responded to his erotic words. "Get out of here, Chase, before something happens neither of us is prepared to deal with."

"No way, darlin'." His touch had a savage roughness that spoke eloquently of his need. "I got a powerful hankerin' for you and I aim to appease that gnawin' ache."

Maggie's eyes grew deep and tawny as Chase's need became her own. Cradling her head in his hands, he let his thumbs caress the prominence of her high cheekbones, her satiny skin, moving in hypnotic circles, reacquainting him with the feel and texture of her. His fingers trembled into the silken mass of golden hair, freeing the curls from the prim bun until they tumbled down her shoulders in glorious disarray.

His kiss was not the kiss of a gentleman, but a bold assault on her mouth that both intrigued and frightened Maggie with its intensity. His tongue plundered, and she answered with quick darting strokes that drove him wilder, crazier. With a will of their own her arms dropped to encircle his powerful back under his denim jacket. She kneaded the massive muscles there, tugged his shirt free of his belt, and raked his bare skin while his kisses rained freely over her face and neck. Slowly and methodically Chase was destroying her senses, turning her into a raw, aching bundle of yearning. Even more incredible was the fact that Maggie was eager and willing to let the cowboy rogue have his way again.

"Take off your clothes, darlin', I want to watch you undress," Chase ordered softly. Without a word of protest, Maggie complied, lost in the soft, swirling heat of his gaze. "I love your body, it's so responsive. Look how tautly your nipples pucker, and I haven't even touched them."

Having shed the last piece of her clothing, Maggie stood before Chase wrapped in nothing but the magnificent golden veil of her hair. No matter what Chase wanted from her, she wanted it too. Why should men be the only ones to feel, to need, to want? Women were equally capable of experiencing those things, though society forbade it. She might be considered a spinster by some, but Maggie was determined to taste fully of life's pleasures. What truly puzzled her was why she chose an illiterate cowboy like Chase McGarrett to share these special feelings with. Then all thought came to an abrupt halt as Chase swung her into his arms and placed her on the narrow bed.

Chase didn't follow but stood beside her and slowly peeled the layers of his own clothing away. Maggie started to close her eyes but changed her mind. The last time they were together like this, she'd seen too little of his body and was curious enough to want to see everything this time. She wasn't disappointed. In comparison to his massive brown shoulders and chest, his waist was narrow, his hips slim. She followed the sturdy columns of his legs upwards to where they joined and her breath caught painfully in her throat. Her tawny eyes lingered there, mesmerized by the stirring sight of his thick manhood leaping forward from a dense copper forest.

Stunned, Maggie's eyes flew upward to find Chase regarding her with wry amusement. "Do you like what you see, darlin'?"

Maggie licked her lips, aware that her mouth had suddenly gone dry. "No—yes. I don't know. You're certainly impressive."

"So I've been told," he grimed wickedly. "I've had no complaints so far."

"Conceited jackass," Maggie muttered, following the line of matted hair from his chest to that part of him that intrigued her most. "My God, Chase, are you going to stand there all day while I admire you?"

"Nope," he said, dropping down beside her. "I'm gonna love you, then you're gonna love me."

"I don't understand."

"You will."

To Maggie's delight, Chase spent long pleasure-filled minutes exploring her body, bringing her to the brink of trembling ecstasy, only to hold her there, suspended. When his lips slid downward over her stomach, Maggie's breath rasped raggedly in her throat. "Chase, no, what—what are you doing?"

The rigid tip of his tongue parted the hair guarding the tender opening between her thighs, gliding along the moist warmth until he found the swelling bud of her femininity. "Chase, please, you can't!" Thoroughly shocked, Maggie never knew such a thing was possible—or desirable. Smiling, Chase proceeded to demonstrate just how little Maggie knew about loving and being loved.

His tongue continued stroking and teasing while his fingers played against her heated flesh, increasing her pleasure until every nerve ending screamed for release.

"Chase, please, I can't stand it!"

"Don't hold back, darlin'," Chase murmured in a muffled voice. "I want to make you happy."

His words had the desired effect as Maggie stiffened, her body a vessel of raw, consuming passion. She opened her mouth to scream, but Chase covered her lips with his own, swallowing her cries as her body convulsed beneath him. Then, with desperate urgency, he thrust into her, feeling her close tightly around him and hold him in the cradle of her warmth. Again and again he filled her, so completely she thought she would burst from the size and strength of him. It was wonderful. He was wonderful. There was an explosion that no words could describe, a brief moment of paradise, then a slow return to reality.

"I thought that first time was incredible, but this— I didn't know such pleasure existed," Maggie whispered breathlessly.

"Just let me catch my breath and we'll do it again," Chase rasped.

"What! Is that possible?"

"It is with me," Chase bragged, his eyes twinkling with amusement. "Only this time, you'll make love to me. I'll be able to hold off longer now and you can ride me to your heart's content." Seeing Maggie's shocked expression, he added, "Don't worry, I'll teach you. Seein' that you're a thoroughly modern woman, I know you'll enjoy it."

She did.

Chapter Seven

"Chase, ending up in bed with you isn't going to solve my problems," Maggie said reproachfully as she watched Chase dress. Deliberately she looked away so as not to be distracted by the sight of his taut buttocks as he shrugged into his pants.

"No, but it sure as hell helped mine," Chase grinned with wicked delight.

"Dammit, Chase, be serious. You know what I want."

"Yeah, my body," he teased, still grinning.

"Ohhh, you're impossible! Just get out of here. I'll find my own way to the Klondike. I don't need a man to take me."

Suddenly Chase sobered. "Promise me you'll do no such damn fool thing."

"No promises, Chase. You'd better go now. Miss Delarue is expecting you."

"Yeah, I don't want to be late for work," Chase grumbled, the words whipping around the door as it slammed shut behind him. "God deliver me from stubborn women."

Two days later Maggie had another surprising encounter with Soapy Smith. He confronted her as she walked through town toward the beach.

"Miss Afton, I owe you an apology," Soapy said, assuming a contrite expression. "I wouldn't hurt you for the world. I abhor violence. It's unfortunate the way things happened in my office. I'm afraid Mr. McGarrett misunderstood."

"I think Chase understood perfectly, Mr. Smith," Maggie sniffed. "If you'll excuse me, I have business elsewhere."

"I understand you're looking for someone to take you to Dawson City."

Maggie eyed him narrowly. He was a pleasant-looking man, if not for his cold eyes. And she had learned that he was a married man with children. "I've decided I don't need anyone to take me. I can get there on my own."

"I admire you, Miss Afton, I think we're a lot alike. But taking off on your own is not only foolish but dangerous. I'd like to help you."

"You want to help me?" Maggie scoffed derisively. "Why is it I don't believe you? Is it because you've thwarted me at every turn?"

"I don't know what you're talking about," he said with feigned innocence, "but I can be of help if you'd let me. I'm sending two of my best men up to Dawson to scout out possible sites for a saloon. I could arrange for them to take you along."

"What's the catch? What will it cost me?"

"You've got me wrong, Miss Afton. It won't cost you a cent other than the purchase of food and supplies."

Maggie waited, fully aware that there was more to come. She wasn't disappointed.

"In return for my help, I ask only that you mention the good I've done for Skagway in any future articles you write about me. I'm not asking you not to write those articles, just temper them by listing my contributions to the community."

Maggie's mind worked furiously. Her interviews had already revealed another side to Soapy Smith. She wouldn't be lying if she wrote about those things, too. But the question remained whether or not she could trust Soapy to keep his word about getting her safely to Dawson. Other than going off on her own, it was the best offer she'd had after two weeks in Skagway.

"All right, Mr. Smith, I'll agree to your terms. How can I be certain you'll not order my death once I leave Skagway? Many *accidents* can happen on the trail."

Soapy looked appropriately aggrieved. "Miss Afton, I assure you I would never do such a thing. I've always cooperated fully with the press. I want to be of help."

"How soon can we leave?" Maggie asked, her mind already made up. Soapy Smith hadn't asked her to do anything to compromise her integrity. Her stories about him would certainly continue, the only difference being that she'd make mention of his good works.

"Two, maybe three days," Soapy smiled, pleased by his easy victory. Obviously he had gone about it all wrong the first time.

"I'll be ready, just send word," Maggie said as she hurried off to begin her preparations. She went directly to the outfitting store to buy food and equipment for her long-anticipated trip.

Maggie's excitement escalated with each passing minute. Finally! She had begun to believe she'd never get to the Klondike, never complete her assignment, never prove her worth as a newspaper reporter.

Chase couldn't believe his eyes when he saw Maggie standing outside the outfitting store amidst a growing mountain of food and supplies. "Damnation! You really are goin' alone!"

"No, I'm not," Maggie smiled smugly, "not that it's any business of yours."

"You found someone willin' to take you to Dawson? Who? Don't you realize how dangerous it is puttin' your life in the hands of strangers?"

"Chase, I know you're going to find this difficult to believe, but Soapy Smith offered his help."

"What! Dammit, Maggie, you've done gone and lost your mind. I won't have it!"

"Chase, please, don't make a scene out here. Mr. Smith is sending two men to Dawson to look for a possible site for a saloon. He offered their escort."

"Sounds fishy to me," Chase grumbled, shoving his hat to the back of his head. "You're not goin' and that's final." Expecting his word to be strictly adhered to, Chase turned and stomped away.

The evening was going badly. Chase found it difficult to concentrate on his work. He looked at his pocket watch for the tenth time in the last two hours. Ten o'clock, still hours to go before closing time. He hated this job, hated the way men gambled away their hard-earned money. But mostly his mind was consumed with Maggie and how important she had become to him in the few short weeks he had known her. She was far too courageous, independent to a fault, stubborn, outspoken, foolish, exasperating, and not afraid to be a woman with a woman's needs.

"Chase, there's an old prospector asking for you. That scruffy-looking character with a gray beard standing at the end of the bar."

The dealer who was to relieve Chase for his first

break of the evening pointed to the man in question.

Chase nodded. "Much obliged, Johnny. Be back in fifteen minutes." He rose and strode over to the prospector who looked as if he'd seen better days.

"I'm Chase McGarrett, heard you're lookin' for me."

The old man glanced up from his beer, somewhat blurry-eyed but definitely not drunk. "If yer Rusty Reed's partner, then yer the man I want. Heard tell old Rusty done broke his leg and is laid up fer a spell."

"You're right on both accounts, Rusty broke his leg and I'm his partner. What can I do for you?"

"My name's Dan Freeman. Got me a claim on Gold Bottom, Fourteen Above. I understand you and Rusty left Sam Cooper in charge of Eleven Above."

"That's right. What about it?" Chase asked warily.

"Old Sam took sick real bad. We been friends fer years. I stopped by before I left Gold Bottom and he asked me ta deliver a message to either you or Rusty. I was comin' to Skagway anyways fer supplies."

"What's the message?" Chase asked impatiently.

"Old Sam is doin' mighty poorly and says fer ya to get up there pronto if ya ain't already left."

"What seems to be the trouble?"

"Don't rightly know, but he needs a doctor and he's afeered of leavin' the claim unprotected."

"Damn," Chase muttered, his mind racing. What was he to do with no money and Rusty laid up?

Cautiously Dan glanced around in all directions, leaned close to Chase, and whispered, "Sam said to tell ya thin's look mighty promisin' at Eleven Above, if ya catch my meanin'. If I were you, I'd hightail it up there before snow flies."

Chase thanked Dan profusely, bought him a drink, and hurried away. He had to talk with Rusty immediately. He knew exactly what he had to do, though he swore he'd never do it. It was imperative he get to Maggie before she took it into her head to leave with Soapy's henchmen. He spied Belle across the room and signaled his desire to speak with her. Belle waited for him to approach.

"What is it, Cowboy?"

"Find someone to relieve me, boss lady, I have to go out for a spell. Business."

"Monkey business, no doubt," muttered Belle crossly. "You got an itch for that newspaper snoop, Chase? Why not let me scratch it? I'm beginning to think I made a mistake in hiring you. You're not the man I thought you were."

"Sorry, Belle, if I led you to believe otherwise," Chase grinned lazily. "When you offered me a job, I didn't know there were strings attached. It's late and I've got to see Rusty before he retires for the night. I'll be back later to finish my shift."

"If you leave now, you're finished," Belle threatened, convinced Chase was going to see Maggie.

"Suits me. I don't like bein' dictated to. My life's my own to do with as I please." Without waiting for a reply, he turned and stalked off.

"Chase, wait!" Belle called, running after him and catching his arm. "Let's talk about this. Come up to my room later, I'll be waiting for you."

"Don't wait too long."

The Hash House was just closing for the night when Chase arrived. Expressing his desire to speak to Rusty, he spent only a few minutes in conversation with Hannah and Kate.

"Chase, what in tarnation brings ya here this time of night? Ain't ya supposed to be workin'?" Rusty asked when Chase burst into his room.

"Yeah, but somethin' important just came up and I need to talk to you."

"What is it, son?" Rusty asked, instantly alert.

"Got a message tonight from Sam Cooper up at Eleven Above."

"Give it to me straight, Chase."

" 'Pears Sam took sick and wants to know why we're not up there yet. His message was to hightail it up to Eleven Above as quick as we could."

A string of curses left Rusty's mouth. "And me laid up with a busted leg and our grubstake stolen. What rotten luck! What we gonna do, Chase?"

"I'm goin' to the Klondike, Rusty."

"You gonna ask Belle fer a loan?"

"Hell no! I don't like the strings attached to her money."

"Since when did you run away from a beautiful woman?" cackled Rusty. "Don't tell me that newspaper reporter is gettin' to ya."

"This is no time for foolish questions, Rusty. We got plans to make."

"What ya gonna use fer money?" Rusty asked, going quickly to the crux of the problem.

"I'm gonna let Maggie grubstake me in return for takin' her to Dawson. It's the only way I'm gonna get up to our claim. You got any other ideas?"

"Nary a one. But Maggie stopped in today to tell me she found someone to take her."

"Yeah, two of Soapy's thugs," Chase spat disgustedly. "I swear she's lost her mind. She's goin' with me and that's final."

"Kinda sweet on that little gal, ain't ya, son?"

"Mind your own business, Rusty," Chase glowered. "I'll arrange with Kate for your keep and pay her in advance. You should be up and about in a couple of weeks if she can find you a crutch."

"Dammit, Chase, I wish I was goin' along."

"Anythin' else I should know before I tell Maggie?"

"Naw, just get up there and take care of Sam. And

take care of Maggie, she's a damn fine woman."

Chase grinned. "I intend to. I'll see you before we leave. Oh, one more thing, Rusty—Sam's message hinted of somethin' big goin' on up at Gold Bottom."

"Jumpin' jehoshaphat! Do ya reckon he's found gold?"

"Don't know, but I aim to find out soon enough. Sleep tight, Rusty."

Maggie's new article on Soapy Smith was coming along well. It was late and she was tired. The knock on her door brought a frown to her face. She had spoken to both Hannah and Kate before she retired and said all there was to say on the subject. They had been so upset over her decision to travel to Dawson with two of Soapy Smith's men that Maggie suspected they had come to continue the argument. She appreciated their concern, but nothing would change her mind. Without hesitation she invited them in, even though she wasn't dressed to entertain visitors. She was clad casually in a prim nightgown and warm robe, her blond hair falling loose and lovely around her shoulders.

The door opened and Chase stepped inside. A small stove warmed the cool night air, and the light from a single lamp spilled a hazy glow over the woman seated at the small desk, her head bent over several sheets of paper.

"I told you both there was nothing you could say to change my mind," Maggie insisted without looking up.

"Can I change your mind, Maggie girl?"

"Chase, what are you doing here at this time of night? You're wasting your time, my mind is made up. I'm going to the Klondike no matter what you say."

"I'm not here to talk you out of goin' to the Klondike."

"I'm not going to bed with you, Chase McGarrett! How dare you come here thinking I'll—"

"Whoa, darlin', that's not why I'm here, either, though I gotta admit the thought did occur to me just now when I saw you sittin' there in your robe lookin' so enticin'."

"Just why *are* you here?"

"To tell you I've changed my mind. You grubstake me and I'll take you to the Klondike."

"Why now," asked Maggie suspiciously, "when I've already made other arrangements?"

"I won't lie to you, Maggie girl. I just received word from the man Rusty left in charge of Eleven Above. He's sick and I need to get up there pronto."

"What makes you think I still want you? I already have an escort. We're to leave soon."

"If you believe you'll be safe with Soapy Smith's thugs, your brains are scrambled. Smith could care less what happens to you after you leave Skagway. Oh, you might get to Dawson, all right—but in what condition?"

"Are you trying to frighten me?" Maggie argued.

"Damn right I am. Don't ask me why, but I care what happens to you. You're still a woman no matter how tough you pretend to be," Chase said, caressing her with his eyes.

Maggie knew Chase was right. Putting her trust in Smith and his thugs was foolish, but at the time it was her only alternative. She knew Chase, knew he'd protect her with his life no matter what, knew she could trust him. The other men were of unknown quality, while she knew exactly what to expect from Chase. Maggie didn't fear Chase, only how he made her feel.

"I want you to know, Maggie, that if we reach an agreement I fully intend to pay back every penny you loan me."

"How soon can we leave?" Maggie asked, her mind

made up. She'd go anywhere with Chase, trust him implicity.

A huge grin split Chase's rugged features. "Day after tomorrow, at dawn. I'll meet you at the outfittin' store in the mornin'. I'll buy everythin' I need then and use my pack horses to carry our supplies over the pass."

"I'll be there," Maggie agreed eagerly. "And Chase, thank you. I was having serious reservations about trusting myself to Smith's men."

"As well you should," Chase chastised. "I'd best be goin' now, I want to collect my pay from Belle. And if I stay longer, I'll forget everythin' 'cept how damn good you feel in my arms, all naked and warm and willin'." His voice was low and husky with desire. "Dammit, Maggie girl, I don't know how this is gonna work when it takes all my energy just keepin' my hands off you."

After one long searching look, Chase left, only too aware that if he touched her he'd go up in smoke. As for Maggie, she was already sizzling.

The outfitting store was a busy place the next morning. Hundreds of men were arriving daily aboard anything afloat. Captain Billy Moore's sawmill on the tide flats was producing lumber at a furious pace to keep up with the demand. Buildings, cabins, and warehouses appeared almost overnight. A major hotel was planned, as well as a church and long narrow docks out into Lynn Canal to facilitate the scores of ships entering the port every day. Maggie suspected she'd hardly recognize Skagway when she returned.

Since Maggie had already purchased her own supplies and equipment earlier, Chase made only a few suggestions, having to do with the type of clothing she needed for the trip. Maggie took his advice, purchasing a sheepskin jacket, long underwear, flannel shirts, thick denim jeans, gloves, and a hat that covered her ears. She also added a scarf and wool socks. She had thoughtfully brought along two pair of sturdy hiking boots from Seattle, and it was a good thing, since nothing at the outfitting store would have fit her. Then Maggie paid for everything with the money provided her by the Post-Intelligencer. It made a considerable dent in her finances, but it couldn't be helped. Soon she'd have money coming in the form of back pay and from the sale of articles sent to a popular magazine that seemed eager for her stories.

"That's it, Maggie, you wait here while I get the pack horses."

"Just a minute, mister, are you forgettin' somethin'?"

One of Soapy's men grabbed Chase's arm before he could walk away. "I think I got everythin'," Chase replied coolly.

"There's a little matter of the fee you owe Soapy fer all the supplies you just bought."

"I believe all that's required is payin' customs tax to Canada," Chase replied, shrugging free.

"Hey, wait a minute, no one gets away without payin' Soapy his cut."

"Tell Soapy he's already got enough of my money, he'll not get another dime."

Soapy's tough was so shocked that he walked away shaking his head and thinking it took a mighty brave man to defy Soapy Smith.

Dawn hadn't arrived any too soon to suit Maggie. The pack horses were already loaded and ready to go. Chase took three of the animals, leaving one behind in the unlikely event that Rusty was able to follow before the passes closed for the winter. He also left all his pay, grudgingly provided by Belle, which he hoped would be enough to grubstake Rusty. At the last minute Chase purchased a sled to be pulled behind one of the horses. Maggie waited outside the Hash House while Chase said his good-byes to Rusty, having already made her own farewells.

"Let's go, Maggie," Chase said briskly as he joined her.

It was only six A.M., but already light as they led the horses to the starting place where men, horses, sleds, and other beasts of burden were in line in that seemingly endless human chain wending its way steadily upward. Maggie thought this trek across White Pass was to be denied her until she actually took her place at the end of the line. It was nearly noon before they even reached the foot of the pass where the trail followed the river and they began the twenty-mile ascent to the summit. The date Maggie recorded in her notebook was September 5, 1897.

The trail led out of Skagway across a succession of hills, deceptively easy for three or four miles, then swung across the Skagway River for another three miles until the road narrowed and was seldom more than two feet wide. Because of melting snow and heavy rains, the route was a seemingly endless series of mudholes, some so bad horses sank in them down to their tails. At places the terrain was steep. Where there was no mud, there were rocks. In some spots a single misstep could send horses and men plunging a thousand feet down to the canyon floor. They reached the first summit, called Devil's Hill, at dark and Chase suggested they stop for the night.

It took a while to find a level place where they could pull off the trail and pitch a tent. By then Maggie was exhausted, cold, and hungry, and she sank to the ground wanting nothing more than to lay her head down and sleep.

"I warned you, darlin'," Chase said as he pulled the horses off the trail. "I told you travelin' to the

Yukon would be rough. It's not too late to go back."

"No!" Maggie cried stubbornly, staggering to her feet. "Tell me what to do."

"Rest while I put up the tent. Afterwards we'll have somethin' hot to eat."

The tent went up easily enough, though the rocky ground made the task more difficult. Soon Chase had a fire going and the fragrant aroma of coffee filled the air. Maggie roused herself long enough to fry bacon and open a can of beans. Meager though the fare was, it tasted delicious.

"Take off your boots, darlin', and climb inside," Chase invited, "you look beat. I'll join you after I feed the horses."

There was little forage for animals along the trail, so stampeders either brought along hay and feed or let their animals starve. Hundreds did and were abandoned. Others were overloaded and driven by cruel masters until they dropped in their tracks. Still others plunged to their deaths on the steep trails.

Nearly as tired as Maggie, Chase crawled in beside her, covering them both with blankets. "Are you awake, darlin'?"

"No," Maggie sighed, "go to sleep."

"How do you expect me to sleep with you lyin' here beside me?"

"Close your eyes," she advised, "it's easy."

To prove her point, Maggie's lids dropped and within seconds she was sound asleep. It was not so simple for Chase, who couldn't seem to find a comfortable position. When Maggie rolled to her side, Chase followed, hugging her body into the warm hollow of his. His hand naturally settled on her breast, and he worked it through the layers of her clothing until he encountered bare flesh. Even in her sleep Maggie acknowledged the intimacy with a shudder. Sighing with repressed longing, Chase

forced himself to relax and enjoy the small concession allowed him. Soon he too was asleep.

The following day was a repeat of the first. Maggie
had no idea the going would be so very difficult.
Soupy mud sucked at her feet so often that Chase
had to help her along in places. Most harrowing was
having to listen to the cry of hapless pack animals
that plunged over the precipice to the canyon below.
The second night they camped near the summit of
Porcupine Hill. The next day proved to be as ardu-
ous as the first two, bringing them to Summit Hill,
which was the customs collection station manned
by the Royal Canadian Mounted Police. A small
cabin housing the customs officer sat in a clearing
at the summit.

The Mountie seemed shocked to learn that Maggie was a woman. Thus far she was the first woman over the trail, though many more were soon to
follow. When the Mountie was told Maggie represented the Seattle Post-Intelligencer, he generously
offered her the cabin for the night. When Maggie
demurred, Chase accepted for her and it was settled.
After enjoying a thorough wash in water provided
by Chase from a nearby stream, Maggie donned
a nightgown from her pack and climbed into the
narrow bunk. Before she fell asleep she thought of
how much she missed Chase's comforting warmth
beside her.

"You smell a whole lot better than those stampeders sleepin' in tents outside," Chase murmured,
nuzzling Maggie's neck.

Maggie jerked awake instantly. "Chase, what are
you doing in here? What if someone saw you?"

"No one saw me, darlin'," Chase drawled lazily.
"I have to love you tonight or else lose my mind.
I've slept beside you for two nights without doin'
anythin' but touch your lovely breasts. I'm a strong

man, darlin', but even I have my breakin' point."

"You're a man of strong passions, Chase," Maggie
acknowledged huskily.

"And you're a passionate woman, darlin'. I'm glad
I'm the one who set them free. The only way to
work you out of my system is to love you 'til I've
had my fill."

Maggie seriously doubted she'd ever have her fill
of Chase's unique loving. Crude cowboy though he
might be, he was the only man capable of setting
her afire. She could no more resist Chase than she
could stop breathing.

"I'd be a liar if I said I didn't enjoy your loving,"
Maggie admitted quietly. "Love me, Chase, give me
something to remember when I return to Seattle."

He helped her off with her nightgown, then
stripped off his own clothes, settling beside her
with a sigh. When she pressed against him, he drew
a quick breath, his body becoming rigid. Suddenly
bold, Maggie twisted to allow her kisses to follow
the thick matting of hair that trailed across his
belly, and he could no longer breathe. Her moist
lips worshipped his skin, and she realized from the
fresh soapy smell that he had just bathed in the
icy stream. Tiny tremors ricocheted through every
nerve ending as Maggie continued her tender torture.
Muscles leaping in response, Chase groaned as her
slender fingers closed over his engorged flesh.

"Damnation, woman!"

He caught her chin between his thumb and forefinger, jerked her head roughly backward, and seized
her lips with his kisses, draining the breath from her.
The passion Maggie aroused in him raged without
restraint through the tense muscles of his powerful
body. His hand smoothed the warm flesh of her hips
while his leg parted her thighs and he slid atop her.
Then he was inside her, flexing his tight-muscled
buttocks to fill her again and again.

Maggie felt the weight of his gaze as he stroked her to completion, watching her eyes turn from brown to the purest gold. His own climax came in a whirlwind of sensation so intense the very air around him exploded.

Maggie was nearly asleep a short while later when Chase curved his arm around her left thigh to lift her leg upon his hip. "Wake up, my lovely Maggie, I want you again." Then, sliding his right leg between hers, he waited for her to mesh their bodies.

Completely awake now, Maggie shifted until they were joined. "You're insatiable, Chase McGarrett."

He made love to her this time with languid ease before the nearly unbearable rapture made him quicken his strokes to bring them to a perfect union.

The descent from the summit of White Pass was as treacherous as the ascent had been. The path went down a narrow funnel for about eight miles, then fanned out into various routes. Maggie was appalled by the conditions. Such a route might have handled a small number of pack trains comfortably, but it was not suitable for the hordes of men and animals who sought to struggle over it. Cruelty to animals was widespread. When horses sank in mud so deeply they could not be gotten out, they were simply abandoned without the mercy of a bullet, often with their loads still on them. Those luckless animals soon died as men and horses climbed over and across them. Whenever they came upon one of those poor creatures, Chase took it upon himself to put the animal out of its misery.

Maggie could easily understand how the trail shattered the health and fortunes of hundreds of men, for scattered along the middle and far reaches were valuable goods abandoned by their owners. No one would buy them or even take them as gifts. After coming this far, Maggie knew why Chase had tried to discourage her from attempting this journey. Though Chase had never been to the Klondike himself, Rusty had told him in detail what to expect and how to proceed. His descriptions were so explicit that none of the appalling conditions shocked Chase as they did Maggie.

Adhering to Rusty's directions, Chase chose the bypass that emerged at Lake Bennet. "Now the real trip begins, darlin'," Chase said as they stood gazing at the thirty-mile-long lake.

The hectic scene at the lake stunned Maggie. It looked much like the beach at Skagway, with hundreds of tents dotting the shore. Men of all sizes, shapes, and descriptions were engaged in one activity—building rafts or crude boats to transport themselves and their goods through a chain of lakes to the Yukon River and then downriver to Dawson City.

"What do we do now?" Maggie asked, awed by the scene stretched out before her.

"We put up a tent and build a raft," Chase said.

"What about the pack horses?"

"Sell them. There'll be men comin' from Dawson every day eager to buy our animals. Or men goin' overland instead of downriver."

As luck would have it, Chase chanced on a man whose partner had just died of an infection and who chose not to continue to Dawson on his own, a decision made by many men faced with the same dilemma. The man and his partner had just completed building a raft when a hatchet cut led to the infection that brought about the partner's death. Chase gladly traded two of the pack horses for the sturdily built raft.

The raft was flat-bottomed, flare-sided, twenty-five feet long by six feet wide, square and wide at the stern. Typically it carried two or three tons of goods and was usually driven by a sail made of a large canvas attached to a stout mast and supplemented when necessary by awkward, heavy pine oars.

"There they are, Bandy." Zeke pointed out when he spotted Maggie and Chase standing by the shore loading their raft.

Bandy Johnson and Zeke Palmer were the two toughs Soapy was sending to Dawson to scout a site for a saloon. They were also to be Maggie's escorts before she had decided to accompany Chase. When Soapy learned that Maggie had already left Skagway with Chase McGarrett, he cursed himself for letting Chase walk away from that dark alley alive. He had done it for Belle's sake, for all the good it did her. Soapy was so angry at Maggie for having welched on their deal that he instructed Bandy and Zeke to take care of the cowboy in any way they saw fit and do what they pleased with Maggie.

"How in tarnation do ya reckon they built a raft so quick?" Bandy asked, scratching his head. "We weren't but a day behind them."

Zeke was equally puzzled until they asked around and learned that rafts were for sale if one knew where to look and had the price. Zeke and Bandy had plenty of money provided by Soapy.

Meanwhile, Chase and Maggie prepared to leave on the first leg of their water journey to Dawson. When it came time to launch, everyone around lent a hand. The wind was stiff enough to capsize carelessly handled crafts, but Chase was proficient enough to keep them afloat, joining in the flotilla headed for the Yukon. It took most of the day to traverse Lake Bennet. At its foot, called Caribou Crossing, they entered a sluggish stream whose four-mile-an-hour current carried them into Lake Nares, four miles long. It was here Chase selected a site to spend the night, tying the raft in a secluded inlet along the shoreline. He wouldn't have found the spot if

Rusty hadn't told him exactly what to look for so it was more or less private. Taking their bedrolls ashore, they slept beneath a stand of tall spruce trees, huddled together for warmth.

"Have you noticed how much colder it's getting, Chase?" Maggie asked, fitting herself into the curve of his body.

"It's well into September, darlin'. In less than six weeks the passes will be closed by snow and blizzards."

"I'll be stuck in Dawson till spring," Maggie mused thoughtfully. "What will you do?"

"Get on up to the claim first and see how Sam is doin'. There's a cabin up there that will provide adequate shelter for the winter. Don't 'spose I'll get much prospectin' done, but I'll do what I can."

"Won't you be spending any time in Dawson?" Maggie asked wistfully.

"No, Maggie girl, don't reckon I will." He wanted to say he'd miss her, but he didn't dare. They'd shared so much these past weeks, yet he could promise her nothing.

Chase had made a commitment when he began this venture, and he meant to honor it. There was still time to earn enough to pay the loan on his ranch, and committing himself to a woman at this time was not in his plans. Maggie wasn't the type of clinging woman who was lost without a man to sustain her. She was a modern, independent woman fully capable of conducting her life without him. She had a career and was astute enough to realize that life couldn't always be the way one wanted it to be.

Chase had to admit, though, that all other women paled in comparison to Maggie, and that if it were possible for him to fall in love now, it would be Maggie he chose. She was passionate, brave, foolish, tender, obstinate, and too damn headstrong for her own good. Yet there was no woman Chase would rather make love to than Maggie Afton.

"Do you think we'll ever meet again after we get to Dawson?" Maggie asked, an odd little catch in her voice.

"It's—hard to say," Chase replied truthfully, unwilling to give hope where none existed. "Do you care so much?"

"I—of course I'll miss you, Cowboy. We've been more than friends these past weeks. A woman doesn't forget her first lover." And likely the last, she wanted to add. How could she let another man touch her after Chase? The answer was simple—she couldn't.

"Maggie, darlin', if there was any way—"

"No, Chase, no promises. I asked for nothing when I let you love me. I wanted it—I wanted you. Whatever happens, let there be no guilt on either side. Our loving is something that happened, something we both enjoyed, and if it must necessarily end at Dawson—well, I'll always remember these nights. Now love me, Cowboy, love me till I'm mindless with rapture."

"I'll always want to love you, darlin'. Let's forget tomorrow and concentrate on tonight."

Chase longed to tell Maggie that if he were free now to love completely, she'd be the woman he'd want to spend his life with. Someday, maybe, if she was still free . . . The thought died when Maggie pulled down his head and he felt the soft imprint of her lips on his.

"There's the raft, Bandy," Zeke whispered as they pulled their own craft into place against the shore. "I knew I saw them tie up here someplace."

"Pipe down, Zeke, they're probably sleepin'. But just in case, I don't want them hearin' us. Do ya see them anywhere?"

"Naw, they musta crawled under them trees yonder. Got the hatchet?"

"Yep, right here."

Bandy handed Zeke the hatchet. Immediately Zeke bent and began prying a board loose just below the waterline where it wouldn't be too conspicuous. By their reckoning, the heavily laden raft should start sinking about the time it reached the middle of the lake—hopefully with the occupants aboard.

"Done!" Zeke crowed, pleased with his sabotage. "Let's get the hell outta here."

Silent as wraiths they slipped off, tying up farther down the shore where they could watch and wait.

Chapter Eight

"Get up, sleepyhead." Chase grinned wolfishly as he swatted Maggie playfully on the bottom. "If I recollect, you were the one who woke up at dawn all warm and willin' and damn eager."

"You were as eager as I was, Chase McGarrett," Maggie grunted, burrowing deeper into the blanket.

"Darn right, sugar," Chase agreed. "But it's time to rise and shine. You have a wash while I fix us some grub."

Chase must have already had his wash, for despite the chill his hair reflected tiny droplets of water sparkling like tiny diamonds in the meager sunlight. Maggie admired the way he moved, his lean lithe grace, the seductive way his hips rolled with each step. He was all man, hard as nails and tough as a two-bit steak—but oh so tender, too, with hands so gentle they drew forth a response with their merest touch. Would their remaining days and nights

132

together be enough to get him out of her system? Maggie wondered bleakly, knowing that even a lifetime with Chase wouldn't cure her of wanting him.

"There's water in the bottom of the boat," Chase called out as Maggie packed their camping gear. Though it wasn't a great deal of water, it was enough to alert a cautious man like Chase.

"A leak?" Maggie suggested.

"It was tight enough yesterday. Maybe I oughta have a look."

"It's probably nothing," Maggie discounted lightly.

"You could be right, but I think I'll have a look anyway."

Rolling up his sleeves, Chase first checked the exposed hull and bottom, finding nothing amiss. Then he plunged his arm into the cold water and began a minute inspection of the hull below the waterline. Because the boat was flat, it wasn't difficult.

"Damnation!" Chase had found the place where Zeke had pried loose a board.

"What is it?" Maggie asked, joining him in the boat.

"If I didn't know better, I'd say we've been sabotaged."

"What? How?"

"Damned if I know. This loose board wasn't here yesterday. I went over the raft with a fine-toothed comb before she was launched."

"Could someone have done it while we were sleeping?"

"Asleep or makin' love."

Maggie blushed. "Who would do such a thing?"

"Beats me, darlin'. All I know is that it's a damn good thing I saw the water and decided to check."

"What can you do?"

"Repair it. There's pitch and spare boards I

brought along just for that purpose. Best I get started."

It was nearly noon before Chase raised the sail and the boat, now watertight and as seaworthy as Chase could make it, slid into the lake to join the flotilla.

Lake Nares was an easy trip as they floated lazily into Lake Tagish, which Maggie thought was a series of lakes instead of the single lake it really was. Halfway down, the Mounties had established the Tagish Post, where each boat was required to register and show a customs receipt for its cargo. It was the only way the authorities had of tracing missing men and it worked surprisingly well. Chase and Maggie tied up for the night beside the post.

Following close behind, Bandy and Zeke waited with bated breath for Chase's raft to sink, and when it did not, they began arguing between themselves as to whose fault it was. But to their chagrin, their devious plans were necessarily put on hold, for they could do nothing that night with the Mounties looking on.

The next day Chase and Maggie entered Lake Marsh through a slow river. Lake Marsh was long, narrow, and almost twenty miles long. Beyond lay Miles Canyon, one hundred feet wide and more than fifty feet deep, through which the Lewes River raced.

"There's a dangerous whirlpool about halfway down," Chase warned. "After that there's Squaw Rapids, then Whitehorse Rapids. Rusty advised me to pick up a pilot before negotiatin' that treacherous stretch of water. Most of the navigators are Indians, but I understand a few white men have joined their ranks. We can pick one up at their small outpost before we enter Miles Canyon."

Not all the boats in the flotilla bothered with a pilot, especially if they were experienced boatmen or familiar with the waterways of the Yukon. Because Chase was neither, he bowed to prudence and Rusty's advice.

"Twenty dollars," the young man replied when asked what he charged to pilot the raft through the rapids.

Chase looked to Maggie, and when she nodded agreement, shook the man's hand. "I'm Chase McGarrett, and this is Maggie Afton from the Seattle Post-Intelligencer."

"A newspaper reporter!" the man exclaimed, regarding Maggie with interest. "I'm Jack London. I do some writing myself."

"What are you doing piloting boats, Mr. London?" Maggie asked curiously.

"Earning money and learning about life." Jack grinned with boyish enthusiasm. "I'll be going up to Dawson before the lakes freeze this winter. Perhaps I'll see you there, Miss Afton. Is Mr. McGarrett your guide?" he asked pointedly.

"Yeah, you could say that," Chase answered before Maggie could form an appropriate reply. "Shouldn't we get goin', Mr. London?"

Jack London proved a capable guide. By keeping to the crest of the waves they avoided the whirlpool. Others were not so lucky, and more than one craft was drawn into the swirling eddy and capsized. Fortunately, the men swam ashore unharmed, and eventually their equipment floated ashore also.

Squaw Rapids proved to be less harrowing, but Whitehorse Rapids boiled and seethed a quarter of a mile through a narrow cut thirty feet high. Maggie hung on for dear life, certain they'd be smashed into smithereens against one of the rocks jutting out from the water. Jack London, young as he was, performed his job remarkably well, carefully negotiating the treacherous waters with amazing skill until they drifted into the serene Lewes River where they bade him good-bye. At that point, the pilots picked up a horse and rode back to the starting place. A good pilot could make as many as ten trips downstream a day. Maggie was relieved to know that no more obstacles stood in the way of their journey to Dawson.

The river widened into Lake Labarge, which Maggie found the most beautifully breathtaking of all with its high ridges, thirty-mile length and two-mile width. A strong wind blew that day, so strong that Chase decided to wait at a place called Windy Arms until weather conditions moderated. The stiff breeze was so cold it pierced through their layers of clothing, forcing them to don their sheepskin jackets, gloves, and mufflers. When the wind showed no signs of abating, they erected their tent close to the shore and crawled inside.

A few yards away, Bandy and Zeke had safely shot the rapids and beached their raft. From a distance, they watched as Chase and Maggie disappeared inside their tent. "Tonight," Bandy said, smiling maliciously. "We'll get rid of the cowboy and have some fun with the woman. She's a ripe piece. She oughta share her favors instead of givin' it all away to that cowboy. I'm sick of them worn-out whores in Skagway."

"Wonder why their raft didn't sink?" Zeke whined.

"Who knows? We'll do it right this time. Once I finish with the woman, ya can have her. We won't kill her 'til we tire of her."

"Just talkin' about her has me so horny I'm hard as a rock," Zeke complained, scratching his crotch.

"Soon, Zeke, soon. . . ."

The wind died down during the night, and before he fell asleep Chase decided they'd be able to continue their trip the next day. But for a few more nights, he had Maggie in his arms to love. For a short time she was his to hold, to treasure, to memorize to his heart's content, until circumstances parted them, perhaps forever.

"Are you tired, darlin'?" he asked, his voice made husky with desire. "If you are I'll—"

"No, Chase," Maggie assured him. "I'm never too tired for you. I only wish . . ."

"No wishes, sugar, I'd hate to see you disappointed. You have to know I care for you, and I believe you care for me. Leave it at that for the time bein'."

"You're right, Chase. I've no right to wish for something that neither of us wants. You have a claim to work and I've a job to do. Both of us are too involved in our own lives to give up any part of it. We're both independent and strong willed," Maggie argued, more to convince herself than Chase, "and I'll always care about you." This was a gross understatement, but she didn't want his pity.

"You talk too much," Chase murmured huskily as his fingers struggled with the buttons of her shirt.

"And you're much too slow," Maggie retorted tartly as she helped him divest her of her clothing.

They made love gloriously, with marvelous abandon, as they always did, and always would no matter how often they came together like this.

When Chase finally thrust into her, he took her with a fierce passion that left her exhausted and magnificently violated, sated for a time, until he touched her again.

Chase awoke with a start, alert even in sleep. What had disturbed him? Then he heard it again, a faint rustling sound. Was someone out there stealing their supplies? Rusty told him to keep a sharp eye out for pilfering local Indians who often resorted to thievery. Glancing over at Maggie, Chase saw that she was sleeping peacefully. Because of the cold, they had donned their clothes after making love and lay fully dressed down to their sheepskin jackets. He smiled when he saw that Maggie had even slipped on her heavy stockings and boots and slid the knife he had given her into place beneath the high-laced top.

There it was again, that noise, and Chase could no longer ignore it. Slipping into his own stockings and boots, and strapping on his holster, he crawled from the tent. He started to rise, his hand on his gun, when a solid blow to the back of his head sent him plummeting to the ground, and he knew no more.

"Finish him off, Zeke, while I get the girl," Bandy hissed.

An uncomfortable pressure jerked Maggie from a sound sleep. Why was Chase lying atop her, pressing her into the hard ground so she couldn't move or breath? "Chase, what—"

Her words were abruptly cut off when someone stuffed a rag into her mouth. Maggie gagged, trying desperately to spit out the offending obstruction. Her eyes leaped open, stunned to find a strange men leering at her through the darkness. Where was Chase?

It took but a moment for Maggie to realize her danger and react accordingly, startling Bandy with her ferocity. She fought like a tigress, kicking, clawing, nearly too much for Bandy to handle. "Zeke, get in here and help me!" Bandy gasped, fending off Maggie's vicious blows. "The bitch is like a wildcat."

Outside, Zeke had pulled his gun, thinking to blow Chase's brains out and finish him off as Bandy had instructed. Then, for once in his life, good sense prevailed, and he realized that a shot would bring men rushing to the scene. Slamming his gun back in its holster, Zeke removed the knife strapped to his waist and aimed for Chase's heart.

At that precise moment two things happened at once. Chase moaned and rolled to his side, spoiling Zeke's aim with his shoulder, and Bandy called for Zeke's help in subduing Maggie. The knife slammed into Chase's upper chest causing great pain but hitting nothing vital.

"I ain't done here yet," Zeke called back, unable to tell in the dark exactly what damage he had done to Chase or if he still lived.

"Forget the bastard. We can take care of him later. I need help with the woman."

Reluctant to leave but accustomed to following Bandy's orders, Zeke joined his partner inside the small tent where a ferocious struggle was taking place. Thinking to end it quickly, Zeke tapped Maggie alongside the head with the butt of his gun. Maggie went limp.

"She's out. Help me drag her outside," Bandy said, panting heavily.

"What about the cowboy?"

"If he ain't dead, finish him off." Bandy scooped Maggie up in his arms as Zeke turned back to Chase.

Suddenly the crunch of footsteps echoed through the icy stillness of predawn. Bandy froze, darting a quick glance toward the neighboring tent, where a man was standing a few short yards away, relieving himself against a nearby tree.

"C'mon, Zeke, let's get outta here," Bandy hissed, shifting Maggie over his shoulder. He disappeared into the shadows, Zeke close behind. There hadn't been time to find out for sure if Chase was dead, but there was enough blood pooling beneath him to suggest he was.

Bright shards of sunlight stabbed repeatedly against Maggie's eyelids, and she tried to raise her arms to shield her face, but they refused to obey. Then came the pain—quick, jabbing, splitting her head in two. Her shoulders ached, her wrists hurt, and her legs felt strangely lifeless. Something hard and uncomfortable stabbed into her back.

"Chase?" Because she appeared to have difficulty

breathing, Bandy had removed Maggie's gag while she lay unconscious. He didn't want her dead quite yet.

"So ya finally decided ta wake up."

Maggie's eyes flew upward. "Who—who are you? Where is Chase?"

"Yer cowboy lover is dead," Zeke guffawed loudly, ignoring Maggie's gasp. "Ya belong ta us now."

"No, you're lying!" Maggie cried. In her mind Chase was virtually indestructible. He was big, brave, bold, and stronger than any man she knew. Nothing ruffled him; he was frightened of no one. "I'm in a boat!" she murmured, finally realizing that she lay in the bottom of a raft trussed up like a prize turkey.

"We left Windy Arm before daybreak," Bandy advised. "Soapy didn't appreciate the way ya backed outta yer deal. Me and Zeke were all set ta deliver ya all safe and sound ta Dawson when we heard ya took off with that cowboy."

"You're Soapy Smith's men! You're the ones who kidnapped me off the street in Skagway," Maggie said, recognition dawning. "What do you want with me? What have you done with Chase?"

"The cowboy's done fer, I seen ta that," Zeke crowed.

A shaft of stark fear shattered Maggie's heart. "What did you do to him?"

"The same thing we're gonna do ta you, soon as we finish with ya tonight. Nobody double-crosses Soapy and lives ta tell of it."

"Please, untie me, my wrists and ankles are numb," Maggie begged, her eyes glazed with pain. "Where can I go in the middle of the lake? I can't swim." It was a deliberate falsehood, meant to mislead the two men into thinking she was helpless. Actually, Maggie was an excellent swimmer, often swimming in the ocean for exercise.

"Untie her, Zeke," Bandy said. "She's right, it's a

long way to shore. Just make sure she stays hidden on the bottom of the boat. Ya never know when one of these other rafts might come up beside us."

Maggie cried out at the numbing pain when the circulation returned to her limbs. She rubbed them vigorously until some measure of feeling returned. At least now she had a fighting chance at escape. Trussed up as she was she would have drowned attempting such a feat.

"Where are we?"

"Still in Lake Labarge," Bandy replied sourly.

"What are you going to do with me?"

"Have some fun tonight after we find a nice private place ta tie up. Bet ya know all the tricks ta drive a man crazy."

Bandy reached out to stroke Maggie's breast, though she felt little through the protection of her sheepskin jacket. "Keep your filthy hands off me!"

"Gonna have more than our hands on ya tonight," Zeke leered owlishly.

"I don't understand. Why are you doing this?"

"I told ya, Soapy don't like bein' double-crossed. He spared the cowboy once, fer Belle's sake, but not this time. He's gonna teach ya both a lesson."

"What do you mean, 'spared him once'?"

"No harm tellin' ya now," Bandy shrugged. "The night we lifted the cowboy's gold, Soapy told us not ta kill him, that Belle wanted him. Woulda done in his partner, though, if we weren't interrupted."

"Chase said all along Soapy was behind the robbery," Maggie said, glaring at the two toughs. "You'd better hope Chase never finds you."

"No chance of that," Zeke laughed, an ugly sound deep in his throat.

"I don't believe Chase is dead," Maggie insisted stubbornly. "He's too smart for the likes of you."

"Believe what ya like, girl, but he won't be comin' after ya," Zeke replied with more assurance than he felt. Truth to tell, he wasn't all that certain the cowboy was dead, but he didn't want to confess his ineptness to Bandy, who would surely upbraid him soundly.

Maggie fell silent. Not for one minute did she believe Chase was dead. She'd feel it in her heart if he was. No, not Chase. He was too vibrant, too alive, too vital to be done in so easily. He'd find her, she was sure of it. Meanwhile, she'd leave nothing to chance and prepare herself to take advantage of any situation. Of one thing she was damn certain—neither of these two men would ever lay a hand on her.

Bandy could hardly take his eyes off Maggie, devouring her face and figure with lustful attention. When he saw her eyeing the surface of the lake with keen interest, he said, "I wouldn't try it if I was you, girl. I can swim good 'nuf ta pull ya out and make ya sorry ya tried it."

Maggie sat back, only too aware that it was a long way to shore and the water ice cold. Best bide her time until conditions were more in her favor, or at least even. She thanked God that Chase had insisted she carry a knife tucked into her boot, concealed by her trouser leg. She could feel its comforting presence against her soft flesh.

"I'm hungry," Maggie complained sullenly.

"Can't take time now," Bandy replied. "Want ta get ta Five Finger Rapids before we tie up fer the night."

Soon they came to the downstream outlet of Lake Labarge, and Bandy expertly steered the boat around a reef situated exactly in the center of the gorge. The going was narrow and dangerous because of the outcroppings of rock jutting from the water. Five Finger Rapids was nothing like Whitehorse Rapids or Squaw Rapids but still could be treacherous to the novice. It got its name from the five great blocks of reddish rock that stuck out like the piers of a bridge. Because it was growing dark, Bandy decided not to shoot the rapids until the next day. He steered the boat into a narrow inlet that completely concealed their small craft. It became obvious to Maggie that Bandy had traveled this route before.

Maggie was unceremoniously dragged from the raft, tied to a tree out of sight of passersby and gagged so she couldn't cry out. A rope around her waist bound her to the tree, and her wrists and feet were lashed together in front of her. Then she was abandoned to contemplate her fate. Meanwhile, Bandy and Zeke built a fire and prepared a make-shift meal. The food smelled wonderful and Maggie's stomach growled loudly, but she said nothing, afraid to draw attention to herself. Evidently her captors had no intention of wasting food on her. What they did intend to do with her became more and more obvious as the evening progressed. While they sat by the fire drinking bad whiskey, Bandy and Zeke grew extremely boisterous.

"Why can't I be first?" Zeke complained bitterly, slanting a lustful glance in Maggie's direction.

" 'Cause I'm the one with the brains and you follow orders," Bandy replied, slurring his words.

A sullen silence followed as they tipped their cups and drank deeply. Maggie realized she had little time left to escape their evil plans. It also became increasingly evident that the two men meant to kill her after they had raped her. She had deliberately defied Soapy Smith, and that alone sealed her fate. Men like Bandy and Zeke needed little reason to kill and rape, except for the enjoyment it gave them.

It was very dark now, and the slack in her bindings allowed Maggie to move her bound hands slowly—very slowly—to her boot, where her knife was concealed. Painstakingly, she retrieved the blade, blessing Chase for honing it to razor sharpness. While her captors drank and argued, she sawed furiously at the rope binding her wrists to her ankles. The going was made extremely awkward because of her lashed wrists, but soon her feet were free and she concentrated on the rope binding her to the tree. She couldn't take the time to free her wrists yet, so she just kept sawing at the thick rope around her waist. She felt the rope give at the same moment Bandy stood up and reeled in her direction.

"Get lost, Zeke," Bandy barked with grim purpose. "Me and the little lady want some privacy. Come back in an hour, then she's yers. Afterwards we can take turns till we're tired of the game."

"Aw, Bandy—"

"Vamoose, Zeke."

Zeke staggered to his feet, hugging the bottle to his chest and stomping off into the trees, muttering darkly to himself.

The rope binding Maggie to the tree fell away, but she had no time to cut her wrist bindings as Bandy approached, swaggering like a cocky rooster. "Now let's see what kept that cowboy sniffin' around ya like a randy goat," he said lewdly. "I got a powerful hankerin' fer that sweet stuff betwixt yer legs."

Bandy reached for Maggie, gasping in shock when he felt the bite of her blade against his open palm. "What the hell!" He was unprepared for Maggie's attack, yet he still managed to lash out with his uninjured hand and deliver a vicious blow to her jaw.

Immediately Bandy was atop her, straddling her slender hips, tearing at her jacket and shirt to get to her breasts. Made groggy from Bandy's hard-fisted blow, Maggie reeled dizzily, unable to fend off Bandy's slobbering kisses and disgusting groping—until she remembered the knife still clutched in her fists. Though her wrists were still tightly bound, Maggie marshaled sufficient strength to raise her arms and plunge the knife into the base of Bandy's neck where it joined his shoulder. It was a vulnerable spot not overly protected by clothing. She felt him slump against her, and a rush of sticky wetness splattered her exposed flesh.

"Oh my god, oh my god, oh my God," Maggie repeated in a litany of overwhelming dismay. What she had just done rendered her stiff with shock. Never in her wildest imaginings had she ever thought she could kill a man. But she had had no choice; it was either use her knife or submit to the vile lust of Bandy and his partner.

Slowly Maggie's wits returned, and she shoved at Bandy's inert form, squirming from beneath him when he rolled aside. Her breath grated harshly in her chest and left her throat in ragged gasps. Fear rode her and survival moved her feet. She spared but one brief glance at Bandy, then at her bound wrists, and at the blade still protruding from his neck. She couldn't bring herself to touch him again, couldn't pull the blade from his flesh. She thought of nothing but escape as she raced toward the shore, and what Zeke would do to her once he discovered she had killed his partner. She had no idea where to go or what to do, until she spied the raft bumping gently against the shore.

Having lived on the coast all her life, Maggie knew the basics of sailing, and seized the opportunity without a moment's hesitation. She preferred drowning in the rapids to facing Zeke's rage.

Her bound hands, so numb her fingers barely worked, fumbled clumsily at the knot holding the raft to a pine tree growing close to the shore. Suddenly she heard Zeke cursing as he stumbled through the trees behind her.

"Finished or not, Bandy, it's my turn. I got so damn hot thinkin' about what yer doin' ta the girl, I'm about ta bust my britches."

Please Lord, Maggie silently prayed, a sob catching in her throat, *let me get out of here before Zeke finds me.*

"Where in tarnation are ya, Bandy?" Zeke aimed his steps toward the tree to which Maggie had been bound. He nearly fell over Bandy's body, cursing violently when he discovered his partner lying still as death in a pool of congealing blood.

It took a moment for Zeke's liquor-befuddled brain to register what had happened, but when it did he erupted in a ferocious frenzy. "Ya connivin' bitch!" he shrieked. "Ya won't get away with this!"

Maggie whimpered beneath her breath, her fingers working furiously at the stubborn knot. If only she hadn't been too squeamish to remove the knife from Bandy's neck. She heaved a glad cry when the knot finally parted, but by then Zeke had seen her small form outlined against the shore and started toward her. The icy water nearly took Maggie's breath away as she plunged into the lake to push the raft away from shore. Zeke's threats and curses lent her the strength to pull herself aboard as the raft entered the river's current and lengthened the distance from where Zeke stood on the bank shaking his fist in furious anger.

Unable to swim, Zeke flew into a frenzy as he watched Maggie, the raft, and all their supplies pick up speed as it entered the current. "I'll find ya!" he ranted, nearly beside himself. "If the rapids don't get ya, I will!"

Exhausted, Maggie lay in the bottom of the raft, the pain in her bleeding wrists nearly unbearable. She couldn't move. All she could do was curl into a ball to conserve her body warmth and shiver in her sodden clothes. It was so dark she could barely make out the shore, trusting the current to propel the small craft forward. She closed her eyes, lulled into an uneasy sleep by the undulating waves slapping gently against the hull. At first light, she thought drowsily, she'd search the bundles of supplies for something with which to cut away her wrist bindings.

Maggie awoke with a start, aware that something was dreadfully wrong. The rhythm of the current had altered, and there was a strange roaring in her ears. Struggling to her knees, Maggie stared in abject horror as the light of dawn clearly defined the monstrous granite rocks jutting out into the river. Five Finger Rapids! My God, she was going to shoot the rapids in a raft she was unable to control! The raft, with her in it, would be smashed into splinters by the boiling current. Then the raft began to buck and whirl, and Maggie hung on and prayed.

The raft was halfway through, and Maggie began to hope, when disaster struck. The craft was slammed into a huge boulder. A section of its stern was ripped away before it was allowed to continue its perilous journey through the rapids. Maggie went flying, landing half in and half out of the water on that portion of the raft that remained intact. But she had sense enough to realize that her hold was so tenuous she'd soon be swept away to her death. Her meager strength failed as she tried to heave herself aboard the wreckage, which was still spinning crazily. As her numb hands lost their grip she began to slide. Gritting her teeth she braced herself for the plunge that would snuff out her life. Then, miraculously, the rope still binding her wrists caught on a piece of wood protruding from the place where the rudder had sheared off.

The strength of that rope saved Maggie's life as the raft shot through the rapids without further mishap, entering the placid Yukon River, which was very wide, broken into many channels and wooded islands. But it still wasn't over for Maggie. When the raft shot over the last yard of churning water, one of the parcels tied to the raft broke loose, hurtling down and striking Maggie in the head. She sank down into a deep, bottomless void, unaware that Dawson City lay upriver but a short distance.

Chapter Nine

The current carried the raft downstream, but Maggie remained comatose most of the time, still lying half in, half out of the water. Numerous rafts floated by, but the river was so wide no one noticed her slight form dangling over the side. Most stampeders were so anxious to reach Dawson they paid scant attention to a derelic raft whose owners probably drowned while negotiating Five Finger Rapids.

Days were shorter in the Yukon where soon only four or five hours of murky light would prevail, and it was already dark again. Maggie shivered uncontrollably, too weak to pull herself onto the raft, too spent to cry out. In the deepest chambers of her brain she was aware that the raft no longer moved at a brisk pace but bumped against some kind of barrier. She had no recollection of the passage of time or of how often darkness changed to daylight. She groaned and moved her head, and pain sent her spinning down into unconsciousness.

"Ya reckon she's alive, Wally?"

"Don't know, Charlie. She looks dead to me."

"You go for the Mounties, I'll wait here. Hurry, mayhap she's still breathin'."

Sometime during her long travail the raft carrying Maggie nudged into Dawson City, where rafts and boats were anchored six deep along a two-mile strip. Wally Cross, whose boat was anchored nearby, discovered Maggie when he awoke early that morning to relieve himself. He and his partner, Charlie Daniels, had arrived only the day before and had slept aboard their boat in order to protect their belongings.

Maggie felt strange, as if she were detached from her body. Her legs were nearly paralyzed and her wrists felt numb from constant, excruciating pain. Her eyes were glued together. Vague, disjointed sounds penetrated her brain, and she concentrated on the hum of words floating around her.

"Who is she?" The voice was deep, low, and soothing to her ears.

"Don't know, Captain Gordon, she musta floated in durin' the night. Wally found her. Is she alive?"

"Just barely," the captain responded grimly.

Tall, virile, and imposing in his impeccable uniform, Captain Scott Gordon was somewhat over thirty years old and extremely handsome, with sunbronzed skin and dark hair. His keen gray eyes contrasted sharply with the swarthiness of his skin.

"I'd like to know the name of the bastard who did this to her," Gordon gritted out angrily. "Look at her hands, they're so swollen and blue I'm not even sure the doctor can save them."

Maggie opened her mouth to speak, but the effort proved too great and she gave herself up to the care of the man who carried her as tenderly as a newborn babe. She felt safe for the first time since she'd been taken from Chase. Thinking of Chase brought an ache deeper than any she'd suffered thus far, and she welcomed the darkness that claimed her.

"Careful, Scott, the pain will be excruciating when you cut away the ropes."

"I know, Doc, but it's got to be done. Poor little thing. I wonder who she is. Even covered in dirt, she's beautiful," Gordon mused thoughtfully.

"Easy does it," the doctor warned as the Mountie carefully cut away Maggie's bonds. Finally she was free. Then the agony began.

Pain, gut-wrenching, grinding, shot up her arms to her shoulders, and Maggie screamed—and screamed and screamed.

"Can't you give her something, Doc?"

"A little laudanum might help." The doctor lifted Maggie's head and held a glass to her lips. At first Maggie fought his efforts until his soothing voice calmed and reassured her, then she gulped the bitter brew almost eagerly.

"That's it, honey, drink it all. It will ease the pain."

Made groggy from the drug, Maggie's eyes rolled crazily before she gave up entirely and drifted off.

"Who is she, Scott?" the doctor asked, regarding Maggie with sympathy. "Where's her man, and who in the hell treated her so shabbily?"

"I won't know a damn thing until the lady wakes up and tells us, Doc," Scott frowned, anxious to get his hands on the swine who would mistreat a woman so badly. "Maybe she has some identification on her."

The doctor had removed Maggie's sodden sheepskin jacket earlier, and Scott picked it up and rummaged through the pockets. In one of the inside pockets, he found a thoroughly wet wallet, opened it, and learned not only Maggie's identity but her reason for being in the Yukon.

"The lady's name is Margaret Afton, and she's a reporter for the Seattle Post-Intelligencer."

"It's unlikely she'd come up here on her own," Doc replied. His words left much unsaid. "She'll sleep for several hours. Come back this evening. She should be able to answer questions by then. Meanwhile I'll take off her wet clothes and make her comfortable. She'll have to be watched closely for signs of pneumonia."

Maggie struggled upward through suffocating layers of thick clouds, confused and disoriented. Her arms were leaded weights, her head a mass of pain and scrambled brains. Her flesh felt bruised and battered, and there wasn't a place on her body that didn't ache. The groan that escaped her lips alerted the man standing in the room looking out the window.

"Margaret, are you awake? Speak to me."

Licking her dry lips, Maggie whimpered softly, "Chase?" But immediately she realized her mistake. Chase never called her anything but Maggie or darling.

A shadow formed before her eyes, at first vague, then slowly assuming a definite shape. It was a man, tall and broad-shouldered, his big hands carefully brushing wayward strands of hair away from her temples. Then he was holding a glass of cool water to her lips and she drank greedily, gratefully.

"How do you feel, Miss Afton?"

Maggie frowned. Where was she? She was certain she'd never seen this man before. Then her vision cleared enough to recognize the uniform of the Royal Canadian Mounted Police.

"I feel—terrible," Maggie croaked hoarsely. "Where am I?"

"In Dawson City, Miss Afton."

"How do you know my name?"

Scott smiled. "I found identification in your jacket. Can you tell me what happened? Who abused you? Who is Chase, and did he do this to you?"

Scott didn't know who Chase was, but obviously he was someone close to the woman, for she had called out his name many times as she struggled toward consciousness.

"Oh, no, Chase would never hurt me," Maggie supplied quickly. "He was—is—my guide. We were attacked at Windy Arm by two men named Bandy and Zeke. They hurt Chase and carried me away. Chase," she gulped tearfully, "was left for dead. Oh God, I don't know what happened to him!"

"Miss Afton, I'm Captain Scott Gordon of the Royal Canadian Mounted Police and I'll do all in my power to find your—companion, but I have to know more. Are you up to talking?"

"Fifteen minutes," snapped a voice from the rear of the room. "My patient needs rest."

The speaker approached the bed, and Maggie immediately recognized the kindly voice that had soothed her during her worst hours.

"I'm Doctor Thomas, Miss Afton. You were brought to my office more dead than alive. Fortunately, you've a strong constitution. Your lungs sound clear despite the long hours you spent in the water."

"Thank you, doctor," Maggie said, managing a weak smile.

Middle-aged and plump, the doctor's lined face broke out in a weary grin. "It's not every day I get a beautiful woman as a patient. Fifteen minutes, Scott," he cautioned as he left the room.

"Now, Miss Afton, tell me what happened as briefly as possible. If I'm not out of here in fifteen minutes, Doc Thomas will toss me out on my ear."

Maggie began her tale, slowly at first, gathering strength as she went on. She revealed her reason

for being in Dawson City and that Chase McGarrett
was her friend and guide. She recounted the attack
at Windy Arm and what happened afterwards.

"I—I killed Bandy," she whispered, her voice sad
and haunted.

"It was self-defense, Miss Afton," Scott countered, appalled by the suffering Maggie had been
subjected to. "Do you have any idea why those two
men attacked you?"

"Have you heard of Soapy Smith?"

Scott's well-shaped eyebrows angled upwards.
"Who hasn't? Even in Dawson his shady deeds
are well-known. How did you get involved with a
disreputable character like Smith?"

"He was angry at me for writing unflattering words
about him for my paper. Then he suddenly reversed
himself and offered me escort to the Klondike if I
altered the articles to reveal him in a more favorable
light. I was so anxious to reach Dawson I unwisely
agreed to his conditions."

"Chase McGarrett is Smith's man?"

"Oh, no, Chase is a—friend," Maggie was quick to
add. "He was angry at me for accepting Soapy's offer
and volunteered to bring me to Dawson himself.
Evidently Soapy didn't like it when I chose Chase
over Soapy's toughs."

"Just one more thing, Miss Afton," Scott said. "Can
you describe the two men who attacked you? And
Chase McGarrett, too. I'll alert my men to keep an eye
out for them. I think it highly unlikely, though, that
Smith's men will show themselves in Dawson after
what they did to you. Dawson isn't a lawless town like
Skagway. The Mounties keep law and order in Yukon
Territory, unlike Alaska where anything goes."

Maggie provided the information Scott requested
and then he left, telling her he'd look in on her
the next day. Maggie smiled wanly and immediately
drifted off to sleep.

* * *

Maggie awoke the next morning feeling amazingly well. Except for swollen hands and bruised wrists, she'd suffered no lasting effects from her harrowing ordeal. When Doctor Thomas brought her breakfast, she learned she was in his combination office and sleeping rooms, and she had probably occupied his bed last night.

Maggie was ravenous, wolfing down every morsel of the hearty fare the doctor provided, though eating was made difficult by the swelling in her hands and fingers.

"Well, young lady," the doctor twinkled, "you seem to have recovered remarkably well. You're very lucky, you know."

"I know," Maggie beamed in reply. "But I am desperately worried about Chase—my traveling companion. I have no idea how badly wounded he is or if he's still alive."

"Captain Gordon is a good man, I'm sure he'll help you. Do you feel strong enough to get out of bed?"

"Yes, I do," Maggie replied gratefully, "thanks to you. Is there a decent hotel in town?"

"You'll be pleased to know that there is. The Dawson Arms is new and comfortable enough for a lady. I'll take you there whenever you're ready."

Maggie was up and dressed a short time later when Scott Gordon arrived. If he thought her beautiful before, now—cleaned up, her hair combed, her body rested—she was stunning. She was not a fresh-faced innocent, but a woman possessed of a mature beauty very young women would have difficulty duplicating. Yet under no circumstances could Margaret Afton be called old or spinsterish. She was vibrantly alive, magnificently fashioned, and beautiful with honey-blond hair and warm amber eyes. She was independent, resourseful, feisty, and had proved herself capable of coping with any situation.

"Do you think it wise to be up so soon, Miss Afton?" Scott asked, concern coloring his words.

"I feel fine, Captain Gordon," Maggie smiled, "and I don't want to deprive the doctor of his bed any longer than necessary. I was getting ready to move over to the Dawson Arms. And please call me Maggie. All my friends do."

"Only if you call me Scott." It was obvious that the Mountie was extremely taken with Maggie. "Something has to be done with the raft, Miss—Maggie," he continued. "It's in pretty bad shape and in danger of sinking with all the supplies aboard."

"I don't own it," Maggie replied.

"Nevertheless, it's yours. I seriously doubt that Bandy, if he's alive, or Zeke, will show up in town. They will assume that you eventually reached Dawson and reported their crime. Everything on the raft is yours. I've already dispatched two men upriver to look for those outlaws."

"What about Chase?" Maggie asked worriedly.

"We'll certainly do what we can, Maggie. Have you decided what you want done with the supplies?"

"No, I—" Suddenly a thought occurred to Maggie. The main reason Chase allowed her to grubstake him was because of a man named Sam Cooper. Sam was ill and needed help. What would happen to poor Sam if Chase didn't reach him in time. Did Sam need supplies? Or a doctor? Was he still alive?

"Scott, Chase and his partner own a claim on Gold Bottom, Eleven Above. A man named Sam Cooper is up there now waiting for them. But Sam is sick and sent a message for Chase to get up there as quickly as possible. If Chase doesn't show up in a day or two, I'd like to take the supplies up to Sam and check on him."

"I'll see to it, Maggie. There's no need for you to go to the goldfields. That's no place for a woman."

Maggie flushed. She'd gotten this far against everyone's advice, and she could damn well go a little farther. "You don't know me very well if you think I'm going to allow someone to stop me now, Scott. My purpose in coming to the Yukon is to report on conditions in the goldfields. I would appreciate it, though, if you'd buy a couple of horses and have the supplies stored somewhere until I'm ready to leave."

Maggie searched her jacket for her wallet and retrieved some bills. Chase had insisted she keep whatever money remained in the unlikely event that something should happen to him on the trail. He didn't want her left without funds.

"Maggie, you're being foolish about this. Women don't go to the goldfields."

"Is there a law against it?"

"No, but—"

"Then it's settled. I'm a reporter, Scott, and I'm not going home without seeing the goldfields and claimsites. It's the reason I'm here."

"You're a stubborn woman, Maggie Afton."

"I've been called worse," she grinned impishly.

"Come along, I'll take you to the hotel. Doc is busy with a patient."

"I want to pay him first," Maggie objected.

"Later. He's setting a broken leg."

"Will you help me get to Eleven Above?"

Scott regarded Maggie with wry amusement, his gray eyes definitely admiring, though somewhat cautious. "Is there no way I can talk you out of this?"

"None."

"Then I'll take you to Gold Bottom myself. I'm due to make the rounds anyway. We'll wait a few days in case your Chase McGarrett shows up and to give yourself sufficient time to recuperate."

The hotel certainly wasn't up to Seattle standards, but acceptable except for the price. During the walk to the hotel Maggie learned that Dawson City was virtually a boomtown, occupying a narrow strip of beach less than one mile wide on the east bank of the Yukon River just north of its confluence with the Klondike River. In late June there was almost continuous daylight, and temperatures averaged sixty degrees but could go up to eighty degrees. In winter only four or five hours of murky daylight prevailed.

"Days are getting shorter," Scott informed her, "and snow could fall any day now. Sometimes temperatures drop to fifty below zero in January. Most stampeders winter in Dawson, but many choose to remain at their claimsites if their cabins are snug. Before snow falls, I usually make the rounds to see if everyone has sufficient supplies to last the winter.

Maggie wasn't prepared for the sight of thousands of tents, shacks, and cabins at Dawson, of wharves lined with boats, of streets crowded with half-built structures. The roar of the Klondike River pouring in from the east was muffled by the high scream of saws, the rat-a-tat of hammers, snorting horses, shouting men, and the tinkling of music from saloons. Many dazed, exhausted men were sampling their first decent meal since leaving home in Dawson's restaurants, which were geared toward the appetites of miners. Scores of rumpled, sunburned, whiskered men turned up in the Klondike hauling their goods on boats, mules, horses, or their backs. The only thing that distinguished the town from Skagway was the presence of the uniformed Mounties, who kept Dawson from becoming a lawless hellhole.

Scott spread the word at the hotel that Maggie was a newspaper reporter under the protection of the Mounted Police before he left her to settle in, not that there was much to settle. All her clothes and equipment remained with Chase.

Thinking of Chase brought a tug to Maggie's heart. How she missed him, all six-feet-four of magnificent male. She missed his teasing, the twinkle in his blue eyes when he looked at her in that special way, his loving. He was so good at it, she thought dreamily—not that she had that much experience. *Where are you, Chase?* she asked in silent supplication. *Are you hurt? Oh, Chase, what did my recklessness bring you to? Whatever you suffered is my fault.* He just couldn't be dead. He was too strong, too vital to suffer an ignominious death at the hands of ruffians like Bandy and Zeke.

But despite all Maggie's optimism, Chase did not appear in Dawson. After several days had elapsed, she knew she had to get to Eleven Above and Sam Cooper. She owed it to Chase. Scott had been more than generous with his help, alerting his troopers and sending men upriver to investigate. One day he informed Maggie that Chase McGarret had been placed on the missing list.

"I'm sorry, Maggie, I know McGarrett must have been more to you than mere guide," Scott said as Maggie fought to hold back her tears. "He could still show up, you know. Perhaps he returned to Skagway."

"No! I—Chase wouldn't go back, not when he needed desperately to get to his claim and Sam. I just have to face the fact that Chase might not be coming back."

"There's something else, Maggie."

"Go ahead, Scott, I can take it."

"A murder was reported at the check-in station at Lake Tagish."

"A murder? Whose?"

"No one seemed to know. The man carried no identification.

"Oh, God," Maggie sobbed, "it can't be Chase."

"It could be the man you said you killed," Scott suggested.

"Yes, it very well could be," Maggie agreed, brightening. "But if that's so, where is Chase? Why has no one heard from him?"

"I don't know, Maggie," Scott admitted, wishing he could take Maggie in his arms and comfort her properly. "Do you want me to make arrangements to return you to Skagway before ice closes the waterways and passes?"

"No, Scott, my mind is made up. I'm going to Eleven Above. It's something I have to do," Maggie said with firm conviction. "When can we leave? Or did you change your mind about taking me?"

"I'll take you, Maggie, if you still insist on going. I've already bought horses with your money. They can be loaded tonight and we'll leave in the morning if you'd like. The sooner we leave, the sooner we'll return."

"Thank you, Scott, you've been a real friend when I needed one most."

"That's my job."

"No, you've gone beyond that and I appreciate it. I'll be ready in the morning."

Maggie had already purchased a few articles of clothing to replace those she had lost, but she needed more, especially winterwear. She also needed to replenish the implements of her trade left behind when she was abducted. Accordingly, the next couple of hours were spent shopping. On the way back to the hotel, she had an uncanny feeling that someone was following her. Whirling abruptly, she saw nothing or no one suspicious. Still the feeling persisted, and when she turned again, she caught a glimpse of a face she hoped never to see again. Zeke! Spinning on her heel, she ran nearly the entire distance to the Mountie station.

Rushing inside, she found Scott sitting in his small office making out one of the tedious reports required by headquarters. He looked up as Maggie burst into his private office; her face was flushed and she was shaking like a leaf.

"Maggie, what happened? Are you all right?"

"I saw him, Scott! I saw Zeke," Maggie exclaimed in a rush of words. "He's in town."

"Calm yourself, Maggie. Who did you see?"

"Zeke, one of the men who attacked me and Chase. I don't know how he got here, but he's in Dawson."

"When did you see him?"

"Just a few minutes ago. He was following me."

She was shaking violently, recalling what they intended to do to her and how she'd been forced to kill to defend herself. Propelled by instinct and a desperate need that had driven him from the moment he saw Maggie, unconscious and helpless, Scott rose and gathered her tenderly into his strong arms. Encouraged when Maggie didn't resist, he slowly lowered his lips to hers, giddy with the need to taste her sweetness. At first Maggie was too stunned to react, realizing that Scott meant only to offer comfort, but when his kiss deepened, she became unwilling to accept his comfort in the way Scott intended. She stiffened, then twisted away.

"Scott, don't. I appreciate all you've done for me, but I can't repay you in this manner."

Scott's face darkened. "I didn't ask for repayment, Maggie, and certainly expect none. I kissed you because I wanted to, because I needed to. I'm sorry if it offended you; it won't happen again. I'll take you back to the hotel now and send some men out to look for Zeke."

"Scott, I—"

"No Maggie, it's all right, really. I should have realized Chase McGarrett holds a special place in your heart. I want you to know I'm here if you need me—in any capacity."

Maggie saw nothing more of Zeke, and Scott reported later that day that none of his men had spotted him either. When they left Dawson the next morning without mishap, Maggie thought perhaps her imagination was working overtime. So did Scott.

Scott bargained shrewdly with Maggie's money, purchasing a pack horse and a mount for Maggie. Scott explained that Gold Bottom was a pup of Bonanza Creek. In miner's language, a pup was an offshoot of an offshoot. Eldorado was the chief offshoot of Bonanza Creek, which was the first spur of the Klondike River. Gold Bottom was a tributary of a tributary. Each miner could claim one hundred square feet, which had to be worked three months daily except Sunday. Beyond the first three months, no requirements existed. Chase's claim, Eleven Above, was the eleventh claim numbered on the upstream section of Gold Bottom, beginning with the original strike claim. Everything downstream was designated with "below" after its number.

It had been snowing off and on most of that first day, and the ground was frozen solid. Even bundled up as she was, Maggie felt the cold penetrating through the layers of her clothing. They camped one night on the trail, and Maggie had been amazed at the variety of wildlife she saw. There were deer, moose, caribou, fox, and others. Scott said wolves abounded in the territory, as well as grizzly and brown bears.

The second day was a repeat of the first, differing only in that they followed a small creek instead of the river. "We're almost there, Maggie," Scott said, pointing ahead. They had passed several cabins and tents along the way, and Scott stopped briefly at each one to talk to the miners.

Now he halted before a snug cabin set back a few yards from the creek. An impressive pile of gravel at the edge of the creek lent mute testimony that someone had worked the claim recently. "This is it. Eleven Above."

Scott dismounted and turned to help Maggie. Then he motioned toward the cabin. "There's no smoke coming from the chimney. Maybe Cooper has already left."

"Do you know Sam Cooper?"

"I'd seen him around Dawson before Rusty Reed hired him to watch the place in his absence."

"Then you know Rusty, too!"

"Yes, but not well. C'mon, let's get this over with."

He removed his glove and rapped on the sturdy door. Nothing. He pounded louder, calling Sam's name. Still nothing.

"Wait here, I'm going inside," he told Maggie when he found the door unlatched.

Reluctantly Maggie waited as Scott stepped cautiously inside. She saw the sudden flare of a lamp and heard Scott shuffling around before he called out, "You can come in now, Maggie."

Maggie stood just inside the door, her eyes slowly adjusting to the dim light. Across the room Scott bent over a figure lying on a rumpled cot. "Sam Cooper?"

"Yes."

"Is he alive?" Maggie asked, moving closer.

"He's breathing."

Kneeling beside Scott, Maggie's heart contracted painfully at the sight of the pitifully thin old man, his emaciated frame nearly lost amidst the pile of blankets. His breath wheezed harshly in his throat, his unkempt gray hair was matted with perspiration, and his withered features were flushed with fever.

"He needs a doctor," Maggie said.

Just then the old prospector's eyes opened, focusing with difficulty on Maggie and Scott. "Who are you?"

"Captain Gordon, Royal Canadian Mounted Police, and Miss Maggie Afton, a reporter from Seattle," Scott replied. "How long have you been like this?"

"Been ailin' fer some time, but up 'til a few days ago, I was still able to get around some. Can I have a drink of water?"

Maggie jumped up immediately, found water in a pan, and poured some into a tin cup she found nearby. She held it to Sam's lips while he drank greedily. No sooner had he drunk his fill than he was seized by a coughing spell that left him weak and gasping for breath. Scott made Sam as comfortable as possible, then drew Maggie to the other side of the room where they couldn't be overheard.

"Pneumonia," Scott said grimly. "It might kill him to move him now, but it can't be helped. He needs immediate care."

Maggie's mind rebelled at the thought of moving a man in Sam's weakened condition. There was another alternative, and for Chase's sake she was prepared to offer it. "The poor man is in no condition to travel, Scott. Let me stay here and nurse Sam back to health. It looks as if there are sufficient supplies to last till he recovers, and longer if need be."

"I admire your courage, Maggie, but what you suggest is not only foolish but impossible. I won't hear of it."

Maggie sighed. How many times had she heard those very same words? She wouldn't be at the Klondike now if she'd heeded them. "It's not your decision to make," she said evenly. "What can happen to me? There's food and water nearby, and when Sam improves we'll return to Dawson together."

"What can happen to you!" Scott exploded. "Good God, Maggie, you have no idea what danger exists in the Yukon, especially for a woman alone. If you get snowed in you'll be isolated for weeks, months. The temperature can drop to fifty degrees below zero in mere hours. Then there's wild animals to contend with—grizzly bears, wolves. Not to mention the two-legged ones, which are the worst kind. Be reasonable, Maggie. We'll bundle Sam up and take him to Dawson. He can ride the pack horse."

"He'll die, Scott."

"It's—possible," Scott admitted slowly.

"What will happen to Eleven Above if Sam leaves?"

"I'm not certain. It's likely claim jumpers will move in, but as long as the claim is registered, the owners can get it back eventually, unless the jumpers can prove it's been abandoned."

"Then there's no question of my leaving. I'll stay until Sam is well enough to manage on his own or Chase shows up."

The stubborn tilt of her chin told Scott that he could talk himself blue in the face and get nowhere. Maggie Afton was one helluva woman. He'd give anything if she belonged to him. That improbable thought brought a chuckle to his lips. Maggie was her own woman; she'd never 'belong' to any man. She'd be partner, helpmate, but never chattel.

"How about a compromise, Maggie?" Scott temporized. "I'll allow you to remain one week. I'll stay the day and night with you, unpack the supplies, see to firewood and make Sam as comfortable as possible. Then I'll continue my rounds. That should take me no longer than a week. When I come back, be ready to return with me, no matter what Sam's condition. If he's still unwell, we'll carry him back to Dawson with us."

"I—"

"I'll hear no arguments," Scott said sternly. "I'm the law in this territory, and I'm doing what I believe is best. Besides, after a week in this remote wilderness, I suspect you'll be good and ready to leave."

It was settled.

The day progressed in a flurry of activity. While Scott tended to Sam's needs, Maggie set about stacking their supplies and starting a meal, which Sam was too weak to eat. When Maggie suggested he needed a nourishing broth, Scott went hunting, returning with a small deer and two squirrels. Then he chopped wood, adding considerably to the pile already stacked outside against the cabin wall.

Maggie was pleased to note that the cabin was snug and comfortable, sporting, of all things, a glass window. It held two bunks, a fireplace, campstove, various cooking and eating utensils, and table and chairs. Supplies and staples were stored in crude shelves built against one wall. The small cabin was well constructed of logs, its spaces chinked with mud so that no cold air seeped through.

That night Maggie took the other bunk while Scott curled up in a blanket before the fireplace, though neither got much sleep. Sam's coughing kept them both awake much of the night. When Scott was ready to leave the next day, he had done all in his power to provide for Maggie and Sam's comfort. But still he hesitated. He had a bad feeling about leaving Maggie alone, even though she had a weapon and ammunition and professed knowledge of their use. Leaving a sick old man and beautiful young woman on their own for a whole week went against all his instincts. But in the end he dared to hug Maggie tightly, bestow a chaste kiss on her cheek, and ride off.

Chapter Ten

After Scott left, Maggie found it difficult to deal with the loneliness and profound silence of the Yukon. Sam slept most of the time, when he wasn't coughing or struggling for breath. Fever still raged in his body, and he seemed genuinely confused by Maggie's presence. Though she'd patiently explained her connection to Rusty and Chase, Sam appeared to understand little of what she said. To pass the time she busied herself cleaning up the cabin, carrying in firewood, writing, and trying to spoon broth down Sam's throat. After two days, Maggie became convinced Sam wasn't improving, and likely never would.

On the third day Sam started babbling about the claim, becoming excited when he told about finding enough gold nuggets and dust to assure the partners that they were on the right track. He mentioned where he had found the gold and where the cache was hidden before slipping into a coma-like slumber.

Sam died quietly in his sleep that night. After a life of hardship and deprivation, made more difficult since joining the stampeders to the Klondike, his heart gave out. His illness and lack of proper medication contributed greatly to his demise, and Maggie realized that nothing she could have done would have saved him. Not even Doctor Thomas could have worked that kind of miracle.

Burying Sam presented a dilemma. Because the ground was frozen solid, Maggie was unable to dig a proper grave. After considerable thought, she wrapped his body in a blanket, intending to drag it to the foot of the hill behind the cabin and cover it with stones until Scott arrived and saw to a proper burial. Fate intervened in the form of two prospectors from upstream, thereby saving her from a harrowing ordeal. They appeared at the door on the morning of Sam's death. The two men seemed shocked to see a woman occupying the cabin.

"Who in tarnation are you?" one of the men asked, genuinely astounded.

"Maggie Afton. Who are you?" At the first knock on the door, Maggie had grabbed the loaded rifle leaning against the wall nearby.

"I'm Bob Croft, and this here is Art Dench. We're neighbors. Our claim is upstream a ways. We heard by the grapevine Sam was ailin'. Thought we'd stop in and see if he needed anythin' as long as we're on our way to Dawson fer supplies."

Maggie's grip on the gun relaxed. The men seemed harmless and anxious to be of help. "Sam died last night."

"Mighty sorry to hear that, ma'am," Bob said, doffing his hat in a respectful manner. "Are ya kin?"

"No, I'm a friend of the owners of Eleven Above," Maggie explained. "Sam was sick and needed help when I arrived, so I stayed on. Captain Gordon from Dawson will be stopping by in a day or two to escort me back to town," she added.

"Is there anythin' we can do fer ya 'til the Mountie arrives, Miss Afton?" inquired Art, the younger of the two.

"I have yet to bury Sam, and I fear the task is beyond me," Maggie confided. "I would greatly appreciate it if you'd see to it for me."

The pair immediately offered their assistance.

Afterwards the men accepted coffee from Maggie, told her their story while she wrote it all down in her journal, and went on their way. Before they left, they volunteered to take her to Dawson. Grateful for the offer, Maggie nevertheless declined, deciding to wait for Scott.

The following day, two feet of fresh snow fell and temperatures plummeted to zero. It was now dark most of the day.

Maggie ventured outside only for firewood and to feed the horses fodder carried up to Eleven Above. Melted snow provided water, and writing in her journal helped pass the lonely hours. That and thinking of Chase. Where was he? Had he made it to Dawson yet? Was he searching for her? Her meandering thoughts took her back to their times together, those wonderous nights when he had filled her with himself, holding back nothing. In return she had offered him her body and soul. Maggie had never thought it possible that a man, any man, could make her feel so wanted, so needed—so loved. Did Chase love her? In his own way, possibly, but certainly not enough to let it interfere with his life.

Before she met Chase, Maggie thought her career was all she needed in life to make her happy. She had her job and her writing, and after this trip no one would doubt her ability again. That was what she still wanted, wasn't it? The answer shocked her.

She'd throw it all away in a minute if Chase loved her enough to want her with him always. It was a statement Maggie Afton wouldn't have made three months earlier.

At the end of the time Scott had allotted her to remain at Eleven Above, Maggie had her things packed and ready to leave whenever he appeared. When he hadn't shown up two days later, Maggie began to worry. When another day passed, she grew frantic, convinced that something dreadful had happened to the Mountie, for he didn't strike her as a man who deviated from his word. When he finally did show up later that day, he was slumped over his horse, his uniform in tatters and soaked with blood. Maggie wanted to scream when she rushed out to help him dismount—scream in outrage and fear.

"My God, what happened?"

"Help me inside and I'll tell you," Scott gasped weakly.

Maggie supported his body as he slid from his horse, then eased him into the cabin and over to the cot just recently vacated by the ailing Sam.

Scott was lying on the cot flat on his back before he noted the old prospector was nowhere in evidence. "Where's Sam?"

"Dead. It happened a few days after you left us. Tell me what happened while I take off your boots."

God, how he adored her, Scott thought groggily. The responsible way she handled emergencies, prepared to face them with fortitude and resoursefulness—her courage, her feminine charms, her beauty.

"Grizzly," Scott muttered, pain and shock bringing a grimace to his face. "Came at me when I stopped by a stream to chop ice to melt for drinking. Thought they'd all be in hibernation by now, but you can never trust a grizzly to do what's expected of him."

"Oh, Scott!"

"I'm all right, Maggie. I killed him. I was lucky, he didn't maul me too badly. As soon as I rest up a day or so, we'll leave."

Though Scott protested, Maggie insisted upon helping him remove his outer clothes so she could cleanse his wounds with disinfectant. Then his longjohns had to go, for his left leg had several large gashes that needed tending. He managed to shimmy out of them while Maggie got the first-aid kit from his saddlebag.

"This one needs stitching," Maggie advised, frowning at the deep gash several inches above his knee.

"Can you do it?"

"I've—never done it before."

"I don't think I can do it myself, Maggie."

Fortunately, shock, loss of blood, and pain caused Scott to pass out before Maggie had taken too many stitches, which allowed her not only to finish the job but to take a few additional stitches in another wound on his chest that needed sewing.

"What next?" Maggie asked herself, finding a spark of humor in the situation. First nurse and now doctor, though truth to tell it was no more difficult than sewing a piece of linen. Relaxing afterwards with a cup of strong coffee, Maggie pondered the events of the past few weeks. She had a wealth of information jotted down in her journal, enough to write a book should she so desire. Was it worth all she'd gone through to get here? Maggie reflected thoughtfully. It didn't take long to search her heart for the answer.

If she hadn't begun this journey, she would never have met Chase—that wonderful, incredible, exasperating cowboy—and learned that love was a powerful emotion, fraught with many pitfalls. Especially when love was one-sided, as she feared hers was. Perhaps Chase hadn't cared for

her enough to search for her after Bandy and
Zeke carried her off. No, Maggie refused to believe
that. Chase might not love her in the same way
she loved him, but he did care about her. If he
hadn't arrived in Dawson yet, it was because Bandy
and Zeke's attack left him unable to travel. It was
the only plausible explanation that Maggie would
consider.

Scott slept through the night and awoke the
next day ravenous, a condition Maggie was happy
to relieve. His hardy constitution literally assured
him of a speedy recovery, though Maggie seriously
doubted they'd be able to leave for Dawson as soon
as Scott expected.

Later that day, Maggie sat on the edge of the cot to
feed Scott the nourishing meal she had prepared for
them. The way he looked at her, devouring her with
his eyes, following her every move, made her squirm
uncomfortably. It was a difficult task to ignore the
adoration in his eyes.

"Don't look at me like that, Scott."

"I can't help it, Maggie, I've never met anyone like
you before. I—"

"No, Scott, don't say it."

"I have to, Maggie. I've fallen in love with you. I—
I want you to be mine."

"Impossible. We just met. You hardly know me.
Oh, Scott, I'm not the woman for you."

"You're all the woman I want, sweet—all the woman I need to make me happy."

Maggie flushed, refusing to met Scott's eyes. How
in the world had her dull, disciplined life become so
complicated in so short a time?

"Maggie, look at me," Scott said, grasping her
chin between thumb and forefinger and lifting her
head. "Do you care for me at all?"

"As a friend," Maggie said. "I value your friendship and all you've done for me."

"God, Maggie, I don't want your friendship, I want your love. Why? Is it Chase McGarret? Do you love the man?"

"I do care for Chase," Maggie admitted, "but nothing will ever come of it."

"Then the man is a fool," Scott snorted, unwilling to believe a man existed who didn't want Maggie. "If you felt that way about me, I'd never let you go. Perhaps I can change your mind."

A mischievous grin hung on the corner of Scott's mouth as he carefully removed the bowl and spoon from Maggie's hands and set them on the floor. He was already propped up in bed, so it took little effort to reach out and draw her into his embrace, wincing when the roughness of her shirt came into contact with the numerous wounds and bruises on his naked chest and arms.

"Scott, what . . ."

A muscle twitched at the corner of his mouth, and his chin with its dark growth of stubbly beard was set in determined lines as he lowered his head and swallowed Maggie's protest. He kissed her with all the love and longing in his soul, his tongue parting her lips and delving inside to taste greedily of her sweet essence. A groan escaped from deep in his chest, and his breathing told Maggie he was aroused by her, a condition that mustn't continue.

What little Maggie knew of Scott told her he was a wonderful man, kind and honest; someone she could depend upon. But he wasn't Chase. Scott's kisses were pleasant enough, but they did absolutely nothing to her. And they had to stop. She had slid her hand upward over his bare chest to shove him away when a loud crash and swirl of wind-driven snow ushered in an apparition from out of her wildest nightmares.

There was an unconscious arrogance in the way he swaggered into the room that Maggie recognized instantly. His heavy coat, fashioned of animal skins, was encrusted with snow; a woolen cap covered his ears and head clear down to his eyebrows. A copper-hued stubble dusted with frost lent him an eerie appearance as his keen blue eyes stared fixedly at the man and woman sprawled across the cot.

"Couldn't you wait long enough to find out if I was dead?" Chase spat, his voice hinting of pain, exhaustion, and bitter disappointment.

Abandoning Scott, who gaped at Chase with obvious confusion, Maggie shrugged from the Mountie's arms and leaped to her feet. "Chase! Oh, my God, you're alive! You've finally come!"

She rushed forward, expecting to be swept into his arms, but she came to an abrupt halt when no such welcome was forthcoming. Instead, Chase slipped out of his coat, took off his hat and gloves, and ambled toward the fireplace.

A silence fraught with mounting tension swirled around them until Chase slanted Scott a disparaging glance and said, "I assume you're Captain Gordon. They told me in town you brought Maggie up here. Where's Sam Cooper?"

Why was Chase acting as if they were strangers? Maggie wondered bleakly. As if there had been nothing between them? Didn't he know how thrilled she was to know he was alive? Didn't he know she and Scott were just friends?

"Scott—Captain Gordon—was attacked by a grizzly," Maggie offered lamely. She made hasty introductions as the two men eyed each other warily. "He arrived at the cabin yesterday and I tended his wounds."

"And did a damn good job of it, I'll bet," Chase muttered sourly.

"See here, McGarrett," Scott said, finally regaining his wits. "I know what you're thinking, and it's not true. I'd never do anything to hurt Mag—Miss Afton.

She's a damn fine nurse. It was fortunate she was here to ease Sam Cooper's passing."

Chase spun around to face Maggie. "Sam's dead? Damn! If I had gotten here sooner . . ."

"It wouldn't have made a difference, Chase," Maggie said sadly. "Sam was too sick and had been too long without a doctor. I made him as comfortable as possible, and his passing was peaceful. Two prospectors from upstream came by that morning and buried him."

"Where was Captain Gordon?"

"I was miles away visiting claim sites," Scott answered, stung by Chase's surly attitude. According to Maggie, McGarrett wasn't in love with her, but he sure as hell looked and acted like he was suffering from a case of acute jealousy. "I arrived yesterday just as Maggie said. I intended to take her back to Dawson immediately, but our return was necessarily delayed due to my injuries."

"Damnation, Maggie girl, when it comes to sense you were shortchanged. Don't you know how dangerous it is for you here?" When he finished with Maggie, he rounded on Scott. "What kind of lawman are you to let a women come out here on her own?"

"She wasn't alone. If I hadn't accompanied her, she would have come by herself," Scott countered stoutly. "Maggie had my escort here and will have it back to Dawson. Don't tell me how to do my job, McGarrett."

"Does your job include layin' buck naked in bed with your hands all over my woman?"

"Your woman!" Maggie gasped, astounded. "No man owns me."

"It's not what you think, McGarrett," Scott sputtered, finding it difficult to like the arrogant American.

"Don't rightly know what you Canadians call it, but you and Maggie sure as hell weren't wrestlin' on that cot."

"There are times you can be downright exasperating, Chase McGarrett!" Maggie said, her amber eyes turning dark with anger. "And you've said just about enough on that subject. Now it's time for some answers from you. Where in the hell have you been the past few weeks?"

For an answer Chase unbuttoned his shirt, peeling it off with the top of his longjohns to reveal the angry raw scar just below his right shoulder blade. It looked as if whoever had tended it botched the job or else it was left to heal on its own.

"Those miserable varmints who attacked us musta used a dirty knife on me," Chase explained, " 'cause infection nearly done me in. My God, Maggie, I was frantic when I woke up and found you gone. What happened? Who were those man and how did you escape them?"

Maggie couldn't help but stare at his bared torso. Chase was magnificent—beautifully rugged, strong, muscles like steel, power like a raging storm, sweeping everything in its path. Not even Scott, who was no slouch in the looks and brawn department, could compare with Chase.

"The men who attacked us were two of Soapy Smith's toughs, Bandy and Zeke. They said I angered Soapy when I abruptly changed plans and chose to accompany you to the Klondike. They were instructed to kill you and—and do whatever they pleased with me."

"Sonuvabitch! If those bastards hurt you—!"

"I'm afraid you've underestimated Maggie's resoursefulness," Scott said with a hint of reproach. Maggie and Chase had been so engrossed with one another that neither noticed that Scott had risen somewhat painfully from the cot and struggled into what remained of his clothes. At least his boots and hat hadn't been shredded by the bear's sharp claws. Fortunately he had replacements in his saddlebag.

"I escaped before they harmed me," Maggie explained, deliberately glossing over her injuries. "I killed Bandy, though. Thank God for the knife you insisted I carry. Then I stole their raft and floated downriver to Dawson."

Maggie made it all sound so simple that Scott felt obligated to add, "She accomplished this with her hands tied together, so swollen the doctor wasn't certain he could save them. When she reached Dawson, she was half-drowned and frozen. The raft broke up against a boulder, and she's lucky to be alive. Not only is Maggie a remarkable woman, but an extremely brave one."

Chase regarded Scott narrowly. It didn't take brains to realize the Mountie was smitten with Maggie. Chase wondered if Maggie returned those feelings. He knew Maggie enjoyed his lovemaking, and that she cared for him a great deal, but they had always stopped short of openly declaring a stronger emotion. Yet the thought of another man touching Maggie in the same way he had drove Chase crazy with jealousy.

"You don't have to tell me about Maggie's courage, or anythin' else about her," Chase declared crisply. "Maggie is one helluva woman, and I'd be the first to admit it."

Suddenly Maggie became aware that Scott was up and fully dressed. "Scott, what are you doing up? Your injuries . . ."

"I'm fine, Maggie. I've been hurt worse," Scott said, limping toward the door. "Thanks to you my injuries will heal with no ill effects. But I really should get back to Dawson. If I don't return soon, they'll send out a search party. How soon can you be ready to leave?"

"Maggie's goin' nowhere with you, Captain," Chase said with firm conviction.

"I think we should let Maggie make her own decision," Scott bit out, swallowing his angry retort for Maggie's sake. "If she remains here much longer, she's likely to be snowed in for weeks. Neither of you seems to realize the danger involved or how harsh fifty degrees below zero can be. It's a shock to your entire system. Exposed flesh can freeze in seconds. If you're trapped here in January, you'll experience the worst the elements have to offer."

"I realize this is no place for Maggie and that she'll be more comfortable this winter in Dawson," Chase admitted. "I don't want her to suffer any more than you do, but we need to—talk. I'll take her to Dawson myself in a day or two."

"Maggie?" Scott asked, praying her good sense would prevail. He didn't think Chase McGarrett trustworthy enough to care for Maggie properly. He seemed the reckless sort, too damn arrogant for his own good and too possessive of Maggie for Scott's liking. "I strongly urge Maggie to return with me now to Dawson." He was dead serious, his voice low and emphatic.

Maggie realized that Scott spoke from experience as well as concern over her welfare. His eyes were softly pleading, but so were Chase's as she shifted her gaze to him. Softly pleading and openly hungering. She could no more resist her body's dictates than she could stop breathing. Besides, there were too many questions that needed immediate answers. What could one more day hurt? If she returned to Dawson with Scott now, she might never learn the answers.

"I'm sorry, Scott, I want to stay with Chase," Maggie said slowly. "Chase will take me back to Dawson in a couple of days. We need this time alone."

Chase must have been holding his breath, for Maggie was certain she heard the hiss of air through his teeth when she announced her decision to stay. Though he said nothing, the look in his eyes spoke more eloquently than mere words.

"You're making a mistake, Maggie," Scott warned ominously. "Is there nothing I can say to change your mind?"

"Nothing, Scott. I'll see you in Dawson in a few days."

"You're past the age to need a keeper, so I'll say good-bye. See that you get Maggie back to Dawson safely, McGarrett, or you'll answer to me." He stomped to the door.

"Scott, wait—you can't go out like that. Your clothes are in shreds."

"I have a change in my saddlebag."

"At least change before you leave," Maggie entreated him. "Have a care for your own welfare."

Scott nodded and left the cabin, returning a few minutes later with a full set of clothing, including longjohns and uniform. In his brief absence not a word was spoken between Maggie and Chase as they stood facing each other, yearning toward one another yet fearing to ignite the flame lest it devour them too soon. So charged was the atmosphere that Scott was able to change without either Maggie or Chase aware of him in the back of the room. He was nearly out the door before Maggie remembered him.

"Scott, thank you."

"No, Maggie—thank you," Scott replied, his voice tinged with sadness. After slanting Chase an inscrutable look, he slammed out the door.

They were alone. The harshness of their breathing reverberated like thunder in the absolute silence of the room, two hearts beating as one. The very air around them crackled with electricity, yet neither Maggie or Chase moved, neither spoke. It was as if a barrier had been erected between them, as each waited for the other to breach the narrow gap. Then abruptly Maggie was in Chase's arms, unaware of how she got there, or who made the first move, and not really caring. She.was where she belonged, where she wanted to be.

Chase's voice was a husky murmur as he repeated her name over and over, his frantic kisses landing indiscriminately over her cheeks, eyes, nose, mouth, anywhere he found an inch of exposed flesh. Then his mouth found hers and he kissed her thoroughly, exploring the inside of her mouth, savoring the texture of her inner cheeks, stroking her tongue with his. Their lips blended in endless kisses, tenderly, aggressively, as he probed for the deepest taste of her. Maggie thought she would die of pleasure. When they finally parted, she was giddy with an emotion she recognized immediately. She loved this magnificent cowboy with her whole heart and soul.

"Damnation, darlin', I've been frantic with worry since those varmints carried you off," Chase said raggedly. Maggie knew he spoke the truth for he wore his concern in the deep lines etched in his face. "I imagined all kinds of things while I lay recuperatin' from this dang wound. You could have been killed, or—or raped and left for dead. It nearly drove me insane. I blame myself, I should have protected you. I'm sorry, Maggie girl."

"It's not your fault, Chase. We had no idea we were being followed."

"Maggie, I—" When words failed him, he kissed her again. With all his experience, he'd never felt so drawn to another human being, or craved to know and be known so completely, to love and be loved.

Maggie knew exactly what Chase wanted. She wanted it herself, burned for his touch, yearned to become a part of him again in the most intimate way possible. Her eyes spoke eloquently of her feelings, and Chase nearly exploded with longing. But when Maggie lifted her lips for another kiss, Chase deliberately denied her.

"I want you somethin' fierce, darlin', but I need to carry in the supplies and get the dogs in the shelter first. I bought dogs and a sled in Dawson. Soon the snow will be too deep to ride. That's why I told Captain Gordon I'd bring you back to Dawson in a day or two." As he spoke he pulled on his shirt and coat and jammed his cap down on his head.

"Are you hungry, Chase?"

"Damn near starvin'."

"While you're tending the animals, I'll heat up the stew I made with the last of the deer Scott shot. I've discovered I've a talent for cooking."

"The talent I'm interested in has nothin' to do with cookin'," Chase said, leering at her.

While Chase made numerous trips outside for bundles of food and supplies, Maggie busied herself with preparing their meal. The meager daylight hours were nearly spent by the time Chase led the animals to the lean-to erected next to the cabin and returned to the welcome warmth of the snug room. Shrugging out of his outer garments, he turned to watch Maggie, pleasuring himself with the sight of her. Maggie felt the hot weight of his eyes and stilled, meeting his look with her own heated gaze.

"Everything's ready," she said quietly. The clear blue of Chase's eyes settled on her with startling effect, sending her appetite flying out the door. She couldn't have swallowed a bite.

Evidently Chase felt the same. "Put the food back on the stove, darlin', it's not vittles I'm hungry for."

They were standing close enough to touch. "I've no pride where you're concerned, Chase. I want you too."

Maggie's golden gaze never left Chase's face as her fingers moved to his shirt, unfastening each button with maddening slowness. Chase inhaled sharply as she kissed his furred chest with hungry lips, teasing and nibbling his flat masculine nipples with an instinctive sensuality, savoring the taste and scent of him.

No words were spoken. None were required. It was as though words would only give unnecessary voice to that which they both felt in their hearts. Kneeling, she skinned his pants and longjohns over his hips, waiting for him to lift a foot so she could remove his boots and stockings. Then he was naked, his manhood rising magnificently from its nest of burnished hair. Drawing her palms down his body, she marveled at the flexing breadth of his shoulders, the lean sides of his waist, the powerful muscles of his thighs. Her fingertips caressed the taut velvet of his stomach and she heard his breathing change, becoming raspy, stopping completely when she filled her hand with the throbbing length of him.

"Oh, sugar," Chase groaned as if in pain. "I don't want this to end before it begins. It's been so damn long. . . ."

Deliberately he removed her hand, burying his face in the soft place between her neck and shoulders as he struggled with the fastenings on her shirt. "Damn," he cursed, "I'm all thumbs. Help me, darlin'."

With impatient eagerness, Maggie tore at the buttons while Chase continued to nuzzle her neck, his tongue a hot brand against her flesh. When the last button fell away, he slid the shirt down her arms and tossed it aside. Her breasts were as beautiful as he remembered, firm, wonderfully full and feminine, crowned with prominent coral nipples. His tongue slid downward and Maggie felt the moist tip gliding along the valley between before he chose a pouting nipple on which to lavish his undivided attention.

A shudder traveled the length of Maggie's slender form as Chase drew the sensitive bud deep into his mouth, nipping with his teeth, then loving it gently with the moistness of his tongue. Transferring his attention to her other breast, he suckled with increasing vigor, causing Maggie to cry out in desperate need. Suddenly her knees refused to hold her, and Maggie would have fallen if Chase hadn't swept her off her feet and carried her to the cot where he stripped her of her remaining clothes, until she lay beside him in naked splendor.

Away from the fire, the air felt cool on Maggie's skin, and she shivered. Recognizing the problem immediately, Chase sought to remedy it by pulling the blankets from the empty cot and laying them carefully on the floor before the fireplace. Then he scooped Maggie in his arms, blankets and all, and placed her on their makeshift bed, falling beside her in a tangle or arms, legs, and blankets.

"Better?" he asked, grinning impudently.

"Ummm, much," Maggie conceded, snuggling into the curve of his body. "You always seem to know exactly what I want."

"That's 'cause we want the same thing."

"Conceited oaf," Maggie teased, answering his widening grin with a giggle.

"Are you laughin' at me, woman?"

"Oh, Chase, you're so many things when we make love," Maggie sighed. "Passionate, gentle, funny— sometimes you make me laugh and other times you're so tender I could cry. You're savage in your need but never so rough that you hurt me."

"I'd never hurt you, darlin'," Chase murmured, her words thrilling him more than he cared to admit.

Suddenly an electrifying thought that had nagged at him for weeks came back to haunt Chase. Did he love Maggie? Love was the last thing in the world he needed to feel at this time. One day he'd have time for

such an all-consuming luxury, but not now. Thus far
he'd been able to talk himself out of falling in love
with Maggie, telling himself that what he felt was
mere hunger—a hunger that nagged, probed, and
forced him to acknowledge it until it was appeased.
But his hunger for Maggie was unlike anything Chase
had ever experienced before, relieved only by the
sight, feel, and scent of her.

"Did I ever tell you you're magnificent?" Maggie
said, her eyes shinning.

"Did I ever tell you you talked too much?" Chase
growled, capturing her lips in a tender kiss.

Her skin was as soft as silk against the roughness
of his palms as he stroked her boldly, from the full
swell of her hips to her finely boned shoulders. A
muted plea fell from her lips as his palms curved
over the gentle rise of her breasts, brushing over their
tempting peaks in a teasing caress. Chase pressed his
mouth to the hollow of her throat, and the touch
of his tongue awakened her nerves into trembling
awareness. Another damp stroke between her breasts
brought her arching against him, groaning his name
as his mouth dragged slowly up the warm slope, so
slowly that Maggie could have screamed in frustration. Finally his lips reached her nipple, and she
purred with pleasure.

Weakly Maggie abandoned herself to Chase's tender torment as her hands wandered aimlessly over
his torso and shoulders, feeling his muscles flex
involuntarily as her fingertips played along his
spine.

"So beautiful," he muttered, his voice low and
ragged as his hooded eyes swept down the curving
length of her slender form.

He'd thought he remembered her exquisite form
perfectly, but he realized now, as she lay nude
in his arms, that his memories had been woefully inadequate. Her silken skin was seductively

soft and smooth. Her tawny curls fell about her shoulders, spilling over the fullness of her breasts and making the lush curves of her figure even more alluring. He was fascinated by her beauty, captivated by her innocent worldliness, thrilled by her bold lovemaking. Maggie Afton was one of a kind, and Chase thanked God for the difference between her and every other woman he knew.

"Chase, my God, do you know what you're doing to me?" Maggie pleaded, desperate for him to finish what he had begun.

"The same thin' you do to me, I reckon."

"Chase, please love me," Maggie begged shakily. She was damp with perspiration and trembling with need.

She swallowed hard with relief as he moved over her, spreading her legs wide to accommodate him, waiting for him to quench the agonizing emptiness inside her. But instead of filling her as she expected, he lowered his head and suddenly his mouth was playing gently between her legs. His hands tightened around her hips, holding her still, and a pulsing pleasure took over any other emotion she was feeling. Painfully aroused, Maggie's hips began to rotate, the devouring sweetness of his delving tongue and mouth continuing until she thought she would faint.

"Chase! I want you inside me!"

Shivering, she heard her incoherent pleas echoing through the darkness, her voice breaking as she begged for him to ease her torment.

"No, darlin', don't struggle against it. Let me take you there. . . . Let me do it. . . ." His tongue flicked maddeningly against the opening of her body, then slid inside, her tender flesh swelling and throbbing against his mouth.

"Oh . . . Chase, please . . . stop."

"Not now, darlin', you're almost there. Trust me."
Tenderly he caressed her damp silken warmth, deliberately sliding the fingers of one hand from her hip to
the moist triangle, searching until he found the tiny
bud of her femininity. With a minimum of effort he
brought her to the fine edge between pleasure and
madness.

Suddenly Maggie cried out, convulsed by a raging delight that crashed over her in great waves.
Her breath exploded in her lungs as ecstasy claimed
her.

"Oh, baby, that's it, let it come," Chase crooned,
thrilled by her response. He held her while the fire
inside her subsided to quiet embers before beginning again a slow arousal.

"Touch me, Maggie," Chase groaned, finding her
hand and placing it on his body.

Cautiously her hand grasped the bold thrust of
his manhood, her cool, trembling fingers gently
encircling him. He was hard and throbbing as she
caressed him, stroking down the length of him, then
upward. Moaning in a combination of agony and
ecstasy, he thrust against her exquisite touch.

Chase muffled Maggie's thin cry with his mouth
as he entered her, taut, heavy, hard with arousal. She
arched upwards, focusing on the pounding force of
him sheathed tightly within her, feeling him press
deep inside until the burning length of him filled
her completely. She clung to him, her arms wrapped
around his neck, her knees flexed as she pushed
against him strongly. Maggie felt the violent surge
of his thrusts all through her body, answering his
driving movements with feverish fury until she was
seized by tremors frightening in their intensity.

Chase murmured tender nonsense in her ear,
cradling her quaking body in his arms, moving
inside her in a way that prolonged her pleasure
long, unbearable minutes. Deliberately he denied

the fulfillment of his own climax in order to thrust into her with slow purposeful strokes.

"Easy, baby," he crooned, "let it last as long as possible, don't rush it. I'm with you all the way."

Feeling her suspended and nearly paralyzed beneath him brought Chase almost as much pleasure as his own release, knowing he had done all in his power to bring her to rapture. Finally he allowed himself the savage delight of reaching his own reward, and Maggie felt the hot spurt of warmth inside her. His muscles tightened beneath her palms and a roar left his throat before he relaxed against her, his head dropping to the warm hollow of her throat. Reaching down, Maggie pulled the blanket over them.

Still intimately entwined, they slipped into an exhausted slumber.

Maggie awoke slowly, her body pleasantly heavy and lethargic. A comfortable fullness filled her and her loins tingled and contracted with painful awareness. A lazy smile tilted her lips when she realized Chase had made himself a part of her again, stroking her awake with exquisite tenderness. It was very dark now, but firelight provided sufficient light to see Chase straining above her, joined to her, his hands and mouth arousing her, claiming her.

"You're as responsive asleep as you are awake," Chase observed, a crooked grin hanging on the corner of his mouth. "I had to have you again, darlin'. It's gonna be a long winter without you."

It's going to be a long life without you, Maggie thought but did not say. How in the world could she bear it? Then all thought ceased as the dictates of her body took over. She buried her face in his throat and sobbed, overcome by an ecstasy so perfect it brought tears to her eyes. Her flesh tightened convulsively around his as the same tremors shook

Chase's body. He found her lips with his and she swallowed his final groan, finding the same burst of fulfillment that had just contracted her flesh around his.

"If your offer of a meal still stands, I believe I could eat now," Chase said when his breathing returned to normal.

"Greedy fellow," Maggie teased. "When you're not appeasing one hunger you're complaining about another."

"I'm a man of vast appetites, darlin'," Chase twinkled, slapping her bare rump affectionately. "Up, woman, before I starve to death and won't be able to take care of you in the manner in which you're accustomed."

Stretching luxuriously, Maggie rose slowly, shivering after leaving the warmth of Chase's body and the tangle of blankets. Chase watched with avid appreciation as she padded to the stove, poured some of the hot water kept in readiness at all times into a basin and washed thoroughly before dressing. Then she saw to their supper while Chase followed her example, tossing the dirty water out the door and adding more wood to the fire before seating himself at the table. While Chase ate the delicious stew of deer meat and dried vegetables that Maggie had prepared, he began talking about the events that prevented him from continuing on to Dawson immediately after the attack by Bandy and Zeke.

"I tell you, Maggie girl, I felt so damn helpless after those bastards took you away," Chase said, chewing thoughtfully. "I had no idea why, who, or what they intended to do with you. I blamed myself for not protectin' you properly.

"Zeke said he killed you, but I didn't believe him."

"I saw the knife comin' and turned aside at the last minute. Otherwise I'd not be here talkin' to you now. I lost a lot of blood before I was found the next day and patched up. It was Jack London who found me. He was travelin' to Dawson to spend the winter. The lakes were already startin' to freeze over. I owe him my life. He even spent hours searchin' Windy Arm for you when I told him what happened. But it was as if you'd disappeared into thin air. I wanted to leave immediately to search for you but had to abandon my plans when a ragin' fever rendered me unable to travel. Zeke's knife must have been filthy to cause such a virulent infection.

"I don't know what pulled me through—determination, I reckon. All I could think of was findin' you and pray you were still alive."

"Scott sent men to Windy Arm, but you weren't there and it seemed no one knew a thing about you," Maggie said, puzzled. "Nor of Bandy or Zeke. Your boat hadn't passed any of the checkpoints between Windy Arm and Dawson."

The Mounted Police had devised an ingenious way of keeping tabs on boats and men entering the Klondike. They established checkpoints on the lakes and rivers, registering boats, men, and home addresses, assigning each boat a number. When a boat failed to arrive in Dawson by an appointed time, a search was initiated and next of kin notified. Chase's boat had been duly registered, but had not appeared at the next checkpoint after Windy Arm.

"My boat was stolen while I lay ill and shiverin' with fever," Chase explained.

"Oh, no!" Maggie cried, devastated by the loss. "Why didn't the Mounties find you at Windy Arm?"

" 'Cause I wasn't there. When London saw how sick I was, and stranded besides, he took pity on me and took me with him. I can never repay him properly. He interrupted his journey by several days when I took a turn for the worse and he had to tie up to shore to allow me time to recuperate. That's why the Mounties had no record of me and my boat. As soon as the fever left me and I started to recover, we continued on to Dawson."

"All our supplies, everything lost," Maggie lamented sadly. "But thank God for Jack London. Where is he now?"

"Still in Dawson, gatherin' material for a book. I wouldn't be surprised to find him knockin' at the door one day. Never know where he'll turn up."

"Where did these supplies come from if ours were stolen?" Maggie asked, aware that Chase had little cash on him.

"I borrowed money from London. He made over three thousand dollars piloting boats through White-horse Rapids and insisted I take a part of it. But I could ask you the same question. You didn't have enough money left for horses and supplies at these prices."

"Everything I brought up to the claim belonged to Bandy and Zeke," Maggie explained. "When I escaped, I stole their raft and floated downstream to Dawson. Fortunately the raft didn't completely break apart when it hit a rock while shooting the rapids. Much of the supplies were left, intact and Scott insisted I keep them. He doubted either Zeke, or Bandy, if he still lived, would show their faces in Dawson after what they did to me. Dawson isn't a lawless town like Skagway. Here Mounties protect the citizens and keep crime to a minimum."

"Why did you come up here to Eleven Above, Maggie?" Chase asked curiously.

"Because of Sam Cooper. I knew he was sick, and when you failed to show up in Dawson I decided to come up here and offer my help. I felt I owed you that much. Naturally I brought the supplies along, having little use for them in Dawson."

"And of course Gordon was happy to act as guide," Chase said with a hint of sarcasm.

"Would you rather I came alone?"

"Hell no! Damnation, Maggie, I didn't know what to think when I saw that damned Mountie kissing you, his hands all over you. And when I saw he was naked as a jaybird, I nearly went insane."

"Chase, it's not—we didn't—"

"I don't want to know, darlin'. I don't want you to tell me you made love with him. You owe me no explanations. Besides, I don't reckon I could handle it if you said you shared with him the same things you shared with me. I'm a selfish cuss when it comes to people I care about."

"I'm going to tell you anyway," Maggie insisted. "Scott and I shared nothing except friendship, and that one kiss."

A tremulous shudder passed through Chase's body, and a heavy weight seemed to fall away. Though no promises had been made between them, he regarded Maggie as his, growing angry and frustrated at the thought of another men possessing her. Would everything between them end when Maggie returned to Seattle? he wondered glumly. No one would ever replace the terrible void in his heart when they parted—as surely they must. A penniless cowboy had no business consorting with an educated woman who'd never give up her independence for someone like him. Why couldn't he have chosen some sweet young thing without a thought in her head except pleasing him instead of an opinionated, stubborn spinster who really didn't need him?

Chapter Eleven

That night Maggie and Chase slept in front of the fire, making love until exhaustion claimed them. Sometimes Chase was like a playful puppy, exciting her with his antics. Other times he was tender, serious, a lover more concerned for her pleasure than his own. Sometimes Maggie played the wanton, driving him insane with need. Other times she was a gentle siren, enticing him with her hands, mouth, and tongue. Chase made her laugh; he made her cry out in a torment of agony. He introduced her to heaven; she took him to paradise.

The following day passed in a blur, too fast for Maggie's liking. The following morning they were to leave for Dawson. As luck would have it, no new snow fell and travel was still possible despite the cold. That night they made love for the last time, and Maggie was never more aware that it might very well be the last time they were ever together like this. In March, when ice began to break up on the rivers and lakes, it was inevitable that she would return to Seattle and a mundane life without Chase McGarrett.

During one of their quiet moments, Maggie revealed to Chase all that Sam had babbled about before he died. "Sam said to tell you he found promising evidence that the claim will eventually produce more than either you or Rusty imagined. He urged that you have the nuggets assayed."

"I noticed the mound of gravel he dug up along the creek," Chase reflected thoughtfully. "Do you reckon the gold came from his diggin's?"

"Sam didn't say, but I wouldn't be surprised if it did."

Together they recovered the nuggets and dust from beneath the floorboard, astounded by the size of of the cache. "My God," Chase said reverently, "if these are an example of what lies beneath the ground, me and Rusty are rich beyond our wildest dreams."

He divided the gold evenly and gave half to Maggie. "I'm payin' you back, darlin', for grubstakin' me. You'll need that to pay for your keep in Dawson this winter. Three-quarters of the stampeders will winter in the city, and prices will soar sky high. I hope you can find a vacant room."

"The room I occupied at the Dawson Arms is paid for the month," Maggie said. "Scott warned me beforehand that rooms would be scarce during the winter."

"Good old Scott," Chase said tightly. "Always eager to help a beautiful woman in distress."

"Forget Scott, Chase, and make love to me," Maggie pleaded, aware that their time together was swiftly drawing to a end. "Give me memories to last for all the empty tomorrows."

"Oh, baby, when I make love to you, there's no tomorrow. There's only today—here—now, you naked in my arms and me lovin' you."

*   *   *

They left Eleven Above the next morning, carrying
a minimum of supplies on the sled and bundled to
the eyebrows in the fur-lined, hooded coats Chase
had purchased in Dawson. They left the packhorses
behind with plenty of feed, for Chase fully expected
to return within a few days. He was excited about
the cache of gold and intended to explore thoroughly the pile of gravel Sam had excavated, even if it
meant bringing it inside the cabin and thawing it a
shovelful at a time.

Unfortunately, a fine blowing snow began swirling around them shortly after they left the warmth
of the cabin, making travel slow. Maggie suggested
they turn back, but Chase knew that if he did they
might not make it back to Dawson before spring
thaw. Chase was determined they reach Dawson
before travel became all but impossible. Four hours
later, the snow stopped abruptly and the dogs literally flew over the expanse of pristine snow.

It seemed to Maggie as if she were in another
world, one all white and shimmering and beautifully
innocent. Around them mountains rose like majes-
tic sentinels clothed in fairy-tale white robes. But
for the barking dogs, the silence was so profound
that Maggie felt as if she existed in a void where
no one dwelled but her and Chase. The enormity
of vast expanses of untouched tundra overwhelmed
her, and she gasped in mute appreciation at the
towering mountains standing in stark relief against
a muted gray sky.

"It's awesome, isn't it?" Chase called down from
his perch behind the sled.

"Unbelievable," Maggie concurred, her words,
muffled by the thick protection of fur and cloth,
snatched away by the wind.

Thank God they weren't on foot, Maggie reflected,
for the going would be rough indeed. Even horses

would have had a difficult time, for their hooves would have broken through the thin crust of ice and become hopelessly mired. Scant daylight hours added considerably to the danger. No wonder Scott had expressed concern.

At the foot of a towering mountain, Chase pulled the dogs to a skidding halt. "This looks like a good place to camp for the night," he said, peering through the frosty twilight at a stand of spruce a short distance to their right. "Stay in the sled where it's warm while I check for the best place to pitch the tent."

Maggie nodded and snuggled deeper into the furs as Chase walked away, his tall figure a dot against the whiteness of the snow. Immersed in her thoughts, Maggie paid little heed to the low rumble that began on the lofty mountainside high above her. When she did become aware of the sound, she looked skyward for the source of the disturbance, thinking she'd never heard of thunder in connection with a snowstorm. But anything was possible in this strange country of snow and ice and darkness. What she saw set her heart to pounding with stark, black fear.

It looked as if the entire mountainside had exploded, sending tons of ice and snow hurtling down on her. Paralyzed with a fright she had never known before, Maggie could do nothing but stare at the churning, grinding mass of snow and rock plowing toward her with amazing speed. She had barely enough time to utter a quick prayer before the unrelenting wave roared over her.

Perhaps the dogs realized what was happening, for at the last minute they set up a terrible howling and lurched forward. But without a firm hand to guide them, they acted independently, each pulling in a different direction. Then blackness engulfed Maggie and the breath, perhaps her last, was driven from her chest with incredible force.

Meanwhile, Chase had found the perfect camping place beneath a stand of spruce that offered moderate protection against the wind. Water wasn't important because snow could be melted on the campstove. His decision made, he started walking back to the sled where Maggie waited. And then he heard it. First the dogs set up a terrible racket, then came the roar of a thousand locomotives. Unlike Maggie, Chase recognized the sound immediately for what it was. Avalanche!

He called her name, a frantic cry so filled with anguish it was more like a sobbing scream. His legs were like lead, refusing to obey, until he willed them to move. A terrible thought made him realize that if he reached her in time, he'd be buried along with her. Not that it mattered. To lose Maggie would be the same as losing his own soul. But despite his best efforts, the thundering mass reached her before he did, plowing, roaring, devouring everything in its path.

Chase was knocked off his feet, floundering in waist-deep snow but not completely buried because he was on the outer fringes of the slide area and to the right of the path taken by the avalanche. Even Maggie and the sled hadn't received the full brunt of the slide, only enough to bury them completely. Chase watched in abject horror as ice and snow devoured her with hungry jaws.

By the time the roar had dwindled to a harmless purr, Chase had freed himself, never taking his eyes off the spot where he had last seen Maggie and the sled, memorizing it in his mind despite the terrible dread churning his insides to mush. Within minutes, nothing remained to mark the spot that Maggie had once occupied but the indelible imprint on Chase's brain.

Panic-stricken, Chase dragged himself on hands and knees to the place he had last seen his love, clawing frantically at the snow, scooping it out with his bare hands regardless of the numbing cold. Chase had no idea that danger from avalanches existed so early in the year. It had to be a freak occurrence, though at the altitude the avalanche originated, the peaks were never devoid of snow, wind, or ice.

The depression beneath his hands grew as Chase worked furiously to free Maggie. His lungs burned, tears froze on his cheeks, his muscles screamed in agony, but he refused to give up. Sobbing in frustration, unbearable anger over the unfairness of fate drove him beyond human endurance. Then, with the horrendous thought of failure staring him in the face, Chase uncovered one limp hand. It was meager encouragement, but enough to give him renewed hope as he increased his efforts. The spurt of adrenelin provided the impetus necessary, and after digging down nearly three feet, Chase finally uncovered Maggie's head.

Anxiously he cleared her face of accummulated snow, his heart plummeting when he noted how still and white she looked. Her eyes were closed, and her breathing appeared shallow and labored. Still unable to retrieve her from her icy grave, Chase continued digging until enough of her body was free to lift her out. Thank God she hadn't taken the brunt of the avalanche!

Cradling her limp form in his arms, Chase caressed her pale cheek, finding it icy to his touch. How long had she been buried? He struggled frantically with the question, unable to put a time to that endless eternity it had taken him to reach her. It could have been seconds, or minutes, or hours even. While he watched in stark terror, his worst fears came to pass. The tiny puffs of breath coming from Maggie's lungs fluttered to a halt.

"Breathe! Breathe!" he implored, his voice a broken sob of pure anguish. Who said a tough cowboy never cried?

Hugging her close, willing her to live, Chase suddenly was at a loss. Was there nothing he could do to reverse this tragedy? Maggie didn't deserve to die. She was too young, too vital, too beautiful and innocent.

"Breathe, damn you, breathe!" he repeated, helplessness moving him to incredible anger. "No, dammit, I won't let you die! Do you hear me, Maggie girl? You're not gonna die! If you can't breathe on your own, I'll breathe for you."

Covering her icy lips with his, Chase began breathing small puffs of air into her lungs, all his tremendous will focused on foiling fate. He never considered failure, not when he was digging Maggie out of the snow and certainly not now. He'd breathe his own life and soul into her or die trying.

Then suddenly Maggie gasped and shuddered, struggling for breath as Chase continued blowing into her mouth. Her eyes fluttered open but she seemed not to recognize him.

"Maggie! Maggie, darlin', can you hear me?" To Chase's consternation, her lids fell over the golden dimness of her eyes, but the steady rise and fall of her chest instilled renewed hope in him.

Lifting Maggie in his arms, Chase staggered to the stand of spruce where he had intended to pitch their tent. He was forced to place her on the icy ground while he recovered their tent and bedrolls.

Returning to the spot where he had found Maggie, Chase began digging frantically, aware that Maggie's life depended on him and his ability to provide warmth and something hot to put into her stomach. Providence was with him, for he located their bundle of supplies beneath the buried sled and dragged it clear. A little more digging produced his rifle.

Instinct told him that it was too late to save the dogs, so he hurried back to where Maggie lay and set up the tent more quickly than he would have thought possible.

Then he placed her carefully inside the shelter, piling blankets atop her to thaw her chilled flesh. Next he built a fire to heat water for tea. Maggie needed something hot inside her, and quickly. She rallied long enough to swallow a few sips of the hot brew before sinking back into oblivion. Thinking of nothing else to do, Chase slid beneath the blankets beside her, pulled her into his arms, and shared his warmth with her.

The howling of timber wolves brought Chase instantly alert, and he reached for his rifle. Poking his head through the opening of the tent, Chase was shocked to see how close the hungry creatures were, too damn close for comfort, their eyes luminous and predatory in the darkness. While he slept, the fire had died down to glowing embers, and the wolves had grown bold enough to approach within twenty feet of the tent. Chase's first reaction was to build up the fire with kindling he had gathered earlier.

"Chase, what is it?" Maggie's voice was weak but the most beautiful sound in the world to Chase.

"Wolves, darlin', nothin' to worry about. I'm gonna build up the fire and scare off a few of the sneaky critters. How do you feel?"

"Weak, but otherwise okay. Wha—what happened?"

"Avalanche. We'll talk later," Chase said when the menacing wolves drew even closer to their campsite.

Chase fed the dying fire until it burst into flames, an effective barrier for keeping wolves at bay. Several well-placed rifle shots helped greatly, but Chase still felt compelled to sit up the rest of the night feeding the flames and firing random shots into the marauding wolf pack.

During the long vigil, Chase contemplated their situation and came to a decision. Because of the recent snowfall, they hadn't covered as much ground today as he would have liked. In fact, according to his calculations they were closer to the cabin than to Dawson. Therefore, because they were without transportation, he felt they should return to Eleven Above, even if it meant being stranded for the winter.

Their supplies were plentiful, sufficient firewood was handy, and the cabin was snug and warm. Chase knew what lay behind them, but not the dangers facing them should they continue on to Dawson. Another thing to consider was the fact that they no longer had adequate transportation or protection from the elements. They would be forced to walk to their destination. When dull, murky light ushered in the morning, Chase abandoned the fire and prepared for their departure.

Maggie still felt a debilitating weakness but was able to walk as they trudged back in the direction from which they had come. Even if he had to carry Maggie most of the way, Chase was determined they should reach the claimsite by nightfall. He wouldn't even consider another night in the open, for he had to abandon the tent and supplies for lack of transport.

As the day progressed, Maggie's flagging strength made it increasingly evident that she wouldn't be able to keep up the pace, but she didn't complain, not when Chase wore a worried frown on his brow. Just when Maggie felt certain she couldn't take another step, the welcome sound of yapping dogs broke through the pristine silence.

"Chase, look!"

"I see, darlin', I see."

Coming toward them at a furious pace was a sled pulled by a frisky team of dogs. One man rode the runners while a second sat atop a load of bundles. The sled came to a skidding halt beside them, and Maggie gave a glad cry when she recognized the men.

"It's Art and Bob, Chase, I know these men!"

Indeed it was Bob Croft and Art Dench returning from Dawson with a load of supplies meant to last the winter.

"Looks like ya could use a lift," Bob said, sizing up the situation immediately. "Kinda wondered who abandoned the tent a ways back."

Once a roaring fire blazed into life, the small cabin became a welcome haven. It worried Chase that Maggie had lapsed in and out of consciousness during the long ride back to the claimsite, but at least she had been snug and warm in the sled. Grizzled though they might be, Bob and Art were virtually angels in disguise. Fortunately, temperatures hovered above zero and no new snowfall arrived to hinder their journey back.

Before long Chase had Maggie undressed and tucked into a makeshift bed before the fire. Then he turned his hand to preparing something nourishing for them to eat while Maggie dozed restlessly. She still appeared deathly pale, and Chase kept interrupting his chores to return to her to make certain she still breathed. Digging her from her icy grave had been the most harrowing experience of his life.

Maggie hummed a tune as she engaged in the housekeeping duties she had undertaken since recuperating fully from the effects of being buried beneath tons of snow. She shuddered when she thought of what might have happened had Chase given up and left her in her icy grave. She owed him her life. He was the strongest person she knew. Nothing rattled him. He was brave and confident in the face of calamity, well-prepared to deal with whatever disaster came his way. He could do anything he set his mind to, even bring her back from the brink of death. The man was incredible. He laughed at fate, dared to challenge God himself if it meant the difference between life and death. And she loved him, loved everything about him despite the fact that one day they'd each go their own way, each find their own destiny.

"Fresh meat, Maggie girl," Chase whooped, bounding into the cabin. It had snowed heavily for the past two weeks, but today was clear and the temperature hovered at zero. Well into November now, Chase decided to use the lull in the weather and scant daylight hours to hunt. "Ummm, smells good in here."

Maggie laughed, delighted with Chase's response to her culinary skills. "I just baked bread, and there's dried fruit cooking. Thought I'd attempt a cobbler today. What did you shoot?"

"A moose," Chase grinned, pleased with himself. "I've already skinned him and cut him up into chunks small enough to handle." Due to the extreme cold, the meat was frozen solid before it was dressed and stored inside the woodbox to keep wild animals from devouring it. "Here," he said, slapping down a good-sized hunk of frozen meat on the table, "once it thaws, cut off a couple of thick steaks for our supper."

Chase removed his outer clothes and lowered his lean length into a chair as he watched Maggie work at her womanly chores. She moved with consummate grace, unaware of the seductive power her body held over Chase or the message each subtle movement transmitted. But Chase was only too aware of every nuance of Maggie's face and form. For two long excruciating weeks, he had slept beside her, held her, soothed her fears, and nursed her to health without once making love to her as he desperately longed to do. The last thing he wanted was to hinder her recovery in any way, or bring about a relapse after her terrible ordeal. She still looked so fragile Chase felt she might break if he touched her. But damnation, he wanted her!

Maggie wasn't impervious to Chase's needs; she had her own needs. But when she had mentioned making love, Chase had deliberately changed the subject, citing her fragile health as a reason for abstaining. But Maggie sensed he wasn't being honest with her. She was perfectly well now, but still Chase remained aloof. Was it something she'd said or done? she wondered desperately. Whatever the reason, she intended to put an end to it tonight.

Actually, Chase did have another reason for refusing to give them what they both wanted—one that Maggie seemed unaware of. Thus far she had escaped pregnancy, but their lusty appetites precluded cheating fate indefinitely. The thought of having a child with Maggie didn't displease him—quite the opposite, in fact. But he knew Maggie would hate him if he made her pregnant at a time when her career meant everything to her. She didn't seem to want marriage as most women did, and a baby would certainly be an unwanted burden to her. Chase reckoned the only way he could be absolutely certain she would leave the Klondike without a living memory of their time together was to refrain from making love, even if it killed him. And the way he felt now, his death was imminent.

Chase watched Maggie as long as he dared, given his desperation, then deliberately picked up a snowshoe lying nearby that needed mending.

"Chase, are you tired of me already?" Maggie asked bluntly, taking the bull by the horns.

"What in blazes are you talkin' about?" Chase demanded, stunned. He wanted her, needed her—

yes, dammit, adored her. Didn't she realize he was denying them for her own good?

"Except for a few chaste kisses, you haven't touched me in two weeks. Dammit, Chase, I'm not made of stone. You taught me to respond, to need you, then you deliberately deny me—deny us. It can't be my health, as you can see I'm fully recuperated. What is it?"

"C'mere, darlin'," Chase said, dropping the snowshoe and holding out his arms. Immediately Maggie plopped into his lap. "Don't you know I have the devil's own time keepin' my hands off you? I deliberately find chores to occupy my hands and mind, dreadin' the nights when your body is pressed close to mine. Damnation, Maggie, I'm no saint. If this keeps up I'll be insane before spring arrives."

"Why are you denying us if it's what we both want?" Maggie asked, truly puzzled.

Chase grinned, shaking his burnished head in dismay. "You're such an innocent, darlin', I find it difficult to believe you've reached the old age of twenty-five without knowin' that if we continue indulgin' our desires, we're likely to make a baby. Unless you know somethin' I don't."

Maggie flushed, burying her head against Chase's chest. She loved the feel of him, his scent, his strength, and she couldn't deny herself their short time together even if they made ten babies. She knew what it meant to be an unwed mother, and with a jolt of sadness she realized that Chase would rather abstain than offer marriage. Yet she was willing to take that chance. Nothing had happened yet, and she might never get pregnant. Even if she did go back to Seattle pregnant, she would love Chase's child and raise it to the best of her ability. If the newspaper fired her because of it, she could put her creative ability and experience in the Klondike to good use by writing and selling stories to magazines. She might even write a book on her experiences. Now all she had to do was convince Chase.

"Having your baby doesn't frighten me," Maggie said slowly. "Living in this cabin with you like brother and sister for the next four months does. Besides, I—I can't have children." It was an impulsive, deliberate lie, but Maggie felt no guilt over telling it. In her mind there was no other way to convince Chase to make love to her without him worrying over the responsibility of fatherhood.

"How could you know that. You were a virgin the first time I took you," Chase said, stunned.

"A—a childhood infection left me sterile," she improvised. "Does it matter?"

"I—no, only in that it relieves my mind. That's one less thing I'll have to worry about after you leave the Klondike. I'd never forgive myself if I hurt you or changed your life in any way. Dammit, baby, I care about you. Maybe some day—"

"Don't, Chase. Remember? No promises. You're not responsible for me. I'm a big girl who's been on her own for a long time. Just kiss me."

"Are you sure, Maggie? About not bein' able to conceive, I mean. Doctors do make mistakes." Chase had no idea why Maggie's disclosure caused a twinge of bitter disappointment, but it did.

"Of course I'm sure," Maggie replied, refusing to meet his eyes. It wasn't the first time a woman had lied about such things, and it wouldn't be the last. She didn't do it to hurt him, but to free him of all guilt and responsibility. "Discussion ended. Now will you kiss me?"

"Oh, baby, that will do for starters."

The force of his kiss bent her head back against his shoulder; the fury of it parted her lips as he delved deeply to explore the inside of her mouth.

"Lift your bottom," Chase urged as his hands frantically sought the hem of her dress. Since she rarely

ventured outdoors, she had taken to wearing the one
dress she had purchased in Dawson.

When her dress rode up around her waist, his
fingers began working at the buttons on her bodice. Then her breasts sprang free, and Maggie felt
the wetness of his mouth tugging at her nipples,
first one, then the other, sending jolts of pure fire
pulsing through her veins. Suddenly his hands were
trailing through the golden forest at the juncture of
her thighs, exploring the tender folds, stimulating
the tiny bud of desire with his thumb.

"Spread your legs, baby," he moaned against the
quivering flesh of her breast.

Maggie obeyed eagerly and a shudder rippled
through her body when she felt his fingers slip
inside, teasing, driving her mad with need. "Oh,
Chase, my God!"

"Easy, baby, take your time, we've got all the time
in the world." He felt her soft flesh contract against
his fingers and used the heel of his hand and thumb
to increase her pleasure.

The sweet agony of what he was doing to her
exploded inside her in a dazzling display of bursting lights and pleasure so intense Maggie could not
speak for long minutes afterwards. When she felt
Chase release himself and ease into her, she shifted
to avoid penetration. His puzzled expression brought
a teasing smile to her lips.

"Not yet, Chase. I want to love you in the same
way you loved me."

Slipping off his lap and taking his hand, Maggie led him toward their bed before the fire. She
undressed him with leisurely slowness, kissing each
part of him she uncovered, until he stood nude and
unashamed before her, his manhood leaping proud
and throbbing at her touch.

"You're magnificent," she said, awed by the
strength and power of him, the broadness of his

shoulders, the muscular sturdiness of his thighs and legs.

"And you're drivin' me loco, baby," Chase growled, reaching for her. Deftly Maggie eluded his grasp.

"I told you I'm going to pay you back for the torture you put me through." Her amber eyes glinted mischievously as she pushed him down onto the pile of blankets.

She disrobed unhurriedly, ignoring Chase's tormented groan as she posed seductively for his benefit. "You little vixen! If you don't stop that, you'll find yourself flat on your back so full of me you'll be sorry you teased me so unmercifully," Chase growled in a torment of agony.

"I doubt that," Maggie murmured as she dropped down beside him.

She thought his restraint remarkable, given the torture she subjected him to. Her hands, mouth and tongue, applied with amazing knowledge and practice for someone who had remained a virgin for the first twenty-five years of her life, explored freely and without embarrassment over every inch of his body. His flat male nipples, the tiny indent of his navel, his long thighs covered with fine hairs that tickled her nose, the bold, thrusting male part of him that gave her so much pleasure.

"Damnation, Maggie!" he gasped, driven to the edge of insanity.

When he attempted to drag her upward and pull her beneath him, she resisted, giggling over the way she had rendered him nearly helpless—the same way he did her. Then abruptly she put his agony to an end when she straddled him, taking him deep— deeper into her moist heat. A strangled cry slipped past Chase's lips as his male aggressiveness took charge, grasping her hips in his huge hands and moving her to fit his rhythm. Grinding hips met with bruising force as Maggie rode him, tossing

back her head in glorious surrender. Though goaded
and teased past the limits of his endurance, Chase
held on, gritting his teeth until Maggie screamed
and contracted around him. Only then did he seek
his own hard-earned release.

November slid into December, but Maggie and
Chase staved off boredom by making love frequent-
ly and talking. She learned every detail about the
ranch in Montana he loved so much, his unlikely friendship with the crusty Rusty Reed, and his
life in the army fighting Indians in the west. Chase
heard how Maggie had developed her passion for
reporting and writing from the dead father she adored, and her short-lived romance with Matt Creed,
the sleezy character who had hurt her so badly.
Maggie discovered that Chase had established no
romantic links with any one woman in particular,
lavishing his attention freely on whores and women
who held no expectations of marriage.

They found their tempers and temperaments
matched, explosive at times, quickly fired to anger
but easily coaxed to forgiveness. During those long,
cold days and nights, Maggie discovered a passion
she never knew existed before meeting Chase. She
fell so deeply in love she wondered how she would
exist without him.

Chase discovered his passion for Maggie did not
cool, no matter how many times he possessed her.
Loving her only made him want her more. He wondered how he would exist without Maggie. Yet, by
mutual consent, all mention of love and commitment
was carefully avoided. Maggie wanted no promises of
love from Chase if he did not truly feel that emotion,
so she deliberately refrained from confessing her
own tender feelings. Chase cared deeply for Maggie,
but knew her career would always come first with
her. It seemed inconceivable to him that Maggie

would be willing to give it all up for a ranch in a remote location in Montana, so he kept his feelings buried within his heart.

While the temperature hovered above zero, Chase began working on the mound of gravel Sam Cooper had excavated near the creek bank. He carried it inside the cabin a shovelful at a time and boiled it in a small amount in water to thaw the snow and clean the stones. He was jubilant when the small pile of nuggets gleaned from the gravel grew daily. Some of the nuggets were so large Chase felt certain Eleven Above would yield a fortune for him and Rusty. Then one day the temperature abruptly plummetted to twenty below zero.

Everything two feet above the hot stove froze. Steam from boiling water formed icicles on the ceiling, which they broke off and used for drinking water. Only a dim twilight prevailed for three or four midday hours. Then, curiously, at the end of December, the snow howling down from the mountains ceased and winds grew surprisingly temperate. Chase decided to take advantage of the brief reprieve and go hunting for fresh meat.

"Be careful, Chase," Maggie said worriedly as he fastened snowshoes to his heavy boots. For some reason she grew fretful and anxious whenever Chase was away from the cabin.

"Don't worry, darlin'," Chase cajoled her with a light, teasing tone. He hated leaving Maggie alone, but for a man accustomed to open spaces and roaming freely, being confined to a cabin for days on end became unbearable. Not that he didn't appreciate having Maggie with him. He would have lost his mind by now if she hadn't been there to share his lonely hours. "If I'm lucky we'll have steak tonight, or a hearty stew."

Maggie tried to keep herself occupied during Chase's absence, baking sourdough bread and

stewing dried fruit for their desert. Perhaps he'd
bring back a moose or caribou, she hoped, and
she'd cook a nourishing stew with potatoes and
onions. It was a constant source of amazement to
Maggie how well she did with the limited variety of
foodstuffs available to her. Many tasty concoctions
had been prepared from the supplies brought from
Skagway.

Faltering daylight slid into blackness, and Maggie
grew anxious for Chase to return. He should have
been back by now, and she feared that something
had happened to him. The blood froze in her veins
when she heard the howling and baying in the distance, easily recognizing the sound made by hungry
wolves that freely roamed this desolate wilderness.
Had wolves attacked Chase? Should she take the rifle
Chase left behind and go looking for him? She discarded the idea immediately. Within minutes she'd
be hopelessly lost out there in all that silent white
tundra surrounded by towering mountains.

Suddenly Maggie was alerted by a sound outside,
and she rushed forward to unlatch the door, calling
his name in mindless fear. "Chase! Darling, are you
all right?"

A blast of frigid air ushered him inside, an apparition out of hell. The door slammed shut behind
him, and he shoved his parka back from his head.
His eyebrows and whiskers were rimmed with frost,
his hair plastered to his head. His eyes were wild,
the grin splitting his face filled with evil promise.
He held a rifle loosely in one hand.

"You!" Maggie gasped in shock and sheer black
fright. "What are you doing here?"

She took an involuntary step backwards; he
pressed forward with quiet menace.

Chapter Twelve

"Did ya think ya'd escape me?" Zeke sneered, his eyes red-rimmed from cold and lack of sleep. "Ya killed my partner. Me and Bandy been together a long time. I can't just forget what ya did ta him. I went through hell ta get ta Dawson after ya stole our boat, and I been dodging the Mounties ever since. Now yer gonna pay—you and yer cowboy lover."

"You came all this way for revenge?" Maggie squeaked, clutching her throat in horror. She was terrified of this wild-eyed creature who had obviously become demented after the death of his partner. Zeke never struck her as the brightest of men, and the killing of Bandy must have sent him over the edge.

"I'd go ta the ends of the earth ta punish the bitch what killed my partner. After I finish with ye, woman, ya'll wish you'da drowned. They're still talkin' in town how ya was found on a wrecked raft, half-drowned and nearly froze. It didn't take much snoopin' ta find out that ya were up here with that cowboy. I'da come sooner but the Mounties had a warrant out fer me, and I had ta hole up fer a spell with a friend."

"I—I'm not alone," Maggie stammered, slowly edging toward the rifle leaning in the corner.

"I know. I saw yer lover leave. I been watchin' the cabin fer hours. I reckon he'll be in fer a surprise when he returns."

Maggie took another step sideways, her eyes carefully averted from the rifle. Keep him talking, she told herself above the furious pounding of her heart. If she could only reach the rifle . . .

"Chase will be back any minute."

"I aim ta take care of him after I finish with you," Zeke bragged, tossing off his heavy coat. "Thought it'd be fun ta let him watch while you and me have ourselves a high old time."

He looked around curiously, sniffing the air fragrant with cooking smells and licking his lips. "Smells good in here. Been a long time since I had a decent meal. Fix me some grub, woman, but remember, I ain't takin' my eyes off ya. If yer smart, ya won't try nothin'."

Deliberately he removed a handgun from beneath his shirt and shoved it inside his belt within easy reach. Then he moved the chair where he could keep an eye on both Maggie and the door. He sat down and leaned the rifle casually against the chair. "Get a move on, woman," he growled when Maggie seemed frozen to the spot. "I want some grub and I want it now."

Surreptitiously Maggie eyed the loaded rifle Chase left her, only a few feet away yet so damn far. Did she dare? Could she reach the weapon before Zeke realized what she intended? If she didn't try, Zeke would surely force Chase to watch while he raped her, then he'd kill them both. It was now or never, Maggie decided grimly as she propelled herself toward the rifle. The sweet taste of success brought a spurt of saliva to her mouth. Her hand touched the barrel, her finger curling through the trigger. But victory turned to bitter defeat when she was yanked viciously backwards and flung to the floor. The rifle left her hand and landed at Zeke's feet.

A sob exploded in Maggie's throat. So close—so damn close. Grabbing her upper arm, Zeke dragged her to her feet, shaking her like a rag doll. "Try somethin' like that again and ya'll be sorry." While Maggie stumbled toward the stove, Zeke picked up the rifle, carefully removed the shells, and tossed it aside.

Zeke devoured every morsel Maggie placed before him, wishing she could lace it liberally with poison. Her worry over Chase became a constant ache, wondering what was keeping him yet dreading the moment he would enter the cabin to find Zeke threatening him with a loaded gun. If only there was some way to warn Chase, she reflected gloomily. Then time ran out as she heard Chase at the door, knocking snow from his snowshoes.

Zeke reacted instantly, his rifle literally leaping into one hand as he grasped Maggie with the other, dragging her behind the door in order to surprise Chase. Maggie opened her mouth to call a warning but the bite of cold steel against her ear persuaded her otherwise. The door flung open and Chase stepped inside.

"Damnation, Maggie, I told you to keep the door locked." Stomping the snow from his boots, he placed his rifle against the wall, removed his gloves, and shrugged out of his coat. "I was lucky, darlin', we'll have caribou steak for supper."

Suddenly, unaccountably, the hair rose on the back of his neck, and a chill of foreboding shivered down his spine. "Maggie?"

"She's right here, Cowboy."

Chase whirled, his heart pounding like a trip-hammer. "Who in the hell are you?" he thundered. "What do you want?"

He glanced at Maggie, her eyes dark and wild with terror. Had this man harmed her? Chase wondered, clenching his fists in impotent rage. He took in everything in one sweeping glance, the maniacal gleam in the man's eyes and the gun pressed against Maggie's sweet flesh.

"We met before, ya just don't remember," Zeke said, cackling mirthfully.

"Zeke, my God!" Chase spewed, comprehension dawning.

"Yep, that's my name. Over there," he motioned with the gun. "Sit down where I can keep an eye on ya. Ya got more lives than a cat."

"If you hurt Maggie I'll—"

"Ya ain't gonna do nothin'. Sit down, I said." The gun gouged painfully into Maggie's neck and she whimpered, bringing about Chase's instant obedience.

"I ain't hurt no one yet," Zeke said, "but I will if ya don't do what I tell ya."

"What do you want? There's a small amount of gold hidden in the cabin, take it and leave."

Zeke's eyes glinted greedily. "Damn right I'll take it. But first I got a little score ta settle with this little bitch. She killed Bandy and she's gonna pay."

"Let Maggie go, Zeke, take your revenge out on me," Chase offered, stalling for time.

"Both of ya are gonna pay," Zeke promised, dragging Maggie across the room. From a pile of supplies stacked against a wall he retrieved a length of rope.

Realizing Zeke meant to render Chase helpless, Maggie cried out, "Don't worry about me, Chase, do what you have to do."

"I—can't, darlin'." Chase choked. "I can't let that bastard hurt you."

"He means to kill us anyway. You have to try."

"Shut up!" Zeke growled, approaching Chase with the rope while pushing Maggie forward with the barrel of the rifle. "Tie him up." Maggie balked, digging her heels in and refusing to move. Abruptly the rifle barrel swung around until it was pointed at Chase's head. "Do it or he's a dead man."

"Do it, Maggie girl," Chase urged, trying to convey a message of hope with his eyes. He didn't want Maggie to do anything to make Zeke angry until he could think of a way out of this mess. He wanted to encourage her, to ask her to trust him, but he feared Zeke's reaction. Chase wasn't frightened for himself, but for Maggie.

Sobbing in frustration, Maggie tied Chase's wrists behind his back according to Zeke's instructions, stretching them to their limits behind the chair he sat in. Zeke tested the rope, then growled, "Tighter!" Gritting her teeth, Maggie complied. "Now his feet." When she finished to Zeke's satisfaction, Chase was trussed up like a Christmas goose.

"You won't get away with this, Zeke," Chase warned. "This isn't Skagway. The Mounties always get their man."

"Shut up, Cowboy. Woman," he barked, motioning to Maggie, "over there." He pointed to the pile of blankets on the floor that served as a bed. "Looks like as good a place as any ta have our fun."

"Don't touch her!" Chase roared, straining against the ropes.

"I been dreamin' of this fer weeks, Cowboy, thinkin' of all the thin's I'm gonna do to the little bitch. Havin' you watch while I diddle her makes it even more excitin'. Take off yer clothes, woman," he growled, rotating his hips in an obscene manner.

"No!" Maggie resisted, raising her chin belligerently. "I'll fight you every step of the way. I'll bite and scratch and make you sorry you ever walked in the door. If you're going to kill us, you might as well do it now because I'll never submit to you."

"Aw, shit," complained Zeke, snorting with disgust. "I ain't in the mood fer no fight. I'm too damn tired right now. I been runnin' behind a damn dogsled fer two days without sleep." He slanted Maggie a baleful glance. "I reckon ya'll keep while I get some shuteye."

A reprieve, even a short-lived one, lent Maggie renewed hope. She directed a meaningful glance at Chase, which he returned with a silent nod of encouragement. Using the rope remaining after trussing up Chase, Zeke made Maggie sit on the floor with her back against the back of the chair Chase sat in. Then he tied her hands behind her, fastening them to the chair. Next her ankles were bound together, rendering her as helpless as Chase.

"That oughta hold ya 'til I can do ya justice, woman," Zeke gloated, yawning hugely. "A couple hours sleep and I'll be rarin' to take ya on."

After feeding the fire, he rolled up in a blanket and fell immediately asleep.

"Are you all right, darlin'?" Chase asked, his voice choked with worry. He had to admit they were in a hellishly dangerous situation.

"Yes, I'm fine, what about you?"

"It's you I'm concerned about. Can you move at all?"

After a few minutes of straining and pulling against her bonds and gaining nothing but bruised wrists for her efforts, Maggie sobbed in frustration and disappointment. "It's no use, Chase, I can wiggle my hands a little, but that's all."

"Take it easy, darlin', relax. We'll find a way."

"Oh, Chase, what if—"

"No, don't even think it. We'll get out of this somehow. Let me think."

Leaning against the back of the chair, somehow Maggie dozed, until she grew cold and woke up shivering. "How long did I sleep?" It amazed her that she could sleep at all.

"Not long," Chase said, his voice ripe with combined frustration and exhaustion.

"Why didn't you wake me?"

"You needed the sleep. I've thought of somethin', and I wanted you rested before attemptin' it."

Maggie's spirits soared. "You've thought of a way to get out of this? Oh, Chase, I knew you would. Tell me."

"Shhh, we don't want to rouse Zeke yet." Speaking in quiet tones meant to instill confidence, Chase whispered, "Before I came into the cabin I thrust my skinning knife into my right boot beneath my pants leg."

"In your boot? But, Chase, what good will that do us? Neither of us can move."

"Listen carefully, darlin'. My feet aren't attached to the chair, just bound together. If I shove them backwards far enough perhaps you can reach them with your bound hands and remove the knife."

"But—"

"Try, baby, just try." Straining forward, Chase thrust his long legs backwards, pulling against the ropes to gain the necessary slack. "Can you touch my feet?"

Her bound hands stretched to the limits as she scrabbled blindly, exhaling loudly when she touched a boot. "Yes! Just barely."

"The knife, darlin', find the knife." Despite the cold, beads of sweat dotted Chase's forehead.

Maggie moved her hands, slowly, painfully, but the ropes severely limited her exploration. "I—I can't, Chase. I can't work my hands to the knife. It's no use." A sob of bitter disappointment caught in her throat and forced itself past her lips.

"Are you gonna give up?" Chase chided, his voice brutally critical. "The Maggie I know wouldn't admit to defeat. My Maggie is courageous and determined and obstinate. Try again, darlin', please."

Chase was right, Maggie scolded herself, angry for giving in to defeat. Their well-being depended entirely on her. Once Zeke was awake, he'd rape her and afterwards kill them both. He was a desperate man wanted by the police and had nothing to lose. Drawing in a deep, steadying breath, Maggie concentrated on locating the knife in Chase's boot. Inch by painful inch she stretched her arms until she thought they'd leave their sockets. When her fingers touched the blade she crowed jubilantly.

"I can feel the knife!"

Relief rolled over Chase's taut body in great waves. "Good, real good, darlin'. Easy now," he encouraged. His legs had begun to cramp from the unnatural position they had assumed, but for Maggie's sake he banished all signs of pain from his voice. "Draw it out, slow and easy. Don't panic and don't drop it. I'm dependin' on you."

"I've got it, I've got it!"

By now Chase's legs were trembling, but Maggie's words sent a surge of adrenaline pulsing through his veins, reviving his hopes and making all his pain worthwhile. But they weren't free yet; the most difficult task still faced them.

"Slide the knife around until you're gripping the handle firmly. Don't drop it!" he warned anxiously. "My hands are just above yours. Hold the knife up and start sawing on the ropes."

"Chase, I can't see your hands," Maggie whispered, casting a wary glance at Zeke, who had stopped snoring and turned over. "I'll cut you."

"Don't fail me now, baby, I need you. Don't worry about hurtin' me, just start sawin' on those ropes. I can take it. Zeke's likely to wake up at any minute."

Tears rolling down her cheeks, Maggie inched the blade upward, stopping when she heard Chase draw his breath in sharply. "Dammit, don't stop!" he hissed from between clenched teeth. "Forget me, forget everythin' but cuttin' me free."

Agonizingly aware that she was probably cutting deeply into Chase's flesh, Maggie grit her teeth and tried not to think about hurting him as she sawed at the ropes with painful slowness. Her hands became wet with his blood, but determination hardened her to his pain. Black fear drove her; blind panic moved her hands. She felt several strands of the twisted hemp give and heard Chase's words of encouragement, bolstering her courage. Grimly she continued hacking away, concentrating so fiercely that her head began to pound. She had no idea how much time had elapsed; all she knew was a terrible desperation to survive and experience Chase's love once more.

Suddenly Maggie felt Chase stiffen, the quick intake of his breath causing her to falter. "He's awake." The warning hissed through his teeth. "Don't move."

Her heart hammering furiously, Maggie heard Zeke yawn and thrash around in the blankets. Then he grew quiet, and she began breathing again, thinking he'd fallen back to sleep. But to her horror, Zeke staggered to his feet and glanced in her direction, his wolfish leer alerting her to his intention. When he started in their direction, Maggie knew she couldn't let him find the knife in her hands, for he'd realize instantly what she was doing. Stealthily, she slid the blade beneath the chair toward Chase's foot. Chase felt it strike his boot and needed no instructions as he acted instinctively. Deliberately he raised his foot and stepped on the knife, completely concealing it beneath his broad boot.

"I'm ready fer ya now, bitch," Zeke said, massaging his groin. "A nap made me hornier than a prize bull in a herd of cows."

Zeke untied Maggie's feet and the ropes binding her to the chair, but paid scant heed to her hands, leaving them bound behind her back. Then he pulled her to her feet and dragged her to the makeshift bed from which he had just arisen. "Lay down," he growled, shrugging out of his clothes. At the last minute, he decided to keep on his longjohns but removed his boots.

"Go to hell!" Maggie shot back. But her defiance did her little good as Zeke muttered something unintelligible and ripped open the front of her bodice.

His eyes popped open as her pale breasts spilled forth. "Gawdamighty!" Zeke breathed reverently, reaching out a thick finger to test the soft quivering flesh. "Just as purty and soft as two white doves. What else ya hidin' underneath them clothes?"

Maggie attempted to turn away, but Zeke's hands prevented her from fleeing as he continued ripping her dress to shreds. Behind him Chase loosed a mighty roar, tugging at his bonds with every ounce of strength he possessed. When Zeke shoved Maggie to the floor, falling heavily atop her, Chase went wild. From somewhere deep within his reserve of strength he found the power necessary to snap the ropes restraining his wrists. Thanks to Maggie's efforts, they had been weakened sufficiently to give beneath Chase's brawn. Zeke was so intent upon Maggie's soft body, arousing him, to raging lust, that he didn't see Chase's numb fingers find the knife beneath his boot and saw at the ropes lashing his ankles together. It seemed like an eternity before they fell away and he was free.

Chase leaped to his feet, nearly falling flat on his face when his legs failed to hold up his weight. Not only were his hands and wrists numb, bruised, and bleeding from numerous cuts, his feet felt like two blocks of wood.

Just then Maggie screamed, a high, thin wail that tore through Chase's pain and prodded his feet. Through a red haze, he saw Zeke slobbering wet kisses over Maggie's breasts, then reach down to release his manhood. Raising his rump, Zeke prepared to plunge into Maggie's wildly resisting body. Two steps took Chase to the rifle lying on the floor, recognizing it as the one he had left for Maggie's protection. Cocking and aiming, he squeezed the trigger, shock shuddering through him when he heard the click of the hammer against an empty chamber. In quick succession Chase pulled the trigger again—and yet again. Nothing.

Poised to drive home his first thrust, Zeke froze at the familiar sound. "What the hell!"

"Chase!"

"Move outta the way, Maggie!"

Scrambling to his feet, Zeke eyed Chase warily. His pistol lay in the tangle of clothes at his feet and his rifle several feet away.

Wrapping the blanket around her, Maggie scooted into a corner, wondering what she could to do help. She spied Chase's rifle sitting by the door, but it was across the room and her hands were still tied behind her. She stared longingly at Zeke's weapon, but the outlaw had the same idea, for he reached for it even as Maggie started to crawl forward.

"Stay outta the way, darlin'," Chase repeated, his mouth set in grim lines. He knew as certain as breathing that this confrontation would end in someone's death. He didn't want it to be Maggie's.

Tossing the useless rifle aside, Chase ducked as Zeke swung around, discharging his rifle at the place where he expected Chase to be. He grunted in pain as Chase slammed into his middle, sending him flying. Chase dove for Zeke and they grappled on the floor, each fighting for the loaded rifle. Suddenly Maggie could stand it no longer. Scrabbling to her knees, she scooted toward Chase and Zeke. The only sound in the room were the grunts and panting of the two men fighting for their lives.

Slowly Zeke's hand felt for the pistol he'd left in the tangle of his clothes. Grasping the butt, he whipped it out. Maggie's warning scream alerted Chase to his imminent danger. In the nick of time he seized Zeke's wrist, but his own maimed hands hadn't the strength necessary to wrest the gun from the desperate outlaw. At that point Maggie decided to enter into the melee, and she threw herself at Zeke. He wore a surprised look as he went skidding across the room.

"Get the gun, Chase," Maggie panted.

Chase reached for the gun, but by then Zeke had recovered and came bounding back, kicking Chase in the groin. Maggie screamed and sought to intervene, but Zeke shoved her hard, sending her flying. His eyes gleaming in triumph, Zeke reached for the gun. Suddenly the door burst open and Captain Scott Gordon blew in with a gust of cold artic air.

"Drop it, Zeke!"

Zeke froze.

Scott's gray eyes fastened on Maggie, overwhelmed with relief when she appeared unharmed. "Thank God I'm in time." His glance slid to Chase. "Are either of you hurt? I came as soon as I heard Zeke was skulking around in town asking about you."

"I'm fine," Maggie said, "but Chase . . ."

"I'm okay, Maggie, just give me a minute to catch my breath. Untie Maggie's hands, Gordon."

Slipping out his knife, Scott obeyed instantly, cutting away Maggie's bonds and rubbing her wrists in order to restore circulation. "Whose blood is that?" he asked with tender concern.

Suddenly aware that the Mountie's attention had strayed, Zeke took a foolish risk. It turned out to be the last foolish thing he ever did. He made a wild sprint for the door, pushing past Scott into the icy deep-freeze of winter, shoeless and scantily clad in dirty longjohns.

"He's getting away!" Maggie screeched, pulling the blanket tightly around the tatters of her clothing.

"He won't get far," Scott said, amazingly unperturbed as he slammed the door on the arctic chill that had begun to turn the cabin into an icebox. "It's twenty below zero outside. He'll freeze to death inside five minutes."

"He probably has dogs and a sled nearby," Chase warned, alarmed at the thought of Zeke escaping so easily.

"I passed it about a mile down the trail. He'll never make it," Scott assured them. "If I thought he'd escape, I'd be out there hunting him down. Nature has a way of dealing with men like him. Are you sure you're all right, Maggie? Zeke had a good head start on me. He didn't—?"

"He intended to rape me and make Chase watch," Maggie said in a quavering voice. "He would have— done it right away, but he was tired and took a nap first. He tied us up while he dozed."

"The bastard wouldn't have gotten the drop on us if I hadn't gone huntin' and left Maggie alone," Chase said with self-reproach.

"Why didn't you bring Maggie back to Dawson like you promised?" Scott asked, accusation bitter on his tongue. "I warned you it wasn't safe out here for a woman."

"It's not Chase's fault," Maggie said, leaping to her lover's defense. "We did start back, just as Chase promised, but there was an accident. A snowslide buried the sled and killed the dogs. I would be dead now if it wasn't for Chase. He refused to let me die in an icy grave. He dug me out and breathed life into me. Fortunately, two prospectors picked us up in their sled and brought us back to the claimsite or we would have been forced to walk."

"I've a sled and dogteam outside," Scott said, his eyes lingering on Maggie. He caught a glimpse of the tattered garment beneath the blanket she clutched about her and had a good idea of the ordeal she'd been put through. "We'll leave as soon as you're ready."

"I—no, I don't think—"

"Captain Gordon is right, Maggie," Chase concurred. "You don't belong here. You'll be more comfortable in Dawson."

"Am I not allowed to make up my own mind?"

"Not when it concerns your well-bein'."

"Have you grown tired of me so soon?" Maggie seemed to have forgotten that Scott stood nearby, trying not to listen but finding it impossible not to.

"Damnation, Maggie girl, I'm not gonna argue with you about this. Pack up your belongin's, you're goin' with Gordon. I feel badly for not protectin' you properly."

Realizing she was wasting her breath, Maggie reluctantly acquiesced to the combined efforts of Chase and Scott. With deceptive calm she collected her meager belongings. Most of her clothing had been left behind at the Dawson Arms, but she had her precious journal and sheaves of notes. When everything was done up in a neat bundle, Scott carried it outside to the sled, giving Maggie the opportunity to change her clothes and bid Chase a proper good-bye.

While Maggie was packing her belongings, Scott had spoken in quiet tones to Chase. His probing questions led him to the conclusion that Chase cared deeply for Maggie. And judging from Maggie's words earlier, the feeling was reciprocated, though

GET YOUR 4 FREE* BOOKS NOW— A $21.96 VALUE!

Mail the Free* Book Certificate Today!

---

4 FREE* BOOKS ❧ A $21.96 VALUE

*Free * Books Certificate*

YES! I want to subscribe to the Leisure Historical Romance Book Club. Please send me my **4 FREE* BOOKS**. Then each month I'll receive the four newest **Leisure Historical Romance** selections to Preview for 10 days. If I decide to keep them, I will pay the Special Member's Only discounted price of just $4.24 each, a total of $16.96 ($17.75 US in Canada). This is a SAVINGS OF AT LEAST $5.00 off the bookstore price. There are no shipping, handling, or other charges*. There is no minimum number of books I must buy and I may cancel the program at any time. In any case, the 4 FREE* BOOKS are mine to keep—A BIG $21.96 Value!

*In Canada, add $5.00 shipping and handling per order for first shipment. For all subsequent shipments to Canada, the cost of membership is $17.75 US, which includes $7.75 shipping and handling per month.[All payments must be made in US dollars]

Name _____

Address _____

City _____

State _____ *Country* _____ *Zip* _____

Telephone _____

Signature _____

If under 18, Parent or Guardian must sign. Terms, prices and conditions subject to change. Subscription subject to acceptance. Leisure Books reserves the right to reject any order or cancel any subscription.

(Tear Here and Mail Your FREE* Book Card Today!)

Get Four Books Totally
FREE* —
A $21.96 Value!

(Tear Here and Mail Your FREE* Book Card Today!)

PLEASE RUSH
MY FOUR FREE*
BOOKS TO ME
RIGHT AWAY!

Leisure Historical Romance Book Club
P.O. Box 6613
Edison, NJ 08818-6613

AFFIX
STAMP
HERE

obviously no promises had been exchanged.

"I want you safe, Maggie, you know that," Chase said once the door closed behind Scott. "I'm not sendin' you away 'cause I don't want you with me. Your safety is important to me. I'm givin' you half the gold for expenses in Dawson." He pressed a weighted sack in her hands.

"I don't like other people making choices for me, Chase."

"I care about you. What we have together is special."

"Evidently not special enough," Maggie sighed regretfully.

"Wait for me, darlin'. Wait for me in Dawson. I'll be there in March. We'll talk then. We've never really discussed the future, but somehow I can't think of a future without you. How important to you is your career?"

Maggie was stunned. Were Chase's words meant as a commitment? Did he love her enough to dedicate his life to her? She knew he loved his ranch in the wilds of Montana and planned to return there. Did she love him enough to give up her career after she'd come so far, done so much, proved she was as capable as any man?

Maggie hesitated so long that Chase felt compelled to add, "I know what you're thinkin', darlin', but I swear it doesn't matter if you can't have babies. I never thought much about kids anyway." A deliberate lie. "Too much responsibility." Another lie. "I—well, dammit, Maggie, I love you."

"You—love me?"

"Did you doubt it?"

"I—no, not really," Maggie admitted. "But, Chase, about babies—"

"Maggie, are you ready?" Scott called through the door. "We should leave."

"Go on, darlin'. We'll talk about this later, when I get to Dawson. Think about what I said, about your career and all. I have a feelin' Gold Bottom is gonna pay off big. We'll be rich."

Maggie wanted to tell Chase that she wasn't barren, that she'd deliberately lied so he wouldn't feel obligated to offer marriage, but there wasn't time. And since he apparently didn't want children anyway, the subject was moot. Would he be disappointed to learn she wasn't barren? she wondered, suddenly sorry she had told that one little lie.

Kissing her soundly, Chase pushed her toward the door. All she managed before she left was a few breathless words. "I love you, Chase, I always have."

"March, Maggie, wait for me."

Maggie stared gloomily at the words she'd just written, her eyes adjusting to the meager light. Resting her elbow on the desk, her mind traveled back to the cold, uncomfortable trip from Eleven Above to Dawson. Bundled in fur robes, she rode in the dogsled driven by Scott over the frozen tundra and breathtaking vistas. The only bad thing that had happened to mar their journey was the discovery of Zeke's frozen, mutilated body a short distance from the cabin. Wolves had already found it, and not much was left to bury. Two days later they arrived in Dawson without mishap.

Maggie had to admit that racing across the frozen white expanses in a dogsled was an exhilarating experience that she wouldn't trade, but nevertheless she was happy to see Dawson. The city in mid-winter had literally swelled at the seams. Wooden shacks along the river sprang up overnight, and every hotel room was taken, often shared by several men. Saloons thrived, supported by stampeders sheltering in the city for the winter, nearly six thousand men,

Scott told her. Yet the town had never become a lawless hellhole like Skagway, due entirely to the Canadian Mounted Police and their vigilance.

There were even two other women in Dawson, besides saloon girls, who had come by ship via St. Michael, Alaska, and the Yukon River in Maggie's absence. Mrs. Adams had a cabin built, and it was rumored she made thirty dollars a day mending and sewing for miners. Mrs. Willis bought half interest in a claim on Bonanza Creek, hired two men to work it, and paid their wages from baking and selling bread for one dollar and fifty cents a loaf and from laundering the miners' clothes. She made enough money to buy the other half of the claim and was now sole owner. Maggie had it all down in her journal and spent most of her lonely hours spinning her tales on paper.

Maggie had been in Dawson a month now, and the weather had turned bitter. Fifty degrees below zero had been reported. At that temperature, the cold was so intense it burned men's lungs and froze their skin. She worried constantly about Chase in his remote cabin, alone with no one to ease his boredom or offer comfort. He was not a man accustomed to being confined to small spaces for weeks at a time. It was due mostly to Scott's attentiveness that Maggie did not suffer the same boredom. Scott's attentions had never wavered despite the fact that she considered him merely a friend.

Maggie hated the perpetual darkness of the Klondike during the winter. In contrast, the month of June boasted nearly constant daylight, providing a favorable climate to grow vegetables and other crops.

Fortunately, Scott had insisted that Maggie's hotel room be kept in reserve for her, else she'd find herself out in the cold. Prices soared with the influx of miners. She was now forced to pay one hundred and fifty dollars a week for her room, a staggering sum, but Chase's gold paid the bill and bought her food, also outrageously high-priced.

One day Maggie met Jack London in the hotel lobby. She remembered the young man immediately, recalling his adventurous spirit and enthusiasm. "Why, Mr. London, it's good to see you again. I've been hoping I'd see you so I might thank you for helping Chase. He might not have survived if you hadn't come along when you did."

"My pleasure, Miss Afton. You don't know how happy I was to learn you were safe. Chase was worried sick about you. I assume he's fully recovered by now."

"Chase was well the last time I saw him about a month ago. Do you plan on staking a claim this spring and trying your hand at mining?" Maggie asked curiously.

"Have lunch with me and I'll tell you," London replied, grinning cheekily.

Maggie thoroughly enjoyed the meal, due entirely to Jack London and the tales he spun of adventure and exploration in out-of-the-way places. He hoped his journey to the Klondike would result in his first break in writing. Already he had a novel in the works which he intended to call *Son of Wolf* and another titled *Call Of The Wild*.

"I have no desire to find a bonanza in gold," Jack said, turning serious. "What I'm gathering is a wealth of information for future reference. Like you, Maggie"—by now they were on a first name basis— "I'm a writer, and quite serious about my profession. I'm also a realist. I seriously doubt there's a claim available any place in the Klondike. I'll stick to what I know."

"You're certainly sincere about your work, Jack," Maggie replied, his enthusiasm catching. "I'd be honored to say I knew the great Jack London when he was a fledgling writer. Of course," she added with a mischievous twinkle, "I'll expect to see my name mentioned in one of your books."

Maggie saw a lot of the twenty-one-year-old London that winter. They had their love of writing in common as well as a sense of adventure. They spent long hours trading notes about their experiences along the Yukon Trail. When Jack wasn't around to cheer Maggie, Scott could always be counted on. But the friendships she formed that winter of 1898 could not assuage her longing for Chase. March couldn't arrive soon enough to suit her.

One day in late February, Scott's gentle probing into her plans for the future took on serious overtones.

"You'll be leaving soon, Maggie," he observed, his words tinged with a lingering sadness. "In March the lakes and rivers will thaw, making travel possible again. Hordes of stampeders will be arriving daily when the passes open. But I fear they'll find nothing but bitter disappointment, for all available claims are already taken."

"That's exactly what Jack London said," Maggie mused thoughtfully.

"An interesting young man. You've been seeing a lot of him lately."

"We've a lot in common."

"Maggie, I don't went to talk about Jack London, I want to talk about us."

They were sharing supper in the hotel restaurant crowded with hordes of men whose voices were raised in raucous laughter and conversation. More than a few were staring at her with avid appreciation. In a town populated with so few real ladies, Maggie was a rarity who captured unwanted attention everywhere she went.

"Scott, let's not discuss this now," Maggie said, shifting uncomfortably. "People are staring."

"Of course they are, you're a beautiful women. But I'm determined to talk about this. Is there no place we can be alone?"

Rather than having their private discussion become the center of attention, Maggie said, "Come up to my room. I know it's not proper, but after spending weeks alone in the wilderness with Chase I've little reputation left."

"I'd never do anything to hurt you, Maggie."

Somehow Maggie believed him. Scott was the kind of man who would always be faithful, loyal, and loving. But so would a dog. Besides, Scott wasn't Chase. Scott wasn't a slow-talking cowboy with a determined twinkle in his eyes and a crooked smile that sent her heart soaring. Only Chase had the power to turn her knees to jelly and melt her insides. He made love as if he invented it.

"All right, Scott, I'm ready to listen," Maggie said once they were alone in her room. She sat primly on the bed while Scott paced the small room nervously.

"I've never met a woman like you before, Maggie. You're daring, brave, and too damned adventurous for your own good. But I wouldn't have you any other way. I've waited a long time for a woman like you. I'm asking you to marry me, Maggie."

"But, Scott, I—"

"We can settle in Seattle if you'd like," Scott continued, warming to the subject. "You can write or continue with your career as a journalist. I won't interfere. I can find work easily enough in Seattle and—"

"Scott, stop, please. I can't marry you. I'm fond of you, but I don't love you."

"How do you know? We've only shared one brief kiss. Do you and McGarrett have an understanding? If you're worried that I'll think any less of you because of the time you spent alone with him, you're wrong. I only know I love you, and nothing else matters."

"You're a better man than I deserve," Maggie said sincerely. "Living in a city like Seattle is far different from the Yukon. You'd never be happy there, and I couldn't live here. No, Scott, I'll always cherish your friendship—but, well, I think you know how I feel about Chase."

"What can McGarrett offer you that I can't, Maggie? A life of hardship and drudgery in Montana? Or do you expect him to make a fortune off that claim of his?"

"Your questions are entirely rational, but I can't supply the answers. I don't even know if Chase and I have a future together. I care for him deeply and he cares for me, but right now I don't truthfully know if anything will come of it."

"McGarrett's a fool if he lets you get away," Scott muttered sourly.

Then, to Maggie's utter amazement, Scott was standing beside her, pulling her into his arms. "I'm going to kiss you, Maggie, whether you like it or not."

His lips were bold and insistent, holding nothing back of himself, willing Maggie to respond. Never had he met a woman he wanted as badly as he wanted Maggie. Uniquely different, she was a woman who inspired him with a love he'd nearly despaired of finding. In his view, losing Maggie to a man who didn't appreciate her was a terrible injustice. Though Scott was a basically honorable man, he was prepared to go to any lengths to make Maggie his.

Scott's kiss was so unexpected that Maggie was slow to react, lending him the courage to continue. His kiss deepened, his tongue parting her lips, then slipping inside to savor her sweetness. A strangled moan low in his throat jerked Maggie abruptly to her senses. Scott's kisses were pleasant, enjoyable even, but he simply wasn't Chase. Chase's loving rendered her incapable of responding to any other man. There was only one Chase McGarrett, and if she couldn't have him she'd remain a spinster. Though Scott was reluctant to release her, Maggie broke off the kiss and shrugged out of his embrace.

"I'm sorry, Scott. You're the last person I want to hurt, but neither do I want to give you false hopes."

"McGarrett again," Scott spat bitterly. "What if he decides he's not ready to accept the responsibility of a permanent relationship? Do I have a chance then?"

Maggie flushed, aware that Chase could very well decide he didn't need her in his life. Of course she would survive, and perhaps even find happiness devoting her life to her work. Maybe one day another man could fill the void, though she seriously doubted it.

"Would you settle for second best?" Maggie asked, doing everything in her power to discourage the determined Mountie.

"With you I'd settle for anything." His voice was low and so sincere it brought tears to Maggie's amber eyes.

"I wish I could love you, Scott. Why does life have to be so complicated? I'm very fond of you, you know that. As to what the future holds, let's just wait and see."

Disappointment tasted bitter on Scott's tongue. "If that damn cowboy hurts you, Maggie, I swear he'll pay."

Chapter Thirteen

The hard, depressing winter was especially difficult for Chase. After the long days and endless nights of making love with Maggie, laughing with her, just having her near, making do without her was unbearable; his loneliness was a palpable, driving emptiness. But no matter how badly he wanted her, she was safer in Dawson where Captain Gordon could protect her.

Despite the excruciating, bone-chilling cold, Chase worked tirelessly on the mound of gravel, separating more of the precious nuggets from the rockpile. As soon as enough snow melted, he intended to dig along the creek bank in search of the vein that produced the gold. Maybe Sam had already found it but died before he could reveal its secret.

Yet even when he toiled until he dropped from sheer exhaustion, thoughts of Maggie plagued Chase's every hour whether asleep or awake. Truth to tell, Chase gave Maggie's surprising words that she was barren more than passing consideration. Though he had insisted it didn't matter that she couldn't bear children, he realized that he wasn't being entirely truthful, that he'd thought often of his sons or daughters, living on the ranch he built. He pictured them playing free and happy beneath the big sky of Montana.

Chase wanted children of his flesh to inherit his legacy. With Maggie as his wife, that wouldn't be possible. Would the love and passion they shared assuage the need for a man to reproduce, to watch a part of his own flesh and blood grow and prosper? Chase didn't know. He knew little beyond the fact that he wanted to spend his life making love to Maggie. Yet that hardly solved his dilemma or eased his mind. As the weeks passed and spring approached, Chase grew increasingly apprehensive about his meeting with Maggie. The day the sun made its welcome appearance, Chase began preparations for his trip to Dawson. He was anxious for the assayer to grade his cache of gold and equally anxious to return to Eleven Above and begin digging in earnest.

Spring at last! By now Maggie had written literally volumes on her experiences, mostly articles and short stories she intended sending to the newspaper and magazines. She hoped Mr. Grant would be pleased with her work. Already the weather was moderating, snow melting and ice breaking up on rivers and lakes. The town was emptying of miners returning to their claims, soon to be replaced by others coming over the passes and downriver in search of riches. It was likely more women would arrive, as well as members of the press, and of course speculators.

Maggie was standing on the bank of the Yukon in late March with Scott and hundreds of others to watch the first appearance of the sun in weeks over the horizon. It was a spectacular sight and exuberantly welcomed after a depressing winter of blizzards, ice, and snow, the worst in several years. The coming of spring meant Maggie's time in the Klondike was limited. Jack London was one of the first to leave Dawson in his continuing search for adventure and knowledge.

Among the first group of miners to arrive that early spring of 1898 was Rusty Reed.

Due entirely to Kate's tender care, Rusty's broken leg had mended properly and he appeared as robust as ever. He was anxious to start immediately for the goldfields to see how Chase had fared during the winter, but he had promised both Hannah and Kate he'd look up Maggie if she was still in Dawson. Rusty's first stop was the Royal Canadian Mounted Police office, where Captain Gordon told him where to find Maggie.

By now Maggie had grown sick of the small, sparsely furnished room in which she had spent weeks writing, pacing, and thinking of Chase. All her meager belongings were packed, and she waited only for Chase to appear before leaving this frozen land of hardship and disappointment behind. This time she intended to travel in comparative luxury in a steamship down the Yukon to St. Michael, Alaska, through the Bering Sea and down the coast to Seattle. It would add nearly three thousand miles to her trip, but she couldn't possibly travel the rivers, rapids, lakes, and passes to Skagway without a reliable guide. That much she had learned from her previous travels. Rumor had it that a narrow-gauge railroad over White Pass was already in the works, and that soon steamship travel would be possible from Lake Bennet at the foot of the pass to Dawson through the lakes and connecting rivers. All these amenities would certainly ease the plight of the stampeders, Maggie thought, considering all the difficulties she and Chase had encountered along the Yukon Trail.

Maggie's mental musings were interrupted by a knock at the door, and her heart thudded with anticipation. Had Chase finally arrived? She flung the door open, gasping in surprise and pleasure to see a grinning Rusty standing on two good legs in the hallway.

"Howdy, Maggie, the Mountie told me I'd find ya here." When the lakes and rivers thawed, Rusty had been one of the first men across White Pass.

"Rusty, you don't know how glad I am to see you!" She dragged him inside, giving him an exuberant hug. "I'm so relieved to see you on your feet again."

"I was powerful worried about ya, and Chase, too. I couldn't wait fer the ice ta break up so I could hightail it up here. Did Chase and Sam winter at the claim or are they in Dawson?"

"Sam's dead. Chase is at Eleven Above, though I'm expecting him in Dawson soon. I can't imagine what's keeping him."

"Old Sam dead? How do you know that?"

"Sit down, Rusty, it's a long story." Then she proceeded to tell him everything that happened from the day she left Skagway with Chase.

"Tarnation! My trip was a picnic compared to what you two went through," Rusty said, amazed. "Imagine Soapy Smith sendin' his toughs after ya. They got what they deserved. If I know Chase, he blames himself fer what happened to ya at the cabin."

"It's over now. I don't want to think about how close we came to death," Maggie said quietly.

"About you and Chase," Rusty hinted, blushing. "Have you—uh, made any plans?"

"If you mean about the future, the answer is no."

"He darn well oughta after spendin' weeks alone with ya in that cabin," Rusty said, indignant. "I'll

have a talk with the boy when I get up there
and—"

"It's all right, Rusty," Maggie smiled, gratified by
his interest in her welfare. "I'm a responsible adult
and knew what I was doing. I'm prepared to live
with whatever Chase decides." Liar. She knew darn
well she'd fight to keep Chase in her life.

Rusty regarded Maggie with renewed respect. If he
had his way, Chase would do the right thing where
Maggie was concerned. But no one knew better than
he did how darn-fool stubborn Chase could be about
certain things.

They parted a short tine later. Rusty intended to
leave for Eleven Above immediately. Maggie had
shown him the nuggets taken from the claim, and
he grew so excited he could scarcely wait to begin
digging. Scott Gordon found him packing his supplies on the broad back of the packhorse he had
recently purchased.

"Did you find Miss Afton?" Scott asked.

"Yep," Rusty replied, being his usual taciturn
self.

"You heading out to the claim?"

"Yep. Any objections?"

"None. I'd like you to deliver a massage to your
partner."

When Maggie told Rusty about Scott and all he'd
done for her, Rusty gained more from what she didn't
say than from what she did say about the handsome
Mountie. Evidently the man was smitten with her,
and Rusty couldn't blame him. Maggie was a feast
for any man. If Chase wasn't careful, he'd lose her.

"What is it you want said?"

"Just tell him that if he doesn't appreciate what
he has, I do. He'll know what I mean."

Nodding curtly, he turned on his heel and left.
Rusty thought the Mountie couldn't have made himself more clear.

*   *   *

Two days later, Rusty arrived at the cabin to find Chase already in the process of packing his gear for his long-delayed trip to Dawson. He had meant to leave much earlier, but now it was already April and long past the time Maggie expected him.

"Howdy, son," Rusty greeted, grinning foolishly.

"You old sonuvagun!" Chase cried, pounding his friend on the back. "All healed, I see. You musta been the first one to leave Skagway. Did you get tired of havin' Kate fawnin' over you?"

"Sort of," Rusty admitted sheepishly. "She's a damn fine woman, Chase, but she understands I had ta get up here. Maggie told me about findin' all them nuggets."

"You saw Maggie? How is she?"

"Looked damn good to me. That Mountie's been keepin' her from gettin' lonesome," he said slyly.

"Gordon?"

"Yep."

Chase spat out a string of oaths.

"Ya got plans fer the lady?" Rusty asked with feigned innocence. "If ya ain't, ya should. She told me she spent weeks alone up here with ya." His voice held a note of censure rare for Rusty. Chase flushed, unaccountably angered. "What if ya got her in the family way?"

"Let me worry about that, Rusty," Chase bit out stiffly. "I'm headin' for Dawson in a day or two to see Maggie. We'll work out our future without your help."

"Ya better hurry," Rusty grunted, "if ya expect Maggie to be waitin' on ya. Cap'n Gordon gave me a message fer ya."

"What kind of message?"

"He said to tell ya he's aimin' ta take yer woman, or words ta that effect. The Mountie's smitten with Maggie, son, and aims ta have her."

An angry calm settled over Chase. Had the Mountie taken his place in Maggie's affections? She had said she loved him, but many things could have happened during all those weeks they'd been apart. Did Gordon know she was barren? Did it bother him that he'd never have a child with Maggie? Had they become lovers? Without the fear of pregnancy, there was nothing preventing Maggie from taking as many lovers as she wanted. Damnation! Why was he thinking like that?

Before Chase left for Dawson, he told Rusty about the gold he'd found and showed him the sizable cache gleaned from the dwindling mound of gravel near the creek bank.

"Looks damn promisin'," Rusty said excitedly. "I'll be interested in what the assayer has to say."

"That's my first stop in Dawson. We've done it, Rusty. Somethin' tells me we're both gonna be rich as kings. I can't wait to get back here and begin diggin' for that rich vein."

"Go to Dawson, son, talk to Maggie, do what ya gotta before ya return. Now that I'm here, I'm willing and able to do my share."

The stern-wheeler steamship *Susie* was due in Dawson City some time in June, 1898. She carried stampeders, saloon girls, whores, wives, and media representatives—in addition to mining supplies, food, and clothing. She was to remain in port a week before returning to Seattle and San Francisco via St. Michael, Alaska. Though Chase still hadn't arrived in Dawson, Maggie realized it was long past time to return to civilization and her job at the Seattle Post-Intelligencer. Surely Chase would come before the *Susie* left Dawson, Maggie reasoned, so she purchased her ticket that afternoon, although it was nearly two months before the ship's expected arrival. With the ticket clasped tightly in

her hand, Maggie became sadly aware that she might
never see Chase again.

"Are you certain you want to leave?" Scott asked
when Maggie revealed her plans to return to Seattle
aboard the *Susie*.

"Positive," Maggie replied with firm resolve. "It's
time I got back to my job. Mail forwarded from
Skagway just recently reached me. My editor
received my first two articles mailed from Skagway
and urged me to return to Seattle."

"I don't want you to leave, Maggie."

They stood in the hallway outside Maggie's door,
having just returned from a leisurely supper.

"Can we go inside, Maggie? I'd like to talk to
you."

"We've said everything there is to say, Scott. We
will always be friends, but nothing you can say will
prevent me from leaving."

"What about McGarrett? I thought you were waiting for him to return from Eleven Above."

"I expect he'll show up before I leave," Maggie said
with quiet conviction.

It broke Scott's heart that Chase had such little
regard for Maggie's feelings. "Please, Maggie, let me
come in for a moment. Perhaps I can cheer you with
stories about my childhood. If they won't cheer you,
maybe they'll put you to sleep."

Despite her somber mood, Maggie bestowed a brilliant smile on Scott, opened the door, and ushered
him inside her room.

Chase McGarrett strode down the upstairs hallway
of the Dawson Arms, his steps light and springy, his
spirits soaring. He had reached Dawson mere hours
ago, and his first stop had been the assayer's office,
where he learned the gold he had accumulated was
of the highest quality. Once he found the vein, it
could yield up to $5000 a day. That alone was cause

for celebration. He had bathed and shaved and was now on his way to see Maggie, eager to tell her of his good fortune and make passionate love to her until exhaustion claimed them. He knew he was late in coming to Dawson, but Maggie had given her word she'd still be here. He couldn't wait to see the look in her amber eyes when he told her he was rich. After a year or two of working the claim, he and Rusty would have all the money they'd ever need. Enough to make his heirs rich. No, he corrected, pained, there'd be no heirs—not with Maggie as his wife. There'd be no children to claim his wealth.

As he neared Maggie's room, his steps faltered. Chase recognized her immediately, standing in the hall. She was even more beautiful than he remembered. But at the moment she had eyes only for the man standing so close that their bodies were nearly touching. Scott Gordon made a handsome picture in his colorful uniform—tall, broad of chest, slim of waist, and obviously in love with Maggie. Chase was trying to decide whether or not to make his presence known when Maggie bestowed a beguiling smile on the Mountie, took his hand, and led him inside her room. Chase waited ten minutes, and when Scott did not reappear, he turned on his heel and fled, ending up in the nearest saloon, where he proceeded to drown his sorrows.

Two hours later Chase was still sober. He wanted Maggie so desperately, the resulting pain rendered the alcohol he consumed impotent. Not even his good fortune seemed important without Maggie to share it with. He left the saloon walking aimlessly along the muddy street, when he spied Scott entering his office. Had he been with Maggie all this time? Chase wondered bleakly. Suddenly he knew he had to see Maggie and learn for himself if the Mountie had stolen her from him.

Determination rode Chase and he hurried his steps. Perhaps he was doing Maggie a grave injustice with his wild conjectures. He desperately needed Maggie to tell him she still cared for him, that it wasn't the Mountie she wanted. Within minutes he was rapping softly on Maggie's door at the Dawson Arms.

Already undressed for bed in nightgown and robe, Maggie couldn't imagine who was knocking on her door at this time of night. Then her eyes fell on the hat resting on the chair. Scott must have forgotten it when he left earlier. She smiled, amused by Scott's forgetfulness, especially when in her presence. She always seemed to rattle the poor dear man. Picking up the hat, she opened the door, holding it out as if in offering.

"Were you so rattled you left pieces of your clothing behind?" Maggie teased archly.

"No, darlin', I'm never too rattled to leave without my clothes."

"Chase! You're here!"

"Obviously you were expectin' someone else." He looked pointedly at the Mountie hat. "Your lover, perhaps?" The grim lines of his face revealed his pain and disillusionment.

"What are you saying?"

"Do you always answer the door in your nightclothes?"

"No, I—"

"Oh, Maggie, couldn't you wait for me? Did you have to take Gordon as a lover?"

Maggie was stunned. She opened her mouth to fling back a scathing retort, but approaching footsteps and loud voices forestalled her. Glancing down the hall, she saw two men laughing and talking and recognized them as the miners who had the room directly across from hers. She didn't want them to see her in her nightclothes arguing with a man outside her door. Chase sized up the situation immediately and slipped inside the open door, closing it firmly behind him.

"I don't know if I want you in here, thinking the way you do," Maggie said tartly. She couldn't believe Chase would read something more into her innocent relationship with Scott. Didn't he love her enough to trust her? Apparently not, or he'd never make those ridiculous accusations.

"What am I supposed to think?" Chase said sourly, flipping off his hat and tunneling long fingers through his hair, revealing his agitation. "I came to tell you my good news and find you alone in your room with Gordon."

"How do you know that?"

"Damnation! I've got eyes. I saw you draggin' him inside. I waited ten minutes before I gave up and left."

"You should have waited fifteen minutes," Maggie remarked, her voice ripe with disgust. "Oh, Chase, must we argue? You're the only lover I've ever had or wanted. Scott has been a wonderful friend, but he's not you."

"You welcomed him readily enough to your room," Chase observed acidly.

"Only because I trust him to act like a gentleman."

"Can you deny he wants you?" Chase challenged. Why in the hell were they trading insults when all he wanted was to love Maggie endlessly?

"Scott asked me to marry him, but I refused. He knows I love you."

Hearing Maggie say those words took all the wind out of his sails. "Oh God, Maggie, I don't know what got into me. When I saw you with Gordon, invitin' him into your room, I lost the good sense I was born with. I was so dang jealous I wanted to kill him for darin' to touch what was mine."

"Am I yours, Chase?"

"Damn right."

"Then prove it. Show me how much you want me. Make love to me."

She released the belt on her robe and let it drop to the floor. Then her hands moved to the buttons at the neck of her prim nightgown.

"No, let me," Chase said, his voice husky with need as he shoved her hands aside.

One by one he released the tiny buttons, his fingers clumsy and shaky. The gauzy material parted, and he shoved it past her shoulders, baring them to his lips. His mouth was warm and moist on her flesh, and Maggie shivered in delight. His lips slipped lower, his tongue caressing the valley between her breasts. Then the nightgown lay in a puddle at her feet, and Chase drew the nipple of one breast deeply into his mouth, laving the erect tip with the moistness of his tongue—nipping, teasing, now sucking strongly.

Maggie moaned, feeling the results of his tender torment deep in her groin. Abandoning those luscious snowy mounds, Chase dropped to his knees, grasping Maggie's buttocks, holding her still as he parted the curling hairs at the apex of her thighs with his tongue and probed gently. Maggie stifled a shriek as Chase used his considerable skill to drive her to the edge of ecstasy. Sliding his tongue along the tender slit, he located the tiny nub of her femininity.

"Chase, please, I can't stand it!"

"Hang on, darlin', you're almost there. Don't hold back, let it come." His fingers dug into the soft flesh of her buttocks as he renewed his efforts, savoring the honey-sweet taste of her passion with the abandon of a man drunk upon the most exotic of wines.

And then she was there, showing him her joy, sobbing and crying out, pulling him closer—closer still. No one, absolutely no one, could make her feel like this but Chase. She felt herself floating, suddenly aware that Chase had swept her off her feet and was carrying her to the bed. Anxious for the touch of his bare skin against hers, Maggie began tearing at his clothes.

"Easy, darlin', don't be greedy." Chase grinned with wicked delight. "We got all night, and the next, and the next, until I go back to the goldfields. Oh, baby, I've missed you. I nearly lost my mind from wantin'."

"Show me, love, show me how much you want me."

With consummate skill and tenderness, Chase slowly roused Maggie to passion again while she rediscovered the secrets of his body. She tasted the texture of his skin, savored the tart saltiness, inhaled the musky odor or his desire.

"Now, Chase," she begged, dragging her nails sharply against his back.

The resulting shock caused him to plunge hard, sheathed completely with his first thrust, her moist depths taking all of him. Vivid waves of light pulsed through her with each stroke. "I've never felt anythin' so damn good," Chase groaned as if in pain. "So tight, so warm, so—" A moan swallowed the rest of his words.

"Harder, Chase, harder." She wanted, needed, to feel his strength pounding against her womb.

"Are you sure? I don't want to hurt you?"

"I'm sure. You won't hurt me."

Their coupling was wild, tender, abandoned. Chase rode her mercilessly, then changed their positions to allow Maggie the pleasure of setting their pace. They mated like animals, neither satisfied with tepid passions, each driving the other to heights never before attained. It ended with an incredible climax that left them both shaken and unable to talk for several long minutes.

"You're magnificent," Chase said, still awed by what he had just experienced. "Damnation, Maggie girl, you plumb wore me out."

"I hope not, love, it's still early," she teased, sliding her hand down the length of his thigh.

"Just give me a few minutes, baby, and I'll try not to disappoint you."

A comfortable silence settled over them until Maggie said, "You mentioned something about being rich. I assume you found more gold."

"You won't believe it, darlin', but with each shovelful of gravel more nuggets appeared. The assayer said they are of exceptional quality and likely to yield a fortune before the vein runs out. We're rich, Maggie, rich. I can buy more land, purchase mares and studs, and have the best damn horse ranch in Montana. It's like a dream come true."

"You love Montana, don't you?" Maggie asked with a strange sadness.

"It's beautiful, Maggie—you'll love it too." He grew so excited talking about his hopes and dreams that he failed to see that Maggie had become quiet and withdrawn. Chase spoke glowingly about Montana while failing to take into consideration her love of writing and need to fulfill her desire to be needed and useful.

Stung by Chase's utter disregard for her needs, Maggie realized that no matter how often she proved herself, it was still a man's world, insensitive to a woman's needs and desires. Chase naturally assumed Maggie wanted what he wanted without asking her opinion.

"Montana is a wonderful place to raise—horses," he amended lamely. He had started to say children but realized abruptly that with Maggie there'd be no children. Maggie thought nothing of the pause, having already forgotten she had told Chase she was barren.

"Chase, are you asking me to marry you?"

Chase looked truly stunned. " 'Course we'll get married, darlin'. I don't plan on stayin' up here more than a year or two and then we can—"

"A year or two! What am I supposed to do till then?"

"I thought you'd come up to the cabin, spend the summer."

"Wouldn't it be somewhat crowded—you, me and Rusty?"

Chase frowned. "I hadn't thought of that. I reckon it's best anyway that you stay in Dawson. I'll try to visit once a month or so. It won't be so bad, Maggie," Chase assured her eagerly. "When we leave here, we'll be rich."

"I'm going back to Seattle, Chase. I've already purchased my passage. The *Susie* is expected in Dawson in a few weeks."

"What! Don't I mean anythin' to you?"

"I love you, but you're taking it for granted that I want the same things you do. I don't *know* if I'll like Montana. I want to have a say in where we'll go and what we'll do. Is that so wrong?"

"But Montana is my home," Chase said tightly. "A wife goes where her husband leads. It's always been that way. Dammit, I love you, Maggie—why are we arguin' like this? I'd much rather make love to you again."

"Then do it," Maggie said with quiet conviction.

"Will you stay in Dawson and wait for me? You can write your newspaper and resign. Or maybe they'll agree to accept your articles from here by mail for as long as you choose to stay. But once we return to Montana, I see no reason for you to continue workin'. We'll have all the money we need."

"I *like* to work. Writing has been my life for so long I'm not certain I can stop. I don't want to spend my days in useless pursuits."

"Do you call bein' my wife useless?" Chase was beginning to grow angry. Why was Maggie being so damned obstinate when obviously they loved each other? "What do you want me to say? That I'll give up ranchin' and my way of life to embrace yours? I can't do that, Maggie. There has to be a compromise someplace, and if there is we'll find it."

"When? In a year or two when you're ready to leave the Yukon? I can't sit idle that long, Chase. I have to go back to Seattle. I owe it to the newspaper. They financed my trip up here quite generously."

"I can't bear for you to be so far away," Chase admitted, "though I can understand why you don't want to stay in Dawson."

"Then you agree that I should return to Seattle? When you've gotten your fortune out of Eleven Above, I'll be waiting."

"Will you, Maggie? Or is this merely an excuse to get rid of me? I'm just an uneducated cowboy, not good enough for the likes of you. Has Gordon offered you somethin' better?"

"Leave Scott out of this. I told you I love you. What more do you want?"

"Is it Montana you're resistin', or the notion of givin' up your job?"

Put that way, Maggie was forced to delve deeply into her heart for an answer. "My job is important, Chase, but there's more to it than that. I'm not sure either of us is ready for this kind of commitment. Your wanting to wait a year or two before we're married proves that your claim takes priority over our love. I might actually like Montana, but I'm uncertain enough about it to doubt our future together. I love you, Chase, I want no other man, but perhaps it's wise to allow us a year apart to make certain."

"You think I don't know what I want?" Chase sputtered angrily. "No, Maggie, it's more than that, there's somethin' you're not tellin' me. Either you stay in Dawson and quit your job or you return to Seattle and forget me. It's as simple as that."

"You're giving me an ultimatum?" Maggie gasped, stunned. "Please, Chase, don't do this to us. I told you I'd wait for you, forever if need be."

"In Dawson? Or at the claimsite?"

Sadly, Maggie shook her head, realizing they had reached an impasse that could split them for all time. "I'll be in Seattle, Chase. You have my address."

"Oh, baby, why does it hafta be like this? I love you so damn much it doesn't even matter that you're barren. We can adopt children to leave my fortune to."

"Barren?" Maggie asked stupidly. Suddenly she recalled telling Chase she couldn't bear children so he wouldn't worry about making her pregnant. It could very well be the truth, she reasoned, for she hadn't conceived in all their times together. Maybe she was too old to have children. "But, I—"

"No, enough has been said. We'll discuss this tomorrow. I'm plumb worn out from arguin'. Let me love you again. Our whole world seems to be fallin' apart, and nothin's real but here and now and you in my arms."

"Oh, God, Chase, I'm so afraid," Maggie sobbed, clutching desperately at this man who had taken over her life.

Why did everything seem to be conspiring against them? The riches Chase hoped to find beneath the ground, her responsibility to the newspaper, the year he wanted them to wait before they married, giving up everything she knew and loved to settle in Montana—the list seemed insurmountable. A realist, Maggie always knew love wasn't easy, but she thought that if two people truly loved each other, things would work out. She had a sinking feeling that she and Chase were about to put her theory to the test.

"Don't be frightened, darlin', trust me. Somehow we'll work out all our problems," Chase promised.

"Perhaps you'd better go, Chase. We both have some thinking to do."

"Not before I love you again. Not before I do this." His bold caress sent the breath whooshing from her chest. "Or this," His fingers penetrated her moist warmth, his mouth found hers, and all thought fled as love claimed them and passion whirled them into a star-studded realm where ecstasy ruled.

Afterwards, when sheer exhaustion plunged Maggie into a deep sleep, Chase eased out of bed, dressed quietly, and left the room. He needed to think, and lying with Maggie's soft warmth in his arms was not conducive to the kind of decisions he had to make.

Chapter Fourteen

Scott locked the door to his office and headed toward the barracks to bed down for the night. It was very late, but with the influx of stampeders his workload was extremely heavy. Besides, thinking about Maggie twenty-four hours a day kept his mind in a constant turmoil. It certainly wasn't conducive to helping him deal with the mounds of paperwork accumulating on his desk.

The sounds of laughter and voices raised in argument brought Scott to an abrupt halt before a saloon well known for its rowdiness. As long as he was here, he decided he might as well look in and make certain everything was in order. Sizing up the situation in one sweeping glance, he saw that nothing warranted his intervention and turned to leave. Then he spied Chase sitting at a table in the corner, and he threaded his way through the crowd toward him. He'd been wanting to have a word with the cowboy anyway.

If not for Chase McGarrett, Scott knew Maggie would return his love. Scott had known men like Chase before, and they weren't the marrying kind. He'd use Maggie, break her heart, and leave her bereft and disillusioned. Why couldn't Maggie understand that all Chase was interested in was the gold beneath Eleven Above? While he, Scott, wanted to give Maggie all she deserved, even if it meant leaving the Yukon and Canada and settling wherever she'd be happy. Was McGarrett willing to offer the same things?

"Mind if I join you?"

"Suit yourself."

Scott dropped into a chair, eyed Chase narrowly, and said, "I suppose you've already seen Maggie. I'm surprised you're not still with her." His voice smacked of strong disapproval.

Chase bristled indignantly. He took Scott's words as a direct insult to Maggie's reputation. "What's between me and Maggie is none of your business, Gordon. Contrary to what you think, I'd never do anythin' to hurt Maggie."

"Why don't I believe that?" Scott muttered darkly. "If you don't want to hurt Maggie, you'd get out of her life."

"And leave her to you?" Chase sneered.

"She could do worse. I love Maggie. I love her enough to leave Canada and go wherever she'll be happy. I want children with her. Do you want a family?"

Chase winced. Certainly he wanted children. Of what use was building an empire if there were no children to inherit? Evidently Maggie hadn't confided in Gordon about her inability to conceive. If Maggie didn't want the Mountie to know, Chase certainly wasn't going to tell him. It stung to think that the Mountie was willing to indulge Maggie to the extent of accepting an entirely different way of life, while he, Chase, had delivered an ultimatum. Still, that didn't mean he loved Maggie any less than the Mountie did, Chase reasoned.

"If you've talked to Maggie lately, Gordon, you'd know it's me she loves," Chase said with firm conviction.

"Maybe so, but you're no good for her, McGarrett. How long do you plan on staying in the Klondike? What will Maggie do while you're up here digging? Did you know she's returning to Seattle soon?"

"Not if I can convince her otherwise."

"Think about it, McGarrett," Scott urged, his voice low and strident. "If you truly loved Maggie, you'd let her go now while she can still overcome the pain of losing you."

"With your help, of course," Chase spat. "I reckon you'll be on hand to console her."

Scott shrugged, denying nothing. "It's your choice, McGarrett. If you want Maggie to be happy, don't take her away from her job and expect her to settle down into a proper housewife. She'd hate it, and you'd hate what you forced her to become. Would you give up your ranch for Maggie? I think not."

Having said all he intended to, Scott rose to leave. "One more thing, McGarrett—money won't buy Maggie. It doesn't matter to her if your claim makes you a millionaire." Then he was gone, leaving Chase to stew in the bitter broth of his words.

Without a doubt Chase knew everything the Mountie said was true. Lord knew, he loved Maggie, and she loved him. Nothing or no one could take that from them. But love didn't always insure happiness. He was an uneducated cowboy and Maggie a bright woman entering a new century where vast new horizons and opportunities beckoned. Soon smart, adventurous women like Maggie would be able to choose their own destiny instead of riding the coattails of men. Not that Chase begrudged them their day. He never did believe in the subjugation of women. Soon all states would follow Wyoming's example and give them the right to vote. It would just take some getting use to.

As Chase sat and drank and pondered the future, he came to the startling conclusion that he had no right to demand anything of Maggie. She had earned the right to do and become anything she wanted. She had overcome all adversity in order to gain recognition as a journalist, and she shouldn't be molded into what he wanted her to become. Maggie deserved to bask in the limelight of her accomplishments. It took raw courage and fortitude to reach the Klondike when lesser men failed. Other journalists had made it to Dawson, but Maggie was the first woman, perhaps even the first journalist of any gender, to traverse White Pass in 1897.

By the time Chase left the saloon for his hotel, he knew exactly what he had to do. He hoped the courage of his conviction would lend him the strength necessary to do it.

Maggie frowned in disappointment when she awakened and found Chase gone. He had exhausted her so thoroughly that she had slept the night away and not even noticed when he left her bed. Since awakening, she had given Chase's words considerable thought. If she hadn't realized it before, she knew after last night that she couldn't—didn't even want to—live without Chase. As much as she loved the newspaper and competing in a man's world, she loved Chase more. She wanted to share everything with him—his ranch, Montana, their children. She'd gladly go anywhere with him in order to remain a part of his life. And if that wasn't enough to satisfy her need to fulfill herself as a woman, she could do freelance writing, or attempt a book about her experience. And of course she'd remain in Dawson until she and Chase could leave together.

Pleased with her decision, Maggie began unpacking her newly purchased suitcase, barely able to contain her happiness. The moment Chase returned, she intended to tell him her news and watch his face reveal his joy. She never considered giving up her job and independence as compromising her goals, for without Chase her goals were of little value.

When Chase finally appeared a short time later, he took one look at the suitcase stretched out across the bed and immediately assumed Maggie was packing instead of unpacking.

Maggie flew into his arms, bubbling with the need to tell him of her decision. "I'm glad you're here, Chase, I've something to tell you."

"And I've somethin' to tell you," Chase replied with a definite lack of enthusiasm. "Do you want to go first?"

Maggie wanted to speak first, but sensing his distraction astutely realized that Chase had something to get off his chest, and she wanted his mind unoccupied when she gave him her good news. "You go ahead, love, mine can wait."

Maggie sat on the edge of the bed while Chase began pacing, a small voice telling her that she should have spoken first, that what Chase was about to say might alter their lives forever. "Maybe I should tell you . . ."

"No, Maggie, this needs sayin'," Chase said with firm resolve. "I've been doin' a heap of thinkin' since last night and I reckon I was bein' unreasonable."

"Chase, I—"

"No, Maggie, don't say anythin' 'til I'm done. It's hard enough to say without you interruptin'. What I'm tryin' to tell you is that I have no right dictatin' your future. I realize now you wouldn't be happy livin' in Montana, and I wouldn't consider livin'

anywhere else. You've fought hard for recognition
as a journalist and deserve the accolades. You don't
need me. You're a resourceful, courageous woman,
Maggie Afton. Maybe someday you'll find a man
who's willin' to share you with your first love—
your work. I'm a jealous man, darlin', I want you
all to myself."

A stunned silence followed Chase's words. What
had happened to change Chase's thinking so dras-
tically? Maggie wondered bleakly. Just last night he
had pleaded with her to remain in Dawson. Did he
suddenly decide he didn't need a wife?

"Is this it, then?" Maggie asked, finally finding her
tongue. "Is it over? Are we to go our own ways and
forget the love we shared?"

Forget Maggie? Forget what they had together,
how she made him feel? Impossible! But for Maggie's sake he had to make it sound as if what they
shared was just a passing thing, too hot to last. "Of
course I won't forget you, darlin'. It was wonderful
while it lasted. But we both know somethin' that
good can't last."

"What brought about this sudden decision? What
made you change your mind? Last night you
said . . ."

"Men say many things in the heat of passion,"
Chase replied, hating what he was doing to Maggie but certain it was the right thing. "It suddenly
dawned on me after I left you last night that I'll soon
be rich. I could have as many women as I want, do
what I please. A wife is the last thing I need."

"So that's it," Maggie said with bitter emphasis.
"A wife would cramp your style, prevent you from
enjoying your wealth to the fullest."

Chase winced. Her words made him seem so shallow. If Maggie really believed he wanted to spend his
money on women and debauchery, she didn't know
him very well.

Maggie couldn't think beyond the fact that Chase didn't want her, that becoming rich and sowing wild oats was more important to him than acquiring a wife. My God, how could she have misjudged him so thoroughly? His love for her was no more than a passing fancy; his passion mere lust for her body. She should have realized back in Skagway that she was a handy convenience to him. She had lost her heart to the handsome rogue and Chase had fed upon her love like a hungry wolf, mouthing words that held no meaning.

"Of course," Chase continued blandly, "if I thought there was a possibility our—mating last night could have produced a child, I might have been tempted to change my mind."

Red dots of rage exploded behind Maggie's eyes. Was a child the only way to bind Chase to her? She'd never stoop so low as to use a child to hold a man, especially a man who didn't want her. She had intended telling Chase she wasn't barren, that as far as she knew she was perfectly capable of producing a child—or children. Now it didn't matter, for she'd never have Chase's baby, unless . . . But of course the thought that she'd become pregnant from last night's encounter was ridiculous. She'd escaped unscathed thus far and would do so again.

"Thank God there's no chance I could be carrying your child," Maggie retorted, assuming a haughty manner to disguise her broken heart. The torment of loving Chase, then losing him was a gnawing ache that eroded the self-esteem she'd carefully nurtured all these years. In a few short minutes he had virtually destroyed her. Only her inherent dignity saved her from begging Chase not to abandon her.

"It's just as well," Chase said with soul-wrenching sadness. Was it really over between them? Had he destroyed the love they had shared so easily? He felt hollow inside, bereft of all he held dear. He wanted to scream, to protest the injustice of loving someone so completely he was willing to lose her rather than cause her years of regret and unhappiness. "Maybe I'll look you up in Seattle," he ventured, grasping at straws.

"Don't bother," Maggie advised. "What good will it do?"

"Well, Maggie girl, I reckon there's nothin' more to say," Chase blustered, assuming a cheerful facade. "It was great while it lasted, and I can truthfully say I've never met a woman like you." Nor likely to again, he thought but didn't say.

"There'll never be another like you, Chase." Maggie choked on a sob, her throat raw from holding back the tears. "You'd better go now. I've a lot of thinking to do, plans to make." Deliberately she kept her eyes lowered to hide her pain.

"Not like this, Maggie, not without so much as a kiss to send me on my way." Chase knew he was deliberately torturing himself by prolonging this, but it seemed his life depended on tasting her sweetness one last time.

Startled, Maggie's lids swept upwards, but it didn't prevent Chase from seizing her lips in a kiss that spoke of fire, and passion—and yes, dammit, love. A love he'd just denied. His kiss deepened, outlining her lips with the tip of his tongue, then parting them and plunging inside to savor her sweet essence.

With a will of their own, his hands curled around her buttocks, pulling her close, remembering with vivid clarity how satiny her skin felt against the roughness of his, the fullness of her breasts, the erect tautness of her nipples when aroused by his mouth. How could he leave Maggie when he needed her so desperately? *It's because you love her that you're letting her go*, a small voice within him answered.

Maggie felt the rise of Chase's manhood against the softness of her stomach and knew she had to break off his potent kiss or be damned forever. It would take very little to lose all the sense God gave her and beg him to bed her, and pride be damned. Exerting all the willpower in her slender body, Maggie pulled free of Chase's arms.

"No, Chase, I won't let you use me again." Her voice was a breathless whisper fraught with profound anguish. "We've been lovers, let's part friends. Don't prolong this parting." She offered Chase her hand.

Chase subjected Maggie to a slow, searching look, the finality of their good-bye all but tearing him apart. Evidently Maggie wasn't as devastated by their parting as he was. The thought served only to reinforce his belief that what he was doing was the best thing for Maggie. Stretching his arm forward, he enfolded her small, cold hand in his, then brought it reverently to his lips. He'd never done such a thing before, but somehow it felt right.

"Before I leave, I insist that you take a share of the gold from Eleven Above," Chase said, still holding Maggie's hand as if he never meant to let her go.

"I don't want it," Maggie refused, aghast that Chase felt compelled to pay for her services. "You've already repaid the grubstake I lent you. I've enough left to take care of my needs until I reach Seattle."

"Damnation, Maggie, I insist! You earned it."

"I refuse to be paid like a common whore! Go, Chase, leave me alone."

She turned then, walking to the window while she waited for Chase to leave. "You know I didn't mean it like that," Chase said softly, stunned by her sordid interpretation of what they had shared. When she refused to answer or even acknowledge his presence, Chase took advantage of her turned back and hid the small sack of nuggets beneath the layers of clothing in the suitcase lying open on the bed. Then, slanting a look of utter despair at Maggie's rigid back, Chase quietly left the room, convinced he had done the only responsible thing to guarantee Maggie's happiness.

"Maggie, I know you're in there!"

Scott had been by twice today, but Maggie had no desire to talk to anyone, so she simply refused to answer the door.

"The desk clerk said you haven't left the room or ordered food all day. Are you sick? Please, Maggie, open up or I'll break down the door."

Maggie sighed, aware that this time Scott wouldn't go away. She didn't want to see him, for he'd demand an explanation for her strange behavior. She just wanted to be by herself and wallow in misery.

"I'm coming in, Maggie!"

This time Scott sounded as if he really meant it and Maggie roused herself from her lethargy. "I'm coming, Scott. There's no need for violence." Dragging herself from the chair, she made her way sluggishly to the door.

"Thank God!" Scott said fervently as the door swung open and he pushed inside. "Why is it so dark in here?"

Until that moment Maggie had no idea she'd been sitting in the gloom. The murky shadows of dusk fit her mood perfectly. She watched with little interest as Scott lit a lamp, then turned to study her carefully controlled features.

"You don't look sick."

"I'm not."

"Then why are you hiding in your room? Has something happened?" Scott had a fairly good idea what was ailing Maggie, but he wanted to hear it from her own lips. He had seen Chase McGarrett earlier today looking as bereft as Maggie.

"Nothing has happened," Maggie denied lamely. "You can see for yourself I'm well."

"McGarrett's in town."

Maggie glanced up sharply. "I know."

"You've seen him?"

"Yes."

"Dammit, Maggie, has McGarrett done something to hurt you? If he has I'll—"

"No, Scott, it's nothing like that," Maggie quickly denied—too quickly. "We—Chase and I—merely decided to—part." Her strangled words told Scott that Chase had taken his advice to heart and done what was best for Maggie, and he respected the cowboy for having the courage to make a painful decision.

"I know you think you love the cowboy, but you'll find out soon enough that he doesn't deserve you. You're better off without him."

"I loved him, Scott, but obviously Chase didn't love me enough to include me in his future. There is only one way to do things—Chase's way. My ideas, my hopes and dreams, were too unimportant to consider."

"I know you're hurt, Maggie, but—"

"No, not hurt," Maggie interrupted in the middle of his sentence. "Mad, damn mad. I don't need an illiterate cowboy to mess up my life. I managed well enough before and can do so again."

Suddenly Maggie realized it wasn't the end of her life. Just because she was an unmarried spinster didn't mean she couldn't live a full life. It wasn't the end of the world, just the beginning of a new phase in her life. One without the solace and benefit of love, for it was a foregone conclusion she would never love again. No man could ever take Chase's place in her heart.

Scott smiled approvingly. He knew Maggie's spirit and gumption wouldn't allow her to grieve for long. The world still held too many mysteries for her to withdraw into a shell of despondency.

"You're a woman in a million, Maggie Afton, and I love you dearly," Scott grinned with warm regard. "Do I dare hope that you and I might . . ." His words fell off, allowing Maggie to draw her own conclusions. Instead she chose to ignore them.

"I'm starved, Scott, any chance of buying a girl supper?"

"I'll take you to that new restaurant. It's reported to be the best in town."

"Give me a few minutes to change and freshen up. Would you wait for me in the lobby?"

"Forever, if I have to. Are you certain you're all right?"

"I am now," Maggie said, forcing a smile. "You're just what I needed."

"I always want to be here for you," Scott said with such profound meaning that Maggie felt almost guilty using his love and offering nothing in return.

Maggie's bravado collapsed the moment Scott left the room. How in the world was she supposed to act normal when her heart was breaking? With a jolt, she realized that she was acting like a sniveling fool, something she'd never done before. She'd gotten along thus far alone and she could do so again. Resolve stiffening her spine, Maggie hurriedly washed and dressed and left to meet Scott, determined that Chase shouldn't ruin her life. She was no silly, simpering female who needed a man to make her whole, Maggie chided herself. There was an attractive man waiting to take her to supper and she was damn well going to enjoy herself.

Surprisingly, Maggie did enjoy herself, as well as Scott's company. He was an intriguing man, handsome, witty, kind, and gentle. She thanked God she had someone like Scott around to keep her from feeling sorry for herself. It was a pity Scott could never take Chase's place in her heart.

The air was nippy as they strolled arm-in-arm back to the hotel. They walked on wooden planks placed close to the buildings in order to avoid the oozing mud of the streets. Blaring music and bright lights from a nearby saloon drew Maggie's attention, and she couldn't help but glance inside when they ambled past. Unaccountably her eyes settled on a table located close to the open door, and her steps faltered.

"What is it, Maggie?" Scott asked, following the direction of her gaze. When he saw what had captured her notice, he muttered a string of oaths and propelled her forward. "Forget him, Maggie, he's not worth it."

What Maggie saw in the saloon was a very drunk Chase sitting at a table with one saloon girl on his lap and his arm draped around another. All three were laughing at something Chase had said, his roguish smile blatantly suggestive. Maggie would have stood there staring forever if Scott hadn't literally dragged her down the street.

Chase should have been happy. He was on his way to becoming rich, he had not one but two voluptuous women ready and willing to accommodate him, and the whiskey was damn good, not the "hootch" so many saloons served but real, honest-to-God whiskey. Yet he was miserable. He didn't know doing the "honorable" thing would hurt so damn much. He smiled distractedly at the women draped over and around him, not really seeing them. They were there only because Chase felt the need to pretend cheerfulness, to celebrate when he actually had little to celebrate. Obviously he could not do what he longed to do, make love to Maggie for the rest of his time in Dawson. In the end he handed the two pouting beauties over to another man, staggered to his hotel and went to bed—alone. The next day

Chase returned to the goldfields earlier than he'd planned.

The days progressed with endless boredom as Maggie waited for the *Susie*. In the meantime hundreds of stampeders passed through Dawson City, either on their way to the goldfields or going home, broken and disillusioned at finding not one inch of land available. Some stories had happy endings, for nearly all the claims along the Bonanza and its tributaries yielded gold. Not all the potentially rich miners spent their wealth wisely; some ended up paupers after selling out and returning to the United States to squander huge sums of money.

The other stories were more common. Especially the one about a Russian miner who sold half of his claim for a sack of flour. Then the buyer hit a paystreak that was forty feet wide and yielded five thousand dollars a day for months. Another man, Alex McDonald, swapped and sold mines and became known as the King of the Klondike. Eventually he would squander his money and die broke.

By June there were two-hundred-and-fifty Royal Canadian Mounted Police in Dawson City and thirty thousand people. The Mounties handled most matters. They were customs officers, land surveyors, police, judge, gold commissioners, and governors. It was no wonder Scott's duties kept him busy long hours each day.

Not only were the crowded conditions in Dawson intolerable to Maggie, but she resented the outrageously high price of food and lodging. A new hotel, named the Fairview, was nearly completed. It was said to be the best in town, boasting three stories lighted by electricity and heated with hot air. Board and room for a ten-by-twelve-foot cubicle was rumored to be set at two-hundred-and-fifty dollars a month. Whenever Maggie ventured outside her hotel, she found herself knee-deep in mud.

Only a small portion of residents were permanent. Most were constantly on the move. Streams of men tramped to and from the gold diggings, in and out of saloons and stores. Hundreds of tents were scattered over the swampy flatlands. A surprising number of stampeders actually expected to step ashore at Dawson and begin picking up nuggets from the ground, and they were shocked to learn that all the gold-bearing creeks had long since been staked.

Two interminably long months had elapsed since Maggie said good-bye to Chase. It was difficult to believe their shared rapture was really over. *Men*, she thought disgustedly. Damn them all to hell and back. Not one of them was to be trusted. First Matt and now Chase. They were all scheming creatures driven by their insatiable lusts. Maggie tried to convince herself that those nights of wondrous passion did not exist. They were memories from a dream that had no place in reality. It was over and done with.

It was light for nearly twenty-four hours a day now, and the *Susie* was expected momentarily. But on June sixth, Maggie received a shock that threw her plans in disarray. Word was received in Dawson that the *Susie* had hit an iceberg in the Bering Sea and had limped into St. Michael for extensive repairs. It would be weeks before her sister ship, *Sarah*, reached Dawson. Unwilling to remain in Dawson any longer than necessary, Maggie learned that the first mail steamer was expected soon from Skagway via Whitehorse and the Yukon River. But even if she booked passage, she'd still have to travel over White Pass to Skagway. When Maggie voiced her decision to take that route, Scott protested vigorously.

"There's absolutely no way I'll allow you to travel over White Pass alone," he objected violently, aghast that she would even suggest such a thing. "Look what happened the last time you made that trip."

"Everything is different now," Maggie argued stubbornly.

"Nothing has changed. It's still dangerous, especially for a woman."

"I want to go home, Scott. I want to leave this place and get on with my life."

"Can't you wait for the *Sarah* to arrive?"

"No, I intend to leave as soon as the mail packet docks."

"Then I'll take you. I'm due a leave of absence. I'll make the arrangements and escort you to Skagway myself. I won't be able to stay long, but at least it will give me another chance to convince you to marry me."

Maggie's eyes grew misty. She didn't deserve a friend like Scott. She would miss him dreadfully, but marriage was out of the question where Scott was concerned.

The stern-wheeler *Bellingham* steamed into Dawson two days later. Maggie was surprised to receive a letter from Mr. Grant urging her to hurry home, that her articles had been well received and he anxiously awaited more firsthand reports. His concern and words of praise made Maggie even more determined to leave the Yukon as soon as possible.

Scott made all the necessary arrangements for their passage aboard the *Bellingham*. When the steamer left Dawson, Maggie and Scott were aboard. Fortunately there was cabin space aplenty aboard the mail packet carrying only mail and passengers. Forty feet long, with three decks and two funnels, she steamed out of Dawson on June 16, 1898. Excess freight was pushed ahead on barges one hundred feet long, controlled by ropes and tackle from the steamer. The trip upriver took four days, and the fare was one-hundred-and-seventy-five dollars. Maggie thought the savings in time and energy well worth the cost.

A look of utter amazement crossed Maggie's face when they debarked at Whitehorse at the foot of White Pass. Two other steamers were loading passengers and equipment for the trip downriver to Dawson. The place was a virtual beehive of activity, and a steady stream of goldrushers wound their way down White Pass. It was difficult for Maggie to imagine that a year ago she was one of the people rushing toward Dawson. So much had happened since then. She wasn't the same green girl who left Seattle those long months ago. A handsome cowboy rogue had loved her and changed her life forever.

Their lack of heavy equipment and mounds of supplies made the passage over White Pass much easier than on the previous trip, and Maggie traversed the dangerous trail without complaint. Her courage and stamina never ceased to astound Scott, and he told her so.

"You possess a unique passion for living, Maggie, a rare determination to succeed. You deserve nothing but the best in life, and I'd like to be the one to give it to you."

"Scott, please, you promised."

From the moment they left Dawson days ago, Scott had constantly pressed his suit, hoping to convince Maggie to marry him after they reached Skagway. He had become so persistent that Maggie had asked him to stop, insisting that she needed time to consider his proposal. Chase had left her raw and hurting and in no condition to think seriously of another man for a good long while.

Despite the normal difficulty associated with negotiating White Pass, they stumbled into Skagway without mishap. Maggie was stunned by the changes that occurred in a year's time.

Chapter Fifteen

Soapy Smith's Parlor was still located in the same place on Holly Street, and the Ice Palace seemed to be prospering, as were dozens of other gambling and dancing halls that had sprung up all over town. A line of small cribs used by whores to entertain their customers sat snugly at one end of Broadway. There was the St. James Hotel and the Golden North Hotel on Bond Street, in addition to several others. Several long piers now reached out across the mud flats into the bay. But most amazing of all was the appearance of a church in this lawless city still ruled by Soapy Smith. There also existed a hospital of sorts in the largest log cabin in town. Women and children were now a common sight on the streets, though most had been stranded in Skagway when their men lost their money by various means—mostly at the hands of Soapy Smith and his band of toughs, who still held the town in virtual terror.

Newspapers had also been established in Maggie's absence, two of which were the weekly, four-page Skagway News and the Daily Alaskan. A bank was now in operation and rumored to be stuffed with gold dust and yellow nuggets. Most hotel safes in town were also crammed with the precious metal. Since the steamers had started operating between Dawson and Whitehorse, the journey to Seattle could now be completed in ten days compared to twenty-six days via St. Michael. Miners were depositing hundreds of pounds of gold in Skagway. In addition there were stores with fancy names and scores of new restaurants. Maggie was happy to see that the Hash House appeared to be prospering, sporting a new addition as well as a fresh coat of paint.

During her stay in Skagway, Maggie learned that fifteen thousand persons still lived in tents, shacks, and improvised rooming houses. There were sixty-one saloons, and as many gambling dives, dance halls, and sporting houses. Music halls had been erected as well as theaters, where some of the most famous entertainers of the day performed.

Maggie checked into the St. James Hotel, too weary to do more than bid Scott good night. She ordered a bath, had her supper brought to her, and fell immediately into a deep, dreamless sleep. The next day Scott appeared early to bid her good-bye, for he was obligated to return to Dawson and his duties immediately.

"I won't ask you again to marry me, Maggie," Scott said, his voice choked with emotion. "But you know how I feel about you. I also know how you feel about McGarrett. I'm willing to allow you time to forget him, but expect me to ask you again soon to be my wife."

"You'd come to Seattle?"

"I'd go to the ends of the earth for you. And when I see you again, I won't accept no for an answer,"

Scott confided. "Will you think about me while we're apart?"

"Of course," Maggie smiled fondly. "You've been more than a friend to me, more than I deserve. It would be difficult to forget you."

"Then you don't mind if I visit you in Seattle?"

"I'd be happy to see you, but how can you get away? What about your duties?"

"My enlistment is up next spring. I'll have thirty days then to make up my mind on whether or not to remain with the Mounties. If things work out to my expectations, I may not go back at all," he hinted hopefully. "I want to kiss you good-bye, Maggie."

Maggie accepted Scott's kiss without protest, thinking it little enough payment for all he had done for her. The kiss was pleasant, enjoyable even. She stiffened slightly when his tongue slipped inside her mouth but allowed him access. While Scott was kissing her, the thought occurred to her that, given time, she might be able to love the handsome Mountie, though she knew she'd never find the same kind of passion she enjoyed with Chase. Besides, she'd be doing Scott a grave injustice by settling for a man she liked immensely but didn't love.

"Look for me in the spring, Maggie," were Scott's parting words.

Later that day Maggie ambled over to the Hash House to visit Hannah and Kate and arrange for her trunks of clothing to be delivered to her hotel. Thank God she hadn't taken all her clothing with her to Dawson, for she'd have nothing left to wear except for what little she'd be able to find in the stores. She was greeted with great enthusiasm by her two friends.

"Hot damn, honey, it's good ta see ya," Hannah boomed, thumping her back exuberantly.

"We've been worried about ya," Kate added, somewhat more subdued than her boisterous partner.

"Did ya see Rusty? He left Skagway in late March."

"I saw him," Maggie replied, "on his way through Dawson."

"Was he well?" she asked eagerly.

"Aw, pshaw, Kate, the man was fit as a fiddle when he left here," Hannah guffawed, knowing full well how Kate felt about Rusty. "That old rooster's got a lotta years left in him."

Maggie swallowed a grin when Kate's face turned beet-red. "Rusty was fine when I last saw him, Kate," she said, easing Kate's concern.

"What about Chase?" Hannah probed. "That handsome rogue is a mighty fine specimen. Took a likin' ta him right off, even though he didn't sell me his cows. Can't blame a man fer wantin' the most fer his investment."

Maggie didn't like where the conversation was leading. "Chase and I are friends, nothing more. I'll probably never see him again."

Hannah and Kate exchanged speaking glances but wisely kept their opinions to themselves. It was plain-speaking Hannah who said bluntly, "Heard tell a handsome Mountie brought ya over the pass."

Maggie stifled a groan. Word traveled fast. "I hate to disappoint you two matchmakers, but Scott is a very dear friend who saved my life in the Yukon."

"I reckon that's a story worth hearin'," Kate opined.

"It's a very long story," Maggie said with a hint of underlying sadness. She had little desire to reveal the harrowing details of her narrow escape from death, not once but twice, at the hands of Soapy Smith's toughs. And her days and nights with Chase at Eleven Above were too private to share with another person. It still hurt desperately to think how easily he had bade her good-bye, with no apparent regrets. "I'd rather not go into the details right now. Instead, tell me how you—"

Suddenly Maggie became aware of a thin man in threadbare miner's garb hovering in the doorway, looking as if he wanted to speak to one of them. She stared so hard at the man that both the other women turned to follow her gaze.

"Which one of ya ladies is Kate?" the miner asked, picking his way around tables and chairs.

"I'm Kate, what can I do fer ya?"

Dangling from the stubby fingers of one hand was a rather wrinkled and dirty piece of paper folded over several times. "I brung this all the way over the pass fer ya," the miner said as Kate accepted the much abused missive. "Friend of mine workin' on the Bonanza asked me ta carry it ta ya." Once the letter was in Kate's hand, he doffed his cap, turned, and left as silently as he had appeared.

"It's from Rusty!" Kate crowed, her voice quivering with excitement as she quickly unfolded and read the smudged sheet.

"Well, what's he say?" Hannah demanded to know.

"They hit paydirt!" Kate shrieked, barely able to contain her glee. "Him and Chase struck a paystreak thirty foot wide and are diggin' out nuggets so fast they had ta hire two men ta help them."

"Glory be," Hannah gasped, flapping her apron back and forth to cool her flushed face. "If that don't beat all. Does my heart good to hear a success story after listenin' to all the down-and-out miners passin' through."

"Is that all?" Maggie asked quietly. "Did—did he mention Chase?"

The two women exchanged knowing glances over Maggie's head. "Just that they're both well and workin' their tails off."

"Did they mention when they're coming back?" Maggie probed.

"Nope. Rusty says the paystreak could play out tomorrow or five years from now."

"Glory be," Hannah repeated, unable to comprehend so much money.

Maggie left shortly afterwards to book passage on the steamship *Portland*, due in Skagway in a few days. Nothing to do now, she thought bleakly, but wait—and think. Think about Chase and those eternal nights of endless passion when nothing mattered but being together and the love they shared. Words were unnecessary then. Their bodies said all there was to say; their hearts and minds were so in tune that parting had been a supreme agony. She wished she knew what had happened when Chase returned to Dawson. At first he wanted her, but only on his terms. Then not at all. Evidently striking it rich had changed Chase, Maggie pondered, despising that shiny yellow metal that had the ability to tear people's lives apart.

The next day Maggie had an unpleasant encounter with Soapy Smith. It happened on the wooden sidewalk outside the hotel where she was interviewing disillusioned miners returning home broke and weary. She thought it an appropiate end to her series of articles.

"Still after a story, Miss Afton?" Soapy asked, his voice revealing his shock at seeing her alive and well in Skagway. "I didn't expect to see you back in Skagway. I thought by now you'd be—er, home." It was obvious to Maggie what he meant to say.

"I'm sure you did all in your power to see that I never returned to Skagway," she retorted, her amber eyes flashing dangerously.

Soapy's smile sent a chill racing down Maggie's spine.

"I don't know what you're talking about," he replied with feigned innocence. "By the way, did you happen to meet two friends of mine, Bandy

Johnson and Zeke Palmer, somewhere between here and Dawson?"

Maggie stifled a smile, thinking it would come as quite a shock when Soapy learned his toughs were dead.

"I don't see your cowboy—friend," Soapy continued blandly, certain his men hadn't failed him completely. Bandy and Zeke were two of his most dependable men. Seeing Maggie Afton in Skagway had startled him, for he had thought her dead long ago. "Did McGarrett remain in Dawson."

"You'll be happy to hear Chase is hale and hearty," Maggie goaded gleefully. "His claim is paying off handsomely. By now he's quite rich," she added for good measure. "If you'll excuse me, I've things to attend to before I leave. Oh, and incidently—I hope you enjoy my articles that will appear in the Post-Intelligencer."

Two days later, Friday, July 7, 1898, Maggie was sitting in her hotel room when a commotion below her window drew her attention. A man stood in a circle of onlookers talking furiously and gesturing with frantic motions. She spied Hannah standing on the fringe of the crowd and decided to join her, her agile mind and nose for news ferreting out a story.

"What's happening, Hannah?" Maggie asked when she joined her friend. The crowd was becoming more hostile by the minute and she pulled Hannah back against the building.

"See that fella over there doin' all the talkin'?" Hannah said, pointing to a young man. "His name is John Stewart, and he ain't been in town but a day or two. Accordin' to rumor, he had a poke of twenty-seven hundred in gold and claims he was robbed behind Soapy Smith's Parlor. Seems like a man named Bowers, a well-known member of Soapy's gang, said he was an assayer from a big minin' company and offered to buy Stewart's gold. When Stewart was taken to the rear of Soapy's Parlor, two pals were waitin' to join Bowers. They overpowered Stewart and took his gold from him in broad daylight.

"Stewart sure is raisin' a ruckus, got the whole town up in arms. The dirty dealin's got Soapy's stamp all over it."

"Perhaps Soapy and his toughs have gone too far this time," Maggie suggested cryptically.

While the two women watched the proceedings, a vigilante committee, long inactive, was hastily reactivated and a meeting called. In her capacity as a reporter, Maggie attended the meeting, convened first at Sylvester's Hall but later moved to Juneau dock, taking notes while the committee formed a list of grievances headed by the demand Soapy Smith bring about the return of Stewart's poke. They set a deadline of four o'clock that afternoon. Even though Soapy promised to have the money back by that time, the deadline was not met. Smith began to drink heavily and talk in a rash and defiant manner.

"By damn," Soapy answered when told there'd be trouble if he didn't return the money, "trouble is what I'm looking for."

By eight o'clock that evening, the money was still not returned and another meeting was convened at Juneau dock. Frank Reid, the city engineer, and two other men were named to guard the dock approach in order to protect it from objectionable characters who might disturb the deliberations of the meeting. Maggie was watching from a distance when Smith tried to force his way into the meeting where he was being accused and "tried" without benefit of a court. He carried a Winchester rifle in his hands. Smith was challenged by Reid, one of the guards at the entrance to the causeway. He walked straight up to Reid and with an oath struck him with the barrel of the gun. A scuffle ensued, and bullets flew; both men fell to the ground, mortally wounded. Smith died immediately with a bullet in the heart; Reid hung on for twelve days before succumbing to his wounds.

The next day an inquest completely exonerated Reid; most witnesses agreed that Smith had fired the first shot. The Skagway News ran the headline, "Soapy Smith's Last Bluff Called By Frank Reid," along with a story that took up two pages. Though saddened by the deaths, Maggie wrote a firsthand report, hoping to scoop all other stateside papers.

All the next day, Saturday, Soapy's gang were rounded up and jailed by the vigilantes. On Sunday, one of the men who supposedly robbed Stewart, "Ole Tripp," came into town and gave himself up rather than starve to death in the mountains where he was hiding with his friends. He was confined to a room on the second floor of the Burkhard Hotel. Acting on Tripp's information, Marshal Tanner dispatched thirty armed men to search for Tripp's three accomplices. The trio—Bowers, Foster, and Wilder—were subsequently caught and placed under heavy guard with Tripp.

Hundreds of citizens congregated that night outside the Burkhard Hotel, demanding justice, but Marshal Tanner's honesty and cool head prevented a disaster. For more than an hour he valiantly fought with the enraged crowd for the protection of his prisoners in the name of the law. Before a detachment of soldiers arrived a few hours later from Dyea to take charge of the prisoners, an unsuccessful rush was made to take the men and hang them.

In desperation, one of the men jumped from the second-story window and attempted to flee amidst flying bullets, which miraculously missed him. He was caught, and it looked as if he'd end up swinging from a rope until Marshal Tanner intervened. Thus ended an era in Skagway history and the end of the worst hellhole on the face of the earth.

During the days history was being made in Skagway, Chase McGarrett arrived in town. His first stop was at the Hash House, where an excited Hannah filled him in on the momentous events of the past two days.

"It's about time someone done that scoundrel in," Chase grunted, thinking of his own poke that had been stolen.

"What brings ya ta Skagway?" Kate asked when they had exhausted the subject of Soapy. "Where is Rusty?"

Chase smiled, aware of the tender feelings Kate and Rusty shared. Who'd have thought a crusty old warrior like Rusty would fall in love at his age? "I'm alone, Kate. There's been such an influx of men to Dawson this spring that food is in short supply. We can't last another winter, especially if it's as hard as the last, on what supplies we have left. I'm younger than Rusty, so I volunteered to make the trip to Skagway for supplies. Rusty sends his best to you."

"Did ya really strike it rich?" Hannah asked, blunt and direct as ever.

"Yep, one of the richest on the Bonanza."

Though Chase should have been ecstatic, a shadow of sadness dulled his blue eyes, as if he were glimpsing a bleak future instead of looking forward to rosy tomorrows living in the lap of luxury. Both women were astute enough to recognize the cause of Chase's apparent apathy.

If Rusty were there, he would have told them how restless and unhappy Chase had been these past weeks, despite the vast wealth they were digging up daily. He would have mentioned how Chase slept little, brooding constantly over something he refused to talk about, although Rusty knew darn well it involved

Maggie Afton. Chase was too damn tight-lipped to talk about the problem, so Rusty remained in the dark as to what happened between Chase and Maggie. It was Rusty who insisted Chase go to Skagway after supplies, hoping to distract him from his doldrums. Hannah knew none of this but managed to put her finger on Chase's problem immediately.

"Have ya seen Maggie yet?" she asked, startled by Chase's reaction to her innocent question.

The mention of Maggie's name seemed to strike a chord in Chase, and he leapt to his feet. "Maggie, here? In Skagway? I thought she left months ago by way of St. Michael. What happened?"

"Why don't ya ask her yerself. Her ship don't leave till tomorrow."

The thought that Maggie was in Skagway stunned Chase. So close—so damn close. All he had ever wanted in life was right here within his grasp, but sadly he had relinquished all his rights to claim Maggie in Dawson. Did he regret it? Damn right he did. Was it too late to make things right with the woman he loved? Ever since their disastrous last meeting he had cursed himself over and over for what he had done. Would Maggie forgive him for being such a damn fool?

He left the Hash House so abruptly that Hannah and Kate could only look at each other in amazement.

"What do ya 'spose is eatin' on him?" Kate asked curiously.

"I'd say that cowboy has a heap of explainin' ta do if he wants ta make things right with Maggie. They're so damn in love with one another they're miserable apart and both too stubborn ta give an inch."

"Maggie's stayin' at the St. James Hotel," Kate called to Chase's departing back.

The streets were filled with people, everyone talking about the death of Soapy and the roundup of his toughs. Chase paid little heed to the gossip, concentrating instead on what he intended to say to Maggie. When he neared the St. James, his steps faltered, his thoughts scattering like ashes before the wind. What could he do to convince Maggie he meant nothing of what he had said in Dawson? At the time he truly felt it best that they part. He had foolishly let the Mountie convince him that Maggie would be better off without him, even though it broke both their hearts. Distractedly he wondered if Gordon had proposed to Maggie and if she had accepted. He'd find out soon enough, he reckoned as he entered the hotel lobby.

The desk clerk gave Chase Maggie's room number and assured him Maggie was in. Chase slowly mounted the stairs, his heart pounding like a triphammer. He was the stupidest man alive to have given Maggie up so easily—and for listening to the Mountie who obviously wanted her for himself.

Maggie sat at the small desk writing in her journal, perhaps for the last time, about the events of the past three days. Beginning with Friday, the day Stewart reported his poke stolen, and ending with the townspeople's aborted attempt an hour ago to hang one of the men responsible. She had it all down on paper, having been present throughout most of the events as they unfolded. She had returned to the hotel when Marshal Tanner restored order and the soldiers arrived, wanting to record it while it was still fresh in her mind. The knock at her door surprised her, for she wasn't expecting visitors. Chase was the last person in the world she expected to find standing outside her door, and her shocked expression showed it.

"Chase! My God! I—what are you doing here?"

"Can I come in? What I have to say is a mite private."

"I thought we said it all in Dawson," Maggie said dismissively.

"I was a damn fool to think I could walk away from you so easily," Chase said with self-derision. "Please, darlin', hear me out."

Maggie sighed, resigned to the fact that Chase was here, in Skagway, likely to break her heart again and she couldn't do a thing about it. Why did he have to show up now and remind her how much she still loved him?

"Come in, Chase. Say your piece, then go. I'm leaving on the *Portland* tomorrow and I still have packing to do."

Chase eased inside the room and closed the door behind him. "You look wonderful, Maggie, lovelier than I remember, if that's possible."

"I understand congratulations are in order," Maggie said, adroitly changing the subject. "I hear you're on your way to becoming a millionaire."

"Tarnation, Maggie, I didn't come to discuss the state of my finances."

"Why did you come? How did you know I was in Skagway?"

"I didn't. Hannah told me you were in town. I assumed you had returned to Seattle weeks ago by way of St. Michael."

"Then why *are* you here?" Maggie was more than a little disappointed that Chase hadn't come to Skagway on her behalf. She was hoping . . . Ah, well, it wasn't the first time the cowboy had deluded her with his sweet talk.

"I'm in Skagway to buy supplies. Everythin' in Dawson is plumb gone. There's been so many people flockin' up to the Klondike that existin' supplies won't last the winter. I aim to carry enough back to last a good long spell. Findin' you here was well worth the trip."

"Why?" Maggie asked, presenting her back. "I thought we parted for good back in Dawson."

Chase spared a few moments to admire the elegant curve of Maggie's slim back before speaking. He loved every inch of it, remembered the satiny texture of her skin beneath his fingertips, recalled vividly the unique way her flesh responded to his touch.

"I never stopped lovin' you," Chase said quietly, causing her to whirl around to face him.

"You have a damn funny way of showing it," she observed with cool deliberation.

"I did what I thought best at the time," Chase ventured. "I—I'm not right for you, Maggie. I didn't want to make you unhappy by forcin' you into somethin' you didn't want."

Maggie appeared unmoved by his words.

"In my heart I believe God granted me this chance to make things right between us. He knows how much I love you. Eventually we would have found a solution to our problems."

"Oh, Chase, couldn't you trust me to know what is right for myself?" Maggie challenged. "I have to go back to Seattle now to fulfill my obligations, but one word from you and I'd have waited for you as long as need be. Given time, we would have found a way to surmount whatever obstacles stood in our way. When you decided we should part, I assumed you didn't love me. If you wanted me, Chase, you had only to tell me and I'd be yours."

"What about Gordon? Did you make him any promises?"

Maggie sighed wearily. "Scott will always be a good friend, but that's all. I don't love him the way . . ."

" . . . you love me?" Chase finished hopefully. "Damnation, Maggie, I was such a dadblamed fool! Tell me you forgive me. Tell me you still love me. Tell me . . . Tell me. . . ."

He reached for her then, almost afraid to touch her, fearing rejection. But she didn't resist, sliding into his arms with effortless ease. Her slanting amber eyes were alive and sparkling; the shaft of sun piercing the window framed the golden halo of her hair. He kissed her frantically, delving, tasting, consuming, until Maggie was shaking like a leaf in his arm and desire fogged her mind.

"I love you, Chase—I always have, even when you didn't want me."

"I never stopped wanting you. Do you forgive me?"

"I—if you're sure."

"I've never been more sure of anythin' in my life."

"Then I forgive you."

"Maggie, Maggie, darlin', love me. Love me for all the empty yesterdays, for all those nights I longed to hold you but couldn't."

His words stroked her gently, creating a shiver of pleasure. His fingers tunneled through the bright tendrils of hair that fell about her cheeks in glorious disarray, his eyes memorizing each detail of her exquisite features. She answered Chase's passionate plea by extending her fingers and one by one undoing the buttons on the front of his jeans, releasing his hot, full maleness, her delicate touch brushing over him, caressing him lightly.

"No, darlin', not yet," Chase groaned, removing her hand. "Let me undress you first. I need to fill my eyes with the sight of you. It's been so long—so damn long. I'm sorry for the pain I caused you."

"Don't tell me how sorry you are—show me," Maggie whispered seductively.

His blue eyes danced mischievously as he undressed her with agonizing slowness. Piece by piece the layers fell away, exposing exciting expanses of white, silken flesh. When he had stripped her down to corset, pantalettes, and stockings, Chase stepped back to admire the perfection of her scantily clad form. A teasing smile lifted the corners of his mouth as his eyes dropped to the outrageously sexy panties that spanned her slim hips.

"Where in tarnation did you find French underwear in Skagway?" Chase asked, pretending to be scandalized by the tantalizing sight.

"Hannah and Kate stored most of my belongings in their storeroom at the Hash House," Maggie grinned saucily. "I brought these from Seattle with me."

"I always was partial to sexy French underwear," Chase admitted, flashing a roguish grin, "and I aim to buy you dozens of pairs when we're married—but right now I'm hankerin' to see you without them."

He stripped them from her with a flick of the wrist, then her stockings and corset, until she stood before him nude and vulnerable to his every desire. When he moved to embrace her, Maggie shook her head, holding Chase at arm's length while she began to undress him, as slowly and deliberately as he had her. She paused often to taste his skin with her mouth, sample the salty texture with her tongue, and gently nip the rippling muscles beneath his flesh.

When Chase could take no more of her tender torment, he scooped her into his arms and carried her the few steps to the bed. Stretching out beside her, he spread slow, sweet nibbles across her flat stomach, teasing and suckling her breasts with tender, moist strokes of his tongue.

His hunger for her made him bold and relentless, wanting to give her pleasure, seeking the ultimate ecstasy, allowing her to keep nothing from him. He demanded her very soul as his mouth sought the sweet essence of her. Waves of wanton rapture poured through Maggie's loins and flooded her slender thighs, and she shuddered roughly, drew a quick breath, and shuddered again. Brutal pleasure wracked her body, but Chase did not lift his mouth from her until her surrender was complete and she lay perfectly still, her breathing coming in hoarse gasps as she whispered his name over and over.

Chase growled deep in his throat. Then he was inside her, lifting her naked hips to his. She quivered, renewed desire rising swiftly as she opened her thighs hungrily, feeling him press deep—so deep, until he had no more to give her. His bold thrusts carried her back into the world of wild ecstasy she had left just moments ago as he stroked her to a second climax as explosive as the first.

A groan of unholy torment erupted from Chase's lips as his body responded to the scent and feel of the extraordinary woman in his arms. He took her mouth with a wild, hungry kiss, his passion honed and sharpened by Maggie's eager response. Suddenly Chase stiffened, his cry smothered in the moist recess of Maggie's mouth. A blossom of sublime pleasure unfolded inside her as her own climax shattered the world into tiny fragments of pleasure.

Chapter Sixteen

Slowly descending from the most incredible experience of her life, intuitively Maggie understood that her life would never be the same. As important as her career was to her, it wasn't as necessary to life as Chase was. Chase McGarrett, a cowboy with little finesse but capable of taking her to untold heights of rapture, was the only man she would ever love.

Chase shook like a leaf, appalled at how close he had come to losing Maggie forever. How could it be wrong or destructive to love someone so desperately, to want that person with every breath? All his wealth meant nothing without Maggie to share it with. During his life he'd had sex with dozens of women, some he was fond of, but nothing compared to what he experienced when he made love with Maggie. No matter what it took, Maggie would be his forever.

Chase slowly ran his hands over Maggie's trembling body, adoring every inch of her luscious curves.

"I don't want to lose you, darlin'," he said, his voice laced with desperation. "Marry me, Maggie girl—now, today. I'm afraid of losing you if we wait."

"You won't lose me, Chase, not now, not ever. I'm yours for as long as you want me."

"That's forever." Chase grinned happily. "Shall I hunt up a preacher?"

Maggie worried her bottom lip with small white teeth as she pondered Chase's question, undecided. They had so little time before the *Portland* sailed in the morning that she hated to waste a moment of it. There was ample time to marry when Chase came for her in Seattle. They could have a proper wedding, one she'd always dreamed about. She'd ask Mr. Grant to give her away. There was still a great deal for her and Chase to decide upon, still much left unsaid and unresolved.

"I haven't changed my mind about going home," Maggie ventured hesitantly. "I've obligations to fulfill. I can't just quit my job after the paper paid my expenses to the Yukon. And the claim will occupy your time for the next several months. I'll wait, Chase, as long as necessary, and we'll be married in Seattle."

Chase considered Maggie's words carefully. "I reckon you're right, darlin'. I'd hate for you to be stranded in the Klondike another winter, or alone in Skagway. It's no place for a woman. I'd rather marry you here and now, but if you want to wait, I 'spose it can't hurt none. Just remember, you're mine."

"Forever," Maggie said, snuggling into this arms. "There's still several hours left before I have to board the *Portland* . . . are you going to waste them?"

"No way," Chase replied, his eyes darkening to smoldering gray. "I'm gonna love you so thoroughly, you'll never forget me. I want enough memories to warm me all those cold, bleak nights to come."

*   *   *

Purple smudges lined Maggie's amber eyes the next morning when Chase delivered her to the quay where the *Portland* docked, but her obvious exhaustion wasn't the cause of her distress. When the actual time arrived to bid Chase good-bye, it nearly tore her apart. All manner of things tripped through her mind. Suppose something happened to Chase in the Klondike? So many dangers existed in this wilderness that just thinking of them filled her heart with dread.

Chase insisted on accompanying Maggie aboard the ship and settling her into a comfortable cabin on the upper deck. Before he left, he placed several gold nuggets into the room steward's hand, charging him with seeing to Maggie's comfort. Then he dropped those remaining in the sack in Maggie's pocketbook, refusing to listen to her protest.

"Consider it an engagement present," he said.

Lumps as large as stones lodged in Chase's throat when it came time to say good-bye, and his eyes grew suspiciously moist. "Come what may, I'll see you in the spring," he vowed urgently as he took her in his arms.

His kiss was sweet and filled with tender promise. Maggie felt his yearning, his fears, the deep conviction of his love. Chase felt Maggie's response, the pounding of her heart against his chest, and marveled that so beautiful and intelligent a lady could want him as much as he wanted her. Then it was time to go.

"Don't forget, darlin'—spring. I'll start down as soon as the ice breaks up on the lakes. No later than April. Plan as big a weddin' as you want. You deserve the best."

"I love you, Chase."

Chase had time for one last quick kiss, then, as an afterthought, whispered in Maggie's ear, "I don't care about the babies, Maggie, I don't need them as long as I have you. The little critters are too much trouble anyways." Part of what he said were downright lies but he wanted Maggie to know he loved her despite her inability to bear children.

Maggie was confused—until she recalled that Chase still thought she couldn't have children. Somehow she never got around to telling him the truth. "Chase, wait!" But it was too late. He was already bounding down the gangplank.

Chase's parting words caused Maggie a twinge of guilt as well as considerable anguish in the days that followed. Did Chase really mean he didn't want children? She knew most men wanted an heir or two. Suppose Chase merely said he didn't want children for her benefit? Suppose he said it to assuage her supposed guilt for being unable to bear children? Somehow she had managed to get herself into an unexpected predicament. The only way out was to admit she had lied, and the sooner she did it the better.

Maggie couldn't imagine a life without Chase's children and had hoped Chase felt the same, but his parting words left a doubt in her mind. The only reason she had lied to him in the beginning was that she didn't want to trap him into marriage should their loving result in a child. If she had become pregnant during their times together, she would never have told Chase unless he had already asked her to be his wife. A forced marriage to legitimize a child was a subterfuge Maggie would never countenance.

The *Portland* steamed into Seattle amid much fanfare, for many stampeders were returning from the Klondike, some of them with tremendous wealth. The gold rush was still big news and people crowded the docks whenever a ship arrived from Alaska and the Yukon. Maggie slipped through the throngs, collected her baggage, and hired a hack to take her to her small flat. She had been gone almost a year and so much had happened in that time that she felt like an alien in a foreign country. Nothing had changed, yet everything seemed different. Loving Chase had altered the entire fabric of her life. She must have been half a woman before meeting Chase. He might be a roguish cowboy, but he was the only man for her.

The next morning Maggie created quite a stir when she appeared at the newspaper. Her first articles had already been published and brought sufficient acclaim to assure her the recognition she'd strived so hard to attain. In fact, her fellow workers held her in such awe, they clamored around her for details of her adventure. Noting that Maggie was having difficulty extracting herself from the group of admirers surrounding her, Mr. Grant came to the rescue.

"Welcome home, Maggie," the beaming editor said. "I began to doubt we'd ever see you again. Was the Klondike so attractive you couldn't tear yourself away? Come into my office where we can talk without being disturbed.

"Maggie, I'm damn proud of you," Fred Grant expounded once they had gained the privacy of his small office. "I must admit, I hadn't planned on your being gone a year, but if your other articles are as good as the first ones I received, it will all be worthwhile. You're damn near a heroine, Maggie, surviving up there in the north country amidst all the hardships. My God, you must have endured hell in the Klondike!"

"It wasn't so bad," Maggie shrugged, thinking of all those endless days and nights spent loving Chase while snowbound at Eleven Above. "Everything is recorded in my journal," she said, plunking her briefcase down on his desk. "There are interviews, firsthand reports of the demise of Soapy Smith and his gang, and my experiences in Skagway and the Klondike. I think you'll be pleased."

"Pleased is too tame a word—I'm ecstatic. I have to admit I was worried about you. I would have blamed myself if anything had happened to you. Are you all right? You look a little peaked, and thinner than I remember."

"I'm fine, Mr. Grant, truly," Maggie assured him.

"Would you like a few days to settle in before returning to work?"

"No, there's too much to do. I want to finish the rest of the articles and get back to reporting. About the photographic equipment—it was wrecked by Soapy Smith's thugs. I'm sorry."

"My God, Maggie, what happened?"

"It's a long story, Mr. Grant, involving Smith and being abducted by his men. I have it all down on paper, including firsthand reports of the events leading to Soapy's death. I'll leave them here so you can look through them."

"Abducted! I knew I shouldn't have given in so easily and allowed you to go to the Klondike on your own. There will be a big raise for you, Maggie, and recognition for your fine work. Your next article will run in tomorrow's edition with your byline in big letters. It's regretable about the equipment, but human life is more valuable. I'm glad you've come back to us safe and sound."

Maggie started to rise, thought better of it, and sat back down. "Is there something else?" Grant asked curiously. "If you need money, I've already arranged for your back pay."

"No, it's not that, it's—I'm engaged."

"Engaged! My word, when did all this come about? Do I know the young man?"

The announcement of Maggie's engagement shocked Fred Grant more than any of the astounding adventures she wrote about. He had assumed her career was too important to her to ever marry. When a woman reached twenty-six, she was likely to be set in her ways and considered unmarriageable. It would take a special kind of man to handle headstrong Maggie Afton properly, and Fred Grant sincerely hoped she had found that man.

"I met him in Skagway—actually, aboard the *North Star*. His name is Chase McGarrett and he owns a spread in Montana," Maggie explained. "He's the man who took me over White Pass to the Klondike. He and his partner own a claim on Gold Bottom. We fell deeply in love."

"Montana, you say?" Grant asked sharply. "Does that mean I'm going to lose my ace reporter?"

"Chase is a rancher. I doubt he'll want to live anywhere but Montana. But we haven't actually discussed it yet. He's promised to return next spring, and I certainly intend to remain on the job till then."

"Is this McGarrett one of the lucky ones with a claim on the Bonanza to hit paydirt?"

"Yes, extremely lucky," Maggie confirmed happily. "He'll return to civilization quite rich."

"I'll hate losing you, but you deserve the best, Maggie. I hope the young man appreciates you, you're one in a million."

Maggie received tremendous satisfaction from seeing her stories and articles appear prominently in the Post-Intelligencer. Some of her work was picked up by newspapers all over the country. Because her picture was shown above her articles, she captured immediate recognition wherever she went. She became an overnight celebrity; people spoke glowingly of her pioneering spirit and love of adventure. Consequently she was courted by large Eastern newspapers and much sought after as a lecturer. What thrilled Maggie most was the fact that her talent and ability were finally recognized and publicly acknowledged. A renowned book publisher had promised immediate publication of a book she was working on in her spare time, a work of fiction involving the lives of stampeders and the families they left behind. If it hadn't been for missing Chase so desperately, her life would have been perfect.

Maggie had achieved so much this past year—recognition, an adventure most women only dreamed about, and love, by far the most important of her accomplishments. But two months after her return, Maggie learned that the love she and Chase shared was soon to bear fruit. A visit to the doctor confirmed her suspicion; she was expecting Chase's child. A child he might not want, if his parting words were any indication.

According to Maggie's calculations, she could continue working for several months yet, at least until the first of the year, if she was careful with her diet and wore loose-fitting clothes. By then her articles on the Yukon would be completed and she could take a well-deserved leave of absence. She could say she wanted time to complete her novel and no one would be the wiser. After much agonizing, she decided she owed it to Mr. Grant to confide in him.

Instead of heaping condemnation on her, Fred Grant showed rare compassion for Maggie's plight. "Is there any way to get in touch with your fiance?" he asked, concern coloring his words. "I'll use all my influence to see that your message is delivered."

"It's already late September," Maggie said, gratified by Mr. Grant's sympathetic response to her condition. "The passes may already be closed and the lakes and rivers frozen over. Sometimes mail reaches the Klondike by dog sled, but I'm not certain Chase will winter in Dawson to receive mail. And—and I'd hate for him to learn something like this in a letter."

"What are your plans? I'll stand by you what-ever you decide. You're a remarkable young woman, Maggie Afton."

"You're a remarkable man, Mr. Grant, and I value your friendship. If you don't object, I'd like to con-tinue working through December. Then I'll request a leave of absence until my child is born sometime in late April. I'd prefer that my fellow workers not know, since they might not be as understanding as you. I can use the free time to work on my book."

During the next three months, Maggie's job con-sumed most of her time. Her initial articles set up a clamor for more of the same and she was pleased to comply. In addition, she sold several short sto-ries using characters she had encountered along the Yukon Trail. She wished her father had lived to see her success but drew comfort from the knowledge that he would be extremely proud of her.

It was the only comfort Maggie received during those long weeks, for she heard nothing from Chase—not one solitary word. As her pregnancy progressed, doubt took root in her brain and refused to be dislodged.

Had Chase forgotton so soon the vows they had exchanged, the love they shared? She berated her-self endlessly for not marrying him in Skagway. Had she agreed to a ceremony back in July, her child would be born with his father's name. But she had grown complacent, thinking she was immune to pregnancy since it hadn't happened before now. What was Chase going to think when he returned and found her bulging with his child? Why had she foolishly allowed him to believe she couldn't conceive? Hindsight was a bitter brew she was now choking on, Maggie reflected glumly, regretting her actions, no matter how well-intentioned.

When Maggie left the newspaper on the last day of December 1898, no one but Mr. Grant knew she was expecting in four short months. The slight curve of her abdomen was well-concealed beneath the loose folds of her clothing, with no one the wiser. Though Maggie felt well, and the doctor pronounced her fit, she had gained little weight. In fact, Mr. Grant had expressed concern several times over her too-slim figure. Small babies ran in her family—Maggie herself had only weighed only five pounds at birth—and the baby seemed to be thriving. Naturally slim, Maggie took her slender proportions in stride, for she'd already experienced movement within the narrow confines of her womb and knew Chase's child prospered. If only she was as certain of Chase as she was of his child.

Maggie didn't venture far from her flat during January and February. By now some of her neighbors recognized her condition, noted her unwed state, and promptly shunned her—all but a friendly older couple who had no children of their own. Ivan and Jenny Greene went out of their way to be kind to Maggie and she greatly appreciated their visits. They never questioned or condemned her but quietly let her know they'd be there should she need them. It was good to know someone besides Mr. Grant cared about her welfare.

As for Chase, he was conspicious only by his absence, though Maggie was convinced he'd arrive in plenty of time for the birth of their child.

April arrived; Chase did not. Maggie attained the great age of twenty-seven.

Standing outside the cabin at Eleven Above, Chase watched the sun rise for the first time after a dismal winter. The harsh months hadn't prevented him and Rusty from working, though. All summer they had dug chunks of gold from the ground, their wealth accummulating at a shocking rate. Just before the first snowfall, they made a trip to Dawson City to deposit their cache in one of the newly opened banks. On those days during the long winter months when they were unable to venture outside due to severe weather, Chase and Rusty spent long hours reminiscing about Montana and their ranch.

Though the Yukon had been good to them, both longed to return to the land of the big sky. Rusty had decided to ask Kate to return with him to Montana and share his life. Chase was cheered by the fact that Maggie waited for him in Seattle. Now, as the sun rose over the horizon, Chase turned to Rusty and saw in his eyes the same kind of longing that plagued his own troubled mind.

"You thinkin' what I'm thinkin', son?" Rusty asked, his gravely voice oddly choked.

"Reckon I am," Chase admitted.

"I ain't no miner, and I reckon I'm rich enough ta suit me. I'm all fer sellin' out ta one of them big Eastern companies and headin' home. This climate makes my bones ache somethin' fierce." He searched Chase's face, hoping his partner's sentiments matched his own.

"It takes a heap of worryin' off my mind to know you feel the same," Chase returned. "I promised Maggie I'd see her in Seattle in April, and I'm not hankerin' to spend another winter up here. We've enough money to buy half of Montana if we wanted to."

"You gonna marry the girl?" Rusty asked bluntly.

"Yep. I love Maggie and she loves me. It scares the hell outta me to think how close I came to losin' her to that Mountie."

"Maggie is a damn fine woman, son, but it ain't gonna be easy fer her ta give up her job and settle down ta ranchin'."

"She's agreed to live with me in Montana, and that's a start. We'll take it one day at a time. I only know I want Maggie in my life despite the fact that she can't—" He hesitated, unwilling to reveal something so personal about Maggie.

Rusty waited for Chase to continue, but when he deliberately remained mum, the older man, not one to deliberately pry, let the subject drop. Instead, he said, "Life ain't gonna be no picnic with Maggie, but it sure as shootin' won't be dull. I can hardly wait ta dangle yer younguns on my knee."

Chase said nothing, and Rusty was too consumed with the happy thought of children to notice the grim line forming around Chase's mouth. Chase was determined that no one ever know how deeply Maggie's inability to have a child disappointed him. He silently vowed never to burden Maggie with those profound feelings, but to find happiness with the life the two of them would make together.

"I'll start packin'," Rusty continued. "Soon's we unload this place, we can collect our gold in Dawson and hightail it down to Skagway. The passes should be open by then. Mayhap the railroad over White Pass is runnin' by now and we can ride over in comfort."

On April 2, 1899, Rusty and Chase signed the deed to Eleven Above over to an Eastern mining company that intended to bring in steam-driven equipment to strip the gold from beneath the surface. To their utter amazement, they received seventy-five thousand dollars for the claim. That sum, in addition to the thousands already deposited in the bank, made them wealthy beyond their wildest dreams.

While in Dawson, Chase saw nothing of Scott Gordon and assumed he was somewhere in the area about his duties. Not that it mattered. Chase cared little for the man who tried to steal Maggie from him. Now that he was so close to seeing his love again, all he wanted was to leave this desolate wasteland as quickly as possible. Something deep inside him drove him to urgency. Some gut feeling told him Maggie needed him. Chase knew it was crazy to feel this way, for Maggie was adept at taking care of herself. But still the feeling persisted. The day he would board the steamer to Whitehorse arrived with a mixture of relief as well as tremendous satisfaction.

With the birth of her child imminent, Maggie rarely left her flat now. Jenny Greene did what little shopping was necessary and looked in on her nearly every day. Maggie still hadn't gained much weight, and though she definitely looked pregnant, she did not appear large enough to give birth any time soon. The air of expectancy grew each day as she waited for Chase. Though he had promised to come to her in the spring, April was nearly gone and Maggie grew apprehensive. Yet each day her excitement increased, knowing every passing day brought Chase closer to her.

Maggie's one consuming fear had to do with Chase's reaction to her pregnancy. He had said he didn't want children and would surely be shocked at her condition. Especially after the deliberate falsehood she had told him. She knew she had a lot of explaining to do and hoped Chase loved her enough to accept her explanation and their child.

One day in mid-April, Maggie felt exceptionally well, but was unprepared for the shock she received when she opened her door to admit a surprise visitor. Though Scott Gordon had told her to expect him in Seattle in the spring, Maggie never imagined he'd actually show up, considering how little encouragement she'd given him. But here he was, bigger than life, handsome as ever, and staring at her protruding stomach with a combination of horror and anger.

"My God, Maggie, I'll kill the bastard for what he did to you!"

"Come inside, Scott," Maggie urged, unwilling to air her problems to prying ears. Seeing Scott again had unsettled her more than she cared to admit, reviving memories of all those months she'd spent in the Yukon and the passion Chase had unleashed in her.

"Why isn't McGarrett with you?" Scott asked the moment the door closed behind him. "Did he marry you before you left Skagway? I heard he was there the same time you were late last summer. I wondered if you two had met; now I can see that you did." His eyes settled accusingly on her stomach. "He was still working the claim when I left Dawson. Does he know about the baby?"

"We talked about marriage when we met in Skagway but decided to wait," Maggie revealed sheepishly. "I—I wanted Chase to be certain. When we parted, I had no idea about the baby. I didn't write him because it was something I'd rather do in person and I wasn't certain a letter would reach him. Chase promised he'd come to me in the spring, and I've been hoping he'd arrive before the baby does."

"You're a fool if you expect McGarrett to keep his word," Scott said with quiet emphasis. "He's rich beyond his wildest dreams. If he's like most men he'll head for civilization with his pockets bulging and wanting to taste life to the fullest. That hardly includes accepting responsibility for a wife and child. His absence when you need him most should tell you what kind of man he is."

"Chase isn't like that," Maggie protested. Somehow her protests sounded weak compared to Scott's knowledge of men and their needs.

"Maggie," Scott said softly, leading Maggie to the sofa and sitting down beside her, "I'm not saying this to hurt you. I'd never do that. I just can't bear to see you suffer because of McGarrett's thoughtlessness. I can understand his wanting you—God knows I've wanted you myself—but he should have taken precautions that this"—he gestured toward her protruding stomach—"didn't happen."

Maggie flushed, aware that her lies had placed her in this awkward position, not Chase's thoughtlessness. She didn't want Scott thinking the worst of Chase so she decided to be brutally honest, even though her integrity would suffer in Scott's opinion. "Chase thought I couldn't conceive."

"What would make him think a thing like that?"

"I told him."

"You! But—I don't understand. Obviously it was a lie."

"It was a lie. I didn't want Chase to feel obligated or his feelings for me be influenced should our—relationship result in a child," Maggie revealed, stunning Scott. "I'd never trap a man into marriage that way. I know it was a deliberate lie, and I should have considered the consequences and how Chase would react should the inevitable happen. I'm scared to death he'll hate me or not want his child."

"Only a fool would not want you or deny his own child," Scott replied, scoffing at so outlandish a notion. "I'd marry you today and claim your child if you'd have me."

Maggie's amber eyes grew misty. Any woman would consider herself lucky to have the love of a fine man like Scott. He deserved someone who could return his love fully, not a woman burdened with another man's child. Besides, she hadn't given up on Chase. She had faith in him, knew he would return just as he promised. Whether or not he'd still want her when he learned she'd been caught in the web of her own deceit was another matter altogether.

The look in Maggie's eyes gave mute testimony to her feelings where Chase was concerned, dashing whatever hopes Scott had built for a future with Maggie. "Do you love him so much?"

"With all my heart," came Maggie's passionate reply.

Defeat tasted bitter on Scott's tongue, and it was with a heavy heart that he finally acknowledged it. But he cared too much about Maggie to abandon her now when she desperately needed someone. "How long before the baby is due?"

"Not long, a week or two," Maggie said shyly, somewhat embarrassed to be questioned so closely about so personal an event.

"I'll stay until McGarrett arrives," Scott insisted, his tone brooking no argument. "I've a whole month's leave and I'll not abandon you when you need all the support you can get."

"I appreciate the gesture, Scott, but it's not necessary. I've taken care of myself for a long time."

"Don't try to dissuade me, Maggie, my mind is made up. Unless you can convince me you've family nearby."

"There's no one, but that's no reason for you to assume responsibility for me. You should be getting on with your life."

Scott's rugged features softened, and he regarded Maggie with a warmth that made her cheeks bloom. "I'd never forgive myself if I left you now. I know what I want from you is impossible, but you need me. Think of me as a relative you can depend upon in a time of need. Have you forgotton how I looked after you in the Yukon?"

"I've forgotten nothing." And she hadn't. Somehow Scott was always there when she needed him.

"Then allow me to continue. At least until your child is born or McGarrett shows up."

"How can I refuse so generous an offer?" Maggie replied, choked with gratitude.

True to his word, Scott secured a room nearby and spent most of the following days with Maggie, lending a hand with shopping and small chores. No matter how vigorously Maggie protested, Scott spoiled her outrageously. Deep in his heart he harbored the wish that Chase would never come to claim Maggie and his child. Then he, Scott, could step in and fill the void in Maggie's life. Her child would become his child, and the life he dreamed of would be theirs. He knew it was an impossible fantasy, yet hope beat eternal in his heart.

The day Maggie experienced mild discomfort and vague pain, Scott refused to leave when it came time to return to his own room nearby, offering to sleep on the floor in case she needed him during the night. Over Maggie's objections, he spread a blanket on the floor and stretched out, leaving Maggie no option but to allow Scott his way. Besides, having someone who cared around at so crucial a time was comforting. She only wished it was Chase instead of Scott worrying over her. Maggie wanted so desperately for Chase to be with her when their child was born.

When Maggie left the room, Scott partially disrobed, removing his shirt, shoes and stockings for comfort's sake. Then he bedded down on the pallet he made on the floor. It certainly wasn't the first time he'd improvised, and he doubted it would be the last. It wasn't late—early evening, really—but Maggie had looked so peaked he insisted she retire early. And with nothing else to do, Scott followed suit, soon falling into a light doze.

Chapter Seventeen

It seemed to Scott that he'd been asleep only minutes when he was awakened by a noise that was as repetitive as the beating of a drum. It took a few minutes to rouse himself sufficiently to recognize what the disturbance meant. Someone was rapping on the door, and quite insistently. Sparing a moment to light a lamp but not bothering to pull on his shirt, Scott stumbled to the door. Grumbling beneath his breath about inconsiderate nighttime visitors, he jerked open the panel, expecting to see Jenny or one of the other neighbors.

Chase chafed impatiently outside Maggie's door. He was so anxious to see her he couldn't wait till morning. After his ship docked, he had been tied up for hours collecting his belongings and arranging for his gold to be deposited in a bank. Then he had settled newlyweds Rusty and Kate in a hotel, seen to the storage of his baggage, and left immediately for Maggie's flat, fully expecting to spend the night

302

with her. After the wedding he promised Maggie, they would all leave for Butte, Montana, together.

By now it had grown dark, but since the hour wasn't all that late, Chase decided not to wait till morning but to claim his woman immediately. His body ached with a terrible yearning that no other woman could appease. He missed Maggie so desperately, needed her so acutely, that he trembled with the knowledge of what tonight would bring—loving each other in all the ways possible for a man and woman to love. Excitement pounded through his veins, keeping time with his pounding on the door. When the panel was finally jerked open, it took several minutes for Chase to accept the fact that a sleepy-eyed man, barechested and disheveled, had answered the door instead of Maggie. Even more astonishing, he knew the man!

"Gordon! What in the hell are you doin' here?"

"About time you showed up," Scott grumbled disagreeably.

"What kinda remark is that? Where's Maggie? What are you doin' here this time of night, and nearly naked besides?"

"Who is it, Scott?"

Maggie had heard the knocking but was slower in rousing herself than Scott. Standing in the doorway with her filmy robe clinging to and outlining her every curve, it wasn't difficult to recognize her condition. And Chase wasn't blind—nor was he a fool.

A terrible dread seized Scott. Suddenly he realized that he was about to lose someone who was very precious to him.

Horrified, Chase's attention was riveted to Maggie's protruding abdomen. How was it possible? Maggie was barren. Yet, here she was, pregnant with Gordon's child. For some unexplained reason

Maggie had told a deliberate falsehood, made him think she couldn't conceive. Was the idea of having his child so repugnant to her she'd say anything, do anything?

"Chase, thank God you're here," Maggie sighed tremulously. As the day progressed, it had grown increasingly evident that her time was near. Chase's appearance when she needed him most was like a miracle.

"Seems to me your husband should be the one person you need right now," Chase drawled, contempt bitter on his tongue.

"My—husband? You know I'm not married." Maggie's brow knitted in confusion.

"If Gordon hasn't married you, he sure as hell oughta. How soon, Maggie—two, three months? The least he could do is give his child a name."

"His—child?" Maggie choked, puzzled by Chase's words.

"You have no reason to talk to Maggie like that," Scott blasted, his face mottled with rage. How could the dumb cowboy hurt her so badly?

"Hell, I don't blame you, Gordon," Chase continued disparagingly. "Couldn't keep my hands off her myself. She's a damn temptin' piece." Deliberately, he turned to Maggie. "What I'd really like to know is why you lied to me. Wasn't a no-account cowboy good enough to father a child?"

"Chase, you don't know—"

"I'm rich now, Maggie, damn rich," Chase continued, ignoring Maggie's futile attempt to explain. "I may still be a rough, uncouth cowboy, but I can buy and sell your Mountie."

Appalled by the way Chase had jumped to conclusions, Maggie searched for words of explanation, sadly aware that he was too hotheaded to accept the truth. "It's not what you think," she offered with quiet dignity.

"Tell me how it is, darlin'," Chase sneered. "Did I start an itch in you that needed scratchin'? How soon did Gordon follow you here? No wonder I didn't see him in Dawson. Did you know that I was determined never to let you know how deeply disappointed I was by your inability to have children? I vowed never to speak of your lack or blame you for it."

"But—you said you didn't want children!"

"All men want to produce someone in their own image. I'm no different. A child assures us of immortality. But I was willin' to accept you as you were 'cause I loved you. You were all I needed in this life, but you managed to shatter every dream I ever had."

"Damn you, Chase McGarrett, why won't you listen?" Maggie cried, overwhelmed by the magnitude of hurt her simple lie had wrought. In the beginning, it was meant to absolve Chase's guilt and save him from making a commitment he might later regret. How could something so insignificant turn her life into utter chaos?

"Why should I listen to more lies? Seems I never really knew you. Next you'll try to convince me the child is mine. Why hasn't your lover married you? Is it because he doesn't trust you any more than I do?"

"I'd marry Maggie tomorrow if she'd have me," Scott spat through gritted teeth. He was so enraged by Chase's unjust accusations that his muscles knotted in anticipation of reacting physically to Chase's verbal abuse. Only his respect and concern for Maggie's delicate condition held him back.

"I'd take the Mountie up on his proposal if I were you, darlin'," Chase said tightly, "you're not gettin' any younger. Marryin' Gordon is better than raisin' a bastard." A hurt so profound it throbbed through his body like a open wound lent venom to his words.

Chase might be sorry tomorrow, but right now it felt good to lash out at someone. Even if that someone was a woman he loved beyond reason.

Maggie's face turned a sickly shade of green as she stared at Chase, unwilling to believe he could attack her so vilely, without reason.

"You low-down, contemptible snake!" Scott roared, by now beyond control. "You're the only bastard in this room. If you'd use the sense God gave you, you'd know—"

"Scott, don't. It's no use, he won't believe you," Maggie pleaded, resigned to Chase's rejection. Hadn't she earned it? All these long months she had prayed Chase would understand and welcome their child, but she realized that Chase was too hurt, confused, and hotheaded right now to think clearly. Perhaps when he cooled off and thought about it, he'd realize the baby was his and accept them both.

"But, Maggie," Scott persisted, "he thinks—"

"I know what Chase thinks. I also know why he thinks what he does. I—I can't bear any more of this."

"The last thing I wanna do is upset an expectant mother," Chase mocked cruelly. "You're welcome to the witch, Gordon."

Chase's careless insult unleashed the full fury of Scott's temper as he delivered a right hook to Chase's unprotected chin. It was so unexpected, it drove Chase backwards through the door, which Scott slammed with such force that it nearly flew off the hinges. Never had Scott received such satisfaction from a single act. When he turned back to Maggie, he found her stretched out on the floor in a dead faint. Horrified, he knelt by her side, chafing her wrists until she moaned and opened her eyes.

"Chase?" Maggie asked tremulously.

"Gone, I hope. Consider yourself lucky to be rid of him."

"Oh, God," Maggie sobbed, distraught as well as devastated by Chase's lack of understanding. Yet she couldn't place the blame entirely on his shoulders.

"Can't you see he doesn't want you, honey?" Scott gently rebuked. "Forget him."

"Forget Chase?" Maggie asked, stunned. "Never. I might learn to live without him, but I'll never forget him."

Disturbed by Maggie's distress and realizing he was partly responsible, Scott said the only thing that came to mind. "After I settle you in bed, I'll go after McGarrett for you. I'll make him understand if it's the last thing I do. Right now he's hurt and upset at finding us together and shocked by your pregnancy. His trigger-temper has cleared his brain of all reason. If you still want the cowboy, I'll bring him back—no matter what it takes. A Mountie always gets his man."

When Scott helped Maggie to her feet, he saw that her face had gone dead white. A grimace stretched across her pale lips and she clutched convulsively at her stomach. "What is it, Maggie? Did the fall hurt you?"

Shaking her head in vigorous denial, Maggie managed to gasp out, "It—it's the baby. I think it's time."

"Jesus! What can I do?"

"First get Jenny, then go for the doctor. Hurry, Scott."

Chase sprawled on the floor outside Maggie's door, rubbing his chin where Scott had clipped him. Deep in his heart he knew the blow was well-deserved, but he had been too hurt and disappointed by what he found at Maggie's flat to bridle his tongue. All those bleak, lonely months in the Yukon, Maggie had been the one constant in his life, the one thing that kept him sane in the land of ice and snow and utter silence. He'd lived for the day he'd make a triumphant return to Seattle and lay his wealth at her feet.

It hurt like hell to learn Maggie hadn't waited for him as she promised. Gordon must have followed her to Seattle within a month or two, judging from her advanced state of pregnancy. She looked to be within a couple of months of delivery. Had she been farther along in her pregnancy or had already been delivered, it would have been another matter entirely. Counting back nine months, he would naturally assume the child was his, started before Maggie left Skagway last July. But any fool could see Maggie was nowhere near delivery. No, the child was Scott Gordon's; his presence in Maggie's flat confirmed Chase's belief that Gordon had fathered Maggie's child.

Chase would have given his fortune to have a child with Maggie and had been disappointed to learn it would never happen. Lies, all lies. Why? If he lived to be a hundred, he'd never understand why Maggie didn't want his babe. Picking himself off the floor, Chase hurried back to the hotel, where he found Rusty and Kate preparing for bed. They thought him mad when he insisted they check out immediately and board the first train to Montana. But Chase was so adamant, so obviously distraught, they complied rather than make a scene, relieved to find a train was expected at midnight.

Chase refused to answer Rusty's questions. Refused to talk about Maggie or what had happened to send him racing for the train station at this late hour. Chase would only say that he didn't belong in a big city like Seattle. Maggie didn't need him—hell, she didn't want him. He wasn't the kind to hang around and have his heart pounded to a pulp.

By the time Scott came charging out the door of Maggie's flat to summon the doctor, Chase was long gone.

"She's beautiful, Maggie," Scott said, staring down at the perfect, tiny face with rapt awe.

The small bundle held lovingly in Maggie's arms squirmed, waved two dimpled fists in the air, yawned hugely, then settled back into a contented sleep. Maggie felt eternal gratitude to Chase for giving her such a precious gift. There was a time Maggie expected never to experience the joys of motherhood, being well beyond her prime. She certainly never expected to be an unwed mother, yet here she was, deserted by her child's father but happier than she'd ever imagined she could be.

Because she weighed barely five pounds, Beth's birth had been relatively easy, hardly requiring the doctor's presence. Just the same, it was comforting to know he was on hand should she need him. Her labor had lasted nearly twelve hours. During that time Scott paced nervously outside her bedroom door, doing all the things expected of a new father. In fact, both Jenny and the doctor assumed Scott *was* the father, and he did nothing to disabuse them of that notion.

Within two weeks Maggie was back on her feet and so in love with her tiny daughter she couldn't bring herself to hate her baby's father. Chase had created a perfect human being and it stung to know he'd never know the contentment or joy of holding his daughter in his arms. Though Maggie needed no one to remind her of her small daughter's beauty, Scott's words brought an answering smile.

"The most beautiful child I've ever seen," she agreed with heartfelt sincerity, "though I must admit I'm a bit prejudiced."

"She looks just like her mother."

Gazing at her daughter, Maggie had to agree. Blond fuzz the color of ripe wheat covered the small round head, and the baby's nose and mouth showed definite signs of resembling her beautiful mother. Her eyes had yet to change from the clear blue all infants enjoyed, and Maggie hoped they wouldn't. She wanted something to remind her of Chase.

"I suppose I'm a doting mother, but I can't imagine life without her," Maggie sighed dreamily.

"I can't imagine life without either of you," Scott offered in a voice choked with sadness. "But I've finally come to realize that there's no room in your heart for me."

He waited for Maggie to utter a denial, and when none came, he continued, "That's why I've decided to return to the Yukon. My leave is up and it's time I got on with my life. There's a telegraph now in Dawson, and if you or my goddaughter ever need me, you know where to reach me."

"You've always been here when I needed you," Maggie choked on a sob. "You've been a better friend than I deserve and I'll miss you. You've so much to offer a woman, but I'm not the one for you. I pray you'll find her soon."

"Will you and Beth be all right? Financially, I mean. I'm not without resources and I could—"

"Thank you, but I'm fine." Maggie smiled warmly. Why couldn't she love this special man? "I'm still able to support myself through my writing. My articles on the Yukon are selling well and I've nearly finished my novel. Thanks to an understanding editor, I still have a job waiting for me. Jenny is more than willing to watch Beth for we when I decide to return to work. It's just that I can't bear to leave her yet."

"Will you accept some well-intentioned advice from someone who cares deeply?"

"If it's from you, I'll listen to whatever you have to say."

"Swallow your pride and go to Chase. One of you has to make the first move. You love him, and no matter how much I hate to admit it, I think he loves you. Allow him the opportunity to know his child. By now he's over his initial anger and will be more receptive to your explanation. You two belong together. Don't throw away your chance to be a family. When Beth is able to travel, pack your bags and go to Montana."

Maggie would never know how much it cost Scott to utter those words.

"I—I'm afraid," Maggie whispered, clutching Beth to her breast. "What if Chase rejects us?"

"Then you'll have lost nothing but your pride, a small price compared to all you have to gain. The Maggie I know and love is feisty enough to fight for what she wants. She's courageous and has more guts than most men."

"I love you, Scott Gordon. You're the brother I've always wanted, and the best friend a girl could ever wish for. Now kiss me and get out of here before I break down and cry."

He brushed her lips in tender yearning, then planted a kiss on Beth's smooth forehead. "Remember my advice," he said in parting, "and keep in touch. If I don't hear from you, you might find me on your doorstep." Then he was gone, leaving Maggie with an empty feeling in the pit of her stomach.

For the next two months, Maggie wavered between following Scott's advice and forgetting that a man named Chase McGarrett ever existed. Beth prospered under her mother's doting care, though it was obvious she would never be a large child. At the age of two months, Beth was the size of most newborn infants. She would be able to travel soon, and Maggie knew the time had come to make a decision. Either she must confront Chase, or forget him.

* * *

Since his return to Montana, Chase was a man driven by the need to erase the past year from his mind. With the money earned from the claim, he and Rusty were slowly building the ranch into a first-rate enterprise, acquiring some of the finest blooded horses available. In time they hoped to offer stud service as well as break and train saddle and race horses. Chase's heart swelled with pride to see fat cattle grazing on the hillsides and corn and hay turning the valleys green. Thankfully, his acres included more than one stream and water was plentiful most of the year. Abundant game was available and Kate had planted a truck garden behind the house to serve their needs.

Though Kate had protested, Chase hired two Indian women, one to cook and one to clean. The arrangement worked well with his expanded household, which now included Kate's niece, Virgie, who had joined them shortly after their return to Montana.

Rusty was building a new house and expected it to be completed by fall. Then Chase would be alone again. Not that he minded having houseguests. Both Rusty and Kate were agreeable company, and Virgie's flighty chatter amused him most of the time. Other times the petite brunette grated on his nerves.

Virgie was an unexpected addition to the family. When Kate had tried to contact her family in St. Louis, she'd learned from their lawyer that both her sister and brother-in-law had died within months of one another, leaving their daughter, Virginia, alone in the world without visible means of support. After receiving Chase's blessing, Kate promptly invited her niece to make her home with them. The vivacious young beauty had arrived within a month of the invitation and promptly set her sights on Chase.

Besides being rich, he was handsome, virile, and the answer to a girl's dreams.

Relying on her considerable charms, Virgie pursued Chase relentlessly, embarrassing him with her adoration. It didn't take Chase long to realize Virgie was everything Maggie wasn't. She was young—just eighteen—clinging, adorably innocent, and totally dependent. Her huge violet eyes were a perfect foil for skin as creamy as magnolia blossoms and hair as black as the darkest night. It seemed to Chase that Virgie's lips were always pursed invitingly, as if begging for his attention. So far he had resisted, but he was no damn saint. Every time he turned around Virgie was at his elbow, thrusting her firm young breasts at him and batting lashes too long to be considered decent. The hot melting center of her violet eyes told Chase she was his for the taking. He wondered how long it would be before Virgie went too far and his male nature seized control of his mind and body. Chase groaned aloud when he spied the object of his ruminations crossing the yard in his direction.

"Chase, I know you'll think I'm a silly girl, but I need the help of a big strong man." Her violet eyes were warm and inviting, and Chase couldn't find it in his heart to refuse so charming a creature.

"What can I do for you, Virgie?" Chase asked, managing a beguiling smile. He seemed to smile so seldom these days.

"There's hot water boiling on the stove and no one around to carry it upstairs for me." Her full lower lip trembled, and a huge tear slipped from the corner of her eye down her cheek. Chase found the mute plea in her huge eyes endearing, her innocent charm quite appealing.

Virgie was a woman who would always need taking care of. That thought immediately conjured up pictures of Maggie struggling over White Pass dressed in baggy men's clothing and shouldering a load most men would find staggering. Unlike Virgie, Maggie was quite adept at taking care of herself. In his mind's eye, he saw Maggie trudging uncomplainingly over snow and ice, determined to prove herself as good as any man. Would he ever forget Maggie or the rapture they shared all those frozen days and nights in the Klondike? Resourceful, brave, smart, exasperating, feisty, and dedicated to the theory that women had every right to be and do anything they wanted to be and do. Ice and rapture. No other words could describe their all too short time together. No other description did justice to their passion. Ice and rapture.

"Chase, did you hear me?" Virgie's plaintive voice brought Chase's thoughts skidding reluctantly back to the present.

"What? Sorry, Virgie, what did you say?"

"I declare, you certainly have a way of wool-gathering. If I didn't know better, I'd think you were pining over someone."

"I've a lot on my mind, Virgie. If you repeat your request, I'll be more than happy to oblige."

"I asked you to carry a pot of boiling water upstairs to my room. No one's around and I'd like to bathe."

"At this time of day?"

"Why not?" Virgie shrugged, batting long lashes at Chase.

"If you're wantin' to cool off, why not use the stream? It's much more refreshin'."

Virgie swallowed a smile while pretending mock horror. Chase's innocent remark was just what she was fishing for. "I know that, silly, but I'm afraid. There might be snakes, or bears, or Indians. I wouldn't feel safe unless you were with me," she declared with apparent guilelessness. "Everyone's been so busy lately. . . ." Her sentence trailed off, but enough had been said to suggest that Virgie had been sadly neglected since arriving at the ranch. And Chase was one of the biggest culprits.

Chase realized that his hospitality had been woefully lacking where Virgie was concerned, but he had driven himself relentlessly these past weeks. His duties left little time for entertaining a vivacious young woman—or room for thoughts of Maggie to creep unbidden into his mind. Guilt prodded him into suggesting something he wouldn't have dared had he given it rational thought. "Get your towel, Virgie, I'll accompany you to the stream."

Delighted that Chase had finally succumbed to her charms, Virgie literally flew into the house to gather towel, soap, and clean clothes, returning even before Chase had finished with his chore. "Ready," she grinned happily.

She was so taken with Chase that she would do anything to earn his attention. She'd gladly give up her virginity if it meant Chase would be forced to do the "right thing" and propose to her. Besides, she was more than ready to lose that bothersome membrane most girls held onto with a tenacity Virgie found amusing. She wanted to experience love, learn what it meant to be a woman—and she wanted Chase to be the man to show her the way.

Falling into step beside Chase, Virgie's romantic fantasies ran amok. Anything was possible within the sheltered privacy of the stream. She knew enough about men to know they were lusty animals, easily aroused, especially when denied the solace of a woman for a length of time. And she was certain Chase hadn't left the ranch in weeks to satisfy his sexual urgings.

Though Virgie was still technically a virgin, she knew more than most young women her age about sex. Unbeknownst to Kate, her timely summons had saved Virgie from a life of prostitution. Left virtually penniless when her parents died, Virgie, pampered by her indulgent parents, was unprepared to earn her own keep. A male friend of her father, who'd always fancied the beautiful young girl, suggested Virgie look up Mrs. Nora Sanders, a kindly woman who took in homeless and penniless young women. Virgie soon learned that Nora Sanders did nothing without demanding a price. In return for room and board and clothing, her girls were expected to service gentlemen who came to the house seeking female company. It was a kind of genteel whorehouse, if there was such a thing.

Each newcomer was subjected to an intensive training period to prepare her for her profession. Virgie was nearly finished with her lessons when the summons from Kate found her. Enough money had been sent Virgie to amply reward Mrs. Sanders for expenditures on Virgie's behalf, though Kate would never know what most of her money was used for. Kate naturally assumed Nora Sanders was a kindly widow who boarded homeless young women. So Virgie had left the madam's care with her virginity intact but wiser in the ways of men than any young girl had a right to be.

Chapter Eighteen

Chase sat with his back to the water, listening to Virgie splash and romp in the creek. If she weren't Kate's niece, he might be tempted to join her. Lord, he needed a woman. He'd had no one since Maggie, and that was longer ago than he cared to remember. Maybe he'd go to Butte one day soon and . . .

"Chase, help!"

Jerked from his erotic thoughts, Chase leaped to his feet, fully expecting to find Virgie being attacked by a ferocious animal. What he did see was all of Virgie, glistening droplets of water dewing her creamy flesh, standing in the waist-deep stream, arms and legs flailing helplessly. The sun reflected off the high peaks of her breasts, their pale pink tips nearly dazzling him. Ebony hair tumbled in disarray around creamy shoulders, and the expression on her lovely features was one of terror.

"S—snake!" Virgie gasped, pointing vaguely into the blue-green water. Her scream thawed Chase's frozen senses and he splashed into the stream—clothes, boots and all.

"Don't move!" he called, finding it extremely difficult to keep from gorging on the luscious feast to his eyes that Virgie offered.

"Hurry!"

In a matter of seconds Chase reached Virgie's side, swinging her up and into his arms. She clung to him like a second skin, thoroughly drenching him, the hard tips of her breasts stabbing against the wide expanse of his chest. She was trembling badly, so he held her tightly, whispering soothing words in her ear.

"I reckon it's gone now, Virgie, don't be afraid. The snake was probably more frightened of you than you are of him. Doubtless it was some harmless variety that wouldn't have hurt you."

"You're so brave," Virgie sighed adoringly. "And strong. I'm never afraid when you're around." Her small hands roamed freely over the ropy muscles clearly defined beneath Chase's wet shirt and she lifted her face, her mouth pursed invitingly.

Every instinct told Chase Virgie was his for the taking, that she was inviting more than innocent kisses. The thought was heady.

"Behave, Virgie," Chase scolded, attempting to ignore the need she unleashed in him but failing miserably. "Think how it would look if someone came along and found us like this."

Virgie hoped it would look like Chase was seducing her. If seduction was the only way to wrangle a proposal, she'd take it. "Would finding us like this be such a bad thing?" she asked coyly.

Splashing to shore, Chase set Virgie carefully on her feet, but he was not yet ready to release her. Her taut young flesh felt smooth and satiny beneath his fingertips and the urge to press her down on the soft ground and bury himself deeply in her softness presisted. He had only to search her features to know she was receptive to him, that she would deny him nothing. But at what cost?

In all fairness he couldn't seduce Kate's niece. Rusty would have his hide, and he wouldn't be able to look himself in the face the next day. If he were considering marriage, it might be a different story, but Virgie was too young and innocent to take, then discard. He could do worse than marry Virgie, Chase reckoned. If he had to have a wife, Virgie was as good as anyone. At least she'd be able to give him a son.

"Chase, did you hear me? What does it take to get you to pay attention to me?"

"You've already done it." Chase grimed with devilish delight. "You're damn enticin', Virgie, but I don't aim to jeopardize my friendship with your aunt."

"Why can't we just please ourselves?" Virgie said archly. She moved sinuously within the circle of his arms, thrilled at the responsive chord she roused in him.

"Damnation, Virgie, stop that. I'm only human!"

"I want you to make love to me, Chase. I want to belong to you. Why are you fighting this?"

"Damned if I know." But Chase did know. Virgie was an alluring young beauty, but she was a child compared to the feisty, strong-willed, independent woman he fell in love with in the Yukon. Damn Maggie Afton! he cursed beneath his breath. She'd ruined him for any other woman. If he wasn't three kinds of fool, he'd wed and bed Virgie and get on with his life. An unfaithful witch had him living like a damn monk, wanting no other woman, craving only Maggie's sweet-scented flesh.

"Kiss me, Chase." Her lips were so close he could see the moistness lingering in the tiny crevices at their corners.

The decision to kiss Virgie was denied Chase when,

impulsively, her fingers tangled in his hair and drew
his lips down to hers. Her mouth was soft and sweetly
yielding, opening greedily to the pressure of his gentle probing. Suddenly Virgie became a living flame in
his arms, hot and seeking, her hands tugging urgently at his clothes. At first Chase was shocked at Virgie's
boldness. There was nothing innocent about the way
she kissed him, or how she thrust her tongue in his
mouth. But when Virgie sank to the ground and held
out her hand for Chase to follow, he balked. Though
every male instinct screamed for him to take Virgie,
his brain still functioned well enough to know he'd
only be using Virgie to assuage his hunger for a
woman. He might be an uneducated cowboy, but
he wasn't a heartless bastard ruled by lust.

"Get dressed, Virgie," he barked. Repressed desire
and anger at Maggie for abandoning him made his
voice harsher than he intended. "I won't take you like
this. You deserve marriage, not some cheap affair."

"Do you mean it?" Virgie trilled excitedly.

"Yep, you need a husband, not a lover."

"Is that a proposal?"

"Proposal?" Chase was stunned. He should have
known that Virgie would misconstrue his words.
"Not exactly," he hedged, "but I reckon it's not too
farfetched. Who knows what'll happen when we get
to know one another better?" Deliberately he turned
away and began gathering up Virgie's clothes, which
lay scattered on the bank of the stream.

Struggling into her clothes, Virgie fumed impo-
tently. She had arranged everything so carefully, set
the stage so painstakingly, to no avail. She was so
certain she had Chase eating out of her hand. What
had happened to chill his ardor? He was so close
to making love to her, she could smell his arousal,
taste his need in his kiss. No matter, Virgie smiled
confidently, she'd have Chase yet. Getting him to
mention marriage was a step in the right direction.

Chase was as good as hooked; now all she had to do was reel him in.

"I'm ready, Chase, you can turn around."

"Come along, Virgie, I'll see you back to the house."

"Are you angry with me?"

Chase looked at her then, his expression softening at the sight of her trembling lips and wide violet eyes. Virgie was so helpless, so endearingly vulnerable, he blamed only himself for what had nearly happened. "You've done nothin' to earn my anger, Virgie. Let's go, I've work to do."

Kate and Rusty exchanged knowing glances as they intercepted another of the silent messages Virgie directed toward Chase at dinner that evening. They knew Virgie was smitten with Chase and had nothing against a match between the two, but they seriously doubted Chase was ready for that kind of commitment. He showed no signs of being over Maggie—if anything he had grown more despondent, more morose as the days passed. He drove himself relentlessly, allowed no one to speak of Maggie in his presence, and become so testy that Rusty and the ranch hands took pains not to rile him.

Chase shifted uncomfortably beneath Virgie's hot glances. He worried that Rusty and Kate would misinterpret their meaning and think the worst of him. Therefore, he wasn't surprised when Rusty asked to speak with him in private at the conclusion of the meal.

"What did you do to the girl, son?" Rusty asked the moment they were alone. "Virgie is young and inexperienced, and I won't have you seducin' her."

"Don't get on your high horse, Rusty. I haven't done anythin' to the girl. She fancies herself in love with me."

"I knew Virgie was smitten, but until today I had

no reason ta think ya even noticed her. You've been so steeped in yer own misery lately no one can talk ta ya," Rusty accused him. "What happened with Maggie back in Seattle? You've been closemouthed about the whole thin'. Get it off yer chest, son, it might help."

"I told you before, Rusty, I don't want to talk about it."

"Ya gotta talk about it sometime. Loosen up, Chase, we been together too long fer ya ta hold back now. It just ain't good fer ya. What happened betwixt you and Maggie ta send ya racin' back to Montana?"

Chase winced. It still hurt to hear her name spoken. "Nothin' special. She just up and decided she didn't want me. While I spent months pinin' for her, she took up with that Mountie."

"Cap'n Gordon?" Rusty asked, stunned. "I knew they were friends but didn't figure they were *that* close. Are ya sure, son? What did Maggie say?"

"Not much," Chase allowed. "What could she say when I found them together dressed in their bedclothes?"

"Did ya listen ta her explanation before ya jumped ta conclusions?" Rusty asked, well aware of Chase's hot temper.

"You don't know the whole story," Chase muttered sourly.

" 'Spose you tell me."

"I hoped to spare you this, Rusty, but Maggie was pregnant with Gordon's child when I saw her in Seattle."

Shock followed dismay across Rusty's weathered features. "Damnation! Are ya dead certain?"

"I know a pregnant woman when I see one."

"Did ya ever consider it might be yer child Maggie's carryin'?"

"Of course—I'm not stupid. I can count as well as you. Maggie wasn't within two months of delivery when I saw her. If she was carryin' my child, she'd have had to be within days of givin' birth. Maggie didn't look big enough to give birth."

"So now yer tellin' me ya know all about women and birthin' babies. Did ya ask Maggie, give her a chance ta explain?"

"There was nothin' to explain," Chase complained bitterly. "The evidence was there before my eyes."

"So ya ran away with yer tail betwixt yer legs. I never knowed ya was a coward, Chase."

"Maggie made a fool of me. She lied to me, and made me believe she loved me. Hell, Rusty, she told me she couldn't have kids. I overcame my disappointment over her lack because I loved her, tellin' myself Maggie was enough for me. Why did she lie to me, Rusty, why?"

"I purely don't know, son, but if I were you I wouldn't have run out before I found out."

"It's too late. Maggie made her choice. By now she's close to giving birth to another man's child. I've lost Maggie, and it's time I got on with my life. Maggie isn't the only woman in the world." Who was he trying to kid?

"If yer lookin' fer Virgie to fill the void in yer life, ya'll have ta convince Kate yer over Maggie fer good. So far yer doin' a piss-poor job of it, and Kate is right fond of her niece. Neither of us want ta see the girl hurt."

"She won't be, Rusty."

"Accordin' to Kate, Virgie is hopin' fer a proposal from ya. Have ya been encouragin' her?"

"I can't say what's gonna happen six months from now, or even three months," Chase replied, "but I haven't been leadin' the girl on. It's entirely possible I'll propose to Virgie one day, and I promise to keep my hands off her until I decide. It's more important right now for me and Virgie to get to know one another."

Chase's words appeared to satisfy Rusty, for they soon parted to join the women in the parlor.

"Aren't you afraid of anything, Chase?" Virgie asked, admiration turning her eyes into saucers of violets. She had been watching him break a fractious horse and marveled at the strength and power of his perfectly coordinated body. Ever since Virgie had tried to seduce Chase by the stream, she was never far from his side. She used every feminine wile available to entice him and felt certain it wouldn't be long before a proposal was forthcoming. Not only did Virgie think Chase a compelling man, but he was a rich one, everything she'd ever yearned for in a husband.

Chase smiled lazily. Virgie's praise did much for his deflated ego and he wondered why he resisted the idea of marriage to the little temptress. Virgie would make a perfect wife and lover, he reasoned. The only thing that stopped him from proposing was the tiny voice inside his brain reminding him that he still loved a woman who made Virgie seem like an untried schoolgirl. He had shared so much with Maggie. Could he find those same things with Virgie?

"I'm afraid of many things, Virgie, but nothin' I can't handle."

Virgie's eyes fastened appreciatively on the damp curling hair visible at the base of Chase's throat. The two top buttons of his shirt were unfastened due to the heat, and the sweat-soaked material was plastered to his back. It was mid-July and so hot even Virgie's pristine skin was beaded with perspiration in a most unladylike manner. The heat, as well as being subjected to so magnificent a display of male virility, made Virgie bold.

"It's beastly hot, Chase—wouldn't a swim feel wonderful?"

Silently Chase agreed, but he knew damn well where that would lead. "Not now, Virgie, I'm too busy."

Virgie pouted, her round little mouth pursed invitingly. "You're always so busy." She stepped closer, the tips of her breasts brushing teasingly against Chase's chest. "What are you afraid of? I thought you could handle just about anything?"

Chase thought so too, but he wasn't certain where Virgie was concerned. She wanted things from him he wasn't prepared to give. She was an enchanting chit, part witch, part child—and all woman.

"You're an encitin' woman, Virgie," Chase conceded grudgingly. "You make a man itch where it's hard to scratch."

"Let me scratch your itch, Chase. You won't be sorry."

"Tarnation, Virgie—" Suddenly Chase's attention was diverted by a cloud of dust rising in the distance. They seldom had visitors, so it was an occasion for curiosity when a wagon came down the lane toward the ranch. "Company comin'," he muttered, forgetting all about Virgie.

Virgie frowned, suddenly apprehensive. Some sixth sense warned her that the visitor would somehow destroy all her plans. She watched with trepidation as the wagon rolled to a stop in the dusty yard.

The startling blue of Chase's eyes settled disconcertedly on the woman seated beside the driver. She sat ramrod straight, hugging a small bundle to her breast. Chase's heart beat a tattoo against his chest as Maggie's amber gaze searched his face for some sign of welcome. He tried desperately to control his rampaging emotions, but his joy at seeing Maggie rattled his composure. "Howdy, Maggie," he said, hardly aware of speaking at all. "You're a long way from home."

What am I doing here? Maggie asked herself as

she stared into the unrelenting blue of Chase's eyes. They were implacable, unforgiving, and remote. This wasn't the Chase she knew and loved, the man who vowed to love her forever. This Chase was cold, bitter, and remorseless.

"Hello, Chase, will you help me down or would you prefer I didn't stay?"

Stay? Maggie wanted to stay at the ranch? Nothing Maggie said made sense to Chase, but he reached up, grasped her slender waist, and swung her to the ground. While they stared at each other with a longing neither would admit to, the driver dropped Maggie's luggage on the ground, clucked the horses into motion, and took off down the lane.

"Who is this woman?" Virgie asked, all too aware of the charged atmosphere. "Where is her husband?"

Just then the baby began to fuss, plunging Chase into cold reality. "A good question. Where *is* your husband, Maggie? I'm surprised Gordon let you travel alone."

Vivid red stained Maggie's cheeks as she deliberately ignored Chase's cruel taunts.

Chase cursed beneath his breath, angry at himself for lashing out at Maggie. She wouldn't have come here alone with her newborn child without good reason. Had Gordon mistreated her? Left her to fend for herself and her child? Somehow he didn't seem the type.

"Chase, introduce us," Virgie whined, angry at being ignored.

"Virgie, meet Maggie Afton. Maggie, this is Virginia Martin, Kate's niece. She's livin' at the ranch now."

"How—convenient," Maggie muttered, taking note of the way the young beauty clung to Chase. Intuitively Maggie knew she was going to have to fight for Chase, but she should have expected it. Lord knew, Chase was no monk.

It had taken Maggie three months of agonizing deliberation before deciding to swallow her pride and come to Montana. She never thought she'd find Chase involved with another woman, but she had mentally prepared herself for any situation she might encounter. Even Chase's interest in a beautiful young woman.

Maggie's decision to travel to Montana was in no way meant to pressure Chase into marrying her. She fully intended to reclaim Chase's love before telling him that Beth was his child. Once he came to love her for herself, with no reservations, she'd feel free to tell him about their daughter. She was prepared to fight for the man she loved, and if little Virgie was an example of what she faced it appeared she would have quite a battle on her hands. If she had any sense at all, she'd turn around and leave now, before Beth grew to love her father. Somehow she had to make Chase understand that she never loved anyone but him, that her lie wasn't meant to hurt but to protect. She couldn't wait for the day Chase realized he had a daughter. But for the time being, she'd take one day at a time until the big cowboy came to his senses.

"Have you traveled far, Mrs. Afton?" Virgie asked innocently. "Are you and your husband friends of Chase?"

"It's Miss Afton. I'm not married. Please call we Maggie. You might say I'm a friend of Chase's." Maggie looked at Chase for confirmation, but he was too busy staring at the squirming bundle in her arms to answer. "We've come from Seattle," she added, turning her attention back to the vivacious brunette.

Virgie was appalled. She'd never met an unwed mother before, certainly not one who seemed unconcerned over her embarrassing state. How and where did this brazen hussy meet Chase?

"Did you and Gordon have a lover's spat? Did the bastard leave you?" Chase asked with growing anger.

"Can we go into this later, Chase?" Maggie asked, suddenly drained of all strength. "It's been a long, tiring trip, and Beth is hungry. If you didn't want me to stay, you should have said something before the wagon returned to town."

"You're welcome to stay, Maggie, and I'm certain I'll find out soon enough what brings you to Montana. Meanwhile, I'll show you and your—daughter, is it?—to a room. I'm sorry we're a little short of space until Rusty's new house is completed, so you'll have to make do."

"But, Chase, there are no empty rooms," Virgie complained. "And mine is hardly big enough to share with another. Beside, the baby will keep us awake all night."

"Maggie can have my room," Chase offered, ignoring Virgie's gasp of dismay. "It's by far the largest and should prove adequate for her and the child."

"I'm sorry, Chase—had I known you were so crowded I wouldn't have come. Where are Rusty and Kate? It will be good to see them again."

"They took the buckboard into town this morning for supplies," Virgie interjected. She had refused to go, hoping to have Chase all to herself today, only it hadn't worked out that way. "I didn't know you knew my aunt. She lived in Alaska for years."

"That's where I met her," Maggie said cryptically as she turned to follow Chase inside the house. By now Beth was squirming furiously, angry at being denied her next meal.

"Quite a temper," Chase remarked with idle curiosity.

"Takes after her father," Maggie replied, tongue in cheek. At least Chase had taken notice of his daughter, she thought, delighted.

Chase chose to ignore Maggie's bald statement, needing no reminder that Maggie had taken up with another man in his absence. Promises meant nothing to her. But now that she was here, he fully intended to discover her reasons for telling him such an outrageous falsehood, why she had led him to believe she was barren. The child resting in her arms certainly was no fantasy. Whatever possessed her to come to Montana so soon after giving birth? he wondered curiously. Why had Gordon abandoned her and their child? If Gordon were here now, he'd wring the Mountie's neck.

Maggie paid little attention to the large, comfortable rooms furnished with rustic but functional furniture that she was being led through. Her attention was riveted on the ropy muscles of Chase's massive torso, the wonderful way his shirt stretched across his broad shoulders, his slim waist, slender hips, and the sinuous motions of his taut buttocks as he walked. He was all man and more ruggedly handsome than she remembered. Why couldn't he realize they belonged together? Didn't he even suspect Beth was his daughter? Men could be such absolute dolts at times.

"Here we are, Maggie," Chase said, opening a door off a long hallway on the second floor. Funny, she hadn't even realized they had climbed stairs. "You and your child should be quite comfortable here."

"Where will you sleep?" Maggie wondered aloud.

An odd expression crossed Chase's features. Was Maggie extending an invitation? "I'll bunk in with the hands."

Satisfied, Maggie nodded. "I know you have a lot of questions."

"Rest first. We'll talk later. And your child needs tendin' to. She's a mite puny, isn't she? Are you sure she's well? She's much too young to be travelin'," he said with mild reproof.

Maggie had placed Beth on the bed, and for the first time Chase got a good look at the tiny infant. Small at birth, obviously Beth wasn't ever going to be large or robust, but she was a healthy child and a good one, rarely crying, smiling often. Chase learned firsthand just how enchanting Beth was when the blond angel smiled up at him with beguiling charm. The pure innnocence of the babe did strange things to the inner workings of Chase's heart. Never had he felt such emotional stirrings as he did when that enchanting infant stared at him through guileless blue eyes.

"Her name is Beth," Maggie offered.

"I'd best be goin'," Chase said, unable to tear his eyes from the tiny girl. "Let me know if there's anythin' you need." He turned to leave.

"Chase, thank you. I didn't intend to put you out of your room."

He nodded curtly. "We'll talk later. I want to know exactly what's goin' on and why you're here." He slanted an inscrutable look in Beth's direction, then went out quickly.

Chapter Nineteen

"I believe your daddy was quite taken with you, sweetheart," Maggie crooned as she nursed her babe. "That big, tough cowboy nearly melted when you looked at him with those big blue eyes. But it's not time to tell him yet. I need to find out first just what is going on between your daddy and Kate's niece."

Oblivious of the anguish and uncertainty plaguing her mother, Beth nursed contentedly, falling asleep when she had drunk her fill. Maggie placed her in the center of the bed and was fastening her dress when a knock at the door announced a visitor.

"Come in." Maggie no idea who to expect but was pleased to see Kate walk through the door. She took one look at Maggie and opened her arms. Maggie needed no prodding as she flew into the older woman's welcoming embrace.

" 'Bout time ya showed up," Kate chuckled, hugging Maggie to her ample chest. "Don't know what happened betwixt you and Chase, but he's damn hard to live with these days. He's as closemouthed as Rusty when it comes ta personal matters."

"Did Chase tell you I was here?"

"Yep. That's all he did say, though."

Kate's voice must have disturbed Beth's slumber, for she chose that moment to let her displeasure be known. Her wail brought instant results. "My gawd, is that a baby?"

Kate's mouth dropped open in dismay as she approached the bed to have a closer look. Chase had said nothing about a child. Just then Beth opened her eyes and gurgled. A stunned expression claimed Kate's features as comprehension dawned. The baby's eyes were the same brilliant blue as her father's. What was going on here? Whatever it was, Kate was determined to get to the bottom of it. She led Maggie away from the bed when Beth stuck a thumb in her mouth and promptly fell back to sleep.

"Do ya wanna explain why Chase left ya in Seattle ta bear his child alone?"

Maggie flushed. She should have known Kate was shrewd enough to guess the truth. She had no option but to confide in Kate and hope she'd understand. "Chase found me pregnant when he came for me in Seattle and, because Scott Gordon was with me, naturally assumed the worst."

"And as hotheaded as Chase is, he probably took off without waitin' fer an explanation," Kate surmised. "Why didn't ya go after him and knock some sense in the big cowboy?" Kate carefully refrained from asking what the Mountie was doing with Maggie.

"Scott offered to go after Chase and bring him back, but the fracas that took place between the two men upset me so, I went into labor. Then my only concern was for my baby. Scott attempted to find Chase later, but learned he didn't wait around

Seattle long enough to find out about Beth."

"Why do I get the feelin' there's more to it than what yer tellin' me?"

"It's a long story."

"I got time."

Resigned to telling secrets she'd rather not reveal, Maggie chose her words carefully. "Seeing me pregnant came as a great shock to Chase."

"Are you tellin' me you and Chase never—that you didn't—"

"No, that's not what I meant. I told Chase I couldn't have children."

"What! If that was true then how—?"

"It wasn't true," Maggie confided. "I deliberately lied, and that untruth came back to haunt me."

"But why, Maggie?" Kate asked, truly puzzled. "Why would ya lie about somethin' like that? I've come ta know Chase, and I believe he'd love ta have children of his own."

"At the time it seemed the right thing to do. I meant to tell him later, but somehow never got around to it. I had no idea I was carrying Chase's child when I left Skagway."

Kate glanced over at the sleeping child. "That would make Beth three months old. Kinda puny, ain't she?"

"That's just what Chase said. It's the reason he doesn't suspect Beth belongs to him. He thinks she's Scott's baby. She'll never be a large child. She takes after my mother, who was a tiny little woman. I gained very little weight during pregnancy, so when Chase saw me in Seattle he never suspected I was so close to delivery."

"Ya never did explain why ya lied about havin' children."

A flash of color crept up Maggie's neck and cheeks. "Chase and I never made any bones about wanting one another. Stranded in the Klondike all those months would have been pure hell if we hadn't been able to—to love each other completely. Chase is a man of honor. Had I conceived during those months, he would have felt obligated to propose marriage. My lie saved him from making a commitment before he was ready. If Chase loved me, I wanted it to be for myself and not because of an unwanted pregnancy.

"I knew pregnancy was possible, but as luck would have it, that's not when it happened. From the beginning I knew I loved Chase and didn't want to force him into anything he wasn't prepared for. It was easier to lie than to have Chase worry about taking care of me and a child. I was willing to assume that responsibility if and when it came. And I still am."

"Then why are ya here?" Kate wondered aloud.

"Because I love Chase and—and Beth needs a father. But only if Chase wants us. That's why I haven't told him yet. I won't use my child to trap a husband. I'm willing to let Chase think what he wants until I learn how he feels about us. He loved me once, I need to know if my lie has turned that emotion to hate."

"Is that wise, Maggie?"

"It's the way it has to be,'" Maggie said determinedly. Then she slid the conversation around to a subject that had been on the tip of her tongue since Kate entered the room. "What is your niece to Chase? They seem—close."

"At first Chase scarcely noticed the girl," Kate admitted thoughtfully. "Poor little thing, I'm all she has in the world and she was thrilled when I invited her ta live on the ranch with us. She's so young and innocent, I'm happy I learned about her predicament in time. She's ill prepared ta care fer herself. It's not surprisin' Virgie attached herself ta Chase— he's mighty temptin' ta a young girl like Virgie."

"What about Chase? How does he feel about Virgie?"

"Ya'll have ta ask Chase."

"Ask me what?"

Both women turned, surprised to find Chase leaning lazily in the doorway, arms folded against his chest. Though he addressed his question to Kate, his gaze lingered on Maggie, his eyes a hot, smoky blue. Maggie recognized the look and flushed.

"I—I was just inquiring if you'd be comfortable sleeping in the bunkhouse," she improvised.

"I'll manage. I came to tell you I sent one of the boys into town to buy a cradle for your baby."

Kate and Maggie exchanged meaningful glances. "I—I don't know how long we'll stay, but I appreciate your gesture," Maggie said softly. "Beth will be much more comfortable in a bed of her own. Thank you, Chase."

Somewhat embarrassed, Chase merely nodded. "I'll see you both at supper." Then he was gone, but not before slanting an inscrutable glance at Beth, who remained blissfully unaware of her parents' problems.

Shortly before the supper hour, Maggie received a surprise when not only did the cradle Chase promised arrive with appropiate linen, but so did a young Indian girl named Spotted Deer. She had been engaged by Chase to care for Beth. Maggie was heartened by Chase's initial response to his daughter. At least he had taken notice of her.

Wearing her prettiest dress, Maggie entered the comfortable dining room just as everyone sat down to supper. The table groaned with an attractive assortment of food, and an Indian girl who could have been the sister to Spotted Deer moved noiselessly about the room serving the diners.

"Maggie, if ya ain't a sight fer sore eyes!" Rusty greeted her enthusiastically.

"It's good to see you, too, Rusty," Maggie smiled warmly.

"I'm right anxious to see that little one of yorn. Kate says she's as pretty as her ma."

Maggie flushed with pleasure. "Prettier."

"Sit down, Maggie," Chase invited. His expression was inscrutable, but the hot blue of his eyes seemed to probe into her very soul.

Everyone in the room felt the smoldering tension building around Chase and Maggie, experienced their emotional upheaval. Virgie saw it, felt it, and flushed with rage. Why hadn't anyone told her about this before? she wondered. What was she to Chase? Why was her name never mentioned when obviously she and Chase were more than mere acquaintences?

The only empty chair remaining was at Chase's right hand and Maggie slid into place, noting that Virgie, sitting at his left, was sending dark messages in her direction. Despite Chase's rather moody silence throughout the meal and Virgie's piercing looks, the meal was pleasant and conversation lively, and Maggie was soon laughing at Rusty's sharp witticisms. Then all too soon the meal ended, and Chase rose to his feet.

"Would you care to go for a walk, Maggie? it's quite pleasant outside."

"I . . ."

"I'd love to go, Chase," Virgie interjected with keen enthusiasm.

Bestowing a disapproving scowl on a beaming Virgie, Chase seemed at a loss for words until Maggie jumped into the void. "I really should check on Beth." Then she politely excused herself and hurried off.

"Come on, Chase," Virgie said, smirking at Maggie's departing back. "After that supper, a walk is just what I need."

Wanting desperately to refuse but hating to disappoint Virgie, Chase offered the petite brunette his arm and they ambled off into the gathering dusk. But his attention wasn't on Virgie's silly chatter, or the blatant invitation in her violet eyes. It was Maggie who captured his thoughts. Maggie and her intriguing daughter. Before the night was over, Chase fully intended to find out what had brought Maggie to Montana and exactly what she wanted from him.

"Chase, you're not paying attention," Virgie complained, pouting.

"Sorry, Virgie, I've a lot on my mind. I'm afraid I'm not very good company."

"It's Maggie Afton, isn't it? What is that woman to you?"

Chase's brow furrowed, deeply troubled by the question Virgie posed. The answer was not so simple. At one time Maggie had been his entire life. The fact that they weren't married and living in wedded bliss was entirely Maggie's decision. For some unexplained reason, she had chosen another man. But to Chase, her cardinal sin was lying to him about an important issue like children. The longer he thought about it, the more he knew they needed to talk. There were too many unanswered questions.

"Chase, did you hear me? Why is Maggie Afton here? Why isn't she married to her baby's father? I'm surprised you'd be friends with a woman of her—kind."

Rage exploded behind Chase's brain. "Maggie is the bravest woman I know and a top-notch newspaper reporter. She surmounted obstacles most women couldn't survive and many men wouldn't attempt. Don't assume havin' a baby out of wedlock makes Maggie a loose woman,'cause nothin' is further from the truth."

My God, listen to me, Chase thought, astounded. He was defending Maggie for the very same reasons he had condemned her. "Let's go inside, Virgie, I'm not fit company tonight."

Chase's outburst left Virgie utterly bewildered. "You never did say where you met Maggie," she persisted. She had to know why this particular woman had such a strange effect on Chase.

"We met aboard a ship enroute to Skagway in the summer of '97," Chase revealed grudgingly. "She came to my aid when I needed help, and I took her to the Yukon with me."

"You—traveled together?" Virgie asked, more than a little shocked by Chase's disclosure. They probably knew each other more intimately than she had supposed.

"Yep, and that's all I'm gonna say about it," Chase said tersely. By now he had steered her toward the front door. " 'Night, Virgie."

Virgie lingered outside the door, but Chase turned on his heel and headed back out into the night. "Chase, where are you going?"

"I'm bunkin' in with the hands, remember?"

Maggie heard Kate and Rusty enter their room across from hers and later identified Virgie's soft tread as she passed on the way to her own room at the end of the hall. Then quiet descended. After nursing Beth and settling her in her cradle, she undressed and lay down on the bed, thinking dreamily that Chase had slept here last night, his head on the same pillow. She imagined she could smell his distinctive scent lingering on the bed linens, a spicy aroma with a hint of tobacco and outdoors. For months she'd thought of what it would be like to be with Chase again, sharing his life, his hopes, his dreams—his love. Now she wondered if it had all been a foolish fantasy. Why would Chase want her when he could have a beautiful young woman like Virgie? Virgie was innocent, sweetly clinging, dependent, and everything a man wanted in a woman.

Perhaps it had been a mistake to bring Beth here, Maggie considered. She certainly didn't want to intrude where she wasn't wanted and definitely wouldn't stay if there was no hope for a reconciliation. Too restless to sleep, Maggie rose from bed and began pacing, finally moving to the window, staring out into the moon-drenched night. The utter tranquility of the setting captivated as well as beckoned. As if in a trance, she left her room, stealthily descended the stairs, and stepped out on the porch, her voluminous nightgown whipping about her legs in the gentle night breeze.

She inhaled deeply, finding the quiet strangely heady. She meant to remain only a few moments, but the cooling breeze was so welcome against her heated flesh that Maggie lingered, staring up at the inky sky and profusion of winking stars.

"It's an incredible night, isn't it?"

Starting violently, Maggie gasped and turned, finding Chase standing mere inches from her. "You frightened me. How dare you sneak up on me like that!"

"Simmer down, Maggie girl, I wasn't sneakin'. I was here before you came out."

"Why didn't you say something?"

"I reckon I was enjoyin' the scenery too much."

Maggie sensed rather than saw his appreciative grin and flushed, realizing how she must look in her thin nightgown. Though she was covered from head to toe, the lack of appropriate undergarments made her feel exposed and vulnerable.

"What are you doing out here anyway? I thought ranchers retired early."

"I've been sittin' here for quite a spell tryin' to decide whether or not to go up to your room."

"Your room," Maggie corrected.

"I didn't want to awaken the baby, but I knew I couldn't sleep until we talked."

"Did you enjoy your walk?"

Chase frowned, puzzled by Maggie's abrupt change of subject.

"With Virgie. She's quite appealing. I realize most men want young, innocent wives."

"What's that supposed to mean?"

"Have you proposed yet?"

Chase flushed, refusing to meet Maggie's eyes for fear she'd see how close she came to the truth. "There is only one woman I've ever proposed to, the only woman I loved enough to marry."

The breath caught painfully in Maggie's throat, waiting for Chase to continue, but he fell silent. When he did speak, he adroitly steered the conversation onto safer ground. "Why are you here, Maggie? What do you want from me?"

Just then one of the hands came out of the bunkhouse to relieve himself and, hearing voices, glanced curiously in their direction.

"We can't talk here," Chase said with a warning glance.

Taking her hand, he led her off the porch and around to the back of the house. The mellow glow of a full moon guided their steps and Maggie followed closely behind, attempting to avoid sharp stones and twigs littering the path. Once she stubbed her toe and stumbled, her whimper of pain bringing Chase to an abrupt halt. Gritting her teeth, Maggie motioned him on. He stopped beside the narrow stream where he had taken Virgie the day she tried to seduce him. Maggie sank gratefully to the bank, dangling her feet in the water.

"I'm sorry, I forgot you were barefoot," Chase said, hunkering down beside her. "Are you hurt?"

"No, I'm fine." The cool water felt good on her feet, and Maggie sighed, tempted to pull off her nightgown and immerse herself completely.

Chase must have heard her sigh and read her mind. "Go ahead, there's no one here to see you. You're probably not accustomed to Montana summers. Sometimes the heat is downright unbearable."

Maggie was sorely tempted but prudently declined. "We're here to talk, remember?"

"I'm findin' it difficult to remember anythin'," Chase admitted, "with you here next to me." The need to take Maggie in his arms and taste her sweet kisses was so compelling he couldn't recall his own name.

"You asked me why I've come to Montana."

"I don't give a damn why you're here," Chase croaked hoarsely, "only that you are. Have you any idea what you've put me through these past months, the questions I've asked myself, the anguish I've suffered? Damnation, Maggie girl, you tore me apart!"

Oh, Chase, Maggie thought in mute appeal, *you did it to yourself. You wouldn't listen to my explanation but took off in a huff.* She opened her mouth to speak but the temptation was too great as Chase seized her lips, probing her sweetness with the hot tip of his tongue.

The first taste of her produced a frenzy of need as his kiss deepened, forcing a hesitant response from Maggie. Tentatively she touched his tongue with her own and he reacted instantly, pulling her close, kneading her breasts, sliding down to grasp the firm mounds of her buttocks. The kiss seemed to go on forever as Maggie's body caught fire and exploded.

"I'm so hot for you, baby," Chase groaned. "No other woman can make me burn like you do. Let me put out my flame in you, Maggie."

He found the hem of her gown and jerked it up to her waist, so eager to enjoy again the special pleasure they shared that he felt ready to erupt.

"How many other women have you had, Chase? How many other women made you burn?" Maggie asked tightly. "Do you plan on adding Virgie to your list?"

"Huh?" Chase grunted, Maggie's words momentarily distracting him. "What in the hell is that supposed to mean? I was more faithful to you than you were to me, and you've got a kid to prove it. Will you hush up now and let me make love to you?"

"No. We should talk first, before we're distracted by—other things."

When Chase refused to loosen his hold on her, Maggie shoved at his chest, her strength catching him unprepared as he tumbled backwards. Before he could right himself, he began to slide down the slippery bank toward the water. Amused by his look of confusion, Maggie began to laugh, but her mirth was short-lived. Before she realized his intent, Chase grabbed her long flowing nightgown and pulled her along with him into the water.

"Chase, no!" But it was too late, as they both tumbled head over heels into the stream.

Maggie came up sputtering and found Chase laughing at her. "You little wildcat, that will teach you to make fun of me."

Then he ducked her again for good measure. Maggie squealed in protest and retaliated by pulling Chase's legs out from under him. He went down, dragging her with him. Somehow, beneath the surface, he found her mouth and they came up joined in a kiss that put an abrupt end to their horseplay.

"Lift your arms, darlin', I'm gonna get rid of this." He tugged at her gown and Maggie eagerly raised her arms. She found her footing in the waist-deep water as Chase deftly removed her single garment and tossed it to the bank, where it lay in a sodden heap. Then she helped him remove his own clothes, which promptly joined hers.

When he kissed her again, there was nothing between them but the cool caress of water. "I'd almost forgotten how good you feel," Chase moaned against her mouth.

His hands roamed urgently over silken flesh, heating the water that churned about them. Nothing had ever felt so wonderful and Maggie encouraged him into deeper intimacies with soft murmurs and sighs. Grasping her about the waist, Chase lifted her off her feet, bringing her slowly down until her breasts dangled just inches from his face. The offer was too tempting to resist as Chase took a rosy nipple into his mouth and suckled gently. Shock registered on his face as he tasted the first hot spurt of milk. Reluctantly he left her breast, thinking how pleasant it must be for tiny Beth to be enjoying this feast several times a day.

"I never tasted anythin' so sweet," he vowed, his tongue lapping the tiny droplet that clung to her nipple. "Open your legs, darlin'." His need was spontaneous and inevitable and too hot to be postponed.

Chase knew he had to be imbedded deep inside Maggie, had to feel her close tightly around him, a warm pulsing sheath for the shaft of his passion. Then he was inside her, his possession so full and deep that their ecstasy soared. "It's not too soon, is it?" Chase gasped, suddenly recalling that Maggie had just recently given birth. Truth to tell, he wasn't certain he could stop even if she said yes.

Maggie wrapped her legs around Chase's waist as he slowly lowered her onto his hardened staff. He filled her completely, the sheer bliss of his possession setting off tiny explosions deep inside her. When it came, his question surprised her. His loving did anything but hurt her.

"Don't, please don't—"

Thinking Maggie was asking him to stop, Chase released a low moan of pure anguish. "Aw gawd, darlin', don't ask me to stop."

"Never," Maggie vowed. "Make me feel again, Chase—it's been so long."

Chase needed no further encouragement as he grasped the perfect ovals of her buttocks and moved her with deliberate slowness up and down the long length of his staff. The exquisite friction brought a groan to her lips, reflecting her impatience to reach that place of ecstasy where no one but Chase could take her.

"Don't be greedy, baby," Chase cautioned, sensing her eagerness. "I'll try to last as long as you need me."

"Now, Chase, I need you now!" Maggie cried, flinging her head back and forcing him to greater speed when his pace proved too slow for her.

Maggie's stampeding passion sparked his own, and Chase began pounding into her wildly, the water churning around them like a raging whirlpool.

"Oh God! Oh Chase!"

The need to spill his seed into her became a terrible ache inside him as Chase poised on the brink of climax. "Hang on, darlin', I want you to come with me." His breath thundered in his chest as a thin wail left Maggie's lips and rapture seized her. Her body thrashed with wild abandon, her arms grasping his shoulders to keep from falling. Only then did Chase unleash the unbridled fury of his own climax. It had been over a year since he'd last had Maggie, far too long for a man to remain celibate . . .

Maggie's legs slid from around Chase's waist. Still too shaky to stand on her own, she was grateful for his support. "Can you make it back to shore?" he asked, still worried that he might have hurt her.

"Just let me catch my breath."

He watched her splash in the water, attempting to cleanse herself, then turned abruptly and waded to shore, picking up his shirt and returning to where he left her. "Here, let me." Wetting the tail of the garment he passed it back and forth between her legs until all traces of him had been removed. Then he scooped her up in his arms and carried her to the bank. Instead of setting her on her feet, he laid her down on the soft, mossy ground.

"Are you ready to talk now?" Maggie asked, still shaky after the heady experience of being loved again by Chase.

"Not yet," Chase grinned, sounding and looking so much like the man she loved in the Yukon that he nearly broke her heart. "A starvin' man eats till he's full."

"Starving? You?" It didn't seem possible that a man as virile as Chase would deny himself all these months.

"I reckon you think I'm lyin'," Chase scowled. "Never thought I'd live to see the day a woman would make a fool outa me. After you, I didn't want another woman."

"What about Virgie—is she expecting marriage?"

"Perhaps," he answered truthfully, "but I promised her nothin'. I admit she's a temptin' morsel, and I briefly considered takin' a wife since you obviously weren't available. Given time, who knows what might have happened?" Chase shrugged. "Virgie made no bones 'bout wantin' me. And she's damn fetchin'."

"And now? Do you still feel the same way about Virgie? Is a match possible between you?"

"I can't think with you in my arms," Chase claimed boldly. "Compared to you, Virgie is a mere child. There's so much I want to ask you, so much I need to know, but I don't want to spoil this moment. Nothin' unpleasant is gonna interfere with my lovin' you again."

This time Chase's kiss was gentle, coaxing, the urgency of their first mating sated. He kissed her eyes, her nose, each cheek, finding the sensitive pulse points behind her ears and at the base of her neck. He lavished excessive tenderness on the sensitive skin of her breasts.

Unwilling to remain passive, Maggie moved her hands freely over the thick muscles that stretched down his back. Her brazen caresses inspected the curve of his hips, the taut planes of his belly. Her tantalizing touch flowed upward to stroke each rib that lay beneath his bronzed skin. Caressing him quickly became an obsession that captivated Maggie. She marveled at the feel of his sinewy flesh and the ominous strength that lay in repose. Moaning, she felt his fingers slip inside her and she undulated her hips in response to his rhythm.

"Oh, Chase!"

Fired by her response, Chase sought to initiate a deeper intimacy, to make her forget Scott Gordon and any other man in her life. Shifting downwards, his mouth found the honey-gold triangle between her legs. Shimmering moonlight gilded her tender, quivering flesh and Chase had never viewed so enchanting a sight.

Her body felt deliciously heavy, as if she were sinking into a pool of rippling passion. He could make her soul sing when he touched her so lovingly. He could send her soaring, gliding toward towering heights. Maggie sighed as his mouth caressed the tenderest part of her, his tongue parting and probing the hot center of her being. When he located the sensitive bud of her femininity, Maggie shrieked in joy, tunneling her fingers in his burnished hair and holding him in place. But still Chase was not satisfied. Grasping her buttocks, he brought her closer still, until her body shook and trembled with the force of her climax. Then he slid full and deep inside her, stroking her to greater heights as he sought his own reward.

Lying exhausted in Chase's encircling arms, Maggie knew existence without this special man would be unbearably dull. Of course she'd always have his child, but there'd be a void without Chase. Yet she'd never intrude where she wasn't wanted. The reason she had come to Montana in the beginning was to learn if there was still a chance for her and Chase without making him feel obligated because of Beth.

Sweet pleasure still flowed like a river channeling through every part of Chase's being, holding him captive in its sweet, undulating current. If he had never sampled Maggie's hypnotic magic, he might have learned to live without her, but after tasting of her sweetness again, he'd never be satisfied with another woman. Few couples ever experienced what they had just shared. Had Maggie come to her senses after Gordon left her and decided she wanted him back? Did he want to be second best? Could he accept another man's child? He hated to admit it, but that tiny scrap of humanity had already gotten under his skin.

"What are you thinking?" Maggie asked, watching the play of emotion on Chase's expressive face.

"I'm wonderin' if you're gonna tell me again that you can't have children. Is there somethin' special you did to keep from havin' my child?"

"I suppose I deserve that," Maggie said with a hint of regret. "The reason I lied to you originally was so you wouldn't feel obligated to make a commitment. I didn't want to force you into anything you weren't ready for, and I knew you'd feel a certain obligation if I conceived while we were together."

"My God, Maggie, I loved you!"

"We came to love each other, that's true, but at first love and marriage had no place in our plans.

I accepted that and took the risk rather than spend all those weeks in the Yukon without your loving. If a child had resulted, I was prepared to raise it on my own. I want a man who loves me for myself, not out of duty or obligation."

Chase chewed on that for a while, deciding that while her thinking might be flawed, he really couldn't fault her decision. What hurt, hurt like hell, was finding Maggie with another man. "If we had created a child, I would have married you even if I didn't love you," Chase admitted. It wasn't exactly what Maggie wanted to hear. She needed to know that Chase wanted her for herself.

"You said you didn't care for children."

"I only said that so you wouldn't feel inadequate because you couldn't have any. Hell yes, I wanted children. What good is all this money if there's no one to leave it to?"

"Would you really have married me in order to claim your child had I conceived while we were together? Even if you didn't love me?"

"What kind of question is that? I did love you."

"But what if you didn't?" she persisted.

"I'd do or say anythin' to claim my child," Chase said at length.

Maggie went still, her mind in a turmoil of indecision. She had yet to hear Chase say he still loved her, that he had never stopped loving her. He had wanted her desperately just now, but was it because he had been without a woman for a long time? That was another shock. Why had Chase remained celibate? Had she done that to him?

If she told Chase now about Beth, Maggie considered, she'd never know if he wanted her for herself or because he wanted his child. Therefore it seemed logical that she withhold her secret until she could make Chase love her again, or he stumbled upon the truth on his own.

"Do you wanna tell, me about Gordon?" Chase asked, realizing the subject could be put off no longer, "and why you're in Montana instead of with your baby's father? Did he run out on you?"

"I don't really want to talk about Scott, except to say that I didn't want to marry him. I assume he's back in Dawson City."

"Is he supportin' his child?"

"Why do you assume Beth belongs to Scott?" Maggie bit out angrily. She wanted to take the mule-headed dolt and shake him until he came to his senses.

"You mean—damnation! What kinda woman are you?" he cried, assuming the worst. "Why are you here? Do you need money? You're certainly entitled to a share of what we earned at Eleven Above."

"Damn your ornery hide, Chase, I don't need your money! I've done extremely well at writing. I want nothing from you."

"Obviously you want somethin', or you wouldn't be here."

"I'll leave in the morning," Maggie said tersely.

"Hold on a dang minute. What if you're carryin' my child?"

"I'll raise it just like I'm raising Beth."

"Like hell! You're stayin'. I don't give a hoot in hell what brought you here, but since you are here and we've made love, I don't aim to let you go 'til I know for certain sure you're not grownin' my seed. No lies this time."

Admitting that he loved Maggie teased the tip of Chase's tongue, but he was leery of making so bald a statement without knowing if his feelings were reciprocated. Something brought Maggie here to him, and if it wasn't a need for money, he damn well intended to find out what it was. If she loved him, he wanted to hear the words with his own ears before committing himself. He'd been through

too much anguish these past months to welcome
her without reservation. Too many questions still
remained unanswered. And there was the child to
consider.

Her temper flaring, Maggie flung herself away
from Chase and dashed back into the creek, hoping
to cool her anger as well as wash Chase's scent
from her. She wanted him to want her, but not this
way. Not because she might be carrying his child or
because he lusted for her. Maggie seriously doubted
she'd conceived after just this one time and made
a solemn vow that Chase wouldn't touch her again
until he said he loved her. She even set a time limit.
If Chase hadn't committed himself two months from
today, she'd go back to Seattle and learn to live without him. A splash nearby jolted her from her reverie,
and she whirled to find Chase rising from the water
beside her.

Every sculptured inch of his upper body shone
like molded bronze in the moonlight. His tension
was evident by the bunched muscles and corded
tendons rippling beneath the smooth surface of his
skin.

"Don't ever run away from me like that again," he
warned tightly. "We weren't finished talkin'."

"I've said all I'm going to say," Maggie tossed
back, heading toward shore. A hand on her arm
pulled her up short.

"If you don't wanna talk, we could . . ."

"No! Not again—maybe not ever."

"What in the hell do you mean by that?"

"I didn't come here to be your private whore."

"Why did you come? How can I help you if you
won't tell me?"

"Right now I'm thinking I should have stayed in
Seattle. Let me go, I need to tend to Beth. She'll raise
a ruckus if she awakens and I'm not there to feed
her. We wouldn't want to disturb Virgie, would we?"

Chase's hold loosened, finding no argument with Maggie's maternal concern. "Just answer one question. Why do you find it so distasteful to have a child with me? I may be a rough cowpoke, but I'm rich enough to support all the children you give me as well as your by-blow."

"Is that a proposal?"

"Damnation, Maggie, don't put words in my mouth."

"Then don't dictate to me, Chase," Maggie flung over her shoulder. "I'll stay two months, and if in that time we find there's nothing left of the love we once shared, I'll leave for good and never bother you again."

"Don't bet on it," Chase muttered darkly.

There was more than one way to make certain Maggie never left Montana. Before long he'd make her love and need him as much as he loved and needed her. Though he burned with jealousy each time he saw Maggie's tiny daughter and pictured Maggie with another man, the fact remained that she had come to him of her own accord and for reasons unknown to him. Chase reckoned that Maggie regretted her mistake and had come to him for a reconciliation. Once she admitted as much he'd forgive her, of course, though he'd make damn certain she'd never have the opportunity to be unfaithful again.

Chase watched with avid appreciation as Maggie walked away from him, her body rising from the water like a gilded Venus leaving her bath. The taut oval mounds of her buttocks and enticing curve of her back brought a flush of arousal to his body, and he was amazed that he could want her again after having tasted unsurpassed ecstasy twice in the space of an hour.

Chapter Twenty

Her soggy nightgown clinging enticingly to the damp contours of her body, Maggie entered the house and quietly found her way to her room. She went first to Beth's cradle, relieved to find her sleeping soundly. She was such a good baby, Maggie thought lovingly, that she already slept through most nights without demanding a feeding. She wanted desperately for her and Chase to be the kind of family Beth needed, but only if he came to it willingly.

Assured of Beth's comfort, Maggie sank down onto the bed, her body heavy and lethargic from exhaustion and sexual contentment. She would have been horrified to know she had been seen with Chase and spied upon returning wet and disheveled after their wild coupling. Unable to sleep because of the heat, and disturbed by the sudden appearance of another woman in Chase's life, Virgie had heard Maggie's steps on the stairs. She rose and followed, hoping to have a few private words with her about her presence at the ranch. She ducked back inside the doorway when she saw Chase step out from the shadows and join Maggie. She couldn't hear what they said, but burned with envy when Chase grasped Maggie's hand and led her off.

Virgie couldn't understand what Chase saw in Maggie when she, Virgie, had so much more to offer. Did Maggie have some hold over the handsome cowboy? What could Chase be thinking? Maggie had to be long past her prime, with an illegitimate child besides. Yet both Rusty and Kate seemed unconcerned about Maggie's unmarried state, or her turning up at the ranch for no reason. Somehow, Virgie vowed, she intended to learn exactly what Maggie Afton was to Chase. Virgie and Chase were meant to be together. He was perfect for her, and no dried-up spinster was going to steal him from her.

When Maggie returned to the house alone, bedraggled and soaking wet, it was obvious to Virgie that more than casual conversation had taken place down by the creek. It rankled to think that Chase had spurned her own efforts at seduction, yet seized the first opportunity to take Maggie Afton. If she didn't do something soon, Virgie reflected thoughtfully, Maggie would trap Chase into marriage.

Surprisingly, Maggie liked Montana and the ranch. The air was so clean and pure Beth seemed to thrive in it. Seattle was beautiful, but the wide open spaces of Montana held a certain appeal Maggie found difficult to resist. Verdant mountains rose majestically above the valleys and forests of Chase's ranch, and often Maggie left Beth in Spotted Deer's capable hands and rode out on a lively sorrel mare Chase had provided for her use. Normally she was accompanied by either

Rusty, Kate, or both, and sometimes Virgie rode along.

After their night of love, Maggie made a concentrated effort to avoid being alone with Chase, which he found both amusing and irritating. Maggie wanted no repeat of their explosive joining down by the stream. She didn't come to the ranch merely to bed Chase, but to win back his love.

During the long afternoons while Beth slept, Maggie satisfied her creative talents by writing chapters for another book and dashing out magazine articles. She missed her work on the Post-Intelligencer and often wished she could both satisfy her love for Chase and pursue her career at the same time. It didn't seem fair for a women to give up a career and all she strived for to follow the dictates of her heart. Was there no happy medium?

Chase tried to stay away from Maggie, aware that it was what she wanted, but as the days passed the task became not only difficult but impossible. He knew Maggie was avoiding him, and all his efforts to ignore her failed miserably. Just seeing her daily, watching her lavish tender love on her daughter, made Chase ache with thwarted desire. Nor did Virgie make things easier. The tempting vixen was at his elbow, luring him with the purple depths of her eyes, suggesting pleasures that needed no words. But at least Maggie was still here, he thought smugly. And, astonishingly, he was getting accustomed to seeing tiny Beth each day. He rather enjoyed having a baby around to liven up his life. If only . . . That thought remained unspoken, for Chase knew from experience that fantasies didn't exist.

One day Maggie watched Chase out the window as he sauntered casually over to where Spotted Deer had placed Beth on a blanket beneath a large shade tree in the yard so that the infant might play and exercise. The Indian girl sat nearby, keeping a watchful eye on her squirming charge. Maggie stared with trepidation as Chase knelt beside the tiny tot, studying her with careful scrutiny. His unfeigned interest surprised Maggie, and she held her breath as Chase picked up the infant, tossing her above his head as she squealed in delight.

Chase had no idea what made him pick Beth up; he had merely wanted to see for himself how she was faring in the Montana climate. But she looked so damned appealing, so artlessly beguiling, he couldn't resist. There was a certain magnetism about Maggie's little girl Chase found difficult to resist. With rapt attention he studied her tiny face, so like Maggie's except for her eyes, which were a spellbinding blue. He'd had the urge to cuddle the tyke like this since the day she arrived but purposely stifled his paternal instincts. Abruptly, he wondered if Maggie had conceived after their mating by the creek and decided to put an end to her foolish attempts at keeping them apart when it was what neither of them wanted. Dammit, he loved Maggie, and deep in his heart he knew Maggie loved him too.

Brushing a kiss across Beth's smooth forehead, he placed the gurgling infant back on her blanket. Turning, he nearly collided with Virgie, who had crept up behind him.

"Don't sneak up on a man like that," Chase scowled, annoyed that Virgie still persisted with her pursuit of him.

"She's a scrawny little thing, isn't she?" Virgie said disparagingly, motioning toward Beth with a careless lift of her shoulder. Though Beth was still small, she had a healthy glow about her that belied Virgie's words. "When are they leaving?"

"They're welcome to stay as long as they like, same as you."

Virgie flushed, recognizing a put-down when she heard one. Virgie definitely wasn't pleased with the way Chase seemed to dote on Maggie's infant but seemed unable to remedy the situation. "Kate has lunch on the table."

"I'll be in directly." He turned away, leaving Virgie fuming in impotent rage. She aimed a hateful glare at Beth, then left in a huff. Maggie turned away from the window, apparently satisfied that Virgie seemed to be getting nowhere with Chase.

Chase was annoyed when Maggie failed to show up for lunch, but Virgie was pleased to have him all to herself for a change. She did her best to entertain him, but it was apparent that his mind was elsewhere. When he rose abruptly and excused himself after choking down only a few bites of food, Virgie knew the time had come to have a talk with Maggie.

Chase was of the same mind.

Maggie had just settled Beth down for her nap when a knock sounded on her door and Kate entered carrying a tray. "Ya missed lunch, honey, so I brought ya a tray."

"That's sweet of you, Kate, but I could have gone down to the kitchen and fixed myself something."

"No need, I wanted ta have a talk with ya anyways." She set the tray on a table and fixed Maggie with a speculative glance. " 'Pears ta me you and Chase ain't gettin' nowhere towards a relationship. Has he guessed about the baby yet? He seems powerful taken with the little mite. 'Course she's sweet enough ta melt even the hardest heart."

"Chase is too cussed stubborn to recognize the truth when it's staring him in the face. Beth is so like him, it's uncanny. The eyes alone give her away."

"What ya gonna do?"

"Hope that he'll open his eyes soon and face up to the fact that he has a beautiful little daughter."

"Tell him, Maggie," Kate urged. "Knowin' Chase, he's apt ta be angry when he finds out you've kept the truth from him."

"Chase has no one to blame but himself. His hot temper sent him jumping to conclusions without stopping to consider the circumstances. It would serve him right if I took Beth and left the ranch."

"Ya wouldn't do that, would ya?" Kate asked, aghast.

"I hope I don't have to," Maggie admitted, taking a bite of crispy fried chicken and chewing thoughtfully.

Chase waited until all the lights in the house were doused and he was relatively certain everyone was sleeping before entering the house and treading lightly to the room he had given up for Maggie and her baby. The door opened noiselessly beneath his hand. Since he knew the room by heart, he needed no light to guide him to the bed. It pleased him to think of Maggie occupying his bed and he peered down at her a few minutes, not really seeing her through the darkness but vividly recalling every tempting, utterly fautless curve of her slender form. How could she deny him what they both craved?

Beth picked that unlikely moment to fuss in her cradle. She had fallen asleep before nursing her fill and awakened now wanting the rest of her meal. Distracted by the baby's soft mewlings, Chase walked to her cradle and scooped her up as if it was the most natural thing in the world. Her tiny rosebud mouth nuzzled his chest, but evidently found nothing to her liking, for her small fists waved angrily in the air and her face puckered up in obvious frustration.

Chase smiled at her antics, his heart contracting with emotions he'd never experienced before. No matter who this enchanting tyke belonged to, he wanted to protect her always; he'd make damn certain nothing bad hurt her. He wanted the same thing for Beth's mother.

Attuned to her every need, Maggie heard Beth whimper and forced herself to respond. When she glanced over at Beth's cradle, the blood froze in her veins. A large shadowy figure bent over her, Beth's small figure nearly dwarfed by brawny arms and massive chest. Maggie opened her mouth to scream, then abruptly snapped it shut when silvery moonbeams produced a halo of light around a head of burnished copper.

"Chase, what are you doing here? You frightened the daylights out of me. Is something wrong with Beth?"

"Sorry, Maggie," Chase whispered sheepishly. "I wanted to talk to you and you've been avoidin' me like poison. As for you daughter, I reckon she's just hungry."

"Bring her here," Maggie said, sliding up in bed and arranging the pillows behind her.

"Do you need a light?"

"No, Beth can find what she's looking for in the dark." Maggie smiled as Chase laid Beth in her arms.

"I've never been very good at seein' in the dark," Chase drawled lazily as he lit and trimmed the wick of the bedside lamp until its warm glow filled the corners of the room.

Maggie lay relaxed against the pillows, Beth's blond head nuzzling at her breast. Her nightgown was unbottoned to the waist and her shoulders and breasts gleamed like polished alabaster. The breath caught in Chase's chest. Never had he seen such an awe-inspiring sight as that enchanting child nursing at her mother's breast. Maggie noted the direction of his gaze and made to cover her exposed flesh.

"No, don't," Chase said, staying her hand. "I've seen you before, there's nothin' to hide. You're so damn beautiful, darlin', it hurts my eyes."

Abruptly Maggie's hand dropped to her side. She shuddered when Chase lightly caressed her breast. "What do you want, Chase?" She had to say something or become completely unsettled. It wouldn't do for him to learn she was putty in his hands.

Chase concentrated for a minute on the slurping noises made by Beth before responding. "Are you carryin' my child, Maggie?" He hadn't meant to blurt out the words in that abrupt manner, but they came unbidden to his tongue.

Maggie flushed. She knew several days ago that she hadn't conceived. "I'm not pregnant, Chase. You're under no obligation where I'm concerned."

Chase frowned. Maggie made it sound as if he couldn't wait to be shed of her when just the opposite was true. He sat down on the bed, enthralled by the sight of Beth nursing noisily at Maggie's breast.

"Is she always so greedy?"

"She fell asleep before she finished her dinner."

Chase ruffled the blond fuzz covering her small head. "She's grown."

"I'm surprised you noticed."

"There's not much around the ranch that escapes my notice. Is she asleep?" Chase asked, nodding at Beth who now lay dozing at Maggie's breast, her rosebud mouth lax against her mother's nipple.

"Yes, I'll put her to bed."

"No, let me," Chase offered, surprising Maggie as he took the babe from her arms and placed her in the cradle with a gentleness that belied his great strength. Then he turned back to Maggie, his hands already working at the buttons on his shirt.

"What are you doing?"

"I'm gonna love you. For weeks you've ignored me, when we both know this is what we want. Just you bein' here on the ranch proves you care for me. Why deny it? Why deny *this*?"

"No, Chase, we can't," Maggie protested urgently. "I didn't become pregnant the last time we made love, but I may this time."

"Is that so bad? I said before I'd take care of you if that happened."

"You mean marriage?"

"Well, dang it, why not?" Chase said thoughtfully, as if the notion just occurred. "If you're carryin' my baby, naturally I'd ask you to marry me."

"Is that the only reason."

"Isn't that good enough?"

"No!" Maggie hissed vehemently. "I always assumed the father of my children would love me."

It was on the tip of Chase's tongue to tell Maggie he loved her, that he'd never stopped loving her, not even when she bore another man's child. But since no such admission was forthcoming from Maggie, he bit back his own words.

"You love the way I love you, the way I make you tingle and burn and cry out in passion. Love has to start someplace."

"It's not enough, Chase."

"How about this?" He stroked her tender breasts. "Your body loves what I do for it."

His mouth slid down the slender column of her throat to take the erect nub in his mouth and suckle with the same delight Beth enjoyed. "Chase, please, don't." Her last words ended in a strangled gasp as Chase's calloused hand crept beneath her night-gown and up the inside of her thigh to that throbbing warmth between her legs.

"Tell me you don't want me," Chase whispered against her lips.

"I—don't want you."

"You're a damn liar." His fingers began a slow, tantalizing massage, first teasing the tender moist flesh, then probing deep inside, his touch a burning brand that set her afire. Her nightgown melted from her like magic.

"Touch me, Maggie, feel how much I need you."

His slow, sensual drawl released the bonds that controlled her response as Maggie reached for him, shocked to find him naked and hard with desire.

"That's it! Oh God, that's good," Chase moaned as her small hand slid down the length of him. "Slowly, baby, that's right." His body moved in tempo with her hand until he knew he had to stop her or shame himself. "Enough, darlin', I need to be inside you now. Lie on your side." Mindlessly, Maggie obeyed, long past the point of protest or question.

She felt Chase mold his body to her backside and spread her legs with his. Then he slid easily inside her, his hands free to knead and tease and tantalize. He sensed her initial reluctance and said, "There's a whole passel of ways to love, darlin', and I aim to teach you every one of them. Next I'll let you get on top and do whatever feels good to you. I'm not hurtin' you, am I?"

Hurt her? It felt wonderful. He felt wonderful. "No, you're not hurting me."

Her words unleashed a demon inside him as Chase shoved himself in deeper, moving, stroking, faster, stoking the flames of her passion into a blazing inferno. And then he took her into its molten center, joining her in an eruption of sublime ecstasy. It was several breathless minutes before either of them could talk.

"Damn you, Chase, I didn't want this to happen again until—" Her words faltered.

"Until what?" Chase asked, his interest piqued.

"Until I decided—what I wanted to do with my life," Maggie finished lamely.

"We're always gonna want each other," Chase stated with firm conviction.

"Like a couple of animals?" Maggie charged, her voice laced with contempt. She was disgusted with herself as well as with Chase.

"Like human bein's who will always need one another."

"Have you changed your mind about Beth? Are you willing to accept another man's child?"

"I don't care who fathered Beth. I don't know what went wrong between us, Maggie, but I still want you. I want you for my w—"

"Fire! The stables are on fire!"

The alarm echoed through the stillness of the night, putting an abrupt end to whatever Chase was about to say. Jumping from the bed, he ran to the window, cursing when he saw flames leaping from the stable roof. "Damnation! My prize stallions are in there!" Pulling on his pants and shoving on his boots, he grabbed his shirt and flew out the door. "You'll be safe enough here. I don't think the house is in danger unless the wind shifts," he threw over his shoulder.

"Chase, be careful!" But he was already out the door.

The commotion awoke Beth, and Maggie struggled out of bed to soothe her back to sleep, forgetting that Chase had stripped her naked.

"You conniving witch, I saw Chase leave your room just now." Violet eyes raked contemptuously over Maggie's nude flesh.

Darting for the robe at the foot of the bed, Maggie shrugged into it before turning to confront Virgie. "I didn't hear you knock, Virgie."

"The door was ajar. You can't deny you were with Chase tonight—the room reeks of sex."

"How would you know what sex smells like, unless—" Her words trailed off as she searched

Virgie's face. "Chase and I are both adults. We don't need permission."

"There's a name for women like you. Why don't you leave Chase alone?"

"I'll leave if and when Chase tells me to. Go back to bed. I need to see to my child. She's frightened by all the commotion."

Deliberately Maggie turned her back on Virgie, leaving the fuming brunette with no choice but to whirl on her heel and storm out the door.

Fortunately, the wind did not shift and the house suffered no damage, but six of Chase's blooded stallions had been destroyed, as well as the stable housing them. Chase spent the following days trying to learn what had caused the costly blaze. Rebuilding the stable was no problem, but replacing the horses meant combing the United States for stock to replace those lost. Of necessity Chase's discussion with Maggie was delayed until the nasty business with the fire was investigated and rebuilding begun. Yet the piercing glances he cast in her direction told Maggie they were far from finished with what they had started that night in her bedroom.

About a week after the fire, Maggie decided to ride into Butte. Beth had outgrown all the clothes she'd brought with her, and she wanted to mail the first chapters of her new book to the publisher. Chase was occupied with supervising the rebuilding of the new stable, and both Rusty and Kate were at their new house, which was nearly ready for occupancy. Only Virgie remained at home, and she offered no comment when Maggie voiced her intention of riding to Butte. Virgie had not spoken above two words to Maggie since the night she had discovered Chase in Maggie's room, and she wasn't about to tell her now how dangerous it was to ride alone in this wild country.

After feeding Beth and putting her down for a
nap, Maggie placed her in Spotted Deer's care. Then
she donned her split riding skirt and went to the
stable where the riding horses were kept. Assuming
she could carry all her purchases in saddlebags, she
didn't bother with a buggy but saddled the gentle sorrel mare Chase had designated for her use.
She saddled the mare herself as no one else was
available, all the hands either occupied with the
new stable or out on the range. Consequently no
one warned her that the fluffy white clouds that
looked like cotton candy were in reality thunder-
heads building overhead. But Maggie felt none of
the oppressive heaviness that hung in the air, nor
recognized the sudden drop in temperature as a
warning of a violent change in the weather.

Maggie lingered in town longer than she antici-
pated, selecting clothes for herself as well as for the
baby. She ate a leisurely lunch, mailed her partial
manuscript, and checked the post office for mail.
There was none. The rumble of thunder and flash
of lightning greeted her when she stepped out onto
the street. Suddenly she became aware of the ominous sky overhead. Hurrying to where her horse was
tethered, Maggie hoped she'd reach the ranch before
the full brunt of the storm unleashed its fury.

Urging her sorrel to greater speed, Maggie tried
not to think of the ruts and gullys beneath her as
the horse's hooves flew over the uneven ground. The
wind rose like a howling banshee across the desolate
range. Then the rain came spewing down out of the
leaden sky. Lightning produced a brilliant display
in the dark heavens, and the sorrel turned skittish,
dancing and pawing nervously.

"Easy, girl," Maggie soothed, thunder and wind
snatching her words away. The next flash of lightning brought the mare up on her hind legs, pawing
the air in terror and sending Maggie hurtling from

her back onto the unyielding ground. Her breath left her lungs in a whoosh as she tumbled over and over, her head coming to rest against a large rock. She lay sprawled in the mud in a narrow gully, rain washing over her in a rushing torrent.

Chapter Twenty-one

The raging storm forced Chase inside. Since it was
nearly supper time anyway, he ducked through the
rain into the house, thinking it a perfect time to find
Maggie and continue the conversation that had been
so rudely interrupted by the fire several days earlier.
Somehow he had to persuade Maggie to marry him,
to convince her nothing mattered but their being
together.

When Chase dashed into the house, Beth was
screeching at the top of her lungs. "What's wrong
with her?" he asked Spotted Deer who was pacing
back and forth in the parlor trying unsuccessfully to
soothe the child. From time to time she paused to
peer anxiously through the window. "Is she sick?"

"Not sick, hungry," Spotted Deer said in halting
English.

"Where's Maggie?" A prickle of foreboding raised
hackles at the back of Chase's neck even before he
heard the Indian girl's terse explanation.

"She not return yet from town."

"Damnation! It's stormin' somethin' fierce out there—a real gully-washer. How long has she been gone?"

"Many hours," Spotted Deer said, her voice rising above Beth's wails.

"Where are Kate and Rusty?"

"At new house."

"The storm musta delayed them."

"What's the trouble?" Virgie stepped into the room, holding her ears. "Can't you stop that brat from squawling?" This was directed at Spotted Deer, who was doing her best to placate the hungry child.

"The child is hungry, Virgie—have you no compassion?" Chase reprimanded sternly.

"Then give her to her mother," the haughty brunette suggested.

"Spotted Deer says Maggie went into town earlier. Do you know anythin' about it?"

"You mean she hasn't returned?" Virgie asked, round-eyed with mock concern. "I knew she was going into town but assumed she'd be back by now. Perhaps she decided to stay because of the weather."

"Not likely," Chase scoffed. "Not when she's the only one who can feed her child. Frankly, I'm plain worried. What am I gonna do with Beth 'til she returns?"

"I don't know anything about babies," Virgie shrugged. "Surely something will satisfy her."

"Of course, why didn't I think of it before!" Chase cried, slapping his knee. "There's bound to be cow's milk in the kitchen, and Bright Leaf is quite resourceful. I'm sure she'll think of somethin'."

He murmured hasty instructions to Spotted Deer, who nodded and hurried from the room in search of the cook. Bright Leaf had birthed several children and certainly would know how to keep a hungry baby from starving. Beth was nearly five months old now and growing rapidly, with an appetite to match. If Chase had waited around, he would have heard Beth's angry screams change into happy gurgles as she devoured the nourishing gruel Bright Leaf spooned into her eager mouth.

But Chase didn't linger. He left Virgie without a word of explanation to dash back out into the howling storm. Maggie needed him—he knew it, felt it in his bones, in his heart. He was in the stable saddling his mount when Maggie's sorrel came back riderless, her sides heaving and foaming at the mouth.

Maggie woke up choking. Water filled her mouth and nose. The narrow gully she lay in was awash with muddy water, and if she didn't extricate herself immediately she was in danger of drowning. After several abortive attempts, she struggled to her feet and staggered to higher ground, cowering beneath the vicious onslaught of driving rain, thunder, and lightning. Pain pounded her head, making coherent thought impossible, yet common sense told her to seek shelter. Though every bone in her body ached, Maggie sloshed through the drenching downpour with dogged determination.

Several times she slipped in ankle-deep mud and fell, picked herself up, and continued on, one painful step after another through the encroaching darkness. Her mind was blank, her thoughts on nothing but survival, sensing that somewhere someone needed her. Unfortunately, Maggie saw nothing that offered shelter, only barren hills, rocks, and water-filled gullys. Still she staggered on, driven by some mysterious force inside her. Her legs were leaden, her body chilled, her brain numb. She was close to succumbing to exhaustion when she spied a small shack through the dense curtain of rain.

Sheer determination lent her the strength to move her feet, one after another, until the shack stood before her wavering gaze. The door opened beneath her touch and she stumbled into the tiny, dank room. Feeling her way through the gray dimness, she located a narrow bunk with a stack of neatly folded blankets at its foot. Fortunately for Maggie, she had stumbled upon one of the line shacks sometimes used by hands required to spend the night on the range. It offered little in the way of comfort besides a bunk and shelter from the elements. But what more could she ask for?

Acting out of pure instinct, she shed her soaked clothes, rolled up in a blanket, and stretched out on the bunk. Within minutes she had fallen into an exhausted stupor.

Chase was frantic with worry. He'd covered the road to Butte and back, finding no trace of Maggie. It was as if she'd disappeared into thin air. If she'd been thrown from her horse as he suspected, he should have found her somewhere between Butte and the ranch. He'd even inquired at all the hotels in Butte and met with disappointment. Torrents of wind-driven rain and sheer blackness finally forced him to suspend the search for the night. But he wasn't giving up. At first light he intended to form a search party and continue combing the surrounding countryside until he found Maggie.

For some obscure reason, Chase felt the need to be close to Beth during her mother's absence, and he spent the long night in his own bed next to Beth's cradle. He slept little, merely watching over the baby, promising her he'd find her mother and keep them both safe for the rest of their days. Sated on the mixture of milk and cereal fed to her by Bright Leaf, Beth slept through the night, blissfully unaware of her father's anguish.

Dawn found Chase preparing to launch a search for Maggie, having already roused the hands from their beds. Most of them were gathered out by the corral receiving last minute instructions when Rusty and Kate rode up in the wagon. All traces of the fierce storm were gone, and pale streaks of pink colored the blue horizon. Rusty and Kate were returning early from their nearly completed house, where they were forced to spend the night due to the storm. The buckboard clattered to a halt beside the group of solemn-eyed men.

"Some storm last night," Rusty said, climbing down from the driver's bench. Chase reached up to assist Kate. "Hope ya wasn't worried none 'bout me and Kate."

"Wasn't you I was concerned 'bout," Chase said tersely.

Kate sensed an underlying current in Chase's words. "What is it, Chase? Is somethin' wrong?"

"Maggie's missin'. She went to town yesterday and never returned."

"Ya reckon she was out in that storm all night?" Rusty gulped, fear seizing him.

"Her horse came back without her. She musta taken a fall," Chase explained grimly. "I went back over the road but found no trace of her. I even went to Butte and inquired at the hotels. It's as if she disappeared into nowhere. Me and the boys are gettin' ready to ride out again."

"I'll join ya," Rusty offered.

"I'd prefer you stayed here in case Maggie returns on her own. No tellin' what shape she's in after bein' out all night."

"I hope he finds her," Kate said after the men thundered out of the yard. "That little baby needs both her ma and pa."

"I'm a mite surprised Chase hasn't guessed the truth by now," Rusty replied, shaking his head.

"I reckon the dunderhead does know deep in his heart but is too dang stubborn ta admit it."

Chase hoped the hands were having better luck than he was. They had spread out in different directions, and each man was to search thoroughly every gully and hill and behind every tree and rock. It was agreed beforehand that two shots in quick succession would signal the others that Maggie had been found.

Around noon Chase stopped by a swollen creek to drink deeply of the cool water and nibble on the dry biscuits and cold meat he had snatched from the kitchen on his way out this morning. He was on his own property now, having found no trace of Maggie on the road to Butte. He had decided to take his search in a wider circle when he suddenly remembered the old line shack nearby, located on a remote section of his property. It was still used occasionally and was equipped with cot and blankets. It was entirely feasible that Maggie had stumbled upon it while seeking shelter, since there were no neighbors within miles. Spurring his mount, Chase raced across the rough ground, praying his hunch was right and he'd find Maggie safe and unharmed at the small hut.

The weather-beaten shack appeared deserted as Chase approached. He wasted no time in useless speculation as he threw open the door and stepped inside. Sunlight streamed through the open door, clearly revealing the blanket-shrouded form curled up on the narrow bunk.

"Maggie, thank God!" Chase breathed gratefully, falling to his knees beside the still figure. She appeared to be slumbering, but when Chase shook her gently she didn't stir.

A frown worried Chase's brow when Maggie failed to respond. Was she hurt? Carefully he unwrapped the blanket and examined every inch of her body, finding no broken bones or ribs, though purple bruises and scratches marred her tender white flesh. Chase covered her again, then smoothed the tangled mass of damp hair away from her forehead. He uttered a cry of dismay when he felt the stickiness of blood against his fingertips. He bent to inspect the injury, cursing when he discovered a lump the size of a hen's egg rising at her temple.

Maggie felt the pulsing pain through the fuzziness of sleep and moaned. The sound sent a jolt of joy surging through Chase's veins. He was ecstatic when Maggie stirred and opened her eyes. Their amber depths were murky with confusion as she stared at Chase without recognition.

"Maggie, can you hear me, darlin'?"

Maggie merely nodded, finding it difficult to work her tongue.

"Can you sit up? We have to get you outta here to a doctor."

Like an obedient child, Maggie struggled to a sitting position, relying heavily on Chase's brawny arms. Her head throbbed so badly that she couldn't think, couldn't talk, could scarcely move.

"Where's your clothes, darlin'?" When Maggie stared at him blankly, Chase searched the room with his eyes until he spied them lying in a sodden heap on the floor. Besides being wet and dirty, they were tattered beyond redemption.

"Not much good," Chase muttered when he saw the condition they were in. "You'll be fine wrapped in a blanket sitting in front of me on my horse." Effortlessly he scooped her up in his arms.

Maggie felt herself floating, and an unknown fear instilled her with panic. A cry of protest left her lips, and she struggled in Chase's arms. She wasn't certain she wanted to go where the big cowboy was taking her.

"Don't be frightened, darlin'—it's me, Chase. You're safe now. I'm takin' you home. Beth is waitin' for you."

Chase? Beth? Maggie wanted to find out more but was too exhausted to ask. Besides, his voice was so soothing, so hauntingly familiar. She relaxed, allowing Chase to carry her outside and place her before him on his horse.

"I gotta signal the boys," Chase warned as he unholstered his gun and fired two shots in the air.

Maggie jumped at the sound despite the warning and snuggled deeper into the protective warmth of his body. Once Chase set his horse into motion, she promptly fell asleep. When some of the hands joined him later, he immediately sent one of them to Butte for the doctor.

"Thank the Lord ya found her!" Rusty called as he came running up to Chase. "What's wrong with her?"

"We won't know till the doc arrives," Chase said worriedly.

"Why is she so still?"

"Sleepin', I reckon. Here, hold her while I dismount."

Once on the ground Chase reclaimed Maggie and carried her in the house and up to her room, where Kate fussed and clucked over her like a mother hen. It worried them all that Maggie hadn't awakened yet.

"Bring Beth and lay her down beside her mother," Kate suggested. "It ain't right fer Maggie ta sleep so sound. Maybe the baby will bring her outta it."

"Maggie suffered a head injury," Chase revealed, anxiety creasing his brow. "She musta got thrown durin' the storm. Don't know how she made it to that old line shack at the north edge of our property in her condition. She seems a mite confused but otherwise uninjured, except for that bump on her head. Could be a concussion."

"Did ya send fer the doc?"

"Yep, I already done it. We'll just have to wait till he gets here."

A few minutes later, Spotted Deer brought in Beth, who recognized her mother immediately. She held out her dimpled arms and gurgled, puzzled when Maggie did not reach out for her. Chase took the tyke from Spotted Deer and dismissed her, leaving only Rusty and Kate in the room with him. Tenderly, he laid the squirming infant beside her mother. Beth squealed in delight, nuzzling frantically at Maggie's breast.

"She wants ta nurse," Kate said. "You men leave whilst I take care of it."

"You think it's okay?" Chase worried.

"Can't hurt. But just in case, we oughta send ta town fer some bottles. With all the cows on the place, milk is no problem."

"I'll go," Virgie offered. Curious, she had come to Maggie's room to see what was going on. "It's easier for a woman to attend to such things, and I know Kate will want to stay with Maggie."

It was so unlike Virgie to volunteer for anything that Chase bent her a grateful smile. "Much obliged. Take one of the hands along. We don't want another accident."

But before Virgie could leave, Maggie moaned and opened her eyes. She seemed frightened as well as confused by the people surrounding her. Immediately Chase tried to ease her fears.

"You're safe, Maggie, back in your own bed. All your friends are here."

"Are you talking to me?" Maggie asked groggily.

"You're the only one in the room named Maggie," Chase smiled indulgently.

"My name is Maggie?"

"Gawd!" Rusty gasped, stunned.

"Of course, darlin'," Chase answered as calmly as his racing heart would allow. "Don't you remember?" Had Maggie's injury affected her memory?

"Everything is so hazy. What happened? Where am I?"

"I hoped you could tell us what happened," Chase sighed. "From all appearances, you were caught in the storm last night and thrown from your horse. You made it to a deserted line shack, and that's where I found you earlier today."

"The storm . . . yes, I remember."

"Thank God."

Then Maggie said something that chilled Chase to the bone. "Who are you?"

"Don't you know me?"

"No, should I?"

Kate and Rusty exchanged worried looks while Virgie seemed rather pleased with the way things were working out.

"I'm Chase, darlin'."

Maggie's face displayed nothing but mild curiosity. "I—I'm sorry, I don't remember."

Just then Beth announced her displeasure at being ignored with a loud squawk. Maggie appeared truly astounded to find a squirming infant in bed beside her. Her eyes flew upwards, searching Chase's face for an answer. Chase was so astonished by Maggie's inability to remember her own daughter that words failed him. Fortunately the doctor arrived just then, shooing everyone from the room. Chase removed Beth from her mother's side and joined the others in the hallway outside the door. Virgie decided it was a good time to leave for Butte and excused herself. Kate also departed to see to household chores, leaving Chase alone with Rusty.

Beth began to whimper and Chase rocked her

gently back and forth, looking helpless. She popped a thumb in her mouth and promptly fell asleep. "She's a fetchin' little thing, isn't she?" he said wistfully. "What will happen to her if her mother never regains her memory?"

"Why, I reckon her pa will take care of her," Rusty said, his voice tinged with amusement.

"If Gordon wanted his daughter, she'd be with him now," Chase muttered darkly. "It's obvious Maggie and Gordon didn't love one another enough to marry."

"I ain't talkin' 'bout Gordon," Rusty hinted slyly. "I never figured ya fer a dim-witted jackass."

"Damnation, Rusty, what in the hell are you jawin' about?"

"A man what ain't got sense enough ta recognize his own young'un deserves ta be jawed at."

Chase's blue eyes flew to Beth, searching her tiny face as if seeing her for the first time. "This is no time for funnin'."

"Ain't funnin'. Did Maggie ever say Beth was that Mountie's daughter?"

"No, but—"

"But nothin'. Beth is over five months old, you figure that one out."

Chase's mind worked furiously. Fourteen months ago he and Maggie had made love in Skagway. Could it possibly be true?

Rusty saw doubt in Chase's eyes and upbraided him soundly. "Hell's bells, son, we all know who Beth's father is. If ya had an ounce of sense, ya'd know it too."

"What is this, some kind of conspiracy? Why didn't someone tell me?"

"It was Maggie's place ta tell ya. She had some damn fool notion that ya'd only want her fer yer child's sake if ya knew. I reckon she'd a told ya sooner or later."

"How much later? Beth is already five months old."

"Didn't ya suspect somethin' when Maggie turned up at the ranch with a baby?"

"Hell, no! Beth is such a tiny little mite, I figured her for a newborn, not a five-month-old infant. I thought Maggie came to me because Gordon left her and she needed someone. She had no family, no one to turn to, and we once meant everything to each other."

"Well now ya know. Let's hope it's not too late."

"I reckon I got no one to blame but myself," Chase said deprecatingly. "I reacted without thinkin' when I saw Maggie in Seattle, pregnant and with Gordon. Naturally I assumed the worst. Maggie looked pregnant, but not nine months pregnant. Besides, it hurt like hell that she had deliberately lied to me about bein' unable to conceive. It was a shock seein' her like that."

"And ya hightailed it back to Montana without askin' fer an explanation."

"I always was hotheaded, Rusty. I wish I knew what Gordon was doin' with Maggie that day."

"Maggie will have to answer that."

"Lordy, I only hope her memory returns so she *can* answer it."

"Mr. McGarrett?"

Chase whirled to face the doctor, who had just emerged from Maggie's room. "How is she, Doc?"

"Gimme the baby, Chase, so ya can talk ta Doc Foster. I'll find Spotted Deer," Rusty volunteered.

"Physically, your wife is fine," the doctor advised, assuming Maggie was Chase's wife. "The bruises will heal in time and the swelling on her head is already receding, but—"

"Give it to we straight, Doc. I know Maggie's memory is gone. Is it permanent?"

Doctor Foster sighed tiredly. It was difficult to

predict what he didn't know himself. A portly man with a ruddy complexion and receding hairline, he clapped Chase on the shoulder and led him off farther down the hall where Maggie couldn't overhear.

"A head injury such as this is difficult to diagnose. I've seen cases where the memory loss lasts only a day. But it could last a week, a month, or even a year. You'll just have to be patient with your wife, Mr. McGarrett. Explain as clearly as possible when she asks questions, and I'm sure she will ask questions, many of them. One day something will jog her memory, and it will be as if nothing has happened."

Chase hung on the doctor's every word. "Are there any instructions or precautions we should follow?"

"Nothing special. Let her get out of bed whenever she feels strong enough, but don't push her to remember. Your wife is confused right now and needs love and understanding. Just see that she doesn't overdo things."

"Much obliged, Doc," Chase said, pulling some bills out of his pocket and pressing them in the doctor's hand.

"Send for me if you need me. I can find my way out—go to your wife. She needs you."

Maggie's eyes were wide and troubled when Chase entered the room. "The doctor said I lost my memory." Her lower lip trembled and she looked like a lost little girl.

"It's only temporary, darlin'."

"He—he called me Mrs. McGarrett. Are you my husband?"

Maggie's innocent question placed a terrible strain on Chase's drained emotions. He'd give his fortune to be able to say he and Maggie were man and wife. "No, I'm not your husband—not yet. We're to be married soon, though."

"The—the baby. Is she ours?"

"Yep," Chase answered proudly. "Beth is our daughter, yours and mine."

"I don't understand," Maggie said, frowning. "If we have a child, why aren't we married?"

"It's a long story, Maggie girl, and I don't want to burden you with it now. When you're feelin' better, I'll explain everythin'. I want you well for our weddin'."

"We're to be married?" Maggie repeated numbly.

"It's about time, wouldn't you say?" Chase hinted slyly. "I'll leave you now to get some rest. You scared the wits outta us last night."

"Chase?"

"Yeah?"

"Our baby, how old is she?"

"Five months old."

"She's still nursing, isn't she? I ache and there's milk . . ." Maggie flushed with embarrassment, but decided that if she had a baby with Chase they were intimate enough to discuss these things.

Chase didn't need a ton of bricks to fall on him to realize what Maggie was implying. "Would you like Spotted Deer to bring the baby to you? There's no hurry, she's bein' taken care of until you're able."

"You don't understand, Chase, I *need* to nurse her." She looked down at herself and Chase followed her gaze, noting that the front of her chemise was already saturated with overflowing breast milk.

"You're right, darlin', I'll take care of it right away."

Maggie watched Chase stride from the room, wishing she could remember him. Never had she seen such an attractive man. He looked so strong, so masculine and virile, yet he had been so very gentle with her. Just the thought that she had known him intimately set her atremble. She couldn't remember his loving, but something deep and profound told her it had been very special.

But there were still so many unanswered questions, so much that needed explaining. For instance, why weren't they already married? Was something or someone preventing their union? Then Spotted Deer entered the room with Beth.

Maggie was hesitant at first, but Beth was so happy to see her mother that Maggie soon lost her heart to the adorable little tyke. It seemed only natural that she bare her breast and offer it to the child. Beth did the rest, latching on to the nipple and suckling greedily. The feeling was so familiar and rewarding that Maggie relaxed against the pillow, sighing contentedly. Though she didn't remember her own child, she loved her already.

Chapter Twenty-two

"A weddin'! Is that wise, Chase?" Kate criticized. "Maggie don't even remember ya."

Over a week had elapsed since Maggie's accident, and she showed no signs of regaining her memory. She had been out of bed for several days now and appeared shy around everyone except Beth.

"Maggie believes what I told her," Chase said tersely. "I said we were planning our weddin' when she had her accident. I explained that we didn't marry before Beth's birth 'cause I was in the Yukon and couldn't get back in time."

"What if her memory returns and she hates ya fer lyin' ta her?"

"I'll cross that bridge when I come to it," Chase temporized. "Maggie will be my wife even if I have to resort to trickery to accomplish it. It's my decision, and if it backfires I've no one to blame but myself."

Privately Kate thought Chase was making a mistake by marrying Maggie when she wasn't herself. But she could understand his motives. There was only one question that needed answering, and if Kate received the wrong reply, she'd put a stop to Chase's wedding plans.

"Do ya love Maggie, Chase? Or are ya marrin' her fer yer child's sake? 'Pears ta me ya woulda asked her weeks ago if ya loved her."

"Call me a stubborn fool, Kate, or an idiot, but I never stopped lovin' Maggie. I was all set to ask her to marry me the night of the fire, but all hell broke loose. Afterwards, rebuildin' the stables took priority and I put my personal life on hold. It didn't even matter to me if Beth wasn't mine," Chase admitted, "I grew to love that little girl like she was my own."

"She is yer own," Kate reminded him.

"I know that now, but it wouldn't have mattered. Maggie and I belong together. Beth bein' mine makes everythin' perfect."

Kate had no objection to Chase's sentiments. Love was an emotion that knew no logic.

Virgie found Maggie alone. She appeared to be in a pensive mood as she sat on the wide porch, staring off into the distance. It was actually the first time since Maggie's accident that Virgie had the opportunity to speak privately with her. Virgie deliberately pulled a chair close so they couldn't be overheard.

"It's good to see you up and around, Maggie."

"I know you're Virgie, but I don't remember you," Maggie said, feeling vaguely on edge with this lovely brunette. "Are we friends?"

"The best of friends," Virgie lied convincingly. "We hit it off the moment you came to the ranch. You told me all your secrets and I told you mine."

"What kinds of secrets?" Maggie asked, her interest piqued.

"For instance, I know why you went to town the day of your accident."

"Was there some mystery about it?"

"No one knew you had even gone into town," Virgie revealed. "You told me you wanted to purchase a train ticket to Seattle for you and Beth."

"I wanted to leave the ranch?" What Virgie said sounded incredible, yet what reason did she have to lie? Why would Chase lie?

"Chase and I were to be married. Why would I leave?"

"It's a lie, Maggie. Chase never proposed to you. You were living here as his—well, you're smart enough to figure it out."

"No, it can't be!" Maggie protested. "I'm not like that. That is, I don't think I am."

"Chase can be mighty persuasive."

"What about Beth? We have a daughter together."

"I hate to be the one to tell you this, Maggie, but Beth doesn't belong to Chase. Her father is a man named Scott Gordon. He's a Mountie you met in the Yukon and fell in love with." No one had actually discussed Scott with Virgie, but when Maggie first arrived she had overheard Chase and Rusty talking about the Mountie. She couldn't hear everything, but she did hear Chase blurt out that Scott Gordon was Beth's father.

Maggie grew still, unwilling to believe Virgie's damning words. "Why am I here if I love Scott Gordon?" she asked quietly.

"I'm not sure," Virgie said truthfully. "Evidently you and Chase were friends, and you turned to him in desperation when your lover refused to marry you."

Maggie's head spun crazily. None of this made sense. Yet it made as much sense as marrying Chase, for her past was a blank. "If what you say is true, why does Chase want to marry me?"

"He feels sorry for you. You came to him for help and he's offering you his name out of pity and to save your reputation. No mention of marriage was made until you lost your memory. Ask Aunt Kate if you don't believe me. Besides, I think Chase rather enjoys bedding you."

Virgie's barbed words were nearly more than Maggie could bear. All traces of color drained from her face and she sucked her breath in sharply. Virgie certainly was being blunt for someone who professed to be her friend. Was everyone on the ranch aware that she was Chase's—whore? How could she bear the shame? Why had Scott Gordon left her and their child? Did pity for her provoke Chase into claiming Beth? Maggie rose stiffly from her chair, moving off in jerking motions.

"Where are you going, Maggie?" Virgie asked, smirking behind her back.

Maggie didn't answer as she walked off in a trance. She had much to think about, many things to consider. She hadn't counted on Kate intercepting her before she reached her room. She attempted to brush past the kindly woman, but Kate sensed Maggie's distress and forestalled her.

"Maggie, what is it, honey, are ya sick? Does yer head hurt?"

Maggie turned to Kate, her eyes blank, her mind in a turmoil. Virgie's cruel words had pierced her heart like well-aimed arrows. Chase had seemed so kind and loving. Was pity all he felt for her? Pity and friendship? Kate would know! Kate had known her since her days in the Yukon. Or so she'd been informed. Dear God, why couldn't she remember? Did she have a lover named Scott Gordon? Was he Beth's father? There was only one way to find out.

"Kate, I need to know something and I want the truth."

"Has someone been tellin' ya things?" Kate asked, frightened by the utter dispair visible in Maggie's golden eyes.

"That's not important. I want to know if Chase and I planned to marry before my accident. All I know of my past life is what Chase told me. I'm depending on you, Kate—please don't lie to me."

Kate sat on the horns of a dilemma. She hated to refute Chase's words, but neither did she want to deliberately lie to Maggie and lose her trust. "Chase always wanted ya fer his wife."

"That's not what I asked, Kate."

"Chase wouldn't take ya fer his wife if he didn't love ya," Kate temporized.

"Chase is a good man. What he feels is pity for me and Beth. Obviously he proposed to save me from bearing the stigma of being an unwed mother." She couldn't bring herself to ask Kate if she and Chase were lovers.

"Maggie, it's not what ya think." Oh, Lordy, how was she going to get out of this one?

"Please answer my question. Was our wedding already being planned when I lost my memory?"

"Not so far as I know," Kate finally admitted. " 'Course, I don't know everythin'. Ya coulda made plans I knew nothin' about. But the baby—"

"Thank you, Kate," Maggie said in a strangled voice, "I've heard enough. I know all about the baby and how she was conceived." Maggie had her answer and knew exactly what she had to do.

In her room, Maggie rummaged through her belongings, hoping to find something to spark her memory. She came across a bankbook from a Seattle bank showing a substantial balance. She examined carefully the writing she had been involved in prior to her accident and the letters in her suitcase. There was one from her publisher, another from a man named Fred Grant. All she experienced was a vague tug at her memory, but it was a start. The doctor assured her she'd remember everything one day. What truly frightened her were the terrible things she might learn about herself. There was only one way to discover the truth, Maggie decided with grim determination. She must return to Seattle and learn all she could about herself. She pulled out her suitcase and began emptying her drawers of all their contents.

"Going somewhere?" Not bothering to knock, Virgie stood in the doorway.

"I'm going back to Seattle."

"So you took my advice and spoke with Aunt Kate."

Maggie nodded. "Yes, and I want to thank you for—for telling me the truth. No one else cared enough about me to do so. I don't want to be pitied, not by Chase, not by anyone. I appreciate your candor."

"We're friends, Maggie. I'd hate for you to make a mistake you'd regret the rest of your life. But I think it best if you don't tell Chase I told you all this. He has a vile temper when crossed." Now that she'd accomplished what she set out to do, she had no wish to face Chase's wrath.

"I won't forget what you've done for me, Virgie, and I promise not to mention our conversation to anyone."

Though Maggie felt gratitude toward Virgie, something about the beautiful brunette bothered her. But without a memory Maggie felt she couldn't trust her own instincts.

Instinct had convinced her Chase loved her when it was merely pity he felt. Leaving the ranch seemed the best thing for Maggie to do under the circumstances. The one thing that puzzled her was her purpose in coming to Montana in the beginning. Had she come seeking solace from Chase because her lover had deserted her, as Virgie said? If only she could remember.

A knock on the door interrupted Maggie's reverie. "Maggie, I've just returned from town and can't wait to tell you the plans I made for us."

"Come in, Chase," Maggie said. She might as well tell him she was leaving now and get the unpleasantness over with.

"I've made all the arrangements," Chase said, bursting with excitement. "The weddin' will be Saturday. The preacher—" His sentence ended abruptly when he saw the open suitcase and clothes strewn haphazardly over the bed and chairs. "What is this, Maggie?"

"I—I'm leaving, Chase."

Chase's blue eyes darkened with shock and the thin line of his lips gave Maggie ample warning of his feelings on the subject. "You're not goin' anywhere."

"You can't stop me."

"You wanna bet? What's this all about, Maggie?" Chase asked, thoroughly confused. "Has your memory returned? If it has, you'll remember how much we love each other."

"My memory hasn't returned. I remember nothing of my past.'

"Talk to me, darlin', tell me what's botherin' you."

"Why did you lie to me, Chase? Why did you tell me we had planned to marry before my accident when nothing could be further from the truth?"

"Damnation! Has someone been tellin' you things?"

"It's not important, just answer my question."

"If someone's been talkin' to you, I'll have their hide for causin' you distress. You've enough problems right now."

"I don't want your pity, Chase. Before my accident I was living here as your whore. You had no intention of changing the way things were between us. I'm going back to Seattle. I have enough money in the bank to support me and Beth."

"You're not takin' my daughter anywhere, and you're certainly no whore!"

Maggie flushed. Did Chase actually believe Beth was his daughter? Didn't he know about Scott Gordon? Everyone else did. "Beth doesn't bear your name and you have no say over what I do with her."

"The hell I don't!" Chase thundered. "We're gonna be married Saturday whether you like it or not. And when I find out who's been feedin' you lies, they're gonna be damn sorry."

"You don't deserve someone like me."

"Are you loco? Why is it so difficult to believe I love you?" Chase's voice softened, aware that Maggie's mental condition required patience and understanding. Someone had placed doubt in her mind, and it was up to him to convince her otherwise.

"What makes it so difficult to believe is the fact that I've been on the ranch for months and you obviously never felt the need to marry me before now. Is it because I'm virtually helpless without a memory and you pity me?"

"Is that what you think? That I pity you? Nothin' could be further from the truth. Have you forgotten my daughter?"

"Your daughter, Chase? Is Beth your daughter?"

"Dammit, Maggie, if you aren't the most infuriatin' woman I've ever known. Whose daughter is she if she isn't mine?"

"Scott Gordon's," Maggie whispered in a tremulous voice.

Chase's expression turned thunderous. "You do remember!"

"No, but your response is all the answer I need. Beth *is* Scott Gordon's daughter."

"Hell no, she isn't! Beth is mine. We made her in Skagway, Alaska. When I left the Yukon and came to you in Seattle, we had an—unfortunate misunderstandin'."

"Don't bother to explain, Chase. I know what I was to you and what I must have been to Scott Gordon. How many other men were there in my life? According to records I found in my belongings, I'm twenty-seven years old. There could have been dozens."

"You were a virgin the first time we made love," Chase drawled, his voice low and seductive as he recalled that day with vivid clarity.

Chase took advantage of Maggie's obvious confusion and pressed on. "Who do you trust, Maggie—me or somebody who doesn't really know you?"

"But—"

"Do you trust me, darlin'?"

"I don't know what to believe, who to trust."

"Do you trust your own feelin's? Will you rely upon your intuition to tell you what's right or wrong?"

"I—it's difficult to have faith in myself when I have no memory, but yes, I would think my intuition would remain intact," Maggie reasoned.

Chase flashed a lazy smile that should have warned Maggie of his intention. "I'm gonna make love to you, darlin', and when I'm done, if you still feel I'm marryin' you out of pity, you're free to leave."

Deliberately he walked to the door, closed it, and locked it. When he turned back to Maggie, her face reflected her panic. "There's nothin' to fear, darlin'," Chase reassured her, "we've done this many times in the past and you've enjoyed it each time."

"But I don't remember," Maggie insisted shakily.

"Maybe it will jog your memory," Chase suggested, unbuttoning his shirt.

"I don't think I'm ready for this. We may have been lovers once, but we shouldn't allow it to continue." She had the feeling that if he touched her she'd go up in smoke. His blue eyes had the ability to reach into her soul and strip away her will.

"You're gonna be my wife," Chase said with a conviction Maggie found difficult to refute. "I'm gonna prove to you I want you for all the reasons a man wants a woman. We're gonna spend the rest of our lives together lovin' and, I suspect, fightin'. Beth will have brothers and sisters, and you can keep on writin' if you've a mind to."

His low, husky voice and passionate words had so mesmerized her that Maggie didn't feel Chase's hands release the buttons on her dress, or lower the bodice to her waist and unlace her camisole. He had already discarded his own shirt, so when he drew her into his embrace she was shocked to feel the hair on his bare chest tickle her breasts. She opened her mouth to protest and Chase accepted the invitation, seizing her lips and thrusting his tongue into the moist cavern, savoring the warm essence of her. He hadn't touched Maggie in weeks, allowing her time to recuperate, and he felt keenly the deprivation. He wanted her desperately, had always wanted her.

Chase realized he was a virtual stranger to Maggie since she'd lost her memory, and he hoped making love to her would restore it. But even if it didn't, he prayed it would convince her of his love. He hoped the least it would do was change her mind about leaving him. Chase couldn't allow that to happen, even if it meant revoking his promise to let her go after they made love it she still wanted to.

Maggie had wondered many times these past few days what it would feel like to kiss Chase, since she didn't remember. She fantasized about their making love, vaguely recalling scattered bits and pieces of lying in his arms, their naked bodies intimately entwined. Now that it was happening she had no idea his kiss would be so electrifying, so thoroughly explosive. His hands were doing wonderful things to her breasts, setting her entire body aflame. Was it always like this between them? If so, she could understand his reluctance to let her go.

"Ah, darlin', your body remembers me," Chase groaned, savoring the way her nipples rose to his touch.

He kissed her lips, her eyes, the tip of her nose, all the while his hands removed her dress, her petticoat, her chemise, until she stood in nothing but shoes, stockings and those skimpy panties Chase adored.

"Your body is beautiful, darlin', you suit me so well," Chase murmured, his eyes glowing darkly. "Do you remember how it always was between us?" Maggie shook her head negatively, unable to speak coherently with his hands on her body.

"That's okay, your body remembers and is respondin' beautifully. Relax, darlin', and let the feelin' flow over you. Don't fight it. I won't do anythin' to hurt you."

"I'm afraid, Chase."

"Of what?"

"That I'll remember and I won't like what I learn about myself."

"Hush, love. Everythin' about you is wonderful. I've never known a woman with more courage. Nothin' frightens you."

Lifting her in his arms he placed her on the bed, then carefully stripped her of shoes, stockings, and flimsy underwear. "You're mighty fetchin' in these scraps of silk, but more fetchin' without them."

Before joining her he quickly shed his pants and boots, dazzling Maggie with the magnificence of his body. She allowed her eyes to roam freely over the manly expanse of his bronze torso, narrow waist, slim hips, and thickly muscled legs. She passed quickly over his thoroughly aroused manhood, then came back to it, drawn and yet repelled by the incredible length and strength of it.

Sensing her thoughts, Chase said, "Don't let it frighten you, Maggie—my need for you is so great I feel bigger and stronger than I ever have in my life. I hope it makes you as happy as you make me."

Maggie was beyond speech as Chase began to kiss and lick her breasts, drawing deeply on each nipple until she tingled and burned all over. She whimpered in protest when his mouth left those tender buds and wandered down her rib cage, tasting her navel and the curve of her stomach. His kisses fell lower, teasing the blond forest growing at the juncture of her thighs as he fondled her buttocks. When Maggie felt the moist tip of his tongue delve into her soft inner flesh, she stiffened and gasped in shock.

Had they done this before? she wondered, his intimacy sending her soaring. Her body grew flushed, her breath left her lungs in jerky gasps, and she feared he'd continue his exquisite torture until she expired from sheer rapture.

"Chase, stop—oh please, stop!"

Chase's answer was to deepen his caress, inserting a finger into her throbbing sheath in order to give her more pleasure. His sensual strokings sent her over the edge as her body convulsed and shook with the force of her climax. Fearing someone would hear her he slid upwards and covered her mouth with his, absorbing her passion as he filled her with his throbbing strength. Maggie was still shuddering and whimpering as he stroked himself to his own reward. Afterwards they remained locked together, kissing, touching, murmuring incoherently.

Suddenly Maggie's eyes widened with the realization that Chase still pulsed hard and strong within her. Her mouth fell open as she gazed at him in astonishment. Chase laughed, a low sensuous rumble deep in his chest.

"See how you affect me? You create an insatiable hunger in me that demands constant feedin'. I crave you like I do food and air. Don't leave me, Maggie girl."

"Is it love you feel for me, Chase, or do I satisfy your lust?"

"Damn right you satisfy my lust. But I love you too. One feeds the other. And at the moment I'm hungrier than I've ever been. I'm gonna make you love me, baby, if it takes the rest of my life."

Then he began to move inside her again, scattering her wits as he rocked back and forth, slowly at first, then with renewed vigor. Maggie responded by locking her legs over his hips and arching toward him as he thrust his body against hers. He stiffened, then paused briefly, then shoved himself deeper within her womanhood, bringing a swift and rapturous ending to their loving.

Chapter Twenty-three

Maggie remained remote and thoughtful while Chase rinsed off at the basin and dressed. He had been correct about her body remembering his. If her body responded so effortlessly to Chase's touch, why not her memory? she asked herself. His loving might not have jogged her mind, but it certainly jolted the daylights out of her body. Despite everything that just happened, the niggling doubt remained that Chase wanted to marry her out of pity. Otherwise, she reasoned with grim logic, they would already be wed. Who should she believe, Chase or Virgie?

"Why so pensive, darlin'?" Chase asked when he turned back to her. "Have you remembered somethin'?"

"No," Maggie said sadly, "my past is still a blank."

"Then what is it? Are you sorry we made love?"

Maggie hesitated for so long that Chase thought he'd go mad waiting for her answer. At length she said, "Truthfully, I don't know how I feel. I'm confused and frightened."

"I want you to trust me, Maggie, and believe in me."

"I don't know who to believe, you or Vir—" Abruptly her sentence fell off, aware that she was about to betray Virgie's confidence.

But Chase caught her slip immediately. "Damn that jealous little witch!" he flung out. "It was Virgie, wasn't it? She's the one who upset you with lies."

"They weren't lies, Chase," Maggie corrected. "Kate wouldn't lie to me, and she verified what Virgie said. We had made no plans to marry prior to my accident."

"I can't understand your preoccupation with dates. What difference does it make when we planned to marry?" Chase retorted, keeping a tight rein on his temper. The next time he saw Virgie, he'd wring her lovely neck. Thank God she'd be leaving his home. Rusty's new house was nearly completed, and the three of them would be moving very soon.

"Evidently I've been here for many weeks before my accident. Why weren't we married before now if we loved each other?" Maggie challenged. "My thinking may be flawed, but it seems strange that we were lovers yet made no lasting commitment. From what I've seen so far you're a compassionate man, and I will tolerate no marriage based on pity."

"Damnation, Maggie, you're just as mule-headed now as you were before you lost your memory."

"I'm being realistic."

"Didn't our lovin' just now prove anything to you? Didn't it mean anything?"

"It meant we enjoy one another in ways that have nothing to do with love. It proved you're an expert lover."

"Are you sorry we made love?"

"No, I have no regrets," Maggie admitted somewhat reluctantly. "I couldn't have responded to you like that if I didn't have strong feelings for you. It makes me feel better about myself. I'd hate to think I'd come to you for mercenary reasons."

"You're not like that, darlin'. You're an intelligent and compassionate woman with compelling strength and courage. You're bold, stubborn, and impulsive, and I love everything about you, good and bad. What you accomplished in the Yukon no other woman would attempt. And you're talented. I'll bet you could run a newspaper single-handed. You gave me a daughter whom I love dearly."

Chase's impassioned words dispelled some of the gloom Virgie had instilled with her lashing tongue, and Maggie flashed Chase a grateful smile. Perhaps he did love her, she reasoned. A man couldn't speak in such glowing terms about a woman if he didn't care about her, could he? Her intuition told her to trust Chase, but her reason warned against leaping headlong into a risky situation she might later regret.

"Do you still wanna leave?" Chase asked when Maggie remained thoughtful. Even if she said yes, he knew he'd find some way to stop her.

"No, it would serve no purpose," Maggie decided, "but I won't marry you Saturday."

"What! Of course you will, it's all arranged."

"Give me two more weeks, Chase. I know I'll regain my memory by then. I'm already beginning to recall fragments from my past. I remember having Beth in Seattle."

"You remember Gordon?"

"No, just the pains and birthing. But I'm certain it will all come back to me very soon."

"And if it doesn't? How long am I supposed to wait?"

"Until I regain my memory?" Maggie offered vaguely.

"If it means not bein' able to love you during that time, then it's too long. I'll give you two weeks but no more. Our weddin' will take place two weeks from Saturday whether your memory has returned or not. You're not escapin' me, darlin. No matter what anyone tells you, you're mine. You've always been mine, despite the best efforts of Scott Gordon."

Dear God, how she wanted to believe him. Chase sounded so sincere that Maggie hadn't the heart to deny him. "All right, Chase, we'll be married in two weeks, if you still want me."

"Damnation, what will it take to convince you I'll always want you?"

"My memory, Chase."

"Unfortunately, I can't do anythin' about that, but I can make you fall in love with me again," he said with a mischievous wink. "I'll start by courtin' you good and proper these next two weeks. I gotta go now, darlin'. Why don't you take a nap? I'll tell Spotted Deer to feed Beth from of one those bottles. She's old enough to be weaned from the breast, though she's not gonna like it. I know I wouldn't," he teased, his eyes twinkling merrily.

Maggie lay in bed a long time after Chase left, not napping as he had suggested, but thinking. If only she could remember everything, not just brief sketches from her past. If she recalled the pain of childbirth, why couldn't she remember everything? She closed her eyes, concentrating on the one event in her past she could recall. Slowly, a scene began to unfold in her mind. She was having Beth and she was frightened, but she wasn't alone. A man was with her, holding her hand, encouraging her, caring for her. Though she couldn't see his face clearly, she knew instinctively it *wasn't Chase*. The man leaned toward her to wipe her brow and whisper softly to her. She heard herself call out his name. Scott!

Dear Lord! It *was* true. Scott Gordon *was* Beth's father! What had she done to make him leave her? She tried to remember more, but her head began to throb so fiercely she gave it up. What made Chase believe Beth was his? she wondered. Had she deliberately lied to Chase in order to trap him into marriage? What to do? she asked herself. Should she continue to allow Chase to think Beth was his or should she tell him the truth?

After searching her heart for answers that eluded her, Maggie still couldn't decide what to tell Chase when she saw him again later that day. Exhausted from her mental musings as well as from vigorous lovemaking, she finally slipped into sleep, not awakening till late afternoon. She awoke refreshed but no closer to solving her dilemma than she was before.

At supper that night, Chase announced that he and Maggie would be married in two weeks. Except for Virgie, everyone expressed delight as well as a certain amount of misgiving. Rusty then informed Chase that his little family would move into their new home the day of the wedding.

"You don't need company on yer honeymoon," he drawled, winking slyly. "Furthermore, don't 'spect to see us fer at least two weeks after the weddin'."

"And we're takin' Beth with us," added Kate. "She likes that bottle just fine, and between me and Spotted Deer, she'll be cared fer right proper."—

"Thank you, but that's not necessary, I—"

"Nonsense, darlin'," Chase interjected, "I reckon Kate wants our daughter to herself for a while. This is a perfect time. Besides, we can use the time alone."

Maggie couldn't argue with Chase's logic and left it at that. Meanwhile, she had another more pressing problem concerning Beth to deal with. But as each day sped by, Maggie couldn't find the words to tell Chase he wasn't Beth's father. He seemed to dote on the adorable tyke, and the feeling was mutual. Though guilt rode her, she remained deliberately mute on the subject, hating herself for being such a coward.

Maggie spent long hours each day exploring the dark void of her memory, coming up blank every time. She was also disturbed by the sullen glances aimed at her by Virgie. Was Virgie upset because Maggie decided to go ahead with the wedding despite the beautiful brunette's warning? Why should it matter to Virgie?

Though Maggie's memory had failed to return, she became more and more certain that whatever she had been or done in the past, she loved Chase. Had probably loved him since the day they met. Her mind might not remember him, but her heart and body did. She was positive they could be happy together even if she never regained her memory.

One day Chase took Maggie into town to meet the preacher and buy a proper wedding dress. She chose a lovely white gown fashioned of lace and satin. Chase wholeheartedly concurred with her choice, adding shoes, stockings, petticoats, revealing night-gowns, robes and those sexy panties she favored. He spared no expense, ignoring Maggie's objection that he was spending too much. Then he bought a new wardrobe for himself and Beth, who at six months had finally begun to outgrow her infant clothing.

Afterwards, Chase treated Maggie to dinner at the best hotel in town, splurging on French champagne to celebrate the occasion of their wedding. It was a perfect end to a perfect day, but Maggie soon learned the full extent of Chase's generosity. Unbeknownst to her, he had recently purchased the local newspaper and presented her with the deed. It was his wedding present to her.

"Chase," Maggie protested, "this is too much. I have no idea how to run a newspaper."

"But you do, darlin'. You're as capable as any man. One day it will all come back to you, you'll see."

"Whatever I did, however I felt before my accident, I love you, Chase," Maggie said, her eyes shimmering with unshed tears.

"No more than I love you, Maggie girl."

They rode home in near silence, guided by silvery moonlight and twinkling stars. Several times Chase paused to kiss her with such longing that Maggie hated to see the ride end. All too soon they entered the yard and drew to a halt at the front door. Chase helped Maggie down from the wagon and carried her packages inside. The house was quiet; everyone had already retired for the night. He offered to carry her packages to her room and Maggie gratefully accepted.

"Shall we look in on Beth?" Maggie suggested, anxious to see how her baby had fared during her long absence. Beth was nearly weaned to the bottle now, and Maggie missed the closeness.

"You haven't lost your maternal instincts, have you, darlin'?" Chase teased, kissing the tip of her nose.

Everything seemed so perfect between them that Maggie couldn't imagine why she had ever doubted Chase's sincerity or his love.

Beth lay asleep in her cradle, only her blond head visible above the covers; these late September nights strongly hinted of winter. Chase thought Beth looked like an angel with her thumb popped in her mouth. Maggie dropped a kiss on her forehead and tiptoed out of the small room that had once been a storeroom but had recently been converted for Beth's use. The bedroom Maggie now occupied alone would be shared by her and Chase after their marriage.

"I don't wanna sleep alone tonight, darlin'," Chase whispered when Maggie stood with her hand on the doorknob. "It'll only be a few days 'til our weddin', and I don't wanna wait. Let me love you tonight."

Her answer was to smile and open the door so they both might enter. No words were needed as they slowly undressed one another, kissing and caressing, until they naturally gravitated toward the bed.

"I love the way you make me feel," Maggie sighed between kisses. "I hope nothing ever changes between us."

"What could change?" Chase scoffed, using his hands and lips with gentle expertise. "I may grow old, but I'll never grow tired of lovin' you. You do believe me, don't you?"

"I was foolish not to trust you," she gasped as his agile fingers found a particularly vulnerable spot and teased it unmercifully. "Chase, please, you're torturing me!"

"Just lookin' at you is pure torture, I want you so badly," Chase admitted, his voice harsh with passion. "Open your legs, darlin', I aim to bury myself so deep in your sweet body you can taste me."

Slowly, so slowly, he filled her, savoring the way she closed tightly about him. Maggie raised her hips to meet his thrusts, her silken arms clinging to his neck and shoulders to keep from drowning in the sea of passion he was creating around her.

"That's it, baby," Chase encouraged her, "move those sweet little hips. This is where I wanna be, forever."

Then speech abruptly halted as Chase toiled effortlessly to bring her to the pinnacle of ecstasy. Only when she clutched him frantically and gasped his name in mindless rapture did he shove himself in even deeper and lose himself in perfect bliss. When their breathing slowed to evenly spaced gasps, Chase moved them to their sides, still joined, reluctant to break intimate contact. Sighing in perfect contentment, Maggie cuddled into Chase's embrace and fell asleep.

Unable or unwilling to leave Maggie to spend the rest of the night in his lonely cot in the bunkhouse, Chase soon joined her in peaceful slumber—but not before his nagging conscience questioned his motives for rushing Maggie into marriage before she regained her memory. Was it because he feared she would no longer want him if she had full control of her wits? Or that he'd discover she still loved Scott Gordon?

Chase meant to rise early and leave the house before anyone realized he had spent the night in Maggie's bed, but it was so warm and wonderful sleeping with his love in his arms that he awakened late. Rusty was already in the kitchen sipping coffee when he arrived. The heat from the stove had warmed the large room, and Bright Leaf was busily preparing breakfast.

"Yer comin' from the wrong direction, son," Rusty said, cocking a shaggy eyebrow.

"A mite nosy, aren't you?" Chase shot back, grinning sheepishly.

"It's a damn good thin' yer gettin' married soon, ya randy young pup," Rusty hinted with sly inuendo, chuckling at Chase's obvious discomfiture. Fortunately, Kate entered the kitchen just then, effectively halting Rusty's playful needling.

Chapter Twenty-four

Maggie pivoted before the mirror, pleased with the way her wedding dress hugged her lithe curves, complimenting her slim figure to perfection.

"Hold still," Kate chided, fussing with Maggie's skirt. "Ain't she a picture, Virgie?"

Virgie maintained a sullen silence, but Kate scarcely noticed, completely engrossed with turning out a perfectly groomed bride. But Maggie recognized Virgie's brooding silence and supposed it was because Chase had chastised the petite brunette for telling Maggie things about her past that were better left unsaid. As for the mystery surrounding Beth's paternity, Maggie decided it would serve no purpose to insist that Chase wasn't her baby's father when she had no actual proof.

Then it was time and Rusty appeared at the door to escort her downstairs. He was to give Maggie away and, along with Kate, act as witness. Sam Wills, one of the hands and Chase's friend, was best man. Virgie politely demurred when Maggie tried to include her in the wedding party.

Maggie was surprised at the number of people crowded into the parlor, which was grandly decorated with white ribbon and bows. Maggie had no idea so many men were employed by Chase on the ranch, and she was even more astonished to note that a few of them had wives. She vowed to make their acquaintence soon.

Everyone was dressed in their Sunday best—high collars, suit coats, boots polished to a high sheen and hair slicked down enough to hold a part. Then she saw Chase, standing straight and tall beside the preacher, and everyone else in the room faded from view.

Chase's new clothes fit him like a second skin, emphasizing the width of his shoulders, the slimness of his waist, and the bulging muscles of his thighs. The deep bronze of his face above the starched collar of his white shirt wore the appropriately solemn look demanded by the occasion, but nothing could disguise the awe and utter delight in his eyes when he saw Maggie walking toward him.

Magnificent, he thought, savoring the warm flush of desire that charged through his veins just looking at her. She resembled an angel, Chase thought, fashioned exclusively for him. It mattered not one whit whether Maggie regained her memory, for she was his till the end of their days. In fact, things had probably worked out for the best, he reasoned. Maggie wanted him now, but he couldn't be certain she'd want him once she remembered how he'd left her to bear their child alone. Under the circumstances it would please Chase if Maggie never regained her memory.

Seeing Chase waiting for her in all his finery, Maggie felt that this was what she had been born for—being Chase's wife, his lover, the mother of his children. Nothing would make her happier, Maggie reflected—except the ability to recall their past relationship.

Then she was standing beside Chase, feeling the warmth of his hand enfolding hers and basking in the glow of his encompassing smile. The ceremony passed in a blur of phrases, repeated vows, and then the kiss. Now she belonged to Chase, not just heart and soul, which had always been his, but legally. Nothing or no one could separate them. Or so Maggie thought.

Then she was surrounded by people—Rusty, Kate, and all the hands—offering congratulations, those brave enough pecking her on the cheek. Only Virgie hung back, her violet eyes as unfathomable as the darkest night.

Afterwards, while guests ate and drank their fill of the sumptuous feast prepared by the women, Chase had to catch Maggie alone and duck with her through the kitchen and into the attached pantry where they might enjoy a few minutes' privacy.

"Are you happy, darlin'?" he asked, kissing the tip of her nose.

"Ecstatic," Maggie sighed, falling readily into his arms. "Even Beth sensed the importance of the occasion; she behaved exceptionally well."

"Our daughter is a precocious little charmer who's as adorable as her mother and stubborn as her father. I'm certain she realizes that we're a real family now."

"A real family," Maggie sighed wistfully. "You never mentioned, do I have any family?"

"No, darlin', not since your father died a few years ago."

"Chase, I . . ."

"No, Maggie, don't think sad thoughts today. Just remember that I love you. Come spring I'll take you on a grand honeymoon—to Europe, if you like. Perhaps when we return, a little brother or sister for Beth will be on the way."

"I want that more than anything, Chase. I love you," Maggie vowed.

"Reckon we oughta get back to our guests?" Chase asked, wishing they were finally alone in the privacy of their bedroom. "It won't be long before they'll leave and I can make love to you like I'm longin' to do."

The kiss he gave her spoke eloquently of his love, his longing, as he pressed her close, his big hands searing the flesh beneath the satin of her dress. When he sought to deepen the kiss, Maggie moaned, molding herself into the curves of his hard body. Lost in a world of their own making, neither heard the commotion taking place in the parlor until Virgie came looking for them a few minutes later.

"Chase, Maggie, where are you?" Her plaintive voice jarred them from their pleasurable preoccupation. "How naughty of you to desert your guests. A surprise visitor has just arrived, and he's anxious to see you."

Maggie suppressed a giggle as she pulled reluctantly from Chase's arms. "What will everyone think of us?"

"They'll probably think I'm anxious to take my wife to bed, and they'd be right." Chase smiled wolfishly. "It's been a hellishly long two weeks."

"There you are," Virgie scolded, throwing open the door to the pantry. "Come along now and greet your guest."

"Virgie, who—"

Before Chase could finish his sentence, Virgie had already turned, expecting Chase and Maggie to follow.

"I reckon we oughta go meet the late arrival," Chase grumbled sourly. "The sooner we get back to the party, the sooner they'll all leave. C'mon, darlin'." Grasping her hand, he led her back to the parlor, which was still crowded with friends and revelers.

The new arrival stood in the midst of a circle of people and all Maggie could see were broad shoulders and dark hair. Suddenly a hush fell over the room and the circle parted, allowing Maggie an unrestricted view of the man whose warm brown eyes and handsome features tugged at the fringes of her memory.

Maggie recognized something hauntingly familiar about this man who gazed at her with compassion and concern—and something else she couldn't identify—something so stirring that every person in the room became aware of the tension, reacting to it with covert glances and embarrassing silence. The breathless calm was nearly unbearable, waiting for something explosive to happen.

Chase held his breath, afraid to speak, frightened of what Scott Gordon's presence might do to Maggie. Why did the Mountie have to show up now? he wondered bleakly. He both hated and feared the effect Gordon seemed to be having on Maggie, who continued to stare at him in a perplexed manner. How did the Mountie know where to find Maggie? With trepidation and wildly beating heart, Chase searched Maggie's face, and a terrible realization seeped up through his bones.

Maggie frowned, aware of the all-encompassing silence around her. She felt herself falling into a abyss, groping, searching for someone or something. A name, a place, a face that danced just beyond her reach as she grasped frantically at the edges of her memory. Then she was spinning, whirling through a tunnel toward a light at the end. As her flightless journey continued, fragments of her past fell neatly into place, like pieces of a puzzle she had misplaced and finally located.

When she emerged into the bright light at the end of the long, dark passage, nothing of her past was denied her. She was Maggie Afton, daring newspaper reporter and author of adventure stories, beloved mother of Beth—and now wife to Chase McGarrett. A look of pure euphoria transformed Maggie's features as she directed a dazzling smile at the man whose friendship she valued, a man who had been there when she needed someone most desperately. Total recall came instantly, and his name bubbled from her lips, producing a sinking dread in the pit of Chase's stomach.

"Scott! Scott Gordon!" Maggie's enthusiastic welcome provided the catalyst that unlocked Chase's frozen senses.

Maggie's reaction to Scott Gordon suspended Chase's thoughts and froze his tongue. The moment Maggie cried out Gordon's name, Chase realized that her memory had returned, and with it the knowledge that it was the Mountie who had stood by her when her daughter was born, not the father of her child, who had abandoned her when she needed him most. Would Maggie recall that today was their wedding day? That she was now Mrs. Chase McGarrett? Would she remember why she and Gordon had parted in Seattle and what had prompted her to bring Beth to Montana?

Chase's blue eyes turned bleak when he saw Gordon open his arms wide and Maggie hurl herself forward into his embrace. The loving display served only to reinforce Chase's belief that Maggie would never have married him were she in full possession of her memory. Their marriage was finished before it began. While Maggie and Scott greeted one another, Chase quietly left the room. Absorbed with the newcomer and his effect on the bride, no one saw Chase leave but Virgie, who wore a satisfied smile.

Deep in his heart, Chase knew Maggie would hate him for lying to her and rushing her into marriage before she recalled their past life and all the differences that lay between them. He had no one to blame but himself, he reckoned, for wanting Maggie badly enough to lie to her. But once he'd learned Beth was his daughter, he'd settle for nothing less than marriage. The sight of Maggie in Gordon's arms was more than Chase could bear, and he rushed from the room, his pride badly damaged. Having his bride desert him on their wedding day was the worst kind of humiliation.

"Chase, wait!"

Chase was halfway up the stairs to the deserted second floor when Virgie caught up with him. Frowning in annoyance, Chase halted. Virgie was the last person he wanted to see. She'd been a thorn in his side since the day Maggie arrived at the ranch. "What is it, Virgie?"

"Do you think Maggie's memory has returned?"

"That's obvious, isn't it?"

"She seems quite fond of Mr. Gordon," she said with sly innuendo.

"What do you know about Scott Gordon?" Chase asked sharply.

"Nothing. Just that he seemed quite concerned when he learned Maggie was your wife."

"I'll bet," Chase intoned dryly.

"Chase, I know how you feel," Virgie sympathized. "It's not easy to accept another man's child. Do you think Mr. Gordon has come to claim Beth?"

"You don't know what you're talkin' about, Virgie," Chase claimed, exasperated with Virgie's meddling. "Beth is mine."

"Of course she is," Virgie agreed blandly, "and I know you love Maggie, but now that she's regained her memory . . ." Her words trailed off suggestively. "Is there anything I can do for you?"

"No, I—" Chase paused, suddenly eager to talk with Maggie privately. A few minutes alone was all he needed to learn if he and Maggie had a valid marriage and whether she returned his love. "Perhaps there is."

"Anything, Chase," Virgie offered eagerly. "Tell me what I can do for you." She stepped closer, letting him feel her willingness, but Chase was immune to all save his desperate need for Maggie. His good judgment fled in the face of his growing desperation.

"You can do me a great service, Virgie, if you tell Maggie I'm waitin' for her in our bedroom. I need to know what regainin' her memory has done to us without benefit of an audience. I need to hear her tell me there's nothin' between her and Scott Gordon, not now, not ever."

Chase's simple request sent Virgie's temper soaring. Couldn't Chase see Maggie wasn't the right woman for him? Her type of woman didn't make good wives, she reasoned irrationally. If she acted with discretion, there was still time to save Chase from himself. Later he'd thank her.

"Of course, Chase, whatever you say," she said with mock sincerity. "Anything else you want me to tell Maggie?"

"Just say that I'll wait one-half hour for her. If she doesn't appear in that time, I'll assume our marriage is a sham and act accordingly."

"Don't do anything rash, Chase," Virgie advised.

"I can take care of myself, Virgie. Are you gonna do as I ask?"

"Right away," Virgie responded as she turned to leave. "I'll relay your message to Maggie immediately."

Maggie hugged Scott exuberantly, surprised but pleased that he'd arrived in time to celebrate her marriage to Chase. She recalled everything now, every detail of her past and present. Her greatest relief came with the certain knowledge that Beth was truly Chase's daughter. How he found out about it was something she intended to learn the moment they were alone. She hoped his eagerness to marry wasn't prompted by his sense of duty to her and Beth, then immediately discarded the notion. These past weeks Chase had told her repeatedly that he loved her. She distinctly recalled her past as well as all that transpired since her accident, and she didn't blame Chase for lying to her. So what if they hadn't been engaged as he said; obviously the love they found in the Yukon had never diminished for either of them.

A mixture of laughter and tears shook Maggie's slender form as Kate and Rusty crowded around her, aware that in the space of a heartbeat something had happened to Maggie.

"It's all right," Maggie said happily. "I remember! I remember everything!"

"Praise the Lord," Kate crowed, giving Maggie a quick hug. "Do ya know what day this is?"

"Of course," Maggie said cheekily, "it's my wedding day." Suddenly Maggie frowned, wondering where Chase had disappeared to. Just moments ago he was standing beside her. "Where's Chase?"

"He was here a minute ago," Rusty puzzled, a frown worrying his weathered features. "Want me ta fetch him?"

"No need," Virgie piped up, having just joined the group. "I'll get him. He's probably saying good-bye to some of the guests. They're beginning to leave now." Smiling brightly, she hurried off. Concerned over Chase's unaccountable absence, Maggie made to follow.

"Maggie, don't go. We need to talk." The pleading in Scott's voice tugged at Maggie's soft heart. "I've come a long way."

She'd be a sorry friend if she couldn't spare a moment for Scott, Maggie reasoned. She had the rest of her life to spend with Chase. "I'd like for us to talk, Scott. It pleases me that you've come on my wedding day. How did you know where to find me?"

"Three weeks ago I received an anonymous telegram stating that you were in Montana, had suffered an injury, and needed me. I came as quickly as I could. Are you all right?"

"I am now," Maggie said happily. Suddenly aware that they were being stared at, she added, "Walk outside with me and I'll explain everything."

Eagerly Scott agreed, slipping with her through the door and into the crisp twilight. The contrasting coolness sent a shiver down Maggie's spine, and immediately realizing the problem, Scott gallantly removed his jacket and placed it around her shoulders. They walked as far as the corral before Maggie spoke.

"I suffered an accident, Scott. I was caught in a storm, thrown from my horse, and sustained a head injury. It caused a temporary loss of memory." Scott surmised that much was omitted in her rather terse explanation.

"Temporary? How long?"

"It lasted several weeks. It wasn't until I saw you just now that my memory returned."

"I'm glad you took my advice and brought Beth to her father. What puzzles me, though, is why you and Chase hadn't married before now. Is there a reason for marrying at a time when you had no memory of him? I can't help but think the person who sent the telegram did so with a purpose in mind."

"I have a good idea who sent the telegram, and she did have a purpose," Maggie said bitterly. "It should come as no surprise that I fell in love with Chase all over again despite the fact that we were virtually strangers after my accident. But even then, there was a strong bond between us that couldn't be denied."

"Then all is well between you?"

"Couldn't be better," Maggie grinned.

"And Beth? How is my goddaughter?"

"You wouldn't know her, she's grown so much."

"I can't wait to see the little imp again. I've missed her, missed you both."

"Have you found someone yet, Scott?" Maggie probed. "You've a lot to offer a woman."

"It's difficult to settle for second best," Scott replied wryly.

"How long can you stay?" Maggie asked, abruptly changing the subject.

"I'll look in on Beth, then take my leave. I won't spoil your honeymoon. I didn't mean to interfere but I had to assure myself you were all right."

"And I'm grateful for your concern, but as you can see, I'm fine. In fact, I've never been happier."

It was that very happiness that made Maggie throw her arms around Scott's neck and hug him without restraint. Then, abruptly, she released him. "Come inside while I find Chase. I haven't spoken with him since I regained my memory and we've so much to say to one another. Don't leave until we both can give you a proper good-bye." Grasping his hand, she led him into the house.

Chase paced his room in endless frustration. The half-hour he had allotted Maggie had come and gone with no sign of his elusive wife. Did she care nothing about him or their marriage? Was Scott Gordon more important to her than her own husband? Restlessly he walked to the window, staring out into the pearly softness of twilight. A movement by the corral caught his attention, and he stared with rapt fascination at the couple intimately entwined. Chase knew immediately that he was viewing a very private moment between two people who cared deeply about one another and shock jolted through him, as if he'd been kicked in the stomach by a mule.

He needed no further proof that Maggie held tender feelings for Scott Gordon. Her absence spoke eloquently of her desire for the Mountie. She had deliberately ignored his summons. So be it. He wasn't going to hang around and suffer the humiliation of rejection. Finding pen and paper, he scrawled a hasty note, then changed from his wedding finery to buckskins, strapping his holster securely around his narrow hips. His saddlebags lay in a corner, and he quickly packed them with clothes and necessities, including a wad of bills from the cashbox stashed away in a drawer for emergencies.

Reluctant to leave without first bidding good-bye to Beth, Chase quietly entered his daughter's room. He didn't know how long he'd be gone, but he couldn't be a husband to Maggie when she loved someone else.

Beth lay in her bed asleep, a thumb filling her rosebud mouth. He loved her so much he nearly lost his nerve, but he was a man driven by jealousy and torn by guilt. Bending low, he kissed Beth's forehead and quietly tiptoed from the room. He left through the kitchen exit just as Maggie and Scott entered through the front door.

Chapter Twenty-five

Maggie tilted back in her chair and gazed around the cluttered room with satisfaction. She'd not been idle since Chase walked out on her on their wedding day nearly six weeks ago. His hasty departure had devastated her, his note providing scant explanation. For the second time since she'd known Chase, he had fled without allowing her the benefit of an explanation. Not that he was due one, Maggie decided with a hint of malice.

Chase's note did little more than apologize for lying and for prodding her into marriage when obviously it was Scott Gordon she loved. Chase went on to say that, despite his best efforts, Maggie's memory hadn't returned until she saw the Mountie. In view of Maggie's feelings, Chase reckoned it best for him to quietly disappear and allow Maggie time to come to grips with her feelings now that she was in full control of her memory. He wanted to do what was best for her. Chase made it perfectly clear, though, that even if she chose to go with Gordon, he wasn't giving up his rights to his daughter.

How could a sensible man like Chase allow his pride to interfere with his thinking? Maggie despaired. Didn't he realize her memory didn't change the love she felt for him? Maggie didn't want Scott. She'd never wanted him—not in the same way she wanted Chase. Scott had been appalled by Chase's desertion on her wedding day. So were Kate and Rusty, for all the good it did Maggie. Their disapproval would not bring her husband back.

"On what page do you want to run this story about the new governor, Mrs. McGarrett?"

Maggie's mental musings skidded to a halt as her typesetter's question jolted her back to the present.

"Page one, John," Maggie replied. "Use eighteen-point type for the headline." John nodded and turned back to his work, allowing Maggie to resume her reverie.

She had moped around the house for days after Chase left, looking for him to ride in at any minute, guilt-stricken and repentant. When Rusty went to Butte to look for him the day after the wedding, he found Chase's horse at the livery. Evidently Chase had boarded a train early that morning for Denver. He could be anywhere by now. Before their marriage Chase had transferred a large sun of money into a separate account for her and enclosed the bankbook with the note he left, so she had no complaint in that department. But money was the last thing Maggie wanted from Chase McGarrett. She wanted her husband. She wanted him to come to his senses and return to her.

Suddenly an icy draught blew a paper off her desk, and Maggie glanced up as Scott entered the small, disorderly office. She'd just recently taken over operation of the newspaper Chase had bought for her and hadn't found the time to sort through all the years of clutter that had accumulated.

"Lordy, it's cold outside," Scott said, slapping his gloved hands together to generate warmth. "I wouldn't be surprised to see snow tonight. Are you ready to leave?"

"Where's Sam?" Usually it was Sam Wills who escorted Maggie back and forth between the newspaper office in Butte and the ranch. Maggie supposed she'd have to think about renting a house in town, for soon travel between the two points would be difficult.

"I stopped by the ranch and told Sam I'd escort you home tonight since I was coming to town anyway."

"Just a few more minutes, Scott."

"You work too hard, Maggie," Scott frowned disapprovingly. "Chase wouldn't like to see you worn to a frazzle."

"Chase isn't here," Maggie reminded him. "The newspaper literally saved my sanity after Chase left."

"I'm confident Chase will show up," Scott confided, "once he realizes how foolish he was."

"Perhaps," Maggie said with reservation. "I just thank God I've got Beth and the newspaper to occupy my time. I feel alive when I'm down here doing what I've been trained to do. It may not be a big operation like the Seattle *Post-Intelligencer*, but it's mine, thanks to Chase."

"Obviously your feelings for Chase haven't changed."

"You didn't expect them to, did you?"

"Not really. That's not the reason I accepted Rusty's invitation to stay with him and Kate until I'm ready to return to the Yukon."

"Why did you stay, Scott?"

"I like Montana," he confided. "I bought a partnership in a claim on Eldorado and made enough money to do as I please. I may decide to settle in Montana permanently. In any event, it's too late in the year to return to the Yukon. Come along now, I'll buy you dinner before we return to the ranch."

Maggie's answer was forestalled when another blast of frigid air ushered in the local postmaster. "I was hoping you hadn't left yet, Mrs. McGarrett. A special delivery letter arrived for you today, and I decided to drop it off to you personally on my way home."

"How thoughtful, Mr. Bently," Maggie said, eyeing the letter with trepidation. She knew it was from Chase. But when it finally rested in her hand, she was loath to open it.

"Read it, Maggie," Scott urged once the postmaster left. "It's from Chase, isn't it?"

"There's no return," Maggie said dully as she tore open the envelope. Deliberately Scott peered out the window in order to allow her privacy. Her strangled sob brought him instantly to her side.

"What is it, Maggie? What did Chase say?"

Two sheets of paper dangled from Maggie's hand. One of them fluttered through her fingers to settle on the floor at her feet. Scott bent to retrieve it.

"Chase wrote this from Denver, but he was leaving the day it was mailed."

Scott half listened as he perused the slim sheet of paper in his hand. He gasped in shock as the words leaped out at him. "My God, Maggie, this is—"

"—A decree of annulment," she supplied dully. The profound hurt Chase had caused her was a hard knot in the pit of her stomach. "He says all I have to do to make it legal is sign it and give it to his lawyer. He wants me to have a chance at real happiness and he's leaving it up to me to decide our future."

"The damn hot-headed fool," Scott muttered, his voice ripe with contempt. "Has he completely lost his mind? What are you going to do?"

"I'm going to think about it for a few days, then I'm going to sign it," Maggie said bitterly. "Obviously Chase wants his freedom and I'll not stand in his way."

"Don't do anything rash, Maggie," Scott advised.

"Rash! Chase was the one who walked out on our marriage. He's the one who initiated the annulment."

"Dare I hope . . ."

"No, Scott, I'm sorry. I'll never marry again. Beth and the newspaper are all I need. Love hurts too much. I'll never allow myself to love again."

"It doesn't have to be that way, Maggie."

"For me it does."

"Will you continue to live at the ranch?"

"No!" came Maggie's vehement reply. "One day Chase will return to the ranch, and I don't want to be there when he does. I intended to rent a house in town anyway. Now, how about that dinner?" Maggie asked brightly, braving a smile.

Chase sat in the Last Chance Saloon in Cheyenne nursing a whiskey—nursing a whole bottle, actually—and thinking of Maggie. Truth to tell, he'd thought of little else these past six weeks. He recalled everything about her, vividly and in detail—the way her amber eyes grew dark with passion, how her body responded to his touch, the sweet sounds she made when aroused; the silkiness of her honey-blond hair spread out on the pillow beside him. Did the privilege of seeing Maggie like that now belong to Scott Gordon? Chase wondered bleakly.

If Gordon was bedding Maggie, Chase had no one to blame but himself, he reflected, snorting in self-derision. Sending that blasted decree of annulment would have destroyed any remnants of feeling she had for him. His uncontrollable temper caused him to walk out on Maggie, not once but twice, both times without allowing himself to cool off and think clearly. Releasing Maggie from her vows was the best thing he could do for her and the hardest thing he'd ever done.

Chase's bored gaze wandered aimlessly around the crowded room filled with riffraff, gamblers, and whores, thinking how well he fit in with the ordinary cowboys and drifters who frequented these places. He'd knocked around Denver for a while, bought a pair of thoroughbred horses that he had shipped back to the ranch, nearly purchased a bank he had no use for before reason claimed him, then wandered up to Cheyenne where he heard about a huge section of grazing land for sale. Briefly he considered running cattle on the land and turning his half of the Montana ranch over to Rusty with the stipulation that Maggie and Gordon could live there until Beth was old enough to inherit.

The one thing Chase feared was that Maggie would take their daughter far away where he couldn't see her. But the idea of leaving forever the ranch he worked so hard for and loved grew increasingly distasteful.

The longer Chase thought about Maggie, the bleaker his future looked. What good was all his money if it couldn't buy happiness? He wanted Maggie desperately, and through his own foolish pride had abandoned their chance for a future together. All they shared now was their daughter. And memories. He cursed himself for three kinds of fool. Why didn't he stay and fight for the woman he loved? Because he couldn't tolerate rejection, a devil inside him prodded.

What he needed was a woman, Chase decided. He hadn't had a woman since Maggie, hadn't really wanted one, but if it assuaged some of the guilt plaguing him, he'd bed a dozen women. That's what brought him to the Last Chance in the first place.

He heard the whores were willing and as clean as any in town.

"Hello, Cowboy." Her voice was low and sexy, and Chase was certain he'd heard it before. "Fancy meeting you here."

"Belle! Belle Delarue! Damnation, what are you doin' in Cheyenne? Did Skagway get too tame for you?"

"You might say that," Belle admitted wryly. "After Soapy was killed, the law moved in and Skagway got downright civilized. Seattle was no better, and I started working my way east. Got as far as Cheyenne and bought the Last Chance. Reckon I'll stay for a spell. What about you? Heard you made a fortune in the Yukon."

"Yep. Put most of it in my ranch in Montana."

"What brings you to Cheyenne? What happened to that newspaper woman you had the hots for?"

I married her, he wanted to say, but didn't. "That's over, I'm a free agent."

"You looking for company?"

"Could be."

"I don't take on many of my customers—I hire girls for that—but I'd be happy to oblige you," she suggested archly.

"If I recollect, we parted on less than friendly terms," Chase said guardedly.

"A lot of water has gone over the dam since then, and you're still the handsomest man I've seen in a damn long time." Belle waited for Chase's reply and, when none was forthcoming, added, "Well, what do you say, Cowboy?"

"Hell, why not?" Chase shrugged, smiling crookedly. "I came here to bed a woman and you're about as fine a woman as I've seen lately." He uncoiled his long length from the chair and clasped Belle firmly about her slender waist. "Lead the way. I reckon I can afford you for the whole dang night. And if you're of a mind, for a whole passel of nights."

"Now you're talking, Cowboy." Belle grinned cheekily as she led Chase up the stairs to her gaudily furnished room.

The moment the door closed behind them, Chase began backing Belle toward the ornately carved bed, tearing at her clothes along the way. "Whoa, Cowboy, what's the hurry?" Belle said, pushing him aside. "I waited a long time for this. Kiss me."

The last thing in the world Chase wanted was to kiss Belle. Kissing was so personal, and there was nothing personal about this coupling. It was merely release he sought—a diversion to take his mind off Maggie. But in the end, he complied, hoping to lose himself, mind as well as body, in soft, willing flesh. He kissed Belle with all the enthusiasm he could muster, but after a few minutes he could tell it was useless. His manhood lay flaccid and uninspired between his legs. After several frustrating minutes of kissing and touching, Chase flung himself away.

"It's no good, Belle! Goddammitt, I'm only half a man!" That horrifying thought was a bitter pill to swallow for a man whose virility had never been challenged.

"Don't even think that, Cowboy," Belle chided sternly. "What in the hell do you think I'm here for?" In all her years of experience Belle never had a man she couldn't please in one way or another, and Chase McGarrett damn sure wasn't going to be the first. She had a reputation to uphold.

"Another time. I'm not in the mood," Chase said sourly.

"Lay back, Cowboy," Belle murmured huskily, pushing him back against the pillows. "I know what to do."

Before Chase realized her intent, Belle had unfastened his pants and shoved them down over his hips, releasing his shaft from its nest of russet curls.

"Relax, Cowboy. When I get done you'll be hard as an ox and raring to go." Her face blurred as she opened her red lips and pressed them to his groin.

"Christ!" Chase roared, shocked by the intimacy he had neither asked for nor wanted. Somehow the thought of any woman but Maggie touching his body in that way sickened him.

Belle fell back, stunned, as Chase leaped to his feet, yanking up his pants as he headed for the door. "This oughta pay for your trouble," he said, reaching in his pocket and pulling out a wad of bills. "It took me a while to come to my senses, but I finally know what I want. I only hope it's not too late."

A blast of arctic wind whipped around the corner of the house and Maggie shivered despite the blazing fire in the hearth and small stoves placed strategically for added warmth. The homey aroma of cinnamon wafted from the kitchen where Bright Leaf baked and cooked in preparation for the Christmas celebration tomorrow. Maggie prayed the weather wouldn't worsen and prevent Kate and Rusty from showing up. Virgie was also invited, along with Scott and the few hands who had stayed on during the winter. Scott had remained with Rusty for the winter, helping out where he could. The chore of caring for the ranch without Chase's help put an extra burden on the older man and Scott's help was much appreciated.

The last few times Scott visited, he had brought Virgie along. It appeared that the petite brunette had transferred all her affections to the handsome Mountie in Chase's absence, and it irked Maggie to think Scott was now the object of Virgie's feminine wiles. Surprisingly, Scott didn't seem to mind. When Maggie questioned him, Scott only smiled and replied that he was man enough to handle the feisty little witch. After that, Maggie let the subject drop, though she couldn't help but worry that Virgie would somehow take advantage of Scott's goodness.

The wind rattled the windows, and Maggie shivered anew at the chilling sound of snow pelting against the panes. It wasn't a fit night for man nor beast, she thought idly as she plucked Beth from Spotted Deer's arms and kissed her good night. Soon both Spotted Deer and Bright Leaf would retire for the night to their separate quarters off the kitchen, and the house would grow silent with memories. Though Maggie had intended to move to town long before now, the paper kept her too busy to look for a suitable residence for her and Beth—or so she told herself. She assumed it unlikely that Chase would return before spring thaw, allowing plenty of time for her move.

Christmas Eve, Maggie thought abstractedly. No one should be without loved ones tonight, yet here she was, bereft of friends and without the man she loved. Due to the uncertain weather, Kate and Rusty had decided not to come till morning, but from the looks of the storm raging outside, Maggie doubted they'd make it even then. At least Sam and the hands would be here for dinner, and Maggie had Beth to remind her that she'd never be totally alone.

Feeling disinclined to retire, Maggie picked up a book she'd bought in town the other day, turned the lamp up, and sat down to read. After a while the cozy heat of the room and the steady pelting of snow against the windows caused her eyelids to droop drowsily. The next thing she knew the door banged noisily against the wall and a blast of icy wind crept up her skirt, chilling her legs.

Sheer black fright turned Maggie's limbs to water. Her first coherent thought was that she had forgotten to latch the door; the second was that the hands out in the bunkhouse wouldn't hear her scream over the wind.

The apparition filling the doorway looked like something out of her worst nightmare. He stood over six feet tall, his shoulders touching the jamb on either side. His clothes were heavily encrusted with ice and snow, and a woolen cap was jammed down firmly over ears and forehead. His eyebrows and lashes were frosted white, as was the thick beard covering his chin and upper lip. Mute with terror, Maggie could do nothing but stare at the bear-like man who slammed and latched the door behind him, advancing toward her in what she considered a threatening manner. Maggie had never fainted in her life, but when he reached out for her, she slumped forward into his arms, unaware of the strangled cry that left his throat.

Maggie came to slowly, floating back to earth on fluffy white clouds that enveloped her in softness. A few agonizing moments elapsed before she realized that she was reclining on her own feather mattress. The stove had been stoked recently and a warm glow softened the darkness. Had she been dreaming? Maggie wondered as she gazed around the room, noting that it was empty except for herself. Suddenly the intruder loomed before her, poised in the doorway. The breath froze in her lungs when she saw that he cradled a sleepy-eyed Beth in his arms.

"Don't hurt her!" Maggie cried, leaping to her daughter's defense. "I—I'm not alone," she bluffed.

The man's head shot up sharply. He stood in the shadows, and try as she might Maggie still couldn't make out his features.

"Where is he?" The man's voice was hoarse and raspy from cold. "I'd swear the house is deserted 'cept for you."

Maggie went still, all her vitals alert. That voice! The hair prickled at the back of her neck, and her heart began pounding as her senses came alive. Could it possibly be . . . ? No, Chase had occupied her thoughts and dreams for so long that she fancied him even in the villainous creature holding Beth captive in his arms.

"Don't hurt my baby," Maggie pleaded, searching the room for a weapon—anything with which to defend her child.

Her words wrenched a cry of anguish from the man's lips. She cringed as he strode forward into the room, noting that he had doffed his heavy outerwear while she had lain senseless. But that's all Maggie registered, for she had eyes for no one but her babe, folded in the crook of the intruder's arms.

"Do you think I'd harm my own child?"

At first Maggie thought she hadn't heard correctly. Then recognition came like a blow to her midsection. His voice had lost some of his hoarseness and there was no mistaking Chase's distinctive tone. Mutely she stared into Chase's face, now close enough to recognize. The beard disguised much of his features, but his eyes were vivid blue pools that pierced straight to her soul. The snow had melted from his hair, and it gleamed a deep copper in the dull light. The craggy ruggedness of his features was as dearly familiar to her as her child's pale complexion, yet his expression was one she did not recognize.

Beth began to fret in Chase's arms, angry at being deprived of her sleep. Noting her obvious displeasure, Chase kissed her forehead and took her back to her own bed. He returned within minutes, scowling fiercely as he approached Maggie, stopping just inches away, his legs spread apart, arms folded across his massive chest. Immediately Maggie pushed herself to a sitting position and glared back at him. He looked so huge and threatening that her temper flared, recalling how he had left her on their wedding day, humiliating her before all their friends.

"Where's Gordon?" Chase asked, looking pointedly at the empty space beside her on the bed.

Ignoring his crude suggestion, Maggie posed a question of her own. "How did you get through on a stormy night like this?"

"Dammit, woman, don't change the subject. I'm here and that's all that matters."

"Did you think you could ignore me for weeks, then blow in with the fiercest storm of the winter?" Maggie taunted. "Did you expect a warm welcome? If you did, you came to the wrong place."

"You know damn well why I left. I'm gonna ask you one more time before I tear the house apart. Where is Gordon?"

"No need to destroy property," Maggie replied sourly. "I'm alone except for Beth."

For a brief moment, a look of pure joy suffused Chase's features, only to be replaced by a scowl. "Did the bastard leave you again?"

"What makes you think Scott is here?"

"I'm not stupid, I saw the way you greeted him on our weddin' day. I know you regained your memory the instant you saw him. I also knew you'd realize I lied to you, that I rushed you into marriage before you regained your memory and discovered you didn't love me."

"You didn't wait around long enough to find out," Maggie accused him.

"I—I couldn't," Chase admitted sheepishly. "Rejection hurts too much."

"What makes you so damn certain I'd reject you?"

"I've got eyes," came his surly reply. "I saw you together. And when you failed to show up in our room after I sent for you, your preference for the Mountie was obvious. I naturally assumed Scott Gordon meant more to you than I do."

"You sent for me?" Maggie asked, deeply puzzled.

"I sent Virgie to ask you to meet me in our room. I gave you half an hour to respond to my summons. When you failed to show up, I knew exactly how you felt about our marriage."

"Virgie!" Maggie spat. "You should have known better than to trust that jealous little chit. I never received your message."

"I waited nearly an hour, Maggie," Chase said uncertainly. "Just before I left, I saw you and Gordon embracing."

"Have you never embraced a woman friend?" Maggie challenged. "Why did you bother to come back if you thought I was with Scott?"

Chase flushed. "I—I—" he began helplessly. "Damnation, Maggie girl, I had to find out for certain if you were with Gordon, and I wanted to see my daughter."

"How good of you to remember you had a daughter. You conveniently forgot you had a wife."

"Do I, darlin'? Do I still have a wife?"

"Chase McGarrett, you're an exasperating, addlepated, mule-headed dolt!" Maggie berated him disgustedly. "What about the annulment I received in the mail? You wouldn't have sent it had you truly wanted a wife. I meant to leave the ranch long before you returned."

"Leave? Where would you go? Is Gordon waitin' someplace for you to join him?"

"Dammit, Chase, will you forget about Scott? We're friends, good friends, nothing more. He's spending the winter with Rusty and Kate, helping with the chores that you should be doing."

Guilt brought a rush of color to Chase's neck. "It took a while, but I finally came to my senses. That's why I couldn't let the storm stop me from comin' home. It wasn't just Beth, or the fact that it was Christmas that brought me here tonight—it was you, darlin'. I had to know if you were still here, if—if you could ever forgive me."

Maggie's heart thrilled to Chase's words, but she wasn't certain he deserved her forgiveness. What if something sent him running off again? This time she'd make damn sure before she'd be a wife to him, if that's what he had in mind.

"Two months is a long time to think, Chase," Maggie said slowly. "Sometimes I think it was wrong of me to come here in the beginning."

"Why did you come, Maggie?" Chase asked curiously. He had asked himself that same question countless times these past months.

A long silence ensued while Maggie formed a reply. At length she said, "I wanted Beth to know her father."

"Then why in tarnation did you let me believe Beth belonged to Gordon?" Chase yelled, his temper flaring.

"Because I wanted you to love me for myself, not because of Beth or out of misplaced duty," Maggie shouted back. "I had no idea how you felt about me after you left Seattle. The only way I could find out was by coming to Montana. Besides," she said reproachfully, "you should have realized Beth was your daughter without being told."

"My God, I loved you, Maggie girl! I've always loved you."

"You had a funny way of showing it. Did you marry me because of Beth? I was so afraid you didn't love me as I loved you."

"Didn't you hear what I just said? I was gonna ask you to marry me before you lost your memory, but then the fire and your accident interferred. Even though I still thought Beth belonged to Gordon at the time, I loved her like my own. I was thrilled when Rusty told me I was her father but hurt that you lied to me."

"I wanted us to be a family."

"I could kill Virgie for the pain she caused us," Chase bit out tightly. "The little witch won't go unpunished. All these weeks of separation could have been avoided had she delivered my message. I love you so much the thought of seeing you with another man was more than I could bear."

"So you ran away," Maggie observed bitterly.

"Forgive me, Maggie, I swear I'll make it up to you and Beth. Would you believe I even tried to bed another woman but couldn't?" he confessed.

Chase was a sensual man, easily aroused, and Maggie couldn't imagine him not being able to perform with another woman, but the thought pleased her. "What about the annulment?"

"We'll get married again, as many times as it takes to make you mine."

He dropped to his knees on the bed, gathering Maggie in his arms. She tugged teasingly at his beard. "This will have to go."

"Later," he drawled in a voice fraught with longing. His blue eyes sizzled with sexual desire and a wolfish grin hung on one corner of his mouth. "After I love you."

Chapter Twenty-six

Maggie wanted Chase's love more than anything in the world, but not just for tonight, or a week, or a year. She wanted it forever.

"How do I know you won't be gone tomorrow? Or the day after that? Or sometime in the future?" she charged. "I can get along just fine without you if I have to." Lies, all lies! "I have my work and my child and can support us without worrying and wondering when you'll disappear again."

Chase looked stricken. Damnation, what had he done to her? "I reckon I deserve that. You have my solemn promise I'll be around forever," he said with such sincerity that Maggie felt inclined to believe him. "I want to see Beth grow up as beautiful as her mother. And I want a son, maybe more than one."

"I'll not give up my newspaper," Maggie said defensively.

"I wouldn't ask it of you. I bought it for you 'cause I wanted you to be happy. Aw, darlin', the hell with words, let me show you how much I love you. I wanna be inside you so bad I'm gonna explode if I don't love you soon. I wanna feel you tighten around me, hear your sweet moans when I take you to heaven. I've missed you, Maggie girl. Welcome me like only you can do."

Maggie cursed herself for three kinds of fool. All Chase had to do was touch her and sweet-talk her and she was ready to throw herself at his feet. It had always been thus, she recalled, from the day they first met. She had fallen hopelessly in love with him despite his rough roguish ways and brash tongue. Then her thoughts splintered in a thousand pieces as Chase kissed her, not waiting for her permission but brazenly taking what he so desperately craved.

A wild and explosive heat seemed to uncoil within Maggie as Chase slowly and thoroughly explored her mouth with his tongue. She felt his hands glide over her body, releasing her clothes, seeking her warmth. His hands were strong, yet they fondled her with amazing gentleness. His kisses were urgent, but tenderly stirring. With fevered impatience he stripped away the layers of clothes that kept him from his heart's desire.

Gently he caressed her thighs, her buttocks, dragging her upwards along the hard length of his body. His lips found the sharp peak of her breast and claimed it, drawing it deeply into the moist recess of his mouth. Chase drew in a tremulous breath, feeling himself drowning in the sweet fragrance of her flesh. She swelled like a morning rain, fresh and clean and scented like wildflowers.

Maggie felt the harsh rasp of clothes against her bare flesh and suddenly wanted Chase as naked as she was. Impatiently she tugged at his shirt. "Your clothes, Chase, take them off. I want to feel your flesh against mine."

Her plea sent Chase's passion soaring as he hastily shed his winter garb, aided by Maggie's quick fingers. When he settled down beside her, the feather mattress and the warmth generated by their bodies provided all the heat they needed. Lovingly she ran her hands over the rippling muscles of his torso, thinking he'd changed little during their week, apart. There was something incredibly potent about the way he looked and how he was formed, with a virility few men possessed in such abundance. His eyes spoke eloquently of forbidden pleasures and dark secrets.

"That's it, darlin', touch me," Chase groaned urgently as he followed his own advice and began a slow, erotic exploration of her body.

He gazed long moments at her breasts before taking the hardened peak into his mouth and lashing it wetly with the rough surface of his tongue, first one, then the other. She cried out when he nipped playfully at the tender nub, then sighed contentedly when he suckled tenderly to make it feel better, all the while his hands teasing and stroking and probing with gentle insistence. Maggie sighed, loving the way he made her feel, the way he toiled so lovingly, so leisurely on her body, wanting to bring her pleasure.

Her own hands and mouth were far from idle, testing the hills and planes of his masculine form, tasting wherever her lips could reach—the tiny nubs of his flat male breasts, his throat, the burnished top of his head. The sounds she made were more animal than human—murmurings and mewlings that only Chase could decipher.

"Chase, please!"

In answer to her mindless plea, Chase abruptly reversed their positions, her legs falling on either side of his narrow hips. "I'm all yours, baby, ride me any way you want. Take me inside you."

Taking him into her hand, Maggie lovingly stroked the magnificent length of him, marveling at the thickness and strength rising from his hard body. It was almost as if it had a mind of its own. His strangled groan told her he was very close to the edge, that his passion matched her own in intensity.

Raising her hips, she took him deep inside her, pushing herself until she had all of him and could feel her narrow passage stretching to accommodate the hugeness of his erection. Immediately he began rotating, thrusting upwards in quick, hard strokes.

"Not so fast, my lusty stallion," Maggie teased, deliberately cooling his ardor. "We've got all night."

"I can't wait, baby," Chase panted. Despite the coolness of the room, beads of sweat dotted his brow and his teeth clenched from the effort of controlling his body's dictates. "It's been too damn long, and I'm too blamed hot for you. I'll try not to leave you behind."

There was no stopping him as he thrust wildly, the tension in him building. Grasping her buttocks he controlled her movement, positioning her to receive all he had to offer. Raising his head, he took her breast in his mouth, lashing it furiously with the mist heat of his tongue, bringing Maggie swiftly and violently to the brink of the abyss where he waited impatiently for her. Then they were falling, spinning, head over tail over the edge into an ocean of unequaled rapture.

"I'm sorry, darlin', I didn't mean this to be so fast. Let me catch my breath, and I promise the next time will be better."

Maggie wanted to say that she wasn't disappointed, but her breath still pounded in her chest and coherent speech was beyond her. Held securely in the cradle of his body, she drifted off to sleep.

Flames licked at Maggie, the heat threatening to

consume her. Hot, so very hot, yet she shivered in delicious agony as sizzling warmth spiraled up from her loins. A sensual smile lifted the corners of her lips and she squirmed uneasily.

"Hold still, darlin', let me clean you."

His voice brought Maggie immediately alert, and her eyes widened when she saw Chase hovering over her. One hand held her legs apart while the other gently cleansed all traces of himself from her with a warm wet cloth. When he saw her eyes on him he dropped the cloth and caressed the inside of her thighs, shoving her legs even farther apart. Then he lowered his head, his lips gently stroking her flesh, seeking until they found the moist, pulsing center of her sensual being. His tongue was a hot piercing lance that sliced her self-control and sent her senses screaming. Once he felt the heated brillance of the wild passion he created in her, Chase grew bold, wanting to bring her to completion with his hands and the hard thrust of his tongue.

"Chase, I can't stand it!"

No answer was forthcoming; Chase's mouth overflowed with sweet, fragrant flesh, preventing speech. Maggie's bright head thrashed mindlessly, rapture licking at her like devouring flames, turning her to molten lava about to erupt. Then she did erupt. Trembling violently, Maggie exploded, nearly bucking Chase off the bed. Then he was pushing inside her, thrusting wildly, bringing himself to climax.

"Ah, Maggie, I missed you so. No one but you can make me feel like this. Look at me, darlin', I want to see the expression on your face when you give to me, and I want you to see mine when I empty myself into you. This is forever, darlin', forever."

How wonderful it was to wake up in Chase's arms, Maggie reflected, cuddling closer to his welcome warmth. The fire in the stove had died, and she pulled the covers up around her chin, too toasty to move. She glanced over at Chase lying beside her and saw that he was awake and watching her. Something warm and affectionate floated in his eyes.

"Mornin', sleepyhead," he drawled, patting her bare bottom. "I'm starvin'."

"Oh," Maggie gulped guiltily, "I'll bet you were hungry when you came in last night."

"I was—for my wife. Or you will be my wife again as soon as we can get to a preacher."

"I'm still your wife, Chase."

"But the annulment . . ."

"I tore it up," Maggie revealed sheepishly. "I wanted to sign it, had intended to, but couldn't."

"Oh, darlin', I love you," Chase said, kissing her soundly. Naturally his hands gravitated to her breasts.

"Stop that," Maggie said, slapping his hands playfully. "I'm certain Beth is awake by now and Bright Leaf has breakfast started. It's Christmas day and company is coming, provided they can get through after last night's storm. I can well imagine everyone's shock when they see you."

"If you're expectin' Rusty and Kate, they won't let a little snow stop them. They've seen worse in the Yukon and Alaska. Lie still while I stoke the fire. It's colder than a witch's tit in here."

Maggie giggled at his picturesque speech, sinking back into the feather mattress as she watched Chase shrug into his clothes. She loved the way he looked. Facing away from her, his buttocks tautened as he stepped into his longjohns and pulled them up over narrow hips, slim waist, massive chest, and shoulders thick with ropy muscles beneath smooth skin with its downy surface of tawny hair.

"You keep lookin' at me like that, darlin', and I won't be able to button my pants," he threatened, "and Lord knows if and when I'll get this dang fire built."

Maggie sighed wistfully, thinking it would be wonderful spending all day in bed with Chase and sorry that they couldn't. "I love you, Chase McGarrett. Now get your chores done, we've got a Christmas tree to decorate. Sam cut a lovely spruce yesterday that reaches all the way to the ceiling."

Their company arrived at noon, trooping in stomping their feet and brushing snow from their clothes. By then the tree was up and decorated, Chase had gotten reacquainted with his enchanting daughter, and the delicious aroma of roasted wild turkey and sage dressing wafted through the house. Rusty had fastened runners to a wagon and they had arrived by sleigh. Unfortunately Chase was in the bunkhouse with the hands and wasn't on hand to greet their guests.

"Why Maggie, you look right pert this mornin'," Rusty said, kissing her cheek. "I swan, you get purtier every day, don't she, Kate?"

Just then Scott walked through the door, followed closely by Virgie. The Mountie gave Maggie a big hug and Virgie managed an insipid smile. "Where's my goddaughter?" Scott asked, glancing around the empty room.

"Spotted Deer is changing her into her Christmas finery," Maggie replied. "Come in everyone, take off your wraps."

"That's a beautiful tree," Kate admired. "Did ya decorate it yerself?"

The tree, rising to the ceiling, stood before the window trimmed with strung popcorn, pinecones, and handmade decorations Maggie had fashioned in her spare time, wanting to provide Beth with an old-fashioned Christmas despite the lack of a father. Her lips curved in a secret smile as she recalled the wonderful time she and Chase had had decorating the tree.

"No, I helped."

All eyes swiveled to the doorway leading from the kitchen, where Chase lounged lazily against the frame.

"Damnation, son, it's 'bout time ya showed up," Rusty chastized his partner reproachfully. "Damn near took off after ya myself, but I didn't know where ta look. Did someone knock some sense in yer head?"

"Chase!" Virgie squealed, and would have rushed into his arms if Scott hadn't placed a restraining hand on her shoulder and hissed into her ear.

"Chase doesn't belong to you, he's married to Maggie. If you run to him now, you can forget me and any future we might have together."

Virgie flushed, old habits dying hard. She had pursued Chase since she first arrived in Montana, and it was difficult to think of him as belonging to another woman. She watched him walk to Maggie's side, place an arm around her waist, and hug her close. The look he bestowed on his wife was so intimate, so filled with love and devotion, that Virgie had to turn away. It made her realize her dreams of Chase were merely fantasies; he had never wanted her, it was always Maggie.

"Are you going to let Chase claim your child?" Virgie asked, remembering that Beth belonged to Scott.

"Beth is Chase's daughter," Scott whispered from the side of his mouth. "There's not the remotest possibility that Beth could be mine, for Maggie has never been unfaithful to Chase. She's loved him from the first day they met. If Chase thought otherwise, he did so out of misplaced jealousy."

Virgie stared at Scott as if seeing him for the first time. He was every bit as handsome as Chase, she thought, amazed that she never noticed it before. He was kind, gentle, and she could do a lot worse. They had grown quite close these past weeks, and she found she thoroughly enjoyed his company as well as his kisses. They hadn't gone to bed yet, but instinctively she knew she'd enjoy that too.

After Chase greeted Rusty and Kate, he deliberately walked to where Scott and Virgie stood whispering together. "I owe you an apology, Gordon," he choked out. Pride was a bitter pill to swallow. "I'm grateful for all the help you've given Maggie in the past. You'll always be welcome in our home." They shook hands. Though they'd never be close friends, it was a start.

"As for you," Chase growled, turning to Virgie with a ferocious scowl, "your meddlin' caused me and Maggie weeks of painful separation and profound anguish." Virgie asssumed an innocent facade, causing Chase to add, "You know what I'm talkin' about."

"What do ya mean, Chase?" Kate asked anxiously. She didn't want to believe her niece could do anything so despicable as cause trouble between Maggie and Chase.

"Wait, Chase, before you say anything, I have an announcement to make." Scott intervened.

He had come to know Virgie quite well these past weeks and reached the conclusion that she was a misguided young woman who was basically honest and sweet. Being deprived of her parents forced her to survive on her wits, and when she met Chase he represented everything she lacked. It's no wonder she latched onto him and refused to let go. If given half a chance, Scott knew, Virgie would be a woman a man could be proud of.

"Virgie has consented to become my wife," he continued, shocking everyone. "I've decided to buy land in Montana and settle down."

Kate stared from Scott to Virgie, surprised but not displeased. Scott Gordon was a good man and Virgie could do a lot worse. She knew Scott had been in love with Maggie for years but decided Virgie was quite capable of capturing his love and holding on to it. "I'm right happy about that," she finally said, smiling. "Virgie is special to me. She's the daughter I never had and my dead sister's only child."

"I wish you luck," Chase said tersely. "She'll be a handful, and I don't envy you. I think you should know that Virgie—"

"Chase," Maggie interrupted, "forget it. I'm sure Virgie is sorry for what she did, and nothing can be gained now from pursuing the matter. I wish nothing but the best for both you and Scott," she said, turning to the couple. Though she had grave reservations about the unlikely match, it wasn't her place to interfere. Scott was a grown man and knew what he was doing. If anyone could handle Virgie, he could.

Virgie flashed Maggie a grateful look, clinging tightly to Scott's arm. She was relieved that Maggie stopped Chase from telling everyone how she had tried to break them up. She was ashamed now of the way she had behaved, but she never thought a special man like Scott Gordon would enter her life.

"If you say so, darlin'," Chase grumbled, far from placated. He wanted to wring Virgie's lovely neck. Because of her he'd lost precious weeks out of his life. But perhaps Maggie was right—accusing Virgie would serve no purpose except to hurt Kate. He and Maggie were together now and would be for the rest of their lives. Let Scott worry about the little vixen from now on.

The day was the happiest Maggie had ever known. Bright Leaf had prepared a virtual feast. Gifts were exchanged by everyone except for Chase, who wasn't expected, and everyone sang Christmas carols before the cozy fire later that evening. The guests were to stay through the New Year, and it was after midnight before everyone retired to their assigned rooms.

While Maggie and Chase made love with wild abandon in the privacy of their bedroom, they had no idea Virgie had tiptoed into Scott's room, where she willingly surrendered her maidenhead to her handsome Mountie.

"I have a gift for you, darlin'," Chase said, rising from bed in all his naked splendor.

"Oh, Chase, that's not fair," Maggie wailed. "I have nothing for you."

"That's not true. You've given me the pleasure of beddin' the best damn newspaper reporter and publisher in the whole damn state. I'm proud of you, Maggie."

"You don't care if I spend my time at the newspaper office and come home with ink on my fingers?"

"Not as long as you come home to me. I wouldn't have bought the paper if I didn't expect you to ran it. You should hire a good editor, though," he suggested, his eyes sparkling. "You won't be wantin' to go to work with your belly in the way. Now close your eyes so I can get your gift."

Maggie squeezed her eyes tightly shut, blotting out the arousing sight of rippling muscles and virile male flesh. Then she felt something slide over her head and settle between her naked breasts. At first it was cold, but it warmed instantly to her flesh.

"Open your eyes, darlin'."

Maggie looked down at the huge gold nugget on its delicate gold chain resting in the cleft between the coral-tipped mounds of her breasts and gasped in delight. "It—it's lovely!"

"Not as lovely as its restin' place," he quipped "I wanted you to have a keepsake of our time in the

Yukon, those months of endless snow and ice and all the hardships you endured."

"And don't forget the rapture," Maggie reminded him, her amber eyes hazy with remembrance. "There was rapture along with the ice."

"Ice and rapture—and the most wonderful, exasperatin', feisty, lovin', beautiful woman all to myself in that frozen wilderness. I'll never forget those weeks when nothin' mattered but the love we shared," Chase sighed wistfully.

"Come back to bed, sweetheart," Maggie urged in a seductive whisper, patting the place beside her. "We can create the same kind of rapture in Montana. We're alone and there's plenty of ice outside our window."

"And rapture to be found in our bed," Chase murmured, more than eager to love Maggie again—and again—and again. Forever.

Author's Note

Con man Jefferson R. "Soapy" Smith was Skagway's most infamous citizen. His life and exploits are celebrated each summer in Skagway in a gala musical drama called *Skagway In The Days Of '98*. To some he was a hero, to others a dastardly villain, but his name will live in Skagway history as the town's most notorious character.

After his death, which took place as accurately as I could describe it, law came to Skagway. But the historical value of the city has not diminished. Skagway will be forever known as the gateway to the Yukon and the Klondike gold rush of 1897–1898.

In the words of the Skagway News, July 15, 1898: "Had Soapy earned his money honestly, he might have been a good man for any community, for he expended it with a lavish hand."

If you enjoyed my story, I would be happy to hear from you. I love hearing from readers and answer all mail. Please write to me in care of my publisher at the address in front of this book. SASE appreciated.

Pirate

Connie Mason

Determined to ruin those who kept him from his heart's only desire, handsome Guy DeYoung becomes a reckless marauder who rampages the isles intent on revenge. But when he finds his lost love, and takes her as his captive, he will not let her go until she freely gives him her body and soul.

__4456-0 $5.99 US/$6.99 CAN

GUNSLINGER

Connie Mason

He blows into Trouble Creek on a raw April wind, a fast gun for hire to the highest bidder. But when Chloe Sommers offers him a job protecting her herd, she has no idea Desperado Jones has a hidden agenda as deadly as his Colt .45. All she sees is a man packing even more raw sex appeal than firepower. She senses right away that his dark good looks and blatant virility are a threat to her peace of mind. But she never guesses what she will discover after a night of explosive loving: Desperado holds a secret claim on her ranch and a far more binding claim on her wayward heart.

___4532-X $5.99 US/$6.99 CAN

Dorchester Publishing Co., Inc.
P.O. Box 6640
Wayne, PA 19087-8640

Please add $1.75 for shipping and handling for the first book and $.50 for each book thereafter. NY, NYC, and PA residents, please add appropriate sales tax. No cash, stamps, or C.O.D.s. All orders shipped within 6 weeks via postal service book rate. Canadian orders require $2.00 extra postage and must be paid in U.S. dollars through a U.S. banking facility.

Name_____
Address_____
City_____State_____Zip_____
I have enclosed $_____ in payment for the checked book(s).
Payment <u>must</u> accompany all orders. ❑ Please send a free catalog.
CHECK OUT OUR WEBSITE! www.dorchesterpub.com

BEYOND THE HORIZON
CONNIE MASON

As the sheltered daughter of the once prosperous Branigan family, beautiful Shannon is ill-prepared for the rigors of the Oregon Trail, but she is still less prepared for half-breed scout Swift Blade. His dark eyes seem to pierce her very soul, stripping away layers of civilization and baring her hidden longing to his savage gaze. His bronzed arms are forbidden to her, his searing kisses just a tantalizing fantasy; but as the countless miles pass beneath the wagon wheels, taking them to the heart of Indian territory, Shannon senses that this untamed land will give her new strength and the freedom to love the one man who can fulfill her wild desire.

___52306-X $5.50 US/$6.50 CAN

Dorchester Publishing Co., Inc.
P.O. Box 6640
Wayne, PA 19087-8640

Please add $1.75 for shipping and handling for the first book and $.50 for each book thereafter. NY, NYC, and PA residents, please add appropriate sales tax. No cash, stamps, or C.O.D.s. All orders shipped within 6 weeks via postal service book rate. Canadian orders require $2.00 extra postage and must be paid in U.S. dollars through a U.S. banking facility.

Name_____
Address_____
City_____ State_____ Zip_____
I have enclosed $_____ in payment for the checked book(s).
Payment <u>must</u> accompany all orders. ❏ Please send a free catalog.
   CHECK OUT OUR WEBSITE! www.dorchesterpub.com

BRAVE LAND BRAVE LOVE

CONNIE MASON

Brave, bold and brash are the traits of the men bred in the land down under, and there is none braver than Ben Penrod. Though Ben is heir to the vast Australian holdings of Penrod station, he has no intention of saddling himself with a wife ...until he meets his match in the most alluring and contrary creature he's ever beheld. With hair like moonbeams and eyes like aquamarines, Tia is only as big as a child, yet her lush curves proclaim her as all woman. And instead of being pursued, Ben finds himself being refused by the one woman who captured his heart for all time!

___52282-9 $5.50 US/$6.50 CAN

Dorchester Publishing Co., Inc.
P.O. Box 6640
Wayne, PA 19087-8640

Please add $1.75 for shipping and handling for the first book and $.50 for each book thereafter. NY, NYC, and PA residents, please add appropriate sales tax. No cash, stamps, or C.O.D.s. All orders shipped within 6 weeks via postal service book rate. Canadian orders require $2.00 extra postage and must be paid in U.S. dollars through a U.S. banking facility.

Name_____
Address_____
City_____State_____Zip_____
I have enclosed $_____ in payment for the checked book(s).
Payment <u>must</u> accompany all orders. ❑ Please send a free catalog.
CHECK OUT OUR WEBSITE! www.dorchesterpub.com